BUILD UNIVERSES

Frank Burkett

View From the Clock Tower

© 2021 **Europe Books** | London
www.europebooks.co.uk – info@europebooks.co.uk

ISBN 979-12-201-0903-1
First edition: April 2021

Distribution for the United Kingdom: **Vine House Distribution ltd**

Printed for Italy by Rotomail Italia
Finito di stampare nel mese di aprile 2021
presso Rotomail Italia S.p.A. - Vignate (MI)

View From the Clock Tower

Some dreams come true, some don't. For me the dream came true when - after a rewarding career in newspapers - Europe Books selected my work for publication. Although the novel's characters live and die in my head, they are inspired by real world people. Inevitably some of these characters are corrupt, but the decent ones include people who believed in me as a fiction writer: family, friends and even co-workers from the newspaper. However, the one person whose faith gives me daily sustenance is my wife Patricia for whom I am very grateful. Meanwhile, I thank Europe Books for their support, patience and professionalism as we embark on this adventure together.

She desperately wanted Jack Bellamy to win. Money versus principle, avarice versus an honest swashbuckler. She could've wept.

CHAPTER 1

It wasn't always like this. Content, comfortable; lying in bed listening to the clock chime six, a light shower scudding across the iron roof. Once it was very different, when there were no friendly chimes, no roof I called my own. Just a clock tower and me up there alone at sunset watching a city fold in on itself.

I'm not a stranger in this place anymore, but I was then.

The story opens in 1939, the year my parents met. Mum was a Rossini and Dad's name was Jack Bellamy, same as mine. They married in 1940 and within nine months Jack had left for war where he collected gallantry medals in North Africa and New Guinea. Following the surrender he returned home but couldn't settle down. Some say it was a scarcity of teaching jobs, others say it was the war, but his story cut deeper than that. In 1947 I was born, then sometime mid 1951 Mum and Dad made the headlines with a boating tragedy in Moreton Bay. According to the records, the only survivor - myself - was dragged from the water by a passing fisherman. Within days a bewildered magistrate threw me into the Nudgee Orphanage where I spent the next twelve years as a state ward.

While most of my fellow inmates had no roots at all, I had a relative of sorts. She was an old aunt on my father's side who came to the orphanage each summer and hauled me down to the beach for a picnic with her idiot son. Although Aunty Nell never talked much, she did say my mum was beautiful and had a film star's hair. She'd run her bony hands over my scalp and whisper in that husky smoker's voice of hers; "You've got Maria's Mediterranean hair (she couldn't bring herself to say Italian), but you've got your dad's nature. He was not a... a... good man, not very nice at all," and shake her head.

Once she ran her fingers through my black curls and her son Lance chirped in, "You look like a wop."

After I had bloodied his nose, a furious Aunty Nell gathered up the picnic things and bundled us into her Vanguard. She lost interest in taking me for picnics after that, and the truth is I never saw her again until one day the car pulled up at the gates of the orphanage and the driver, who I'd never met, told the nuns that Nelly was dying and wanted to see me. The other kids thought I had pulled off the big one; you know, where a mysterious driver collects a kid who turns out to be the lost child of a renowned actor/surgeon/politician... you name it. That was the toughest game played at the orphanage. Anyone could join in. Just invent a life, any life, but make sure it ends right. I've seen kids cry after playing this game, but I never dreamt of a perfect life, I only wanted to know what happened to the one I was given. In any case, the nuns slicked down my hair and shoved me into the back of the car from where I stared at the outside world like a wide-eyed refugee.

When we reached Mt Olivett Hospital, Aunty Nell was stretched out pale and still in her narrow bed. Undeterred, the driver pushed me into the room and approached her. "The boy's here, Nelly."

She lifted a withered hand from the sheet and crooked a finger. I shuffled across. "Jack, you hear me?" she whispered.

"Yes, Aunty," I whispered back.

"Speak up, boy," the driver boomed from his chair in the corner.

"Jack, you probably think your parents died in a boating accident. Would I be right now?" Before I could answer she gulped a mouthful of air and went on; "Well, it didn't happen like that, God forbid, but it was a terrible thing he did. Shooting them both, cold-blooded like a Fenian, and him brought up in the faith."

I didn't recoil at her news as I already suspected Mum and Dad's death was no accident. A few years earlier one of the orphanage gardeners had sidled up from behind the cricket shed and said, "Are you Jack Bellamy?"

"What if I am?" I replied cautiously as gardeners were dimwits who earned their keep stooging for the nuns.

"If Jack and Maria and Pinch-me went down to the river to bathe," he sang, "And if Jack topped Maria then himself, who do you think was saved?"

"Pinch-me," I said to humour him.

"Pinch-me-Jack," he cackled and slithered off to his compost heap.

And there were other clues, but nobody had come out with it like Aunty Nell did that day in hospital. She then reached under the covers and dragged out a pouch fastened at the neck with green cord. After untying the cord, she tipped out a folded sheet of paper which she handed across. "That's their wedding certificate. Don't go losing it." Next she shook out three medals I couldn't see too well, but they were attached to ribbons and dark with age. "Help me out of bed," she ordered.

After we stood her up, she tottered across to the window that had a cliff-top view over the Brisbane River. She gave me one of the medals on a faded ribbon. "That is your mother's St Francis of Assisi medal. The divers recovered it from her body. Do you know who St Francis was?"

"Sort of. He was a happy old monk who fed the squirrels."

"St Francis was the gentlest of men. Your mother was a gentle woman. You must learn to be like them."

Then she held up two bronze medals. Both were tarnished and all I could see were the shapes - one round and the other an ornate star.

"Your father was awarded these during the war. He won them in battle. It's a pity he wasn't shot instead."

I reached out for the medals but she turned and flipped them out the window. Horrified I watched as they sailed over the cliff face, pretty ribbons fluttering in their wake, then plop-plop into the Brisbane River. So that was the end of Dad's war history according to Nell.

CHAPTER 2

Years later I searched through old *Courier-Mails* and found Aunty Nell was right about Dad receiving two medals. But she'd told only half the story. The writer described my father Jack Bellamy, a school teacher from Brisbane, as a 'distinguished war hero' who had been captured by the Italians in North Africa. After suffering 'unspeakable torture', Lieutenant Bellamy escaped and went on to fight in several more campaigns. The newspaper described the shooting in Moreton Bay as a double tragedy. I also got a mention; 'Rescuers pulled the four-year-old son unharmed from the water.' My infancy recounted in eleven words; floating in the bay one minute with dead parents, the next dripping wet in a rescuer's boat. Nothing before or since. The inquest closed with a finding of murder-suicide that nobody questioned, although Dad's former commanding officer did say, "Lieutenant Bellamy was the finest young man I ever met." Does that sound like a man who'd shoot his wife then himself? Not to me, it didn't.

At sixteen I was released from Nudgee Orphanage, and as the nuns didn't like ex-inmates hanging round the place I was chased into the city. Most mornings before daylight I found work unloading bags of produce at the Roma Street markets where, after sterile Nudgee, it was a pleasure indulging in the rough and tumble of grown men. When the markets closed late morning, I would catch a tram down to Woolloongabba to watch the trains shunting in the yards, and sometimes the engines would steam right through the Fiveways behind a guard ringing a bell. I'd lean on the fence and dream of trains taking me places. Big wheezing engines that radiated a spirit of freedom.

One Friday the young guard escorting the train snapped me from my reverie. To my astonishment he was none other than cousin Lance. After the touch-up at Nudgee Beach I somehow thought it was the last we would see of each other. He had lost his chubbiness and was now a lanky streak wearing a Queensland Railways uniform that fitted like hand-me-down pyjamas. When he noticed me, his brain flicked through the same card index, spitting out the same connection. He glanced away, but it was too late, and besides I was standing in the path of the engine.

"Get off the track," he shouted at the stray dog.

"It's not bloody Lance?" I said, moving to one side.

"Lancelot to you," he corrected.

"Lancelot," I guffawed. "Kind of rhymes with idiot."

"How's life in the orphanage, Jack? Did the nice nuns let you out for the day?"

By now the train was level and I had to walk parallel with Lance on the opposite side of the engine. Common sense told me to mend my tone as Lance was a rare if not endangered link with the past.

"No, I'm finished with the orphanage. Got a job, like yourself."

"With the railways?"

"No, at the markets, but I like trains."

A set of points approached and the train driver tooted the whistle, jolting Lance back to his work. As he scurried ahead to throw the lever, I noticed an odd twitch he'd picked up since the days of Nudgee Beach. The twitch started in the left jaw, rippled across his left shoulder then down his ribs to finish with an outfling of the left leg. Oblivious to this quirk, Lance perched on the lever until the train had squealed into a siding, then threw the switch back to its original position.

I walked up to him, mindful to stay on his right. "Sorry about your mum." I said.

"She died four years ago," he replied.

"Four years? Crikey, that long. Sorry." No fertile ground there. I shifted tack. "When do you knock off for lunch?"

"At the usual. Why?"

"I want to ask a few questions about Dad and Aunty Nell. Never really knew them."

He glanced at the clock above the Woolloongabba rail yards. "I go for lunch in thirty minutes. We can meet at the back of the platform, over there," he said pointing to an area of deep shade. "I don't know much about your dad, apart from the stuff in Moreton Bay."

"Anything will be a help."

As he jogged after the steam loco I wandered across to a pie shop in Stanley Street. Twenty minutes later I climbed onto the platform and strolled to an open-sided shed where workers sat in groups playing cards. They munched on sandwiches and drank from tall, brown bottles that could've held anything. I walked past them to an empty bench and ate my pie while waiting for Lance who finally arrived with the ubiquitous Gladstone bag and hot flask. Four years my senior, he was pale, thin and liberally pimpled across a horsey face. His hair was stiff and dark and sported a cut that was pre-war shear on the sides and shaggy Beatles at the back. While from behind he looked half modern, from ahead he was the faithful railway porter.

"G'day," he said, plonking his bag on the floor between us. He released the clasp and furtively drew out a sandwich. After taking a moment to admire the contents, he stuffed half into his mouth and mumbled, "What is it you want about my mother?"

"For a start, where does she fit in with Dad?"

"Well, there were four kids in the family, three girls and one boy. My mum Nelly was the oldest, Jack the next, then Aunty May - who died of consumption as a kid - and Aunty Ursula who married a copper."

"Are any still alive?"

"Ursula was killed in a tram accident last year, but I think her husband, the cop is still around. His name is Kevin Cleary. Going back five years he was a sergeant down at Fortitude Valley. Probably retired by now."

"At least," I said.

"He might be mid-sixties," Lance conceded, "but that's all. Mum was fifty-eight when she died of cancer."

My eyes popped from my head. I thought Aunty Nell was over seventy when I had visited her at Mt Olivett.

"What do you remember of Dad?" I asked.

He was at once uncomfortable, and I couldn't blame him. "Not a lot. Jack was a teacher and war hero, but I only know what people said after his death."

"Your mum didn't like him."

"What do you expect? My dad died in the last weeks of the Pacific war when a bomb exploded near the road he was fixing. Nobody had touched it or anything. It just went off. So poor Dad, who'd kept his head down, got killed by accident while Jack took all the risks and came back a hero. Then instead of being grateful, he shoots Aunty Maria and himself. Mum was very bitter about all that."

"Lance, do you think my dad was the killer?"

"What sort of question is that?"

"You might've heard something that didn't make sense."

"Not really, though there was one thing. Years after your parents died, Aunty Ursula came over and spent a weekend with us. Not sure why as she and Mum weren't all that close. Anyway, they were in the laundry chatting like normal sisters when they got into a barney. Mum claimed Jack was a bad man, but Ursula flared up and said Mum wouldn't know half of it."

"Half of what?"

"Dunno. Mum had the stronger personality, so it was brave of Ursula to rip into her."

Lance packed the remaining sandwich into his mouth. Even as he chewed, the left side of his jaw twitched, followed by the shoulder, ribs and leg. He poured himself a cup of tea from the plastic flask, then after a moment's hesitation slopped tea into the lid and handed it across. The drink was hot, black and sweet.

"Thanks," I said. "Now what about Uncle Kevin, the cop? Did he go to war?"

"Almost. He had polio as a kid and somehow got recruited into the military police in Townsville. A year or two later they transferred him back into the civvy police. I'm told he wasn't happy about that."

"Why not? They're all coppers." I said.

"No idea. It's just what I heard."

When a whistle blew in the distance he climbed to his feet, releasing the jumpy leg. Awkwardly we shook hands.

"Do you really like trains?" he asked.

"Yeah, love them. One day I'll get work in the railways."

His smile was broad. "Sorry Jack, there ain't no rail jobs in Brisbane. You have to go up to Maryborough where they make the trains."

"How far away is that?"

"Several hours."

He twitched across the platform towards a steam loco panting at the head of a dozen wagons. Meanwhile the train crews packed up their cards and strolled back to their duties. As I watched them I felt the outsider's twinge of loneliness. However, I couldn't say I yearned for a funny haircut and a day throwing switches in the freight yard.

With this encounter fresh in my head, I caught a bus from Woolloongabba back into the city then walked to my digs in Quay Street. Although the monthly rent and a welcome mat can never be the same, the boarding house was the closest thing to a home that I knew. Featuring squat verandahs and sash windows, the century-old house resided among its companions like a row of shabby spectators watching over the Brisbane River. The houses, however, were not alone in this activity. Reg Byrne the landlord kept records in a notebook of the coal and gravel barges plying the tidal water: coal downstream from Ipswich and gravel upstream for the houses spreading westward to the Great Dividing Range. When asked, Reg said he was a compulsive note-taker from his job during the war, the nature of which he never revealed though he let us believe it had been highly dangerous. Barefoot and unshaven, his preferred dress in retirement was cotton shorts and a black singlet he had kept from his stint in the mines. He was into his fourth mug of tea and second pack of cigarettes when I poked my head through the door.

"You're late for lunch, and Mrs Byrne ain't happy," he said.

"Sorry, but I met an old relative."

He snorted. "You ain't got any rellies."

"Now I do."

"Well, who is he?"

"Not he, they. A cousin in the railways and an uncle in the police."

That knocked Reg back on his heels. Like others in the boarding house he imagined Orphan Jack had come from outer space, which sat easier than the official line that an Australian war hero had married one of the enemy before taking both lives in a fit of madness. But, to be fair, no relatives of the couple were ever mentioned in the papers. Just the kid found drifting on an oar.

"So you have a cop for an uncle? What's he like?"

"I haven't met him yet, but I plan to. And I'll tell you another thing. My dad is innocent."

"Says who?"

"My cousin."

He laughed. "That'll make 'em tremble."

"Well, I'm going to prove him right. Me and my uncle. You got any beer in the fridge?"

"As if you didn't know. Leave a dollar in the tin."

Reg owned five houses and half the share market, but still wanted a dollar for a beer. I left the money in small coins, took a beer and returned to the table.

"Where does this copper work?" Reg asked.

"Did," I answered. "He worked down in Fortitude Valley."

"You going to chase him up?"

"Sure. Straight after lunch."

"You might as well go now." Reg said, climbing to his feet, "because lunch is finished."

Reg Byrne was right. His missus, who had a soft spot for me provided I did the right thing, had scraped my lunch into the bin and cleaned up the kitchen. A note in Reg's handwriting was pinned to the cupboard. 'Lunch at 12.30pm. Tea at 6.30pm. No exceptions.' He followed me from the dining room to watch I didn't sneak any food.

"If you're hungry, you'll have to go to the shop."

"I'm always hungry." I replied, taking my dollar from the top of the fridge. "See you tonight."

I strolled out the front door then down to Central Station where the trains departed for Fortitude Valley. It was now mid-afternoon Friday and the bars along Ann Street were full of public servants who hadn't returned to the office. They wore long white socks and dress shorts with the flat, dreamy stare of men who rarely left a footprint, even in the sand. As sons and grandsons of public servants they avoided criminals, saints and loose women, although some had skeletons in the cupboard, or worse a brother who had toured Vietnam and was now a hippie. Unavoidably, I saw my teacher dad among these timeless men and I couldn't believe that a nerve in his brain had snapped, leading to the death of his wife and himself. There had to be provocation or an unknown third hand. Surely to God.

    A suburban diesel took me down through the city and into Fortitude Valley where the inhabitants were Irish and Chinese, poorer than folk up in the city and less pretentious. Leaving the train, I strode up to the colonial police station in Brookes Street where cops lazed about waiting for their Friday shifts to end. Benches dotted with hapless souls littered the reception area while faded posters warned against the crime wave that was about to crash on the Valley. Behind the desk a husky sergeant blocked all-comers from the sanctuary beyond. Without glancing up he laboriously completed a form that required each entry in square, copybook capitals. After five minutes I rang the bell under his nose. He straightened.

    "You want something, lad?"

    "No, I'm a phantom bell ringer."

    He laid his big palms on the desk, lowered himself to eye level and glared. "Ever seen a square arse, lad?"

    "No, sarge."

"You will shortly, and you'll need a mirror."

For a solid minute I held his stare, which wasn't difficult. I'd had lots of practice with the nuns.

"Well?" he said.

"I'm looking for a man."

"Name?"

"Sergeant Kevin Cleary."

He digested the name. A barest flicker in the green eyes.

"Why do you want him?'

"He's my uncle."

"So what's your name?"

"Jack Bellamy."

He rolled the name round in his mouth. "Jack Bellamy, eh? Sounds familiar. You related?"

"He was my father."

When he raised an eyebrow, I added hastily, "My mother was Italian, hence the curly hair and suntan. Anyway, did you know him?"

"I've heard of him. Like most people."

We locked eyes again. He was probably three times my age, twice the weight and half as fit. For a man in a hurry he was dragging out the helpfulness.

"Where can I find Sergeant Cleary, sarge?"

"Townsville, I believe. He left the force three years ago."

"Retired?"

"That's one way of putting it."

"Is there another way?"

He glanced at the clock. "Lad, I have twenty of these forms to complete before five. Your uncle Kevin's story is a long one. I don't have time for it."

"When will you have time, sarge?"

He squeezed the bridge of his nose and sighed. "Okay, tomorrow at twelve. I break for lunch. Come and see me then."

With that he returned to his forms and I let myself out the door.

When I awoke early next morning, I had the feeling that at last the Jack Bellamy saga was hitting the road. I was no longer gazing into the depths of a black cave. The view was more into a faintly lit tunnel where human forms were visible in the distance. Although the faces were blurred, one had a name; Kevin Cleary. Long before daylight I was out of bed and into my jeans ready for work at the markets. Pink light brushed the cliffs at Kangaroo Point and a fog clung to the tugs moored along the South Brisbane wharves. It was that sweet, crisp time of day I loved. In an orphan's world it was the hour before kids plunged into a mayhem of prayer, breakfast and class rooms. In the post-orphanage world it was the hour when the farmers, newspapermen and milkos prepared the city for a new day.

When I arrived at the markets my boss Bernardo Maroni was already setting up his stall under the arc lights. A good-humoured but tough Italian, Bernie was a grower's agent who brought in the produce from north Queensland: bananas from Innisfail, zucchini and melon from Home Hill and tomatoes from Bundaberg. As the trucks caked in red dust began rolling into the long shed, Bernie climbed onto a crate to direct traffic.

"Hey Jackie," he called to me, "Take-a dem spuds off-a dat truck, eh. And be-a careful. Spuds don't-a bounce on concrete."

Right on sunrise the customers arrived. At the front, as always, were the Asians with slick black hair and stained aprons buying for their shops in the West End. Although born to haggle, they were sorely tested against Bernie up on his box, hairy fists punctuating his mangled English.

"Too ripe-a, my arse." Bernie swore at a sniffing Indian. "Dem tomatoes *sono perfetti per la cucina. Belissimo.*" He kissed his fingers. "I ortta charge you twice-a da price. Twenty-eight cents a kilo, and notta cent less."

Bernie punched his palm to close the deal, and as the Indian backed away his space was taken by a short-sighted, flat-faced Chinese who, Bernie claimed, had walked into the Great Wall for a laugh. By late morning the sales were finished. I helped Bernie stack the crates and sweep up the discarded fruit and vegetables. After hosing down our square of market, I changed into respectable clothes.

When Bernie saw my fresh outfit, he thumbed his glasses to the top of his head. "You in big-a hurry, Jackie. You gotta girl?"

"No Bernie. I've found an uncle."

"An uncle? You never tell-a me."

"I didn't know until yesterday."

"Hey, take-a care, eh Jackie."

"Why take care, Bernie? He's an uncle and a cop. There's no harm in that."

Rising from his crate, he walked across to me. "Don't-a kid yourself, Jackie. Folks not like-a see orphan boys. Specially you bein' half *Italiano*. And your papa and mamma, well, I smell-a funny bus'ness in dat."

When his Italian face crumpled with concern, I smiled. "Thanks Bernie. I'll take care. Promise."

The police sergeant sighted me through the glass doors and held up his hand to wait outside. After five minutes he pulled on a fawn civilian jacket and joined me on the steps of the police station.

"Want a sandwich?" he asked, and before I could answer plunged into the pedestrian tide along Wickham Street. I followed in his wake two blocks north and one east until he reached a small café that had its doors shut and a flip-over sign reading *closed*.

The sergeant pushed open the door and stepped inside.

"G'day, Mick," he called to a man in a navy apron mopping the floor.

"'Afternoon, Harry," the man said, glancing at his watch. "Sorry but we're shut for the weekend."

"You don't look shut to me." Harry said and pulled out a chair at a small table. "Four cheese and tuna sandwiches, lots of pickle. One coffee and one milkshake."

"I don't drink milkshakes." I protested. "I want a Coke."

For the first time since leaving the station Sergeant Harry noticed me. "How old are you, lad?"

"Gone seventeen, and my name's Jack."

"You're still a kid. You should be drinking milk." He leant back in the chair. "So how come you're an Eyetie and your uncle Kevin Cleary is milk-white Irish?"

"I told you yesterday. Dad married an Italian woman while Kevin married Dad's sister. They were brothers-in-law, not brothers. You ought to remember all that."

"Why should I know your family history?"

"It's all part of the Jack Bellamy story, the murder-suicide in Moreton Bay."

"Don't get too excited. I had nothing to do with the investigation. Everything was done out of head office in Turbot Street." He leant forward and studied my face. "Fancy the little kid in the water being a wop. That was never mentioned."

"I'm not a wop." I said defiantly.

"Don't get touchy." Pulling out a crumpled pack of Camels, he lit one and called, "Hey, Mick, where's that sandwich?"

"It's coming," Mick grumbled. He pushed open the servery hatch and dropped a plate of sandwiches on the table in front of us. He then fetched a coffee and milkshake.

"I told you I don't drink milkshakes." I said to Mick. "I want a Coke."

"You'll get a clip over the ear instead."

"Just fetch him a Coke." Sergeant Harry sighed. "You can't force a boy to drink milk."

"Sarge," I said, grabbing the fattest sandwich off the plate. "Yesterday at the office you were about to tell me something about Uncle Kevin. What was it?"

Unhurriedly, Sergeant Harry laid his paw on a sandwich, stacked it onto another then piled the lot into his mouth. Not until the tongue could move freely did he speak. "Your Uncle Kevin was a bent cop. Not even his mates could trust him. Caught a dose of polio as a kid and I think that put a chip on his shoulder. Always resentful, and always on the take. His cousin was the Assistant Commissioner, which might explain how he entered the force in the first place. He spent his first years of service in the Valley then took a posting up north, Townsville mostly but other places as well. Calen was one I believe. From what I recall he started out quietly enough, even joined the military police during the war. Anyway, at some point things went askew. The army changed their minds about him and used the polio excuse to transfer him back to civvy duties. But he wasn't the same bloke after that. Turned nasty, real nasty. Some reckon it was the old Kevin coming to the surface, like he was on a private vendetta. If he couldn't get at the well-heeled who he really despised, he took it out on others. Blacks for one. Mention a black and he'd froth at the mouth. Italians and Germans didn't rate either, but that's understandable with the war on. One story went that under national security precautions he rounded them up by the dozen, unless they had money. Then he was Mr Saviour himself."

"Mr Saviour?"

"Yes, saviour; like in, I'll 'save-ya' for a price."

Sergeant Harry burped loudly and ordered more coffee. Mick the owner was not pleased, but apart from a faint grumble made no attempt to evict us. After dumping the coffee on the table, he went back to his mop. I slurped at the milkshake.

"I thought you didn't drink milk." Sergeant Harry said.

"It can fill a hole."

"Is that how they filled you in the orphanage?" he asked quietly.

"Yes, lots of milk. Milk, bread and pineapples. Anyway, what happened to Uncle Kevin?"

"Well, he was smart enough to do his exams and make the rank of detective sergeant. Sometime in the early fifties he was posted back south because of complaints in the tropics. When he arrived in Brisbane, it wasn't long before he tried the same game. You could smell the rot in him a block away." He lowered his voice. "The brass weren't all that upset he was bent, they just wanted him to crawl up a log and disappear."

My skin began to prickle. "You shouldn't tell me these things, sarge. You don't know who I might blab to."

"Tell them what?" he laughed. "There are bent cops in Queensland? Every force in the world has 'em. The only name I've mentioned is Kevin Cleary who got chucked out on a pension."

"Well, I don't care if he was bent double. I'll find him one day and clear my dad's name. That's all I want."

"Cleary wasn't the sort of bloke I'd like as an uncle." Sergeant Harry said. "You know his wife killed herself, jumped under a tram. Couldn't take the shame."

"It might've been an accident."

"Maybe, but I've seen people go under trams before, and it's rarely an accident. Not here at least. Trams so slow you could play cricket in front of them."

I thought carefully about my next question. "Sarge, do you think Dad was innocent?"

"Well, I wouldn't have been so quick to find him guilty. He seemed like a top bloke who'd done his country proud." He stretched and rose from his chair. "So what's next, lad?"

"I don't know. Everything's happening rather sudden."

"Ever thought of joining the police?"

"Not likely. I might become a bent wop cop."

He laughed easily. "Yeah, can't have that."

CHAPTER 3

Following my *tete a tete* (I got that from Mother Superior who was big on *tete a tetes*) with Sergeant Harry and cousin Lance, I came to realise a man can't spend his life unloading potatoes and watching trains. Although aching to know the truth about my parents, I had to face reality. Fruitless years could be spent on the quest, and I had no desire to be like the doomed falcon riding the drafts in search of an invisible prey. Cousin Lance had said train jobs were in short supply in Brisbane. When I checked this with a driver, he agreed that my best chance was to head north to Maryborough and apply for an apprenticeship in the loco shed. I liked the idea and caught the 8.25am Bundaberg Mail to Maryborough where I readily found work with Walkers Limited. Although the company was now making giant diesels that pulled wagons the length of the state, my first weeks were spent cleaning rods on the last of the steam engines, an undemanding task that placed me next to men whose honest faces revealed their love for simple, beautiful machinery.

In my late teens life wasn't so bad. After a brief stint with rag and polish, I signed the papers as an apprentice boilermaker, but even that became a struggle when they threw me into a classroom and told me to brush up on my maths. I just wasn't suited to a scholar's life. I was happiest when my hands touched steel, cutting out shapes and welding them into sections for a train. I was also happy in the foundries where they cast massive cogs for sugar mills, and I enjoyed the hot smell of leather and sweat in the big sheds that echoed with hammer on metal. Meanwhile, my workshop mates had girls we fooled about with, and although the occasional girl liked a hands-on ride in the back seat, nobody seemed too bent on getting married. Or certainly not from where I stood. Most nights after footy practice or a session at the Tatts Hotel I'd return to my boarding house and fall into bed alone and exhausted, but not unhappy.

I guess I could've set up my home in that industrial city. Memories of the orphanage were fading into the distance, and even the image of dead parents stopped invading my sleep. One Friday afternoon however, all that changed.

I recall riding my pushbike into the city for a haircut. Afterwards I stood on the Town Hall Green admiring the ornate Maryborough City Hall whose Tuscan columns supported a domed roof and clock tower. While staring up at this symbol of conquest over an ancient land, I was distracted by the elderly curator who shuffled past jangling a set of keys at his belt. He wore a flannel vest over his shirt and a leather brace on the outside of a gammy knee. All he lacked was the hump.

"How old is this place?" I asked him.

"Built in 1908," he sniffed and gestured at a plaque. "It's all on there."

"Can anyone go inside?"

"Of course. It's a public building." He tilted backwards to glance up at the clock. "You'd better hurry. I shut the doors in eighteen minutes."

"Can I climb right up to the clock tower?"

"Not on your own."

"How about tonight?"

"Why tonight?"

"Is that a problem? You don't shut for another eighteen minutes."

He shifted his weight onto the good leg. "Do you live round here?"

"Yes, of course I do. My name is Jack and I'm an apprentice at Walkers Limited."

That seemed to impress him. Anybody with a job at Walkers had to be among the chosen.

"Alright," he grumbled. "Let's go."

He led me behind the Tuscan columns then up a spiral stairway to a balcony where signs pointed to the Council Chambers on the right and the Committee Room on the left. In the centre an arched doorway opened to the stalls above the auditorium. After selecting an iron key, he shuffled across to the Committee Room and unlocked the door. Inside, the room brooded like a thunderstorm with its panelling in dark oak and images of past mayors. To one side a grandfather clock kept Maryborough apace with the universe, while to the other plush leather chairs were set evenly round a solid table. The curator selected another key and opened a door into what appeared to be a broom cupboard. Once inside, a tapered stairway reached into the gloomy heights.

"Follow me," he ordered. "And don't fall off. I've got a sick missus at home and can't be late."

With surprising agility the curator mounted the stairs until he reached a trapdoor. He slid back a bolt, thrust open the door and climbed onto the parapet. Ignoring my hand, he grabbed my collar and pulled me through. I was now on a wide, square area surrounded by four arches that supported the clock tower and flag pole. One could see clearly in every direction. To the north was the Post Office tower, to the west St Paul's bell tower and to the south-west the Fire Tower silhouetted against a red sunset. On the fourth side, facing east, houses pressed against a forest of trees that ran all the way to Sandy Strait. Nearer to hand the Mary River coiled through the city like a python whose belly at times swelled into the mangroves and sugar fields. Within the python's length were thousands of timber houses radiating in grids from the City Hall.

As I studied this landscape, I was overcome by a profound sadness. The roots of those houses were deep, and my workmates had parents and grandparents, uncles and aunts, brothers and sisters, all living there, all woven into the city's thatch. This was their city and their history, but it wasn't mine.

After a time I climbed that clock tower whenever I could, and the bells chiming each quarter were a painful jab at an orphan's conscience. I could never set up a new life until I had taken care of the first.

As the weeks passed my Maryborough routine lost its discipline. First I was late for football practice, then I missed training altogether. Next I dropped out of the Friday night sessions in the Tatt's front bar and I gazed at trains more often than I worked on them. Trying not to hurt my friends, I invented small excuses while inside I hummed like a fly trapped against the glass. I desperately needed to break free. One afternoon I opened Aunty Nell's leather pouch that still held the St Francis medal and my parent's wedding certificate. It showed they were married at a whistle-stop town called Kolijo about an hour's journey north of Mackay. Since I had no Brisbane leads on Kevin Cleary, and cousin Lance appeared to be Dad's only known link with the south, I bought a 1967 Norton Commando motorbike and headed for the tropical canefields.

CHAPTER 4

The journey up the coast was a discovery in itself. Like a winding, uneven road that keeps drawing a man into his future past, the *Doctor Who* theme on endless replay. I rode across the plains at Rockhampton and thought, is there a clue to my parents' death in this? The same with the ranges behind Sarina where the forest rushed at me like a green-garbed army. Was this the backdrop for Act One in their tragedy? Where are the dark clouds here? North of Mackay it was more hot sky and muddy rivers cleaving the terrain. Somewhere in this landscape had lived a couple whose tormented souls I would find, God willing, and lay to rest.

Three days after leaving Maryborough I rode into the township of Kolijo which had been cut neatly down the centre by the national road and rail line. To one side of the divide sat a tidy little shop and two fuel pumps, to the other a handful of timber houses. My first impression of Kolijo was not of a romantic haven, nor even the kind of town to get hurriedly married in. It just squatted there, astride the highway with sugar cane on three sides and mountains to the rear.

I propped up my bike near the front of the shop and walked inside. A pleasant fat blonde in her thirties greeted me. "Havin' a nice day?" she beamed.

"I am, thanks. And you?"

"If it was any better, I'd be in heaven. Where you headed?"

"Kolijo."

"Right here to this town?" She clapped her hands together. "Well, ain't that something!" Taking a Coke from the fridge behind her, she plonked it on the counter. "You could do with a drink, and for town guests it costs nothing."

I accepted the Coke in both hands like a tribal gift, then explained my visit. "My name is Jack Bellamy. I'm looking for some history on my parents. They were married here in 1940, then after the war died in a boating tragedy."

"How dreadful."

"It sure was. Have you been here long?"

"Two years. Why?"

"I don't see any churches. Would they have got married in a house, or shed maybe?"

"Could do. What were their names?"

"Jack Bellamy and Maria Rossini."

Disappointment clouded her face. "Sorry, never heard of them though the district is teeming with Italians. But that house at the end," she pointed through the glare to the opposite side of the road. "Was originally a church. I know that because the bird bath was a christening font."

The roof of the house did have a peak like a country church, but it was set on high stumps with a covered verandah on both sides.

"The owner's name is George," the woman said. "Go and cheer him up."

After waiting for a convoy of caravans to slog past, I sauntered across the highway. Twenty metres beyond the road and rail line a smaller line split off into a disused siding. In years past the trains running to Brisbane would have stopped at Kolijo, but the siding with its proud but faded lettering was now a museum piece waiting to be reclaimed by vines and guinea grass. A dozen houses, separated by picket fences, backed onto the siding. Connecting them at the rear was a narrow path that paralleled the rail track then turned left at the last house and disappeared into the township. I followed the path to the house-church and let myself into an untidy yard. After climbing the stairs I tugged on a bronze lever that rang a bell in the kitchen.

Moments later George emerged scratching his armpits. Unshaven and half dressed, he grumbled with sleep.

"What can I do for you, mate?"

"My name is Jack Bellamy." I said politely. "My folks were married in this town back in 1940, and I'm told your house was a church."

"Yep, that's right. Catholic church."

An awkward silence hung between us. "Do you know if the wedding took place in this house... church?"

"Could've done, but you'd have to ask a Catholic."

I plodded on. "Was a history kept of the place?"

"Dunno, mate. When I bought the house ten years back it was already converted, so I wouldn't know who got blessed in it... or shagged, for that matter. And seeing they're mostly wops up here - no offence - you'll have to root around in their tip."

He glared at me. "Anything else?"

I looked beyond him into the tip he called home. "No, mister. That was it."

"Good," he said, and kicked the door shut.

Back at the shop I told the jolly blonde about George and his grouchiness. "He's often like that," she giggled. "Sour as a cane toad's bum. Must be all the old sins peckin' at him."

"More than likely." I agreed though I'd not heard of such a torment, even at Nudgee.

When I asked directions to suitable lodgings, she pointed me down the road to the Jolimont Creek Caravan Park.

"It ain't flash, but it's clean and tidy," she said, then added: "A good lookin' young fella like you doesn't need to live in a caravan."

"How is that?"

"Well, I mean... you could always board. A single mum would be glad of the extra quid."

I smiled. "Thanks, I'll remember that."

The Jolimont Creek Caravan Park was clean and spacious as the blonde had said. Graceful figs blocked out the worst of the sun and a wire fence separated the back of the park from fields of cane. To the northern side Jolimont Creek flowed sluggishly out to sea while several boats lay up on the grass like sunbaking walrus. The old couple who ran the park handed me the keys to an empty on-site van then lectured me on park rules. "We got nothin' against young blokes," the woman muttered, "but youse forget yourselves when you've had a rum or two."

"I don't drink rum, missus."

She studied my curly hair. "Vino is just as bad. Anyway, make yourself at home and if you need anythin', bang on our door."

Moving in was simple. I parked my bike under a fig, undid the two panniers and dumped them on the narrow table. And so had ended a productive first day. I had discovered George's house was once a Catholic church - in which Jack and Maria were possibly married - and I had established a base from where I could unravel the mystery of their life and death.

Over the next two weeks my plan was to find work while exploring as far north as Townsville where Kevin Cleary was thought to have moved. I imagined that at some point I would cross his path or the Rossini's. However, my search radius proved unrealistic as Townsville was over four hours away, and earning a living had become a priority. As it happened, I was down to my last few dollars when the harvesting season began. I followed a tip from the park owners and scored a job hauling cane at Pindi Pindi, which wasn't that far from Kolijo. The work was tough, but it was fast paced and the pay was good. From Monday to Friday we cut and hauled cane to the rail siding, on Saturdays we helped out if needed, and on Sunday, with phone book in hand, I would throw my leg over the Norton and hunt for clues. I soon learned that finding information on Mum was no easy task. Although heaps of Italians were scattered around the district like the shop lady had said, they were unhelpful. At one door a youth had stared at me and bellowed over his shoulder; "Dad, there's a Jack Bellamy here asking after a sheila called Maria Rossini." His old man trundled to the door, gawked, then said, "Nope, never heard of her." As the days passed I began to think Mum's death must have cast a hex over these remote northerners.

One morning with fewer than ten bins on the line, the sugar mill broke down, and we were sent home. With little else to do I rode to Calen, the business centre for the district and just across the creek from Kolijo. Apart from a spread of weatherboard and fibro houses, Calen's hub was predictable: a school, pub, police station, two halls and a mix of shops. At the intersection with the highway I noticed a blue and white sign pointing to a Catholic Church which, in hindsight, should've been on my radar from the start. Mounting my bike, I crossed over the main street and up to the church that stood beside the presbytery on the western edge of town. After thumping on the door, I waited in the porch while reading the notices pinned to a slab of cedar. Father Michael Burke was the parish priest, and according to a separate notice, Mass was celebrated on Sunday mornings at Calen and Saturday evenings at Mt Charlton. Shortly I heard the crunch of footsteps on gravel and turned to find a priest making his way from the back of the presbytery. Somewhere close to sixty years of age, Father Burke was podgy and bald with a circle of grey hair that detoured at the forehead into a single gull-wing eyebrow. His pale blue eyes squinted against the glare while his fleshy nose hung like a folly over a soft mouth. He thrust out his hand.

"How can I help, young man?" he asked in a faded Irish accent.

I briefly recounted my story and asked if his records might reveal anything on Jack Bellamy and

Maria Rossini. I'd swear he blinked twice, like Sergeant Harry had done at the Valley police station.

"What's your name again?" he said.

"Jack Bellamy, same as my father."

"I don't recall the name," he said after a pause, "but we get lots of seasonal workers. Some meet a local girl and marry, though we don't encourage it." When I stood in front of him waiting for more, he said without enthusiasm, "I suppose you'll want a gander inside?"

"If you have the time."

He glanced at his watch. "I can make time."

Taking a key from his pocket, he led me into the church where he started pointing out things of interest, like the altar rail that had come in pieces from Italy. However, my eye was drawn to the back wall and the sketch of an early bush church.

"What church is that?" I asked.

"Kolijo," he shrugged. "But it doesn't exist anymore. Hasn't done for years. Now, those statues either side of the altar came from France. Very cosmopolitan, our parishioners."

I ignored the statues and peered at the sketch. The building was of rough timber that vaguely followed the Gothic form. At either end was a steeple and bell tower, both of which could be dismantled to convert the church into a dwelling. When I had finished with the sketch, I turned to Father Burke who sat patiently at the end of a pew.

"Do you have anything more on Kolijo?" I asked.

"Like what?"

"Records. Photos."

He reached into a cupboard and lifted out a heavy cloth-bound volume that bulged with memorabilia. As he opened the book loose pages fell to the floor. Unconcerned, he retrieved the pages and shoved them into the cover before handing the book across. Sorting through the scraps of paper, I found another sketch of the Kolijo church in 1938, two years before my parents were married. I skimmed through the register and although the name Rossini appeared several times, there was no mention of Jack Bellamy.

"Why do you think that happened?" I asked.

"Two reasons, I'd guess. Either they were never married here, or the records were lost."

"Well, they did marry in Kolijo because I have the wedding certificate, and I don't believe parish records just disappear. Some pages are torn. Where are the rest?"

"In those early years nobody cared for records," he said indifferently. "The poor devils were stretched trying to make a living. And besides, Kolijo was never a big deal."

After locking the church door, he led me through a screen of trees to the rear of his presbytery where a fridge hummed noisily in the laundry. Unlatching the fridge he lifted out two cans of beer which he punctured with a blade hanging by a monk's cincture from the roof. He glanced at his watch. "Just gone ten," he said, "and a man could die of thirst. Can't let that happen."

Once he had taken a seat on the laundry steps, he motioned me to a pineapple crate. When I was settled he said, "Bellamy is a common name. I imagine heaps of Bellamys came through here over the years."

"Maybe, Father, but they didn't all marry Maria Rossini."

"Don't take this the wrong way, lad, but Bellamy is an Irish name, and you look, well, Italian. Nothing very Irish about you. Sure you've got the right dad?"

"I'm certain alright. Irish is the weaker gene. Thought everyone knew that." In fact, I knew nothing about genes, and by the look of the priest's face he knew even less.

"Steady on," he said. "I'm only pointing out the obvious. Where were you born?"

"No idea. Orphans aren't told that stuff. Might upset the foster parents."

"So what did you learn at the orphanage?"

"The usual. Why?"

Draining his beer, he reached across and grabbed a fresh can. "Jack, orphanages are terrible places and can lead a man to do strange things, go on strange journeys, get strange ideas."

"Not with me they don't." I replied bluntly. I wasn't letting this priest chase me off the scent.

"I know what I'm saying because I was an orphan like yourself. Does that surprise you? Perhaps not. The Black and Tan killed my folks when I was a wee feller, and I was tossed into a house for strays. I was tainted, you see. My dad was in the IRA and my ma had fallen in love with the wrong man. When they shot him, they shot her too. They said my parents were traitors to the king, but the poor sods only wanted a roof over their heads and the right to go to their own church."

When he fell silent I said, "That's a weird coincidence. My folks were shot too."

"I'm sorry to hear it. Truly sorry."

Sitting his can on the step, he stretched out his legs. The bottoms of his trousers were frayed at the heel and the soles of his shoes had repair rings like an old tree. Despite not seeming to care about his appearance, the place had a smell of money. For a start the beer we were drinking was premium lager.

"When I left the orphanage," he said, "I took the only decent option and joined the priesthood. It was either that or dig spuds for a living. What choice did you have?"

I told him about Maryborough and my apprenticeship with the trains, and that I wanted to lay my devils to rest. "I'm here because they say Dad was a murderer. That's ridiculous. He was a respected war hero and a teacher."

"Can I give you some advice, Jack. For your own sake let it go. Believe your dad is innocent, but move on."

I shook my head. "Mum was a Rossini. I'll keep searching until I find her family."

"You'll need a ton of luck. Tribes of Rossinis live up here. I see them most weekends, and any hour of the day when they're sick."

"I guessed as much," I said without enthusiasm.

He scratched at the beer label while choosing his next words. "Not meaning to be a pain, Jack, but you don't even take after the Rossinis."

"What are you getting at, Father? First you say I'm full-blown Italian, no Irish. Now I'm not even a Rossini. Keep this up, and I'll doubt I was born."

"What I'm saying is that the local Rossinis come from the south. You look like somebody from the north."

"Didn't know there was a difference."

"There is. Northern Italians are taller and fairer. More Austrian and Swiss in their blood."

"Lighter skin? Then that's the Irish in me."

"No, it's a different sort of colouring."

I rolled my eyes. "Here we go."

"Jack, friend to friend. I'm trying to be realistic while you're doing your head in. Seriously. With so many Rossinis around, all different to yourself, you could chase your tail to the moon and back. Take my advice. Go back to Brisbane and start with the State Registry where proper records are kept."

What was the priest's caper? If he was questioning my pedigree, I couldn't figure it out. Since I was half-Rossini according to my parents' wedding certificate, it didn't matter how tall, dark or thin I was. The water was already murky without the priest making it worse, and I wasn't retreating to Brisbane for anyone. I rose from the pineapple crate.

"Before you go, Jack, let me tell you a story."

"I've heard enough, Father."

"Suit yourself, but you're not alone in this world."

"Meaning what?"

"Meaning you should listen."

"Okay, give it to me," I muttered and resettled myself on the crate. I should've been excited but wasn't. I felt I was trapped in a game where the dealer knows, sooner or later, the mug always loses.

He wasted no time. "Like I said, at seventeen I had two choices; be a priest or be a nobody. I had barely started training in the seminary when an uncle, an elderly priest himself, came to the gate. He told me that after my ordination I was expected to join the IRA in the north. Naturally I objected as I wanted a quiet parish in the south. He then explained I had a debt to the IRA who had funded my education. So it was no surprise that on the day I walked out of the seminary in a clerical collar an IRA car was standing at the kerb. I stayed with them two years, trying to keep my nose clean, but that would've been tough to ask of anyone. It came to a head one day when soldiers raided my church in Armagh and stood me against the wall. They gave me a choice. Either I hand over the gunman Joe O'Reilly who was hiding in the belfry, or they shoot me and burn down the church. I was no hero, and anyway Joe was one of the cruellest feckers to ever walk this earth. I turned him over to the British, and the soldiers kept their word. They dressed a body in a priest's cassock and dumped it on the beach at Lough Neagh. Next they blindfolded me, and twenty-four hours later smuggled me into Liverpool where I was given a new name and loaded on a ship to Australia. I worked in a parish at Fortitude Valley for a few years before I moved up here. And this is where I expect to remain until I'm done."

His story ended in silence broken only by the fridge motor. Although a remarkable yarn, I couldn't see the relevance to my dad. Did all Irish Catholics belong to the IRA or something?

I waited for more, but he just stared at me.
"You were... um... lucky," I said.
"That I was, Jack."

As the silence deepened, it occurred to me that he had mentioned Fortitude Valley. Was that the single grain amongst all the chaff?

"Father, while in the Valley did you meet any cops?"

"Irish cops? For sure. The place is full of them."

"Did you know one called Kevin Cleary?"

I watched him closely but he had a can to his mouth. "Hard to say. Cleary is Irish, right enough."

"You would remember him. He limped from a polio infection."

"I seem to recall a man with a limp. What about him?"

"He was my dad's brother-in-law."

Father Burke scratched at a mole on his cheek. His hand shook, but I put that down to the grog. "Sorry lad, I wish I could help. I only mixed with police who had family. You know... church picnics, baptisms, funerals, that sort of thing."

He gazed reflectively at the laundry wall then crossed to the fridge where he pulled out another beer. This was his fourth in under twenty minutes. With his back to me, he lifted a carton of Swan Export from the floor and loaded it into the fridge among several clear bottles. More bottles stood in two lines near the doorway. This priest had enough liquor to defy the apocalypse.

"It could've been me, you know," he said, facing me.

"Infected with polio?"

"No, the body they threw into Lough Neagh." He was blinking rapidly and a web of capillaries now showed in his eyes like cats-claw. "I betrayed a man and one day I'll pay for it. God's truth, he's not the first or the last."

"Sure, Father."

He snorted. "Once you kiss the devil, there's no going back."

I scoffed at his melodrama but as I later discovered, he and his story deserved more respect.

After farewelling the priest who had staggered out to the front to see me off, I rode thoughtfully back to the caravan park. Granted he had filled himself with beer, but why a narrative on mixed loyalties and betrayal? Was it a Sunday homily he couldn't deliver to a packed church? Save it for the unwitting stranger who was partial to a good yarn? I suspected there was more to the story, but it wasn't his past I had come looking for. It was mine, and that's what I found intriguing. He claimed he never knew Maria Rossini whose murder would've been the talk of the district; the good Catholic family who needed the support of their local priest. Meanwhile he had raised other issues, like my dodgy blood lines. Even so, I was certain the name Kevin Cleary had meant something to him. He had dismissed it too quickly. The cop with a limp? A parishioner in the Valley? But knowing Sergeant Kevin Cleary's link with vice, I guess only a fool would admit a connection.

My time with Father Burke had added to the frustration. I had seen drawings of the old Kolijo church and I had found the name Rossini in what remained of parish records, but that was it. Not even the priest's eagerness to see me high-tail it back to Brisbane had a credible explanation. I was stuck on

GO with a dice that kept rolling off the board. Worse still, time was running out. The cane harvest was expected to finish in November and I'd be forced to return to my old job with the trains. Maybe I was the doomed falcon after all.

After my meeting with Father Burke I stopped zipping about with a phone book in which roads were rarely mentioned, just localities, and settled on a two-stage plan. Stage One was to visit all the farms on the right of the highway as far north as the Goorganga Plains. I had chosen the plains for my northern limit because logically anyone living beyond that would have been married in the sugar town of Proserpine. The detective work was slow as endless gravel roads led to farm houses, and often when I arrived the house was empty. Most of the farms grew cane, some had cattle, and others a crop of old cars and rusted machinery.

I had finished doing the right (or ocean) side of the highway and was into Stage Two, the western side, when I struck gold. A wizened farmer at Yalboroo heard the bike in his driveway and after listening to my story untied the gate. He then directed me to the shade and was about to sit down with a pannikin of tea when his brows leapt skyward. A mob of ducks had sneaked into his vegetable garden and were taking it to pieces. In the chase that followed most creatures did the right thing and escaped to the open, but two old ducks led a gang into his fibro house. As the farmer tore in through the back door, the old ducks flew out the front. Behind them novices crashed into walls while a panicked cat set off three dogs that had been watching from my feet. Ten minutes later the farmer fetched his lukewarm tea and apologised for the spectacle.

"No need," I said, reflecting how much I missed good TV.

Once he had regained his breath he explained Maria Rossini wasn't a relative of his even though she had the same surname. He added that in some parts of Italy the name Rossini was very common, and if you wanted to claim kinship you'd have to unravel lineage all the way back to Nero. Meanwhile, Rossini was an offshoot of Rosso, which was even more common, and that Rosso and Rossi were the same depending on whether you came from Brindisi or Brescia. My eyelids were beginning to droop when he remarked that yes indeed, he did know the family, and he certainly remembered the wedding of Maria and Jack. It was a big event for those times, especially for homesick Italians, and the reception was an all-night affair at her parents' farm on the O'Connell River. He had never met Jack, 'that school teacher bloke from the south', but he'd heard Jack had a weakness for the underdog; blacks wanting to play club footy, or poor kids craving an education. According to the talk he was also a wild one but fitted in readily enough. After all, he was a Catholic like themselves and had a prestigious job, which school teaching was in those small towns.

"I reckon he was lucky the war started 'cos he punched a fella at Calen and would've been sacked for sure. Don't know much more because we had our own worries being Eyetie and all." The farmer frowned, recalling his days behind the internment wire. "Mind you, all that torturing in North Africa must've got to him. Why else would a war hero go about killing folks at home? His wife Maria was the catch of the district. Italian studs queued for miles to have a crack at her, but she dumped them all for Jack Bellamy."

The wrinkled farmer studied me. "I heard there was a kid involved, but I thought he didn't survive."

"He did and the kid's me."

"You were lucky, well, maybe not so lucky. That's life. Anyway, Maria's older brother Carl now runs the farm and he owns most of the valley upriver from the bridge."

CHAPTER 5

The next weekend I didn't get a chance to look up Carl Rossini because the Farleigh Mill broke down on Friday, and we had to cut cane Saturday. That's when the days were long. After loading your rail siding with extra bins Friday night, the mill expected the contractor and his haul-out drivers to go hard all next day to fill them. Sometimes we'd be dropping the last bin onto the tramway just as the sun faded into the Clarke Ranges. All the same, day's end brought its own contentment. The machines suddenly quiet, the soft purples of the forest melting into the green cane, and the blokes in the gang thirsting for a beer at the Calen Hotel. It was times like this I enjoyed the job. I could feel it made sense to be Italian in this climate, where the sun was hot and the opportunities endless. Hard work was rewarded with prosperity and the fertile land stretched from the mountains to the sea like a ripe virgin. Sadly the virgin wasn't yet stretching out for me, or at least that I could tell.

Saturday a week later and with the mill's crushing on schedule, we had the day off. Mid-morning I spruced myself up and rode along the highway to the O'Connell River bridge. It's a mighty impressive river from the new bridge and the farms along both sides looked successful, but I couldn't see any homestead, only a few fibro houses, sheds and cane cutters' barracks. I rode back to the turn-off, at a place called Cathu, then along a gravel road until I came to another bridge, which I crossed and kept going. Five minutes later the road traversed a narrow spur then entered a valley that opened out to large blocks of cane on the left and cattle paddocks on the stony, uneven right. On a rise in the middle of the flat area where the river had taken a deviation, stood a spacious brick farmhouse, deep verandahs along three sides and lawns shaded by poinciana and mango trees. To one side of the house sprawled a group of machinery sheds, and further back a causeway that led over the river to cattle yards. Against the foothills a tractor worked the loam to an escort of crows, while nearer at hand the zing of cicadas filled the bright morning air.

I climbed off the bike and walked across to the sheds where a man with grey hair and overalls serviced a harvester. When he saw me he straightened from the chain he was adjusting and wiped his hands.

"Good day," I said. "I'm looking for Carl Rossini."

"That's me," he answered and stuck out his hand. "And who might you be?"

"Jack Bellamy."

You'd think I had slapped him with a wet fish. First he was startled then he frowned, then his face went thunderous black. Not that colours were easy to identify as Carl was a wire-headed Italian whose skin was burnt to teak.

"Jack Bellamy," he grunted after his blood pressure had settled. "So who was your father?"

"Same name," I said, shaken by the response.

He took a deep breath. "It's been good meeting you, Mr Bellamy, but I've a stack of jobs to finish. You can do me a favour and return the way you came." With that he turned aside, grabbed a couple of spanners and buried his head under the elevator chain.

This was weird. I coughed politely and said, "I never knew Dad."

"Then you were lucky."

"He married your sister?"

Carl withdrew his head. "Maybe he did. And maybe he was the mongrel who killed her."

"She was my mum," I said, holding my ground.

"Yeah, that was rough. But I don't want the name Jack Bellamy fouling this air."

"Hey, mister. Her death had nothing to do with me. I was the little kid lashed to the oars."

"I know the story, but that chapter's closed, permanent. So if you don't mind, I'm busy."

Some things get me riled, and being told to piss off is one of them. "Listen, old man, I've come looking for Mum and Dad. I never knew them and I've spent half my life in an orphanage. So don't give me crap about fouling your precious air."

He tossed a spanner in his hand as if weighing a club then turned back to the harvester. "Like I said, boy, I've work to do. So jump on your bike and go home."

I glared at his back considering my next move when I realised we had the same mop of curly hair. The old coot was undoubtedly my uncle and since blood is thicker than water, I discarded any idea of leaving empty-handed. With that I gazed about the farm, concluding that I probably stood on the very land where Mum had grown up, the actual bit of earth where she had played oblivious to the tragedy awaiting her. There was nothing for it, I'd have to show myself around. I wandered into the shed and took in the smell of oil and sweat. Tools hung on the wall and piles of greasy rags and bits of machinery littered the benches. In one corner a giant tractor waited on blocks for somebody to replace the rear wheel. I didn't get any vibes about my mother in that shed, and as the back door stood open, I walked through to a couple more sheds, a sprawling hen house and a small orchard of persimmon and custard apple. Across to the left at the rear of the house stood a clothes line with dry sheets flapping in the breeze.

As Carl still hadn't appeared, I stuck my nose into the two sheds that were identical, even down to the weather beaten slabs. One was a bits-and-pieces museum from pre-war days, and the other contained saddlery, bridles and leather that appeared still in use. While I studied the horse gear I tried to imagine Mum as a little girl who kept her saddle here and helped the men with the cattle. She would've liked the outdoor life and her horse would've been her best mate. Shrugging off the ghost of a mother I never knew, I turned my attention to the house. It was typical north Queensland: two big water tanks on stands, the laundry out back near the tanks, a concrete path from the clothesline and three short steps leading to a screen door that stood wide open.

I was now certain this was Mum's home, and I was determined to locate her presence in it somewhere. Closing the door on the saddlery shed, I was halfway to the house when Carl powered through from the front. His fists were bunched, and he didn't look pleased. "You're trespassing on my land," he roared. "Now beat it."

Two could play this game, so I squared up to him. "Carl, you're my uncle, and you've got rotten manners."

At that instant a young woman ran out the back door with a laundry basket in her hands. Midstride, she heard my voice and skidded to a halt at the bottom step. I gaped at her, she gaped at me and Carl swung his head back and forth like an old bull. Aside from the shock of the moment I had good reason to gape. This woman was a knock-out. She would've been aged about twenty and was a genuine Italian beauty with the dark hair and creamy skin of a Vespa photo-model.

Her eyes swept me up and down. "What's going on, Dad?"

"This young fella was about to hop on his bike."

"No I wasn't," I said.

"Who are you?" she demanded.

"Jack Bellamy."

For a moment the eyes widened but that was all.

"And you?" I asked.

"We own this farm. What are you doing here?"

"I've come looking for my mother, Maria Rossini."

That one landed. She did a double take like her old man. "I'm Maria Rossini," she said quietly, "and I'm not your mother. You've obviously made a mistake, Mr Bellamy. Please leave."

"I've made no mistake, Miss Maria," I said, imitating her hoity tone. "Your dad and my mum were brother and sister."

She stared at her father. "Is that true, Dad?"

"No, it's not bloody true. I've never met his mother. Never."

The girl couldn't drag her huge brown eyes from Carl who was on the brink of a seizure.

"Please leave us, Mr Bellamy... Jack," she said.

I knew I had struck lucky, but the show was going nowhere. Jamming my helmet on my head, I left the scene. Half an hour later as I roared down the highway towards Mackay I let out a long happy whistle. Mum's family had been unearthed. Later I tried to picture her as a beauty like her niece. According to the aged farmer at Yalboroo, Italian studs had queued for miles to have a crack at her. The sons of those studs were probably licking their lips over young Maria who was back at home with a washing basket in one arm and an apoplectic old man in the other.

I also got to thinking that I couldn't come so near to Mum and Dad then let them disappear.

Next Saturday I was back at the farm and Carl was ready for me. The sheds and laundry were empty, but when I climbed onto the verandah he came to the door and handed me a scrap of paper.

"My sister Loretta lives at this address in North Mackay," he mumbled. "Her married name is Townsend. She'll confirm what I've already said."

"Thanks, but one thing. Did Mum live here until she got married?"

He took a long time answering. "I said I don't know your mother."

"Okay. Did your sister Maria live here until she married?"

"Yes."

"And did she marry a bloke called Jack Bellamy?"

The pain was so visible in his face you could touch it. "Talk to my sister."

CHAPTER 6

I had been hoping to catch a glimpse of Maria but as that now seemed unlikely, I jumped on the Norton and rode across to a row of timber houses near the Gooseponds in North Mackay. All the houses were the same; weatherboard, up on high stumps, and partly bricked in underneath. Each had the obligatory palm out front and a paling fence that struggled for authority over the rampant grass. I knocked on Number 27 and after a while the door was opened by a plump Italian woman in her fifties. She had greyed round the edges, and although she was no longer handsome she had young Maria's cheekbones and mouth.

"Loretta Townsend?" I asked.

She looked me over before answering. "You Jack Bellamy?"

"That's right."

No raised eyebrows, just a gruff question, "What do you want, lad?"

"Um… my mother was your sister. She died when I was little and I want to learn all about her."

Loretta Townsend was taking no chances on letting me into her house, and who could blame her after the description Carl had probably given. She planted herself in the doorway. "Well, as you might've guessed, and assuming Maria was your mother, she grew up on the farm. She was the sweetest kid on earth until Jack Bellamy showed up. They got married. He went off to war, came back half crazy, then in a state of drunken lunacy shot her."

I wasn't ready to buy that yarn and I had a feeling she was testing me. I shook my head. "They were on a boating picnic in Moreton Bay. That's not the style of a drunken lunatic."

"Maybe he was a sober lunatic. It made no difference." Then she studied me frankly. "If you're the young Jack, you were a pretty boy. What happened?"

"I was brought up in an orphanage. Somebody broke my nose."

"Like father, like son. Always into fights."

"So you agree Maria was my mum. Can you tell me how they met, that sort of thing?"

She still wasn't ready to let me inside, but she eased back on the prickliness. "It was at the dances where most folk gathered in those days. It would've been late '39 during the crushing. I wasn't long out of school when she came home with this cocky Australian. Good-looking, full of mickey. And he knew how to turn a girl's eye. Dad never took to him, but Mum had her own ideas. Teachers were somebody you looked up to."

She was about to tell me more. Her face had even begun to soften, then she said abruptly, "Sorry, lad, but I've got scones in the oven. I'd better see to them."

I wasn't making progress with anyone. They certainly knew how to carry a grievance. I guess the disappointment showed in my face. "Thanks, Mrs Townsend."

"Look, your dad boarded with the Avolio family at Pindi Pindi. Paulo Avolio was a few years older than your father. His people know the story better than most."

"Why's that?"

"Ask him."

With that she glanced back at the kitchen. "Must go. See ya." And pulled the door shut.

At least Loretta had given me a lead to follow, and the timing was perfect as we were due to harvest Avolio's cane that same week. Sure enough, no sooner had we arrived at his farm at sunset ready to light the canefield when Paulo turned up in his utility. The harvester driver had a quick word with him before we split into groups and spent the next half hour burning the leaf from the crop.

After the blaze had settled, I walked up to Paulo and offered my hand. "My name is Jack Bellamy. I'm told you knew my father."

In the flickering light of the embers he squinted at me and said. "Jack Bellamy? Do I know that name?"

"You should, Paulo. My father boarded with you before the war."

He wasn't a very good actor. "Oh, that Jack Bellamy?" After shaking my hand, he fiddled with a wad of tobacco and papers.

"So you were the kid they pulled from the bay."

"Yes, that's me."

"You've grown into a fine young man."

"I won't argue with that," I said, then got to the point. "What do you remember of Dad?"

The guy was nervous, which was odd. Even assuming Carl had warned him of my visit, we were talking about events from the forties, and earlier. He settled himself onto the tailgate and told a yarn that sounded like a rehearsed speech. Much like Loretta's in a way. "Your father was a new boy to the district. You probably guessed that, but you mightn't have known he was somebody to be wary of. Liked fighting as much as he liked a good time. And he was all class at rugby league. Captained Calen District the year we won the finals. I remember we all trotted along to watch, then hung about to clap his black players who got presented like they were on special leave from heaven. Normal stuff today, but it was embarrassing back then. After the war he flipped his lid, but considering what happened in Africa who could blame him? Still, you'd have to be crazy to shoot your missus, then tie your kid to an oar hoping he'd float."

Paulo inhaled on his cigarette and blew plumes of smoke through his nostrils. He didn't have the grizzled Italian features like Carl. His face was thin European, and his high forehead and hooded eyes gave the appearance of a rogue lawyer. But they weren't hostile eyes, just watchful. Right now they studied me.

"Did you and Dad get along?" I asked.

"At first, sure. We all did, but they were early days, and we were taken by the larrikin in him. After a time others like Carl saw him in a new light; too good-looking, too superior, too whatever."

"And you?"

Paulo's lips twitched in a half smile. "He was okay. Actually, I found him easy to get along with. Maybe because we were from opposite poles, him the smart white teacher, me the dumb Eyetie farmer.

And, of course, he played up when it suited. No family around to embarrass."

"Perhaps he wanted family when he married Mum. How did they meet?"

"There's no point glossing over the story. I remember the night well. There was a dance in Cohen's Hall at Calen, just a block up from the pub. Four of us - Carl Rossini, Jack Bellamy, my brother Guido and myself - arrived in Carl's old flatback truck. Maria came too, but she sat in the front with her sister Loretta. It was some dance. Blokes and sheilas were there from miles about." Paulo stopped and puffed on his smoke. I thought he'd forgotten me, but after fogging his lungs he continued. "Maria was the… ah… belle of the ball. Real eye-catcher. Like a Hollywood star, and she knew it. Folks often said she'd be strife. Too pretty for a joint like this."

"Did she have a boyfriend?"

"You could say that. She was declared to my brother Guido."

"Declared?"

"Yes, Italian custom. Goes back centuries. They were going to marry."

I frowned. This wasn't in the script. "They were engaged?"

"As good as."

"Did Dad… um… know this?"

"Everybody did. It was no secret, hadn't been for months, though that meant bugger-all to Jack. He saw a pretty girl and he wanted her. Which didn't seem to bother Maria. She might've been cute, but she was no angel. Jack wrangled two or three dances out of her, then when it came time to leave, Guido said he wasn't sharing a vehicle with the likes of

Jack. Jack said, please yourself, but he wasn't walking home. So Guido jumped off the back and tried to force Maria to stay with him. She didn't, of course; six miles in high heels would've been deadly. I don't know how long the walk took, but Guido was at breakfast with the rest of us. He didn't say much, not that he ever did, poor bugger. Maybe if he'd spoken up none of this sad business would've happened. Anyway, a month later they held the cut-out dance, the biggest night of the year. We were all there and tensions were high. The next minute Jack and Guido started fighting. Jack won the fight and the girl."

"Even though she was *declared*?"

"Yep. A line was crossed that night."

"And you saw the fight?"

"Everyone did. The hall's not that big."

"Were they matched?"

"Not really. Italians prefer the good life, sadly for Guido."

"So nobody tried to break it up?"

"Take on Jack Bellamy? Get real."

Paulo toyed with a box of matches and I couldn't help thinking he had seen aggro of his own making. It mightn't have been in the face or eyes, but he had strong, smooth hands that coiled and uncoiled over the matchbox.

"As I was saying, I got along with Jack but I felt for my kid brother. He lived for Maria, then along comes a playboy from the city and steals her. Not that she won any friends out of it. Behaved like a trollop, despite her being your mum." He spat out a strand of tobacco and maybe it was the taste of Mum he didn't like. "Poor Guido was never the same. And you've got to remember we're a small community here. He expected to marry his sweetheart, buy into a farm and breed a family."

"So why didn't he find another girl? You said the cut-out dance was huge. Must've been Italian girls by the truckload."

Paulo's hooded eyes went cold then he chuckled. "There was only one star in the heaven for Guido. Anyway, once Jack had his trophy he wasted no time showing her off. Even used a Norton to cart her round. Funny thing but you ride a Norton, must be the old man in you." When he got no response, he went on. "Well, Jack and Maria were married down the road in Kolijo. After the wedding they lived at the Rise and Shine in the original Rossini farmhouse. Jack stayed on teaching after the war started then he signed up with the infantry in Mackay, and Maria went back to her parents. When the war ended they lived for a short time at the farmhouse then he left for Brisbane and took her with him."

Paulo's mixed feelings in the story were understandable. Although he felt for his brother, he had a grudging admiration for Dad and everything would've been rosy had Maria stayed loyal. But you had to wonder if she and Guido were truly matched. Even if Dad hadn't showed up, countless other young men were knocking at her door. However, I kept my trap shut. Paulo was talking even though he had the fidgets, like he was breaking rank to chat with a stranger. Apart from cicadas rasping in the distance the evening was quiet as haul-out drivers walked round the block with knapsacks on their backs. An ember on the headland flared and the men sprayed it with water. I got to thinking about Paulo's story.

Although it was informative, it hardly put anyone in the frame for murder as men had fought over women since creation. The winner took first prize, the loser cast about for a second girl and life went on.

"How well do you know Carl Rossini?" I asked.

"We are not drinking buddies, but we're farmers in the same district. And we knocked about as kids."

"Do you know his daughter, Maria?"

For the first time Paulo's eyes glowed. "Of course. She's a sweet lass, that one."

"Does she resemble my mother?"

"Yep, very similar. But there is a difference. Unlike young Maria, your mother fell for the rat with a gold tooth. No disrespect of course. She wasn't content with the one good man she had, she wanted another."

"Paulo, is it possible Mum fooled about while Dad was away?" I asked carefully.

He broke apart his dead cigarette and tipped the unburnt tobacco into the packet. His hands were no longer steady. "She might've done, who knows, but that's not the point. She chose Jack and a life in Brisbane away from family. She could've been happy in Calen. This is where she belonged. She upset everybody."

Fair comment, I thought, but I wasn't here to cry over Calen's misfortune. In any case I wanted to hear about the good side of my mother - the *gentle woman* of Aunty Nell's description - which Paulo was not giving me. I had an idea.

"Paulo, I'd like to meet young Maria, but her old man won't let me near the place."

"Do you blame him? He's seen what happens when a stranger named Jack Bellamy comes to town."

"We can't all be judged by our fathers. Where does Maria work?"

"I'm not saying. Only mugs let history repeat itself."

"According to who? History's like lightning. Never strikes twice in the same place."

He leant over the side of the ute to trim the wick of his burner. You could see the anger in his face. "I told you, Jack, let Maria be."

By now the fire had died away leaving the caramel smell of burnt molasses. The men from the gang were throwing their tools into the back of the utes and heading for home. I grabbed my bike helmet about to give up on Paulo when he tapped me on the arm. "They decorated Jack because he risked his life for his mates. Maybe he was like that at war, but a man who shoots his wife is no hero. That's how people remember him around here, so take my advice and stop digging up the past."

Although his voice had changed - now threatening like Carl's - I had come a long way to find my roots. I said again, "Where does Maria work?"

"Jack, bugger off home. You'd do everyone a favour."

That did it. I walked back and pushed my visored face into the bridge of his lawyerly nose. "Paulo, mate, where does she work?"

His eyes were two hooded lights. "Venardos in Sydney Street."

CHAPTER 7

That night after leaving Paulo's farm I rode slowly down the highway watching the sporadic glows in the sky as farmers torched their blocks of cane. The sun had long gone and stars struggled to appear through the clouds of smoke that followed each blaze. The nearer to Calen the bigger the fires, as if neighbours were trying to out-glow each other on bonfire night. Since my goggles were fouled with soot, I called into the pub at Calen to wait out the inferno. Several men sat in the bar, among them an Irishman named Eamon who hauled cane for a small contractor south of the river. He was a roughly dressed, thickset man with a pelt of hair and a smorgasbord of tattoos circling each arm like medieval scrolls. However, his eyes were intelligent and his voice educated whenever he dropped the boozy Irish accent. Hired on a temporary visa, Eamon often said the path to residency was via a woman's bed.

When the barmaid had poured me a beer, I drew up a stool beside him.

"What sorrows are you drowning, Eamon?"

"Ah, my friend, I be reflectin', not drownin'."

"Go on."

"Tat lass behind te bar, what do ye tink of her?"

I studied the girl. She was somewhere between twenty and thirty with fair hair and a vague, homely face. She wore a full blouse sheltering a mountain of breast, and on her arms a string of bangles that tinkled as she moved.

"She's okay, I guess."

"Okay? Begorrah. She's a comely lass. Heavy wit' sadness, waitin' for a good man."

"She won't find him in Calen."

He peered at me like the priest had done in the laundry. The gaze was shrewd despite the impression he was all beer and piss. "To be sure, a good man sits beside Jack, and he cannot see it."

"Have you spoken to her?" I asked.

"Aye."

"Well?"

"Hard to know. She t'inks I talk funny." He measured the girl from her sturdy feet to her plain face. "Ah, she would make a grand wife."

"Then ask her out. She looks bored enough." I changed the subject. "Eamon, do you come from the north or south of Ireland?"

"I were born in a wee town called Shillanmore."

"Where's that?"

"County Fermanagh."

Still none the wiser, I asked, "Are you a Catholic?"

His eyes were shrewd again. "Tat's a dangerous question, my friend."

"I'm not prying into your faith. A few weeks ago I met an old priest who said he'd been in the IRA. He came to Australia because his life was at risk."

"Irishmen, Jews, Poles. Lots of poor devils flee t'eir homes."

I outlined my conversation with Father Burke. "Can anyone join the IRA? Such as the priest, say?"

"Ah, tat crowd give and take as tey choose. T'is best tey be left alone." He studied me carefully. "Does sometin' about te priest trouble ye?"

"No. But it's odd he would talk about his betrayal. Surely he'd take that secret to the grave."

He was about to comment, then stopped and affected a matey, tipsy voice. "Ah, tis te drink and te sun. A sad old priest who has no friends, and who in Calen cares? Tey're all Italians who tink IRA is a Latin swear word. Do yeself a kindness and forget him." He laughed and beckoned to the girl who leant against the taps filing her nails. She looked up and smiled.

As the cane fires had died away, I emptied my beer. "See you next week, Eamon."

"No, my friend. Next week I'm in Sydney. Job on te wharf. Ye be careful now. Real careful."

"You too, and take the girl with you."

Work in the canefields was a revolving door for men who had no ties to the north, but I hadn't expected Eamon to leave so soon. He was a respected driver who seemed content with the money and lifestyle. Still, a job on the wharves was close to ideal; legendary pay coupled with minimal work and lifetime security. It was an exclusive career handed down from father to son. So how had Eamon managed it? *When this business is over I'll look you up*, I thought to myself. *Get a job there too*. Meanwhile, his advice about the priest was sensible. Who indeed cared if he had invented a life in the IRA or been sent to Australia to save his skin? All that mattered was he denied any knowledge of my father and mother or the cop Kevin Cleary. So I moved both the priest and Eamon's names from the 'possible' to the 'unhelpful' list, which was expanding by the day.

Back at the van I lay on my bed and flicked through a vintage *Playboy* magazine I had found in the laundry. Mostly at night I read about trains because steel wheels on steel tracks got a man dreaming of exciting places, but the girls in *Playboy* could do that too. Tonight however, I threw away the magazine after a few pages. Apart from the endless merry-go-round I had found myself on, Eamon's sudden departure, with or without the barmaid, had depressed me.

A week later we encountered one of those rare harvesting days when the cane was straight and clean, the rows long and the bins all finished by midafternoon. With hours to fill before the evening fire, I was horsing about with a grease gun when the boss swore loudly and ordered me to Mackay to fetch spares for the harvester. I completed the errand, and although I looked a grub - cane ash and grease everywhere - I drove across to Venardos and asked for Maria Rossini. In no time she emerged at the front counter, but I was too filthy to be recognised. The same couldn't be said from my end of the lens. Although now wearing sensible office dress, she confirmed my first impression of an Italian beauty.

"Hi Maria."

She frowned as recognition dawned. "Oh, hello… What are you doing here?"

"I came to fetch tractor parts. Thought I'd take a minute to say hi."

"Well, I appreciate that, but I'm awfully busy. So if you don't mind." And turned to leave.

"Whoa…" I said throwing up my hands. "I just wanted to ask one thing."

"Okay, but keep it quick."

"Do you have a boyfriend?" I felt myself going red under the soot.

"Is that it?" she asked, incredulously.

"Well... no. Yes. Actually, what I'm asking..."

"Please..."

I blundered on. "If I scrubbed up and all, would you eat with me tonight?"

"Thanks for the invite but the answer is n-o. No."

"You don't have a boyfriend?"

"I do. No was to the second question."

"So I'm out of luck?"

"Look - Jack, isn't it? - we appear to be on different wavelengths. I love my father very much, and he's not... um... keen to have anything to do with you. Nor am I. Sorry." She smiled apologetically which made her even more appealing. "So please, let's go our separate ways and forget the silly games."

I tossed my last card on the table. "Maria, I'm an orphan. You know, the kid that's got no folks. In the last few weeks I've located their ghosts, and when I ask about them I'm treated like a leper. You're my cousin, the only cousin I know apart from a dill in Brisbane, so what's the crime for reaching out to family?"

"Jack, please. You're treading on peoples' feelings. Let it go, okay?"

"I'm sorry, Maria, but my mother died violently before she was thirty. How can I?"

The battle inside her was impressive. She drummed her nails on the counter before giving a little toss of the head. "Okay, tonight seven-thirty at Maguire's. In the lounge bar."

With that she turned on her heel and was gone. When the girl on reception said, "Excuse me, fella, you're spreading muck on the floor," I snapped out of my trance and headed through the exit, punching the air. Dinner tonight with Maria, and who cared if her old man would love nothing more than to boot me off a cliff.

CHAPTER 8

That night I dug out my best jeans and shirt and fronted up to Maguire's Hotel. I was early and Maria was late. Real late. Just when I thought she'd caught a bout of cold feet she arrived, flustered and tense.

"Sorry," I said quietly.

"What for?"

"This is a big favour you're doing me."

"Please, let's get it over."

She had changed into baggy jeans and a loose shirt, pulled her hair into a tight knot and scrubbed off her make-up. She didn't want me getting any ideas; this was an information session, end of story.

After letting me buy her a lemon, lime and bitters she sat across from a small table.

"Have you eaten?" I asked.

"No." And without looking at the board she murmured, "I'll have the barramundi and salad."

Once the girl had come and taken our orders I said, "How long have you worked at Venardos?"

She ignored the small talk. "You wanted to ask about your mother. What was it?"

"Well, for a start you could explain why your dad hates me."

"Dad doesn't hate anyone. It's not in his nature. He's a good man. What happened to his sister is still painful, and he wishes people wouldn't snoop around."

"I'm not *people*, I'm his nephew. That must carry some weight on the family tree."

"Jack, why don't you leave it alone? There's nothing will come from raking over the past. Dad's had to live with losing Aunty Maria for twenty years. He loved her dearly, and he sees in your face the man who took her away."

"That's a bit harsh. While Jack was at war, Maria lived at home. He didn't take her from anyone."

"After the war he did."

"Only as far as Brisbane. That's not the end of the earth."

"He also shot her."

"That's not true."

"And you'd know, of course."

She played with her cutlery waiting for the food to arrive.

"Do you get on with your folks?" I asked.

"Like most kids, I suppose."

"Maria, do you understand where I'm coming from? Maybe not. If you haven't been to an orphanage you couldn't know what it's like. The word 'parents' is banned. Nobody wants to talk about the black hole we came out of. We're in the orphanage because folk don't know what to do with us, and they don't try to make our lives easier or more pleasant. We're treated like nuisances that had to be chucked into a kids' prison for our own good. That's tough for a little fella who's done nothing wrong. I can't help that Mum and Dad died of gunshot wounds. But it's like I'm wearing the blame. Carl takes it out on me when I only want to learn about Mum and where she came from."

"You can't expect Dad to be friendly when the name Jack Bellamy still burns a hole in him."

"And you? Does Jack Bellamy cut you up?"

"No, Jack, it doesn't," she said curtly, "but you have to remember your father ripped this community apart. Before the war - before your father arrived - everything was fine. People were happy." She took a deep breath and for the first time lifted her face. "I think that... no, I don't know why I believe this, but I do... in the early days Jack Bellamy was popular. From all accounts he had the gifts. He was brave, he was good looking and he had charm, probably too much of everything. Did you know he stole Aunty Maria from one of Dad's friends, Guido Avolio?"

I nodded.

"He didn't win any mates out of that. It was by fighting, of all things"... she pulled a face... "and at a dance, of all places. Even the cops kept their distance."

"Cops are like that."

"Not up here. They loved the sport of Italian bashing."

"Watching, or taking part?"

"Both. Loretta tells of one whose leg should've kept him out of fights, but didn't."

"Leg? You mean he had a bad leg?"

"I guess so. Do you know him?"

"I know one who had polio. His name is Cleary." I tried to remember what Sergeant Harry had told me in the Valley café. "And I think he was stationed at Calen."

That's all I said. It wasn't the time to mention he was Dad's brother-in-law.

"Anyway," Maria went on, "by the outbreak of war your father was no longer popular, especially with Guido's family. He had stolen the girl who was to rear the next generation of Avolios. When he returned after the war everybody was at first understanding - hoping he'd leave, I'd guess - but the mood didn't last. Bear in mind what I'm telling you I learned later as I grew up. Stuff people talked about at night. Events that hurt them badly." She stopped, realising she had said too much.

"What kind of events?"

"Oh, little things really. But at the time they seemed huge."

"What little things?"

She just clammed up. On an impulse I reached out and took the hand that was playing with the cutlery. Her skin was soft and the fingers trembled like a bird. "Maria, tell me what you know."

She withdrew her hand and stared into my face; a flash of concern, or was it anger? Hard to tell under the pub fluoro. "After the war, Jack came back to the O'Connell River and while he was waiting to get demobbed he found work on the local farms. He liked that better than teaching, but they said you had to be careful with him. He wasn't all charm like before. Sometimes he got morose and nasty, and he drank a lot. Before returning to the Rise and Shine they lived at our house and Mum said she could hear them talking late, then he'd start crying. She says it was awful to hear a man so broken. Next morning Maria would come out dark-eyed and Jack would disappear without so much as a cup of tea. Although this went on for weeks, Mum refused to condemn him. He'd just returned from a dreadful war."

"So what was the bad event?"

She lowered her face and I bent forward to hear better. "One day Jack and Guido went hunting for feral pigs in the ranges at the top of the valley. There was an accident and Guido got shot."

"Guido, the ex-boyfriend?" I asked, astonished.

"Yes. The police said there wasn't enough evidence to prove your father pulled the trigger, so the coroner wrote it off as an accident."

"Did the locals believe the coroner?"

"No."

I let out my breath. "So that's why everybody is so touchy. They think Dad went gun crazy. First he shoots the boyfriend, then takes his wife to Brisbane and shoots her too."

Maria was miserable. She was trying to keep her composure, but when she sniffled I unwrapped her napkin.

"In any case," I said after an awkward pause, "why would Dad shoot Guido? Was the man playing around with Mum?"

"They're both now dead, Jack. I shouldn't have told you."

"Well, if Guido was hopping back fences at night, your father has a nerve treating me like a pariah. Besides, Guido sounds an idiot."

"Don't talk like that."

"Well, he'd be an idiot to go hunting with the man he's cheated on."

"You're rushing to conclusions. Most likely your mum was a faithful wife. In those days Italian women had to be. They lost everything if they weren't."

By now my steak and three vege had arrived. I pushed Guido's death to one side and ate hungrily, washing the food down with a pot of lager. After Maria had picked at her barramundi and played with her drink, she started glancing at her watch.

"Maria, I'm not the mongrel people think I am. I'm just a bit rough round the edges from living in an orphanage. And I do want to find my roots. I'd like to tell you sometime about what I saw from the clock tower in Maryborough. Can I see you on the weekend?"

"I don't think that's wise, Jack."

"Well, how about Monday after work for a coffee. We finish our bins by three o'clock, and I do stuff-all until dark."

She forced a weak smile. "Okay. Five o'clock Monday. I'll meet you at the entrance to Caneland Plaza. And remember it's coffee only."

Maria drove home and I found my way into the main bar where I swallowed another two beers. A young couple were playing ping-pong on a TV screen, and a team of navvies in matching shirts were halfway through a competition on the dartboard. I perched on a stool and gazed sightlessly at the bar while my thoughts spun in circles. According to the locals Dad had lost the plot badly. After years at war he involves himself in a shooting 'accident' with his wife's old boyfriend, then sometime later kills his wife who happens to be Calen's star chicken. No wonder they haven't treated me like a prodigal son.

CHAPTER 9

The rest of the weekend was fairly quiet. On Saturday afternoon I took the bike for a spin up to Proserpine where I turned right on the Bowen side of town and threaded the two peaks of Mount Julian and Mount Marlow. Then it was down through the canefields to Airlie Beach. The handful of shops facing each other in the village were closed and long-legged herons picked through shells at the low water mark. Airlie was a quiet joint in those days. You were either a cane grower, a fisherman or itinerant, depending on the clothes you wore. Although the coppers frowned on anyone who didn't seem local (it was their job I guess), I often rode up to Airlie and spent the night. The little village was one of those places that made the heart sing. A man could stand on the pub verandah at sunset and watch the blues fold into pink across the Coral Sea, and later drink with the visiting yachties. That Saturday was one of those times. Half of me buzzed with the excitement of another meeting with Maria, and the other half grappled with my latest discovery on Dad. The rich colours of the Whitsundays were solace to a confused soul, and I wound up drinking vodka with a German girl who played Pink Floyd endlessly on the jukebox. Sometime later we collapsed on a moonlit sand that palms had cut into shards of clear, glittering silver. Even at that drunken hour the pair of us were neither friends nor strangers, together nor alone, happy nor sad. When I woke at daylight the depression in the sand beside me was empty and a soft rain was blowing in from Mandalay Peninsula. I climbed on my bike and rode home.

CHAPTER 10

Next Sunday night we again torched cane on the Avolio farm, but Paulo didn't appear. His son Sam, who was roughly my age, came out to lend a hand. Although of good height and build, Sam looked too poncy to be a farmer. Long, dark curls framed a chiselled, olive face and everything about him seemed too fashionably arranged. But it was Sunday and I guess a man needn't wear overalls every day of the week. The fire went okay, and I was riding back to the Jolimont Creek Caravan Park by seven-thirty.

That was the only weakness with a seasonal job. Once work was over for the day, time was the enemy. We were too knackered to go fishing or boating, and on the nights of a burn we rarely got home before eight, followed by a five o'clock start the next morning. Mostly we burnt every third night, but sometimes the fires escaped, and we'd have to cut solidly on one farm for a whole week. Not that runaway fires were always our fault. In the old days when steam locos hauled the cane to the mill, fires were a constant hazard. Sometimes it was the loco spitting hot coals, but often it was canny old farmers wanting to harvest their crop while sugar was at its peak. They would throw a match after the loco had past, knowing burnt cane lasted only five days before turning to alcohol. As a consequence of the runaway fire, all harvester operators in the area would be ordered to the farm where they'd work feverishly to bring in the crop. One year an old Yugoslav's farm burnt out 'unexpectedly' the third season in a row, and again right after a loco had driven past and his cane was at its prime. Disgruntled neighbouring farmers watched the fire roar through to the creek and did nothing. Not during that day, nor in the next week. Some say the Yugoslav was unlucky, but his cane never burnt unexpectedly again.

However, that night, as there were no runaway fires, I called in at the Kolijo store to replenish my pantry. Since arriving in the north I'd been forced to learn the mysterious art of cooking. In the orphanage tucker had been stodgy, but it filled our bellies. After the orphanage I lived in boarding houses where older women cooked, and although we were expected to wash up at night, we never so much as boiled an egg. But once alone in the caravan with a two-burner stove taunting me, I had two choices - cook or perish. Bravely I opened a cupboard to discover, apart from a saucepan and frying pan, gadgets for peeling, straining and mixing. Deciding to experiment, I rode to the store and bought silverside, potatoes, pumpkin and peas. Back at the van I cooked up an undemanding meal of boiled meat and three vege, which became my staple for the next several weeks.

As it happened, the pasta menu entered my life entirely by chance. Having mistaken a can of tomato puree for baked beans, I held the offending item under the store lady's nose. "What am I supposed to do with this *puree* stuff?"

Surprised by the question, the blonde laughed and said, "Make pasta sauce like your rellies do."

She then grabbed a packet of noodles, pointed to the recipe on the side and fetched the ingredients from her shelves. Back in my kitchen I was mildly encouraged by my first attempt. And I had reason to be pleased. During my orphanage years I had loathed spaghetti because it was wop food, but in the north pasta was standard fare, which I discovered at lunch on the first farm we cut. More to the point, my pasta dishes awoke in me the cultural reverse my mum would have encountered when she chose to leave the Italian circle.

Next day we cut Avolio's cane and I never laid eyes on Paulo or his son, Sam. By mid-afternoon we had dumped our eighty, four-ton bins into the Pindi Pindi siding. After filling out the weighbridge docket I rode back to Jolimont Creek where I showered and changed before heading to Caneland Plaza, the new shopping centre on the edge of the city. I was a good ten minutes early and sat on a concrete gnome watching the scurry of last-minute shoppers; women scanning from their lists while the blokes sprinted in their wake with miscreant trolleys. Shortly after five Maria emerged from the car park. Even when troubled, as she appeared now, she had the beautiful, enigmatic face Romans sculptured out of marble, and her office dress though a functional white blouse and navy skirt, understated the classic body. As she entered the mall she saw me and waved, but her face was no-nonsense. Not even the hint of a smile.
"We'd better hurry," she said. "They don't take orders after five-fifteen."
I didn't care about the coffee, I only wanted this time together, and I suppose in my mind she was becoming two people: Maria the desirable young woman, and Maria the niece of the mother I had never met.

We sat at a formica table and ordered coffees despite a scowl from the girl who had finished wiping down and stacking the chairs.

"You wanted to tell me something about the view from the clock tower," she said.

"That's right. But it wasn't an ordinary tower. After doing my time in the orphanage, I found myself in Maryborough where there's a City Hall and ornate clock tower. I became friends with the curator and sometimes after work he'd unlock the door in the Committee Room and let me into the tower. There was something special about climbing that long narrow stairway. And at the top is a hatch that leads onto a broad parapet from where you can see to every corner of the city. Well, there were thousands of timber homes with contented people living in them. Some of those people traced their roots back three or four generations, others to their grandparents in Scotland or Germany. But I had nobody except this silly old aunt…"

"Silly?"

"Yes, silly as a wheel. She was Dad's sister and over a couple of years took me for picnics at Nudgee Beach. When the picnics stopped I didn't see her again until just before she died. I remember the day well. The old biddy levered herself out of bed and chucked Dad's war medals into the river before…"

"She threw away your father's medals?"

"Yes, into the river. She said they blundered giving him medals. They should've shot him instead."

"How awful."

"I know. And it doesn't get better. She had a bad-mouthed son."

"What did he say?"

"He called me a wop."

Maria giggled. "There are worse names than that."

"Not the way he said it."

"Do I look like a wop?" she asked.

"Yeah, maybe… if wops can be pretty."

She smiled and blushed, then said not unkindly, "Thanks, Jack. You're okay for a wop yourself."

It was my turn to feel pleased. "Thanks, Maria. It's cool when you put it like that."

We were both silent, and a little embarrassed at the unexpected intimacy. I wanted to keep the mood alive.

"Maria, did you ever enter a competition?"

"What sort of competition?"

"You know, Miss Sugar Harvest, Miss Surf Girl. That sort of thing."

"Jack, you're heading down a dangerous path. Stay off it."

"Why, Maria? You are… well… heaps prettier than other girls I've known. You must've thought about it."

"What interests me in life is irrelevant. I am your cousin, remember."

"Being pretty is not irrelevant," I said.

She lowered the cup she was cradling and pushed her blouse off one shoulder. I stared in horror. A disfiguring burn spread from her upper arm to her shoulder where the bra strap crossed it like a white bridge traversing a sea of tortured flesh.

After seeing the reaction in my eyes she adjusted her sleeve. "I told you, Jack. Don't go down that path."

"Does it hurt?"

"No, it doesn't. I don't even think about it. Now what were you saying about Maryborough?"

I took a steadying breath. "Well, when I looked over the city from the clock tower, I badly needed roots like other people. I wanted family. That's why I was so keen to find you. You and Carl are my blood relatives even if it pains you to know it."

"Now you've found us, will you go back to Brisbane?"

"Is that what you really want?"

"Dad's feelings are what matter, not mine. When you're about he's unhappy, and that hurts us both."

"Where's your mum?"

"She died in a car accident while I was still at school."

"I'm sorry."

She opened her palm dismissively. "It was years ago. Now I look after Dad."

"So you don't have time for boyfriends?"

"Yes," she replied. "I do have a boyfriend. His name is Sam, and he lives on a farm at Pindi Pindi."

It was my turn to be smacked with a wet fish. "Sam...? You don't mean that ponce, Sam Avolio?"

She frowned. "Yes, that's the Sam and he's not a *ponce*. He's a lovely man."

"Lovely?" I said, and hooted. "I hope nobody says I'm lovely. He wears these tight pants and funny coloured shirts. And that's when he's ploughing the farm."

"Don't be awful. Sam's a good man."

"Calen would be full of good men. That doesn't make them special."

"I don't care. Sam is my boyfriend and we love each other."

I couldn't help myself and laughed.

"What's so funny?" she demanded.

"Well, it is kind of weird that your boyfriend is an Avolio, same as my mother's first choice. He was Guido Avolio."

"That's just coincidence." She pushed back her chair. "Anyway, it's getting late. I'd better go."

"Any chance of another coffee sometime?"

"I'd rather not. Please Jack, you've found what you wanted. Let's leave it at that. Maybe we can write to each other or something," she finished lamely.

"No, Maria, I'm not disappearing to Brisbane. Now I've found my family, I want answers. And I promise to behave myself."

CHAPTER 11

Harvesting the cane went like clockwork over the next four days. The wheels of machinery hummed, and on the large board outside Farleigh Mill a foreman wrote the magical figure of five-hundred thousand tons of cane crushed. When Thursday afternoon arrived the harvester driver announced that as he had a funeral to attend next day, we would cut until dark then have the Friday off. I immediately elected to use the free day to ride up to Townsville and search for this mysterious Uncle Kevin Cleary. Right on daylight Friday morning I kicked over the Norton Commando's 750cc engine and headed north. By breakfast, I was at Proserpine scoffing buns from the bakery in Main Street, by nine-thirty I had skirted the tidal city of Bowen, and by noon I was pulling into the outskirts of Townsville. Bougainvillea shimmered in purple veils as I waited at the lights in Charters Towers Road for a train hauling endless wagons of cattle. With the engine off, I took in my first impression of Townsville. The illusion was of a tropical city sleeping in the narrow corridor between Cleveland Bay and Hervey Range, but one could sense a raw, frontier quality and even the crows wheeling above Castle Hill looked strangely inoffensive.

I drew into a café on Flinders Street and sat at a table thumbing through a phone directory while an Asian girl fixed me a hamburger. The directory was full of people named Cleary, but only three had a first name that began with K. As two of the Clearys appeared to be married - and none with a wife 'U' for

Ursula - I decided to try the single K who lived in the inner suburb of Railway Estate.

Few areas in Townsville can match the bravado of Railway Estate. Backed on one side by the mangroves protecting Ross River and fronted on the other by the city's industrial rail link, Railway Estate had the hardy resilience of an underfed street kid. The houses were a series of timber cottages built off the same plan with the same time-worn, weatherboard and louvre weariness. Mango trees alternated with Alexandra palms in front yards, and picket fences were replaced here and there by link wire. But despite this tough exterior there was an underlying pride of ownership. The footpaths were trimmed to the kerb, backyard gardens overflowed with flowers and vegetables, and paw-paw trees bowed under the weight of fat yellow fruit.

I pulled up at the gate of the second last house in Brooks Street. Although matched roughly to the buildings either side, the house boasted one clear difference; security screens protected every window and a locked, iron-framed door guarded the porch. Pushing open the narrow gate, I walked up the front steps and knocked. No response. A venetian blind twitched in the windows next door, and when I glanced over my shoulder a curtain shivered. At least the street was awake. I knocked again, louder. A few minutes later I heard a scuffle behind the door, the handle turned and an eye peered at me through a safety chain.

"What do you want?" a gravely voice demanded.

"I'm looking for Kevin Cleary."

"And who might you be?"

"My name is Jack Bellamy. Kevin is my uncle." In the darkness all I could see was the pale blur of a face. "Are you my Uncle Kevin?"

"Maybe not."

"You are or you aren't?"

"You don't want to know me, kid."

"Why is that?"

He ignored the question. "What have they said about me?"

"Not much. You were married to Dad's sister, Ursula. You are a retired police officer. That's about it."

"That's all there is. Sorry you wasted your time."

"No, Uncle Kevin. That's not all," I said, jamming my foot in the door. "I was raised an orphan because no family had the decency to take me in. I wasn't a bad kid, just unlucky, and I want to hear about the father I don't remember. You knew him."

"I didn't know Jack Bellamy. We never mixed."

"Uncle Kevin, please let me in. Everyone in the street is listening. Let's talk over a coffee."

"Lad, bugger off. Your Aunty Ursula and your Dad are both dead. I don't want to talk about them."

I wasn't taking my foot out of that door. "Please."

He swore loudly before unlatching the chain. "Ten minutes, that's all."

"Ten minutes is fine," I said as I followed him down the gloomy hallway. He wore a cardigan, even in Townsville's heat, and his dry bony skull was like a dull lantern that caught the light at every window. However, his most distinctive feature was the shuffling limp. The cop with a bad leg.

In the kitchen that was clean and neat - an old army discipline perhaps - he beckoned me to a chair and flicked on the hot water jug. He then selected two mugs from a cabinet, placed them on the table and ladled in equal amounts of coffee powder and sugar. Next he took milk from the fridge, plonked it on the table then stood with his back to me waiting for the jug to boil. He had not spoken nor made eye contact since opening the door, which gave me plenty of time to study him. Although once a tallish man with good shoulders, he was now stooped, leaning on chairs for support. His narrow features were grey and drawn like a man who has spent hours in a sick bed.

"Is it okay to call you Uncle Kevin?"

"Call me what you like."

"Why can't you talk to me?" I pressed him.

"I came here to escape all that."

"What do you mean *here*? You were stationed in Townsville for years. It's your second home."

"Second home? Crap."

"It's not crap. And what do you mean by *escape all that*?"

He still hadn't faced me. "Who have you spoken to?"

"Sergeant Harry at the Fortitude Valley police station. He's a big fellow, and he served with you."

"What did he say?"

"He didn't know you that well, but…"

"But what?"

I thought carefully about my next words. "He said you received your pension early."

Kevin snorted and spun on me. Although red splotches burnt his cheeks, the eyes were cold.

"Friggin pension, eh? Look at the place. This is what a police pension gets you. A scrawny house in a scrawny friggin suburb."

Offended by his language, the jug wailed. After splashing hot water into the two mugs, he shoved one across. I tested my luck with his hospitality.

"You wouldn't have a biscuit?"

He shook himself angrily. "Yeah, maybe," and opened a painted tin that held a dozen, stale milk-arrowroots.

"What else has Harry told you?" he demanded.

"That you got offside with your superiors."

"My superiors! They were thieves, the whole bunch of them. That's why the dirty bastards hated me, because I was straight. I guessed their little tricks: the envelopes full of cash, a pimp here, a drug dealer there, the cafés that didn't want trouble."

"Harry never said you were bent."

"Rubbish. He was into the same trough. I bet he took you to a café run by Irish Mick. If you're a cop in the Valley, that's what you do."

As I hadn't come to hear about life on the beat, I changed the subject. "Were you at Mum and Dad's wedding?"

"Of course."

"Were you Dad's best man?"

"Not likely. His best man was a teacher. Nobody wanted a cripple on the altar, bad for photos."

"When Dad signed up in 1940, he was sent to Africa. Later when the Japs started invading the north, he was posted to Townsville. You would've seen him many times, probably even had a drink together."

"Us drink together? Get real. Jack never had time for my type. Six months after enlisting he was made sergeant. Always going places was Jack Bellamy." He looked at the clock. "Your time's up."

"Two more questions then I'm gone. The first is, did you attend the fight in Calen between Dad and an Italian named Guido Avolio?"

"The wops were always fighting in Calen."

"Maybe, but you would remember if Dad was involved."

"Your old man was a pest. That's the best I can say for him."

"Uncle Kevin," I said patiently, "did you attend any fights involving Dad?"

"Why is it important?"

"Because he was my father."

Pretending to think, he tugged at one ear. "Nope. Don't recall any specific incidents."

It was time to throw in some dodgy evidence. "Witnesses have described the officer who attended the fight. They say he had a limp."

He parried the claim easily. "There must be a dozen cops with a limp. So what's your second question?"

"Were you the officer who investigated Guido's death?"

"Sure was. A cut and dried accident. The gun fell over and bang, clean through the chest. Wops and guns go together like kids and matches."

"Is it possible that Dad might've pulled the trigger?"

"Would've suited me if he had, but the wop took a stray bullet. End of story."

"Uncle Kevin, do you mind if I ask one further question?"

He glanced at the clock above the stove. "You said two questions. Okay, be quick. I have things to do."

"Did you play any role in the investigation into Mum and Dad's death?"

"Hardly. The bosses looked after that, and typically made a cock-up. First of all they appointed a moron detective who grew up in fairyland. After reaching the dumb conclusion that a third party was involved, he was sent off to a shrink. Any halfwit could see that Jack Bellamy and Maria were alone in the boat. So the bosses chose another detective, 'somebody with experience', who found that war hero Jack holed the boat, then shot his missus and himself."

"After tying his kid to a floating oar," I said.

"Yeah, that's right. Conscience must've got to him."

"Or that a third party *was* involved. Somebody else made sure I lived."

"Believe what you like, kid, but it was murder-suicide. Is that all?"

"Yes, I'm finished for now. Is it okay if I call again?"

"Don't bother. I buried all that shit when I retired. I'm not tramping through it a second time."

With that he limped to the front door and held it open. As I edged past I offered my hand, but he slammed the door in my face. I walked down to my bike, ignoring the eyes that followed from behind curtains. Kevin Cleary was one bitter retiree. Sergeant Harry reckoned the polio was at fault but maybe his current illness, whatever it was, had a bigger influence on his state of mind. It made me recall a nun at the orphanage who'd been one of our favourites. She brought us treats, and was one of the few who didn't mind us skylarking after tea. But one morning she took sick, staying in bed for months. A girl in the upper school said she had hephalytis, which old nuns and pygmy women die from in the jungle. Whatever the cause, Sister Gertrude was a changed woman after that. She turned resentful, no more sweets or little games, even blaming us kids for the disease. The same thing could be taking place inside Kevin Cleary; ailing in the body, but already cactus in the head.

I rode back into the city following the railway line until it crossed Boundary Street, then I turned right and into the central district. Cars and bikes jostled for space along the palm-lined streets that led towards the wharf where men in overalls loaded the barges for the trip across to Magnetic Island. Skirting the heavier traffic, I rode down Flinders Street and parked my bike against an 1890s shop whose awning crackled in the tropical heat.

Kevin Cleary's hostility clung to me like a bad migraine. I walked over the Ross Creek bridge and gazed forlornly at toad fish nuzzling the muddy banks of an incoming tide. Near the centre of the bridge an elderly Aborigine dangled a hand line into the water. At his feet lay an open hessian bag that held bits of fishing tackle, a few bananas and a bottle of water. Three Aboriginal children fished with him, but on my approach they wound up their lines and disappeared.

I leant against the railing and said, "Any luck?"

"Not really, bro. Fish not hungry."

"What sort of fish?"

"Bream. Good bream in this creek."

Abruptly the line dipped, snapping the old man into watchfulness. When the line twitched a second time his hand jerked upward, snaring a fish that had ventured from the piles. Chuckling, the old man hauled in a silver bream flashing and twisting in the light. Once he had landed the fish on the bridge he pulled the hook from its mouth and threw it back into the water.

"That boy too small, too bony. Next time I catch his daddy."

Reeling in the line, he dropped it into the hessian bag with a packet of bait that lay in the shade of the decking.

"Not today. Maybe tomorrow," he added.

"You off now?" I said.

"Yeah, bro."

"Where?"

"What's that to you, bro?"

"I'm looking for my father. You might be able to help."

"How can I help a white boy?"

"I'm not white."

"A white Eyetie boy."

I beckoned to a giant fig. "Can we sit a minute."

"Okay bro," he said reluctantly.

After leading the way to the tree, I sat on a bench covered in bird dung. At our feet lay a bottle still sheathed in a paper bag from the previous night.

"My name is Jack. What is yours?"

"Philip."

"I don't want to keep you, Philip, but I'd be grateful if you heard me out. My father was shot in Brisbane twenty years ago, and I think events in Townsville during the war had something to do with it. In 1940, he married my mother, an Italian girl from Calen. It wasn't a mixed marriage, but it upset lots of people. While Dad was here, and for some time after the war, the town was serviced by a cop with a limp. Would you know of such a cop?"

"That war finished a long time ago."

"I know, but you were a young man then. You would remember that cop."

Philip had developed the fidgets. "Many cops in Townsville. Heaps of 'em. Some have a crook leg, some a bad eye."

"Yes, but one cop in particular. A white man about my height. And he walked like this." I stood up and imitated Cleary's limp. Philip refused to look at me.

"You remember him, don't you? He gave you a hard time."

"White cops always treat us bad," he said softly.

Coming from an orphanage, I wasn't sure how to answer that. Like him, I had been typecast, though admittedly not for life. "Perhaps that's true, Philip, I wouldn't know. I only seek the cop with a limp."

He stared into the mangroves then he said, "My cousin can help, maybe."

"Where is he?"

"Wait here. I'll bring him."

Leaving the hessian bag at my feet, he ambled along a well beaten path that followed the creek before turning left into a line of trees. Fifteen minutes later he emerged with a snowy-haired

Aborigine who walked stiffly erect like he was the last of his tribe. His prominent brow shaded a broad, flat nose and wide lips. His dark eyes were watchful.

I stood up as they drew closer.

"Bro, this is my cousin Godwin."

We shook hands then sat under the tree where I asked the same question. "Godwin, would you know of this cop with a limp?"

"I know of him. It has been a long time, bro. Why ask now?"

"Because he claims he was the only cop in Townsville doing the right thing. What can you tell me?"

"You believed him?"

"No."

"So who are you, another copper?"

"No, an orphan looking for his father."

Godwin studied my face, then without speaking leant forward and pulled his shirt over his head. Ugly weals cross-hatched his back. Although now healed, they were evidence of a beating years earlier.

"Mr Cleary did that. The cop with a limp. He nearly kill me."

"Mr Cleary. Are you sure of that name?"

"Everybody knows Mr Cleary."

"What had you done?"

"Be a black fella, that's all. Mr Cleary patrolled these streets at night. If he found a drunk black fella, he cuffed him to the door handle and beat him. I wasn't drunk. I was asleep. He crept up on me and put a knife in my face, then he beat me. He beat lots of blacks - old men, women, kiddies. It got real bad. Everyone frightened."

"When did it stop?"

"Near the end of the war. By a teacher fella in the army. One day he was fishin' at the mouth of this creek, tryin' to land bait. He was catchin' nothin', but havin' a good time. I showed him how to cast a net, and he shared his army lunch. Later he saw the blood on my back and asked about it. When I told him, he said he would fix it. After that, no more beatings."

"Do you know the teacher's name?"

"Yes, we call him Boss Jack."

"Did you know him too, Philip?"

"Yes, bro. All the Murries knew Boss Jack."

I exhaled slowly. "That was my father, I'm sure of it."

"No, he was a white man," Godwin said.

My Italian skin had again triggered the wrong response. "My father was white," I said.

"What was his name, bro?"

"Jack Bellamy, same as mine. He died when I was a little kid. I never knew him."

"I am sad to hear Boss Jack is dead."

"You're not alone. But tell me, how did he stop the beatings?"

"I dunno, bro. One night they just stop. Boss Jack was a sergeant and he never tell us why. But after he saw my back, he took me to the American first-aid man and had me fixed up. He also told us to stay our side of the river while the coppers were about. Sometimes Boss Jack and me fished together, then he left in a big ship for the war. He was still very happy, but no more sergeant, just a corporal."

"Why was that?"

"I dunno. He never say."

A young couple had crossed the bridge with lunch packets in their hand. They were looking for a shady tree but the only available bench was occupied by two Aborigines and their mixed-race companion. When they stared at us, Philip became restless. He climbed to his feet and slung the hessian bag over his shoulder.

"Look after yourself, bro," he said and shuffled upstream to a patch of land that was hidden from shops and houses. He turned back to Godwin. "You comin'?"

As I clasped Godwin's outstretched hand, I said, "Where can I find you?"

"Here, bro. Every day a Murri is here fishin'. But you don't want to find me. Like Boss Jack, the past is dead."

"That's not true." When I tried to explain that it was a mistake to bury the past, Godwin listened politely then shrugged and walked after his cousin.

Once he was out of my sight, I let the young couple have the bench and returned to my bike. Boss Jack had to be my father. There was no other possibility, and Godwin had remembered him as a kind man who stopped the beatings.

CHAPTER 12

I still had one visit to make in Townsville, the police station where hopefully an older cop would remember Sergeant Kevin Cleary. It was now midafternoon and too late to reach Jolimont Creek before darkness, kangaroos and giant trucks claimed the highway. I booked a room at the Great Northern Hotel and sauntered up to police headquarters. At the entrance I walked through a colourful honour guard of hydrangeas and into the forecourt where officers scuttled about on private Friday afternoon business. A female clerk, barely out of high school, sat at the counter filing cards into a long narrow box.

"How can I help you?"

"My name is Jack Bellamy, miss, and I'm chasing information on my uncle Kevin Cleary who was a sergeant here twenty years ago."

"Does he have a record?"

"I guess so. He was a permanent officer."

"Then you will have to see Personnel. Through that door on the left and up the stairs. You'll find another counter like this."

"I'm not after his police record, miss. I want somebody who might've served with him."

"Well, I'll leave a notice in the lunchroom if you like. Where are you staying?"

The nuns had educated me in this sort of palaver. "I was hoping to talk to an older officer today, miss. Somebody who's been here twenty years."

"There won't be many of them."

"True."

She stared at me, filing card in hand.

"Please, miss," I said.

"Wait here, Mr Bellamy. I'll see what I can do."

She was gone ten minutes, returning with a pear-shaped senior constable whose red face glowed like a dance floor. His age was hard to judge, maybe early fifties, but good living was his next of kin.

"G'day, son," he said, berthing his stomach against the counter. "I hear you're looking for Kevin Cleary."

"Well, not exactly looking for him, officer. He is my uncle and I know his address. Did you serve with him?"

"Sure did, and proud of it. Why?"

"Well, I've heard... um... conflicting things about Uncle Kevin. Some good, some not so good. Would you say he was a good cop?"

"Is there another kind?"

"That would depend, I guess."

He glanced at the paper the girl had handed him. "Jack Bellamy, eh? Have I seen that name before?"

"It's possible. I'm named after my father."

"Well, Jack, I did work with Kevin Cleary, and he was an outstanding officer. Legendary, I'd say. Yeah, a bloody legend. I was on probation when I first met D.S. Cleary, and he taught me day-to-day policing. I can tell you, ratbags never gave cheek to Mr Cleary."

"The limp didn't bother him?"

"Not Kevin Cleary. If anything, he was tougher for it. All the same, you'd be dumb to mention polio in his hearing."

"How about the general public. Was he hard on them?"

The constable frowned. "Mr Cleary only punished those who broke the law."

"Punished?"

"Arrested."

"What about Aborigines?"

"Son, while Mr Cleary patrolled this city, a girl knew it was safe to walk home alone at night. Drunken abos learned to stay in their camps across the river. And hoodlums kept their hands in their pockets."

"What about Italians?"

"Funny thing but he got on well with the Eyeties unless they were, you know, enemy aliens. Somebody had to look after the blighters. Just imagine, without 'em the sugar industry would've gone belly up."

Rolling the slip of paper into a tube, he held it to his eye like a telescope. "Jack Bellamy? Now I remember that name. Teacher from Calen. Married an Eyetie girl. It's coming back to me. Soldier during the war. Fancied himself in the ring. Matey with blacks. I heard he and Mr Cleary were related, cousins or something, but I didn't know anything about a kid."

"I wasn't born then."

The constable grinned, displaying a row of yellow teeth that matched the shape of his paunch; big donkey teeth at the front descending to small ones at the back. "Your dad went up and down the ranks like a yo-yo. While, in Townsville he got busted to corporal. That would've hurt."

"Maybe, but I don't recall the story."

"Well, it did the rounds for years because it showed Kevin Cleary was a cop with principles.

During the Pacific War he was attached to the military police at the same time your dad was camped in Townsville. All went well until a bunch of soldiers, your dad included, applied for a week's leave. It was the time when the Japs were smashing down our front door. The soldiers got their leave and were about to hot-foot out of camp when orders arrived that all leave was cancelled. A few pretended they hadn't heard and slipped past the sentries. Naturally the brass posted MPs at the railway station to catch any blokes going AWOL. As it turned out Mr Cleary was at the station when Jack Bellamy waltzed into his arms. Bellamy lost a stripe over that, and I don't know if he ever got it back."

"He did. He was discharged as a lieutenant, but not before he received medals for bravery in North Africa and New Guinea."

"Good for him. But up here Mr Cleary was the law. It was his job and he did it well."

"It wasn't fair on Dad. He was going back to Calen to see his wife. Married two years and hardly saw her."

"Yeah, war can be tough."

The phone rang and the girl jotted down a few notes which she handed to the constable. He took the paper from her, read it and frowned. Pushing his belly away from the counter, he said, "Duty calls, son. I hope you find your uncle," and disappeared through a batwing door.

"Thanks, mate... for all your trouble."

He had already gone and the girl was bent to her files. I walked out the station past the line of dog-faced residents waiting for service. In truth I didn't know what to think. Dad was admired by some and condemned by others. But nothing I had uncovered suggested he would recklessly kill two people, one of whom he loved.

CHAPTER 13

A few days later we again finished harvesting early. With two hours until nightfall I changed out of my rough clothes and rode down the highway towards Mackay. On either side of the road farmers watched nervously as ugly, black clouds gathered above the Clarke Ranges. Big rains halfway through the crush were never welcome; machines got bogged and burnt cane was left to rot in the field. Suddenly drops of rain splattered against my goggles and cane trash hurtled across the road in the gusting wind. By the time I reached The Leap, a rocky outcrop north of the city, the squall was ripping through the trees. Not wanting to be drenched I called into the pub, but it was an early storm that disappeared out to sea as rapidly as it had formed. I climbed back on the Norton and rode to Loretta Townsend's house to find out what she knew of these escapades, especially Guido's death after the war.

When I arrived she was in the front garden knocking grasshoppers off her hibiscus with a cricket bat. Most of the hoppers survived her cuts and drives and clattered over the paling fence to land in the neighbour's bushes. Propping the bike near a lamp post, I walked up to the gate. She saw me appear and swished the bat like a schoolboy waiting to take a strike.

"Those grasshoppers are buggers of things," I said to her.

"That and all," she replied guardedly. "And what can I do for you?"

"Well, *Aunty* Loretta," I said, testing out the word. As she didn't bite, I kept going. "I want to ask a couple of questions about Dad and Guido. You know, Guido's death."

She lowered the bat and ambled across to the gate. "You have been digging round."

"Well, I didn't come north for the sun."

"Who've you been talking to?"

"Paulo... and others. What do you know about the shooting?"

"It was a tragedy. Should never have happened."

"Do you believe it was an accident?"

"That was the police verdict."

Straight bat for the first two balls. Next delivery. "What did your brother Carl think?"

"You winding me up?"

"'Course not, Aunty. But if Carl agreed with the cops, why is he so cranky with me?"

"You're getting Guido's death confused with Maria's."

"No, I'm not. There's no proof Dad killed anyone."

"Okay then. Carl has always believed Guido was murdered."

"By Dad, I assume."

"Correct. The *unofficial* verdict."

End of the over. No wickets lost, no runs made. She stood the bat against the fence and opened the gate. "You might as well come inside."

I followed her square hips up the stairs and through the lattice doorway onto the verandah. Pot plants hung from the rafters and a pair of deep chairs watched over the street. Loretta pointed to one of the chairs. "Sit down. I'll make a cuppa."

While she bustled around inside, I studied the house. The verandah smelt like old timber that has survived a hundred monsoons, the hardwood floor needed re-nailing and the wooden venetians along the northern side were thirsty for paint. At the opposite end of the verandah a sash window opened onto a bedroom and curtains furled softly over the ledge. For all its tiredness, the home was friendly and the street quiet, and I closed my eyes imagining if this was the kind of house I'd like to raise a family in.

"Cranky old bastard!"

My hair shot up and I leapt from the chair.

"Cranky old bastard!"

Peering cautiously into the living room, I found a sulphur-crested cockatoo perched on a stand. "You're the cranky bastard," I snapped. He lifted his beautiful white feathers and screeched.

Just then Loretta reappeared and silenced him from a tin of Arnott's biscuits. "Who's the cranky old bastard?" I said.

Loretta laughed. "Your dad taught him to say that. Cocky might be an old bird but he's got a long memory. Shortly after the war Jack and Maria stayed with us on the farm, but Jack never saw eye to eye with Cocky. By the end of the month they were swearing at each other."

"I've heard many things about Dad. Was he hard to get along with?"

"He was different to us, which caused its own problems, but actually he had a good nature. Though, I'll tell you something queer. Cocky hasn't sworn like that for months. He must know a thing or two."

Rising from my chair, I walked over to the bird. "I'm a nice boy, Cocky, and I'm not old."

"Cranky old bastard," he replied unmoved.

"Loretta," I said, returning to the verandah, "you were about to say something about Guido's death."

She took a slurp of tea and lowered her cup into the saucer. "How do I know I can trust you?"

"Others do."

"Name one."

"Maria. She told me about the shooting."

"That's common knowledge up here. It was in the papers."

"Come on, Loretta. Stop playing games."

She drank more tea. "Okay, Jack. What I'm about to tell you I've kept to myself all these years. I never told anyone, not even the police, and I'd be obliged if you did the same."

"You must let me hear it first, but I'm no gossip."

"Alright. On the day Guido and your father went hunting, they took only one rifle, Guido's. At first Jack was upset he couldn't find his own rifle and wanted to search for it at the farm. Guido argued that as they were running late, both could shoot with his, so the two of them headed off in Guido's ute with Guido's rifle. Yet - and here's the strange thing - when Guido was found dead, the bullet had come from Jack's rifle."

"An inquest would've picked that up."

"No. The only firearm ever mentioned was Jack's."

"Are you telling me Guido was killed by a gun they never had to start with?"

"That's right."

"Dad's might've been in the car all the time. He didn't search hard enough."

"Jack was a good soldier, he knew how to look. Anyway, it was a utility, not a car. Men don't leave precious rifles to bounce round in the tray of a ute. I tell you there was only one rifle, it was Guido's, and it was on the rack behind their seats."

"So why didn't you tell the cops?"

"The police were convinced Guido's death was bad luck. Their theory was simple. One of the men, Jack, trips over a log and accidentally fires the rifle. Next moment the other man, Guido, drops dead. Against that theory would be a silly teenage girl, myself, imagining I saw them set out with a different rifle. What would a girl know? But don't forget I grew up on a farm. I know what I'm saying. Although the rifles were both .303s, Jack had carved a small Australian flag on his. It was the sort of thing he did. Besides, the police mentality was post-war Australian. Jack was a war hero and the dead man was a wicked Italian who deserved what he got."

"It can't have been that bad."

"You don't know what it was like to be Italian. The snide glances, the whispers and, to make it worse, the racist cops."

"Especially the cop with a limp."

"You have been busy."

I tapped my nose, but she didn't think I was funny. "Sorry, Loretta, the cop with a bad leg is - like you say - common knowledge up here. Everyone seems to have a story about him. He attended the shooting."

"I know. He was an officer from Townsville who kept bobbing up in Calen. He had a mean reputation long before Guido died. As far as I recall he decided in less than a day that Guido's death was accidental."

"Who did he speak to?"

"Don't know exactly, though he did come to the farm to see Papa and Carl. I guess he would've seen the Avolios."

She let me chew on this news while she fed the cockatoo more biscuits. The law knew Guido had been shot with Dad's rifle, but only Loretta seemed to know the rifles had been swapped. To me, it was a crucial piece of evidence in Dad's favour even though it made no sense.

I decided to leave the guns aside and probe deeper into the cop with a bad leg. "Loretta, the investigator's name was Kevin Cleary. I've already met him."

"Don't worry, we know his name. Detective Sergeant Cleary. The boys and Papa called him D. S. Cruelty. If you want the truth, we hated him. He'd been given the job of unearthing Italians who posed a security threat to Australia, and since they couldn't detain all the farmers, D. S. Cruelty used extortion to separate the so-called sheep from the goats. If he found an Italian with a suspect past, or had written letters home during the war, he arranged a meeting to discuss options. But there was only one option, money. If the unfortunate man couldn't pay a bribe, he was shipped off to an internment camp."

"I've heard about that. Do you know who might've paid bribes in Calen?"

"No, I was too young and anyway Carl, Maria and myself were native Australians who had never been out of the country."

She stared down at her farm-worn hands, unhappy that her country of birth could be so mean to its own citizens. Despite her initial misgivings she had been frank with me, so I opened my closet hiding a Bellamy skeleton. I knew the view wouldn't be pretty.

"Loretta, there's a third reason why people might think Dad was not charged with Guido's death. He was Kevin Cleary's brother-in-law."

Loretta stared at me. "Brother-in-law? Jack Bellamy and D. S. Cruelty were related." A look of horror crossed her face. "Do you mean that your father could've shot Guido after all?"

"Certainly not, and in any case Dad and Cleary despised each other. Last week I rode up to Townsville and found where Cleary lives. Later on, I learned how he went about at night as a military policeman harassing blacks who had strayed across the river. Dad was a sergeant in the army while stationed in Townsville, and somehow put an end to the practice. A few weeks later Cleary took his revenge when Dad went AWOL trying to sneak home. Dad was caught and punished, getting demoted into the bargain."

Despite herself Loretta laughed, covering her mouth like a schoolgirl. "Sorry, Jack, but your father was always a scoundrel, disappearing from camp. He hated sitting round bored when he could be at home. Even train drivers sympathised with the soldiers and slowed near Yalboroo to let them jump off. I remember hiking with Maria up to the railway and hiding in the bush for the train to arrive. Sometimes military police would be standing on the carriage balconies waiting, but they never caught anyone."

"They must've been blind."

Loretta giggled. "Well, blind to the jumping men. The women took it in turns to create a diversion."

"Like?"

"Flashing their breasts, or worse. They did it on one side of the track while their men jumped on the other. You could've knocked the coppers' eyes off with sticks, poor devils. And of course, soldiers in the train cheered for encores."

"It must've been a popular spot."

"It was. But those places were everywhere. I read in the paper that Australia charged more soldiers with AWOL than any other Commonwealth nation. Isn't that terrible?"

"Hard to say really," I said, not seeing any harm in going AWOL. We often did it at Nudgee. "In any case, Loretta, D. S. Cleary took his revenge at the train station, then after the war he arrived in Calen to investigate Guido's death. Maybe his presence was pure chance, but it has to be treated with suspicion."

Loretta was silent as she climbed to her feet and fed the cockatoo that wasn't in the least bit hungry. After a time she returned to the verandah and sat down. It was apparent from the set of her mouth she was troubled.

"What is it, Loretta?"

"If Jack was innocent, why did he need collusion with a bad cop?"

"Perhaps there was no collusion. It could've been an accident, even with the second rifle. The two hunters might have stopped at Guido's place to exchange the guns... got distracted..." I ended unconvincingly. "Anyway, we can't ignore the possibility that an unknown person wanted Guido dead. You say he was part of a big happy family. Maybe he wasn't."

Loretta pouted. "A lot of people envied Italians who worked hard and did well."

"I mean, apart from the Italian angle. We know D. S. Cleary was into extortion. Were there other rackets Guido could've been involved in?"

"Such as?"

"I've no idea. Drugs maybe."

We stared glumly at the floor.

"Loretta, is it possible some Italians were unaware Kevin Cleary existed?"

"I doubt it. Why?"

"Well, when Paulo Avolio told me about the fight at the hall, he said nobody intervened. He didn't mention the police. Surely he would've recalled a cop with a limp."

"Jack, those pre-war dances were the end of the good times. A lot of awful things happened after that, stuff best forgotten. I can understand why Paulo wiped Cleary from his memory."

Loretta lurched out of her chair and disappeared inside, returning five minutes later with a fresh pot of tea which neither of us wanted. It was more an excuse to take fresh air. As my first cup had gone cold, I tossed it over the railing into the hibiscus where grasshoppers were making up for lost time.

While Loretta refilled the cup, it occurred to me that although different stories were emerging about Guido Avolio, I couldn't picture him. I put the question to her. "Loretta, what was Guido like?"

"He was okay."

"You don't sound excited."

"I'm not."

"Go on."

"Well, the three of them - Guido, Carl and Maria - were mates from when they were little, though it was mostly the boys doing things on their own. They had push bikes Nonno had found on the tip in Mackay. He repaired and painted them - one for Carl and the other for Maria - but as she was too young to ride Guido took it. With their bikes and a cut lunch the boys fished in the river, toured the valleys behind the farm, and on weekends cycled down to St Helens Beach. Of course Carl didn't entirely forget his little sister. He made a pillion seat for her and mounted a basket on the handle bars. Not so thoughtful was Guido who saw her as a nuisance. Maybe she complained to Papa, I don't know, but as she grew older she joined in their games. You have to remember that Maria was the proverbial ugly duckling. Mamma bobbed her hair short and dressed her in tomboy clothes, which was Maria's preference anyway. It wasn't that she didn't like pretty stuff, it was more she idolised her big brother, and wherever he was, she wanted to be. For all that she was a good friend to me, her younger sister by six years. We shared things when we were small, including a room, and then clothes and shoes as we grew up. But I was always miles behind her. She was a full-blown tomboy while I was still in rompers, and she emerged from her chrysalis while I was still playing with dolls.

"As for harvest dances, I was at primary school when the trouble began. But don't imagine that because I lived in Maria's shadow, I was blind. Over a few short months at the end of high school she came of age. It happened quickly and I'll never forget the night of her transformation. Nonno and Nonna had organised a party at their house for her seventeenth birthday. She had stayed with them overnight while the rest of us drove across in Papa's truck. It was a warm night, too lovely to be indoors, and we sat on the verandah drinking tea and red wine. I recall I was on the steps playing with a kitten when Maria appeared from the hallway dressed in a beautiful gown Nonna had brought from Italy. Everybody fell silent. It was like a scene from a movie. Where once there had been a rough and tumble little girl, there was now a stunning princess. I remember rushing up and hugging her. She was so beautiful. Mamma and Papa were so proud of their daughter, but I think secretly they wished she was plainer, like they had gotten with me."

Loretta shrugged off the last comment with a laugh, then continued. "Guido was placed at the head of the queue for Maria's hand. He had jumped in smartly when he discovered the ugly duckling was a beautiful swan, and he also had Carl's backing. I must be honest and admit I never liked Guido. He was a braggart and to my thinking he was cruel. Like the time he killed a frog with a stick. I guess most boys do that, but Guido got a thrill from watching us watch it suffer. And like all cruel people, he was a coward underneath. I've seen him run when the tables were turned. I suppose I had no reason to like him. For a start he called me Loretta the wetter. I was much younger than him, and probably hadn't even started school. We were playing out in the yard, and somehow I wet my pants, and he made such a thing of it. The way he behaved hurt Maria too. He never really changed as he grew up, and during the war he poked fun at stories about your father in North Africa. That didn't sit well in the pubs because Jack was a hero by then."

"It doesn't sound clever letting them drive off together with a gun."

"I think Carl and Paulo were meant to join them, but they had to stay and work the farms."

"Well, if they'd all gone, Dad would've been outnumbered three to one. A bit one-sided."

"He could handle himself, don't worry."

In the silence that followed I asked, "You wouldn't have any photos of Mum or Dad?"

"I've got plenty of Maria, but only one of your father. When Maria died, Carl destroyed every photo of Jack that he could lay his hands on."

"Can I see them?"

She went inside and returned with an album bulging with photos. Some were in frames but most were an untidy jumble. Selecting one of the framed photos she handed it across. "That's Maria, Carl and myself at a picnic at Seaforth. Those people in the left background are my mamma and papa with Guido, and on the right are friends from Calen. The photo was taken for Carl's 21st, which puts Maria around eighteen."

Mum was very attractive and in the photo she shared a joke with her brother while facing away from boyfriend Guido who had slick hair and a conceited face. The resemblance between Mum and young Maria Rossini was striking. Loretta next handed me a group shot that contained my father. The photo was of several bareheaded men on motor bikes, all wearing cane cutter's shorts and shirt sleeves rolled above the elbow. Dad was at the front of the group, and he did look cool, perched on the seat like James Dean, cigarette hanging from the corner of his mouth. But if there was any similarity to me, I couldn't see it. I said as much to Loretta.

"Sure, Jack was very Irish, fair skin and tousled hair," she replied. "But you have other traits in common. He was self-confident and quick with his fists. You're a chip off the block."

"My quick fists have nothing to do with Dad. Fists are an orphan's survival tool."

"You've got a brain and the nuns gave you an education, that's what you should be using," she said tersely.

"I don't have Dad's brains or his looks. And Mum was beautiful. She's not a wop, like I am."

Loretta flared up. "Don't use that word in this house again. You are Italian, I'm Italian. So was your mother. That's something to be proud of."

Loretta cooled down as she flipped through the photos. After an awkward minute she turned to me. "Do you understand what I've told you about the hunting trip?"

"Yes. Somehow a third man was involved. And he had arrived with Dad's rifle."

"And…?"

I spoke deliberately. "This man knows exactly how Guido died - maybe even did the killing - and let Dad take the blame."

"That's right, Jack. I believe your father was innocent, and I don't care what evidence Mr Cleary buried."

"Why are you telling me this, Aunty?"

Grimacing, she said, "Don't call me that, lad. Too much water's flowed under the bridge."

"Not with me, it hasn't."

She gave a little snort and slid the photos back into the album.

"Do you know Sam Avolio?" I asked.

"Of course. He's the son of Paulo, though from your position he's Maria's boyfriend."

"What do you think of him?"

Her eyes narrowed. "He's a good, solid boy. Nothing remarkable, but that's okay. Get too choosy and you will die of heartache."

I couldn't help myself. "She's knock-em-down pretty, and he's a bloody ponce."

"Ponce eh? Well, that's nice coming from a penniless drifter. You have more in common than you think. They're happy, so leave them be."

At that she grabbed my cup and plate, which was a powerful hint to leave. After standing up to thank her, I ducked into the living room. "Cranky old bastard," I flung at the startled cockatoo and bolted down the steps.

Behind me the cockatoo screeched obscenities while Loretta stood at the rail wagging her finger. When I grinned back at her, the finger relaxed into a small wave. Yes, I reckon Loretta wasn't that upset to learn she had a nephew.

CHAPTER 14

As I rode back along the highway to Jolimont Creek Caravan Park, the Norton's engine sang between the tall rows of cane and bugs dived for the single beam headlight. Up ahead the last of Corvus drifted across the Clarke Ranges, and the tang of burnt cane blended with the scents of October rain, ripening mangoes and nesting fruit bat. I couldn't help but wonder why Loretta had told me about the two rifles. The men had set off with a single rifle, but it wasn't the one that killed Guido. And Loretta had told nobody until now. Not her father or brother, and certainly not the cop with a bad leg. I couldn't see where she was headed with this. Why tell an orphan boy after all these years? Did she feel sorry for me, or was I the only one taking her seriously? Guns aside, I was also puzzled by Kevin Cleary's role in the story. Paulo never mentioned him, which was odd, whereas Loretta remembered him for his spite. But before I could broach Uncle Kevin with this fresh evidence, I needed to visit the upper streams of the O'Connell River where the killing had taken place. I sensed there was a reason why Guido had died where he did. I also wanted to meet Carl Rossini again, and I figured the only way of achieving both was through young Maria.

That Monday, following a trio of electric storms, the fields were judged too wet for harvesting. When the boss gave us the day off, I changed my clothes and rode down to Mackay, pulling up outside Venardos shortly before lunch. This time I was clean and tidy, not that it mattered to the woman on reception. When I asked for Maria she lifted the phone and paused with one finger over the dial. "Excuse me, what's your name again?"

"Sam."

"Sam who?"

"Sam's enough. She knows who Sam is."

She dialled a couple of numbers. "Hello Maria. I've got Sam wanting to see you. Okay, sure." Then she turned to me. "Maria will be right out. Take a seat."

I settled myself on the vinyl lounge and thought to myself, "If she really loves Sammy, she'll be out like a rocket." As it happened, ignition was not spontaneous. After a five-minute delay she came through the doorway with a warm smile. The smile faded. "I thought Sam was here," she said, puzzled.

"He's getting his hair done."

She pressed her lips together, then said tiredly. "What do you want?"

"Maria, I want to visit the place where Guido died. Are you familiar with it?"

"Can't that sort of thing wait? We're busy right now."

"Well, it could. But you're hard to catch."

"If only. Anyway, I can't describe the place on a map. It was somewhere upriver."

"Does your father know?"

"Of course. He helped recover the body."

"Would he have any problem showing me?"

"What do you think?"

"No harm in trying my luck. This Saturday morning at ten. Will you be home?"

"Not if I can help it."

"Well, I'm riding out to quiz your father. If you're home, he might just cooperate."

"Please, Jack. You'll be hurting Dad for no good reason."

"Maria, just have the kettle on."

She rolled her eyes and muttered something inaudible.

"See you Saturday," I said, pushing open the glass door. "And you should work on that smile of yours. It's a game changer."

I didn't catch her reply, but as I jumped on the bike I knew I'd do my best to force Carl into revealing where the death took place, and if he was slow on that one I'd ask him about the second rifle. Sorry Loretta, but if the first question didn't stir him up, the next would, and I needed to know what smouldered inside that woolly head of his.

CHAPTER 15

All week we worked hard in the cane, making the most of the clear weather. The routine of a day's harvest was simple. At prelight the team collected the machinery from an open field and assembled on the headland at the start of the first row. While waiting for daybreak we'd stroll about in the cool air, chatting quietly and avoiding the burnt cane that left sticky smudges on hands and clothing. Then as dawn washed over the Coral Sea the boss would announce, "Time to go, boys," and we'd fire the big diesels into life. That first half hour was always special - the slickness of a well-run gang, the sense of urgency, the vibrant colours of a tropical sunrise. Not that we ever spoke about it, or tried to. Our aim was to have the first six bins on the line as the sun cleared the hills at Seaforth. By mid-afternoon when the 80th bin had been filled and our quota finished, the mateship bonding the gang made the ache in our backs worthwhile.

As my Saturday mornings were generally free from work, it was nice to dawdle over breakfast and read snippets of news in the Daily Mercury. The lazy breakfast also separated me from the people who washed clothes on Saturday. I guess I was a bit contrary there since I found it easier to crank up a washing machine at night and hang my clothes on the empty lines. It also removed me from the rounds of park gossip which I found tiresome. As I soon discovered, there were three layers of resident in the caravan park and each had its quirks. The first layer was the permanent residents, the park elite who tendered small vegetable gardens, screened in their privacy with potted crotons and knew everybody else's business. The second layer was the seasonal workers like myself, temporary residents who adapted readily to the permanent lifestyle because, in truth, we had no other home. The final layer was the overnighters, towing their vans north to escape the southern winter, then reappearing southbound at the first sign of a hot, humid summer.

Among the first layer was a Thursday Islander named Jimbo who had lived in the park for years and, like myself, was immune to gossip. A heavily built man, Jimbo had the smooth dusky skin of a Torres Strait fisherman. He was unmarried, of indeterminate age and dwelt in a rusty van at the farthest end of the park. To one side of his van Jolimont Creek flowed lazily out to sea, while to the other a row of leichhardt trees shielded him from the endless rows of sugarcane. Scattered among the flotsam he had collected over the years were oil drums planted with herbs, and, either side of his door, rows of carrot and ripe, red tomatoes. Jimbo was a man of the sea who earned his income during the harvest as a navvy on the narrow-gauge train lines. In the wet, which was the growing time for cane and a period of northern idleness, he augmented his income by selling fish to the park occupants. Around the district it was said that Jimbo in his boat with a line in hand was the most contented man you'd ever meet. Indeed, that contentedness helped chase my ghosts back into the recesses where they belonged. Often of a weekend I would amble across to his van and sit in the doorway as he prepared for a day on the water. On these mornings he lectured me on the do's and don'ts when casting for tidal prawns, fishing for barramundi, or handling a live crab. But, more importantly, he taught me about survival from within.

This morning I sat on an upturned dinghy and asked him about himself. "Jimbo, do you have a mum and dad?"

"Yeah, bro. Dey be at home on Murray Island," he said, repairing a hole in a small net.

"Do you ever see them?"

"Not much."

"Isn't that a bit sad?"

"We a big family, not a sad family. Some of my bros live on de island with dere little kids and pigs and chooks."

"Jimbo, you should live there too, and marry a nice girl who'll give you tons of kids. And you could sit with them in the shade, fishing all day."

He smiled calmly. "Bro, when a man is hungry for sometin', he never be happy. So mind dem belly pangs."

I nodded in agreement (well, I *was* hungry for sometin'), and walked back to my van where I fiddled with the Norton's suspension as I waited for midmorning. When I thought it was around coffee time for Carl Rossini, I kicked the bike into life and rode up to the farm.

Carl's harvester and haul-out tractors stood outside the shed like a hen and her chicks, but the place was otherwise empty. I lifted the bike onto its stand and stuck my head into the main shed. "Anybody here!" The only sound came from a radio on the shelf tuned to 4MK and the announcer reading the sports draws. I walked through the shed and out the rear, shouting politely as I went. The second and third sheds were empty, as was the laundry.

"They've fled at the voice of Jack Bellamy," I said to a cat sniffing haughtily from the tank stand. I stepped onto the front verandah and rang a bell that echoed down the hallway and out the back. Not a soul.

I rang the bell again, and a voice shouted from the kitchen, "Hang on. I'm coming."

Maria rushed into the hallway wiping flour from her hands. "Oh, hi," she said as though surprised to see me, then untied her apron and tossed it into the kitchen with the towel. She wore casual shoes with a smart print dress whose sleeves, I now knew, concealed the burn on her shoulder. Her hair shone as if freshly washed and her face glowed with wellbeing.

"Sorry about the mess," she said. "I've just got home from town and Dad's out checking the cattle. Sit down and I'll fetch that self-invited cuppa. Anything else you wanted?"

"Did he know I was coming?"

"I told him, but the farm always comes first."

"Where are these cattle?"

"Couldn't say."

"Come on, Maria. He doesn't need a daughter to protect him."

"Jack, you're a p..." She bit off the word.

"What Maria? A poor lost cousin?"

"I was about to say pain in the neck; massive pain. He's in the yards on the other side of the causeway. I'll make a flask of tea and drive you."

I sat on the verandah while she fussed noisily in the kitchen. She then disappeared into another room to return minutes later in faded jeans and a country shirt. "See you near the shed," she called.

I wandered down the side of the house, pausing to grab a guava off a heavily laden tree. I ate it carefully, watching for the fruit fly that enjoyed spoiling the sweet flesh. Ironically, guava was a tree that held strong associations. At the orphanage the single tree was declared out-of-bounds so that a cleaning lady could make jelly for the nuns' table. As it happened the nuns rarely saw a pot of jelly between them. What the fruit fly couldn't eat, the kids did.

Just then Maria hurried down the back steps wearing a battered western hat and riding boots. "I didn't expect to see a hootin' tootin' cowgirl," I said.

"What did you expect?"

"Not this. You struck me as a... sort of... well, covergirl girl."

"The day is already awkward, Jack. Don't make it worse."

Maria climbed into the driver's side of an ancient Land Rover and I scrambled over junk into the passenger's seat. Five minutes later we had rattled across the causeway and parked beside a ute that sat alone under a fig. When Maria turned off the clattering engine, the silence was filled with the bellow of fifty cattle that had been herded into a series of tight yards. Heavy steel gates and a race took up one end of the yards while a loading ramp dominated the other. Carl was moving along the rails from where he inspected each animal before spraying it against insect pests. When Maria tooted the horn, he lifted his head and waved. She called "Smoke oh," and a smile creased his face, then his eyes fastened on me and the smile died. Undaunted, I grabbed the picnic box and walked across to an open-sided shed that held a rough bench and table. Maria and I stood together in the shed for a few minutes then when it appeared Carl was in no hurry, she strolled across to the yards while I defended the box against marauding ants. Some minutes later he finished the last animal and shouted to Maria to open the gate. After the cows had been shunted into a river paddock, she fastened the gate before returning to the shed.

"I hope you're not planning to upset him," she said, pouring the tea.

"Of course not."

"If you do, Jack, I'll never speak to you again. Never. I mean it."

"Maria, I'm not what's bothering your father. Something is, but it's not me. I only want a friendly chat. Tell him that."

"You tell him," she said as Carl stepped under the shelter drying his hands on a rag.

It was easy to see where Maria got her taste in farm wear. Carl had the same jeans, boots and western hat. Actually the gear had character and I thought it wouldn't hurt to add a dash of cowboy to my wardrobe. Certainly better than the untidy hippie clothes that were still fashionable.

"What are you doing here?" Carl demanded.

I stuck out a hand. "Hello, Uncle Carl."

Despite himself he took my hand. Maria offered us each a mug of steaming tea and opened a tin of buttered pikelets. When Carl grabbed two of the pikelets, I followed suit.

"Uncle Carl…"

"Don't call me that."

"Mr Rossini…"

"I'm not a school teacher. My name's Carl," he said gruffly.

"Carl, can I ask a favour?"

"Depends what it is."

"I'd like to visit the site of the shooting accident. Pay my respects to Guido where he died."

"You can visit the cemetery in Calen. His name's on a stone."

"It wouldn't be the same."

"Well, it's a long way upriver and I haven't the time."

I gazed into the mountains where the O'Connell River began its short rush to the ocean. "I'm busy too, Carl. We could make the time."

"Damn it. Stop pestering me."

"Sure, if you tell me what's wrong. I didn't come here to cause trouble. I'm an orphan looking for his roots. You know lots of things that could help but you won't open up."

"I don't want to talk about it."

"The truth shouldn't hurt."

Maria sat on a bench, watching her father. She felt for him but her poise suggested she also wanted the boil lanced. It had festered too long.

Carl quietly munched on his pikelet. You could tell he was a farmer. No matter how much he churned inside, the jaw remained calm. Maybe he was too composed, too rigid. "Guido and I were good mates, right from the day we could walk," he said eventually. "So it was only natural that when my sister arrived she knocked about with us. As we shifted up through the years, Guido and Maria grew closer and by the time we finished our schooling it was obvious they were going to marry. They weren't just a matched couple, they were happy. Then along came Jack Bellamy - a fine cut of a man, I'll give him that - but he was city smart and cocky. Maria fell for his charm and, looking back, I guess we were too protective. Maybe if she'd gone into town and mixed with other blokes, she would've seen the danger coming. As for Guido, his downfall was his soft nature. He didn't notice the bad side of Jack until it was too late; got drawn into a fight at the dance hall and paid the price. Much as he loved my sister he never stood a chance against the bully from the south."

"Carl, it takes two to tango," I said, uncomfortable with his portrait of Dad. "So what actually happened?"

"There'd been trouble before, but it boiled over at the cut-out dance. Lots of people in the hall, lots of drinking and skylarking. Although Jack had plenty of sheilas to choose from, he wanted Maria. I don't think she was keen at first, but she was a pretty girl and Jack was like a dog sniffing a bitch. When Guido told him to piss off, that was it. Somebody bundled them outside, and I remember this ring of spectators on the grass and others craning their necks from the windows. It was all over in a couple of minutes. Even less really. When Jack knocked Guido to the ground, the place went quiet. Then somebody shouted, "You won't get away with this, mate." I don't know who it was. Could've been Paulo, or any one of fifty people. Half an hour later the cops arrived and asked questions, but nobody was talking. In the meantime a teacher drove Jack to a house in Mackay and Paulo took his brother home. As you can guess, that was the end of Jack's stay with the Avolio family. They weren't keen on feeding a boarder who assaulted their son."

"Was Guido hurt?"

"What difference did it make? He lost the fight and his girl. Most people felt sorry for him. At least his friends did. Others like Jack's footy pals thought it was great entertainment. Even the cops sniggered at Guido."

"Perhaps they weren't laughing at him. Some cops like prize fighting. It's in their blood."

"No, they laughed at Guido. Thought it was real funny."

"Did one of the cops have bad legs?"

"It's possible."

"Would you remember his name?"

"Can't recall that detail. Too far back."

"What if I suggested Cleary? Detective Sergeant Kevin Cleary."

"Could've been. I never took much notice."

All this time Carl avoided looking my direction. He had settled on the bench near his daughter, sipping from a second cup she had poured. The way he stared at the yards you'd think he was counting heads, but it wasn't cattle he saw.

"Yes, I remember Cleary," he finally muttered. "He was a mongrel dog - sorry, love - all pretence about how he cared for Italians, but hated them, and I think he was sorry Jack hadn't given Guido a proper beating."

I was tempted to mention that my father and Cleary were unlikely to agree on anything. I let it slide.

"To my mind that fight was the end of the good days," Carl went on. "The three musketeers - Guido, Maria and myself - stopped knocking about together and Jack took to displaying Maria like a carnival prize. Even worse, he hung round the farmhouse like a bad smell. Sometimes he'd eat with us. Sometimes he and Maria would haul off together, and when they came home you could tell he'd been having his way with her."

Carl wasn't only pricking the boil, he was landing punches that Guido never managed. "That's a big call," I said. "She might've loved him."

He glared at me. "Loved him? Humph!"

"That's right, loved him," I said defiantly. "At the very least she didn't mind his company. That's how love starts."

He snorted. "My sister didn't need the likes of him. She was a good girl. She and Guido were made for each other."

"That's not what Loretta said."

"Loretta was only a kid. She'd have no idea what Jack was like."

I had to be careful that I didn't get riled up. Carl knew everything, too sure of the faults of others. But losing my temper wouldn't help. "Okay, that aside, why can't I see where the shooting took place?"

"Because for twenty years I've wanted to put this behind me. And still do."

"How many rifles did they go hunting with?"

"Two I'd guess. Why?"

"Loretta saw them off that morning. There was only one rifle in the ute. Guido's. And it was not the one that killed him."

Carl stiffened. He could respond alright if the needle hit its mark. "She was probably mistaken. Girls are prone to imagining things."

"She expected you to say that."

"Then she expected right."

"You forget Loretta was almost finished school. She was a young woman."

"Did she tell the police?"

"No."

"Well, that's how important it was." He glanced at his watch. "Anyway, we've wasted enough time. I've two hundred head to spray before dark. Maria will see you off."

In spite of his rough dismissal I sprang up like a cricket, keen to show I was the wholesome nephew. "Thanks for your time, Carl. I appreciate your honesty. It's helped fill in the picture."

The old bastard was caught off guard. A glimmer of warmth crossed his face. "Has it? That's good. Your father could've been a decent man in another place, the city maybe where he grew up, but this is the bush here. He destroyed the heart of this community and might've got away with it except for the war. Those years cracked him open, and once he was exposed he plunged into hell, taking your mother and Guido with him."

His good humour had vanished, and I guess he would never admit that in all likelihood Dad and Mum were happy, and the tragedy after the war wasn't entirely of Dad's making. But while Carl refused to see Dad's good points, he was also blinkered to the flaws in Guido. Loretta saw him as nasty, but Carl remembered him as his best mate. I helped Maria collect the tea things and in silence we climbed into the Land Rover and lurched back to the farmhouse.

As we entered the yard, Maria pursed her lips then asked carefully, "Is that... um... true about the two rifles?"

"God's honour. Loretta told me during the week. She's been a goldmine."

An eyebrow arched ten millimetres. "Loretta a goldmine? So what's she think of it all?"

"Well, assuming she saw correctly - and I believe she did - there had to be another man in the frame. Who it might be, she has no idea. Meantime, the law concluded there were only two likely scenarios: either it was an accident, or Dad deliberately shot ex-boyfriend Guido. Because of Dad's war record they gave him a free pass. However, if they'd done their job right, they would know Dad was genuinely innocent and the 'accidental death' was impossible."

I lifted the picnic box from the Land Rover and slammed the door before any junk fell out. Maria came round the back of the car and took the box from me.

"To make it worse," I said, "the locals wasted no time branding Dad a killer."

"Which locals?"

"Every Italian from here to whoop-whoop."

"Are you suggesting a local farmer killed Guido? That's absurd."

"Maria, it's not absurd," I said, tiring of the constant Italian denial. "To make you feel better, though, my gut instinct is that the killer was a stranger who's kept his mouth shut, and may even live here. He didn't operate alone, I'm sure of that."

"Well, I can see you won't let it rest. Who's next for a grilling?"

"This ain't *Homicide*, but I'll chat with Paulo again. He might know something about the second rifle. And I guess I'll keep talking to Loretta."

"When will that be?"

"I caught up with her last Monday. I'll do the same this week."

"Do you mind if I… um… tag along?"

I studied her closely. An hour ago she wasn't keen on anything to do with Jack Bellamy - myself or my father - but the gaze she returned was candid enough.

"Sure, Maria. Five-fifteen at her house. By the way, is she married?"

"Her husband died from bowel cancer years ago. They had two kids who did their schooling in Brisbane and rarely come home. She didn't remarry."

"That might explain her prickliness."

Maria almost let a smile escape. "You'd make anyone prickle."

CHAPTER 16

That afternoon I walked through the rows of caravans to Jimbo's place. After exchanging weather notes ("Looks fine for tomorrow, Jimbo."

"Yeah, dat be right, bro."), we launched his dinghy and motored down Jolimont Creek with a pack of Fourex and two fishing lines. Above our heads a lone eagle patrolled the mangroves and the occasional prawn skipped across the dinghy's bows. We dropped anchor mid-stream, fed out our lines and snapped the top off our drinks. Good as the beer tasted, even better was the thought of Maria's company which she had offered voluntarily. Maybe she was starting to warm to me, see my other side, but reality prevailed, and I was forced to admit that, unlike most locals, she probably did seek the truth. Shortly after four in the afternoon the tide changed and as the dinghy swung its bow seawards, I pulled in a king salmon. I don't know what caused that salmon to strike my bait because all afternoon I had done nothing but feed the crabs. In any event, the caravan mob ate well that night.

The following Monday, right on five-fifteen, I parked the bike outside Loretta's gate. I think she'd been expecting me as she was at the hibiscus smacking grasshoppers with the cricket bat.

"I'll never plant these hybrids again," she said. "Everything eats them." She stood her bat against a house stump and opened the gate. "What's it about this time?"

Just then Maria drove up and stepped from the car. She was still in her office dress. "Hello Aunty. Not too late for a cuppa?"

The two women embraced. "What are you doing here, *bambina*?" Loretta asked.

"Oh, just dropped by with eggs from home."

Loretta narrowed her eyes. "I'll swear you pair have been talking."

"Well," I jumped in, "I did say I had more questions."

"And I didn't know if he's trustworthy," Maria added, handing over a bag of eggs.

"Alright, you'd better come in," Loretta said and led the way upstairs. Once on the verandah she showed us to chairs then bustled in the kitchen while the cockatoo screeched, "Cranky old bastard."

"He'll cranky his way to an early death," I said.

Maria took celery from her pocket and fed him. "Do you know he learnt that from your father?"

"Yes, Loretta told me. Apparently Dad could teach bird-brains."

"Would you like to be a teacher?"

"No, I hated classrooms, especially anything to do with maths. Reading and writing was okay because, well, once you've cracked the code you're away. Still I couldn't teach it to kids."

"You can go to college where they teach you to teach. You come out with a diploma."

At the word college I pulled a face. "What I enjoyed was sport. We had a strong footy team at the orphanage, but we played only a handful of matches because of the fights. Not so much with state schools, but with the private schools who thought we were vermin. Maybe they inherited it from their parents, maybe it was the way of uppity schools, but a slap or two in the scrum helped wipe the smile from their dials. The general view was that we played dirty. We weren't dirty, we had no honour to play for."

"That's sad."

I decided her concern was genuine. "The whole business of orphanages is sad. Kids thrown together, no parents, no families. Nuns who treat seven year olds like army squads. If you cried, they cuffed your ear. And if you touched a girl, even held her hand, they caned you for having dirty thoughts."

"I'm sorry," she said. "Were they all like that?"

"No, not really," I admitted.

Although Nudgee had its share of cruel nuns, they were mostly good people following their vocation. Yet it was the bad apples you remembered; the darkness prevailing over light, and afterwards, sometimes years later, the light pushing back in unexpected ways. Like now. I wanted to touch Maria, touch softness, be touched in return. Hold her hand. Feel what it was like to be close to a woman who cares. But I didn't touch her. I smiled brightly and she smiled back.

"We had our little wins," I said after an awkward pause. "Sometimes we'd escape at night and steal cakes from the bakery. Cripes, they were delicious. And we'd be home in bed before the nun patrol caught us."

Maria laughed as Loretta arrived on the verandah with a pot of tea and a plate of biscuits.

"If you prefer a beer, Jack, there's a bottle in the fridge. It's been there since Christmas."

"I'll take you up on that," I said and wandered down the hallway, checking out the house as I went. Loretta's house was divided down the centre, bedrooms on the left and living rooms and kitchen on the right. The entire place was built from hoop pine, including the high ceilings and the tongue-and-groove walls that had fanlights separating each room. Little tables stood in every corner cluttered with enough trinkets to start a china shop, and prints hung three deep on the walls. In the lounge room that opened onto the verandah, she had a plump sofa, a TV, piano and the cocky's cage. Her sleepy old house oozed comfort like a well-worn slipper.

I found a beer at the bottom of the fridge and returned to the verandah.

"Maria was saying you rode out to see Carl again," Loretta said.

"That's right."

"I asked you not to mention the second rifle."

"Sorry, but I wanted to see his face."

"And?"

"It startled him. Then he said you imagined it, being young and all, and besides if it was true you would've gone to the cops."

Loretta set her cup on the tray. "Carl knows about that rifle. One day he'll admit it. The awkward thing for Carl is that the rifle was legally his and Jack borrowed it whenever he came over. Jack was handy with a rifle which made the farm boys envious, especially Paulo who fancied himself as a crack shot. Carl was different. He used a rifle only when he had to."

I was a stranger to this world of guns. In Brisbane only criminals or soldiers carried guns, not even the cops. Guns aside, I wanted young Maria to hear a different story about the romance. "Loretta, you probably knew Mum and Dad better than most. Were they a match?"

"It wasn't easy at the start. Maria had broken her promise to Guido, if I can put it that way, and given her heart to Jack. So it was awkward for everyone, especially for Papa who held with tradition. And who knows, Papa could have been right. It's very possible that Guido and Maria could have lived a comfortable life among family. However, when Jack came along, he offered Maria something she'd been denied: choice - freedom of choice to be exact - and she chose Jack. For all his ways I'm convinced he loved her and tried to make her feel special."

"It must've been hard going to war straight after the wedding."

"He didn't join up at once. He was still teaching when they moved into my grandparent's old house at the Rise and Shine."

"Where's that?"

"It's a small farming valley south of Carl's place. When the government balloted this land back in the 1920s, my grandfather Nonno drew a block in the Rise and Shine. Papa came out on the same ship and drew his block in the O'Connell River where Carl now lives. But while the O'Connell River land was flat and fertile, Nonno's was rough and uneven. I remember he ran a herd of dairy cows and grew small crops that he sold from the back of a sulky every Friday in Calen. When Nonno died in a horse accident in 1937, Nonna moved in with us on the O'Connell River, and we rented the Rise and Shine house to cane cutters. After Jack and Maria married in 1940, the house was freshened up and given over to them. Maria soon turned it into a nice little home."

"Were the two farms near each other?"

"On a map they look close. By car, it's only twenty-five minutes, but by foot it's a couple of hours. There's a track crossing the ridge that separates the two farms. We used to walk it as kids, but we had to be careful not to stray. In some places it was barely a mark through the trees."

"So it was kind of isolated?"

"You could say that. Few people in those days had a car. Once or twice a week I walked across to their house, and sometimes on a Saturday afternoon, they'd walk over to us and stay the night."

I turned to Maria who had been listening in silence. "Have you ever walked the track?"

"A few times. Nobody lives in the house anymore and Dad runs cattle on the property. When we go there now we drive in from the main road."

"I'd like to see it one day," I said.

"It's easy to find," Loretta answered, and reached for a notepad and pen. "I'll draw you a map."

Before Loretta could start sketching, Maria said, "I can take you. It won't be any trouble."

The pen slipped from Loretta's fingers and rolled to the floor. As I bent to pick it up, Maria brushed hair from her face. She was talking quickly. "Dad wants to mend a fence there next Saturday and I promised to help. It's a lot quicker if two people do it, and some of those posts can be hard work."

"Fencing is like that," I agreed. "I've seen the movies."

Without a further word we finished our drinks and made noises that it was time to move on. When

Maria offered to show me the farm, I felt a shift in wind direction. Maybe it was our progress with this wartime mystery, but I think it was more to do with a thaw in attitude. Loretta was almost perky as she waddled down the stairs after us.

I held the car door for Maria. "What time Saturday?"

"Meet me at the Rise and Shine turnoff at nine," she said, turning the ignition key. "And Jack, this is not an invitation to something else. I'm showing you Nonno's old house, that's all."

"Message understood." I clicked the door shut. "And Maria… thanks."

Once she had pulled away from the kerb, I kicked over the Norton's big engine and waved cheerfully to Loretta who watched from the gate. The three of us had created the makings of a team, and in a vague kind of way, I was experiencing the closeness of family.

CHAPTER 17

The next week was a disaster in the cane. First up the sugar mill broke down on Monday night when a sprocket on one of the crushers worked loose and fell into the mill. Bits of metal chomped their way through all sorts of vats and conveyors. The mill manager reckoned that as it would take forty-eight hours to fix the damage, trucks could take the harvested cane across the river to the Marian Mill. But that mill had its own problems. So they turned the trucks around and sent them down to Pleystowe Mill. However, that was only part of the drama. Different cane varieties reach their peak at different times, after which the sugar content falls, and since farmers earn bonuses on the CCS (commercial cane sugar) content, tempers were flaring in the paddocks and boardrooms. Meantime the poor devils cutting the cane, fellows like me, were being jigged about like gnats on a string. One moment we were told to cut a block on Harry's farm, but after driving across with all the machinery we were ordered back to Wacko's place. The contractors were upset because their payment came from the tonnage they cut, and the haul out drivers, that's me again, earned nothing but sore bums for all the driving about with half empty trailers.

Worst of all, I saw my Saturday jaunt with Maria getting the flick. But as luck had it, the mill bosses decided to cut an extra thirty per cent on Thursday and Friday, and if additional make-up time was needed, the Farleigh Mill would crush until late November.

Saturday morning dawned gloriously. Lorikeets flashed through the grevilleas along the creek bank and sunlight danced on waters that rippled and sang. I walked across to the shower block and splashed water over my face. Although Maria was only cousin, my circuitry was running hot. I scrubbed my teeth, and after a quick shower and shave studied myself in the mirror. Not a lot to be excited about, especially the broken nose, but I decided that if I was to spend the morning with cowgirl Maria, I needed to look the part. Shortly after eight I rode into Calen and bought a western shirt, jeans, rodeo belt and big hat.

It was now twenty minutes to nine. I stuffed the new hat into the front of my shirt and rode northwards through the settlement of Pindi Pindi to the turn-off for the Rise and Shine. Apart from a cheerful signpost and newly graded road, there wasn't much about the valley to up-and-at-em as the name suggested. I leant the bike against the fence behind some trees then sat on a log where I moulded my hat into a cowboy shape. It was very quiet on that road. From somewhere in the east came the rise and fall of a tractor engine, and closer to hand the occasional rush of a car down the highway, but those sounds were remote. Right there, on the log, a sense of peace flowed out of the landscape. Maybe I was getting my search for roots out of perspective. What happened to Dad, Mum and Guido was history, and Carl could be right in wanting to let sleeping dogs lie. But as I watched a goanna tackle patiently the entrance to a native bee hive, I thought I must do the same; unearth one riddle at a time.

Bye and bye Maria's Land Rover came chugging down the highway. She flipped on the indicator and pulled to a dusty halt beside me.

As she slid open the window, her eyes widened. "Wow. Hi cowboy."

"Howdy y'all," I grinned. "Yo goin' my way, lady?"

She shook her head in disbelief. I swung open the door and settled in among the junk which included the picnic basket. Her eyes hadn't left me.

"Where did you buy that stuff? Roy Rogers' estate?"

"My agent flew it in last night."

She laughed. "Ever ridden a horse?"

"Once. The nuns took us to a fair in Nudgee and for sixpence we rode the carousel. My horse was black and silver."

"Did you fall off?"

"No, I was clamped to the thing."

She fell silent as she handled the clumsy Land Rover along the narrow gravel road. At a fork that had a one-room state school in the apex, she swung right and drove round a series of low hills before the valley opened into an expanse of green pasture dotted with trees. She stopped and pointed to a farmhouse that stood alone at the base of the timbered ranges. "That's where Nonno and Nonna lived, and you see that dip in the first hill behind the house? That's the track crossing to our farm."

Three minutes later we turned off the gravel road onto a two-wheel track that led up to a gate. I opened the gate and after Maria had driven through, closed it behind us. We then bumped and lurched along the track towards the farmhouse. Big red and white cattle grazed either side and at times Maria changed down a gear to manoeuvre past them.

"What do you like best, cattle or cane?" I shouted above the engine.

"I was raised with both, and I like both, but the cattle are more interesting. The cane really is just tall grass and the harvesters big mowers. On the other hand, horses and cattle belong together. If you love one, you love the other. I learned to ride as a kid and I adore saddling up and working a herd."

As we drew closer to the farmhouse I could see the yards and a couple of sheds where a group of horses lazily swished their tails in the shade of a tree. There were no other cars. No utes, nothing. Maria pulled the Land Rover to a halt beside the verandah and shut down the engine. Unhurriedly she scrummaged through the mess in the back. When she had located a small box of machine parts she carried them up the stairs and dropped them on a bench.

I followed with the picnic basket and leant against the verandah rail. "A man could grow to like this," I said, breathing in the landscape. Before me lay the splendid valley and on either side like two encircling arms were the spurs of the Clarke Ranges. Cattle grazed contentedly and a pair of hawks circled over a distant field. Maria gave the scene a cursory glance before moving inside where she thrust open doors and windows.

"Where is the fence your dad is mending?" I called to her.

"He must've finished."

"Fast worker. It's not even ten."

She emerged through a side door. "There is no broken fence. I made it up."

"You've taken a risk, young lady," I said, turning to face her. "Up here on your lonesome with Roy Rogers."

She stared right back. "I brought you here to show you the house. And if you're fit enough, I'll take you up that hill behind us. From there you'll find sections of the old track, and you'll see the bridge over the O'Connell River." She pulled off her hat and slapped at dust on the table. "Do you want to eat now or later?"

I actually wanted her to join me at the verandah rail, but I said; "Let's climb the hill."

She led the way through overgrown grass past the remains of an orchard that was now three untended trees - a loquat, mango and bush lemon - and onto a cattle pad that wound into the foothills. One massive bull blocking the path turned his head arrogantly as we strode towards him, but when Maria thumped him on the rump he ambled away like a baby. Once into the lower slopes the path ascended rapidly and I was glad of all the cane bins I had pushed onto trailers. Sweat was dripping off my chin and my pulse beat like a hammer. Up ahead Maria strode along happily. Occasionally she paused to be sure I followed and once she offered a bottle of water. "What's the hurry?" I gasped.

"You're unfit for your age," she said, poking her stick at my belly, "and you probably drink too much."

"I'm not unfit," I protested. "And I'm teetotal."

"In your dreams."

In a direct route to the top of the hill it would have been two hundred metres, but the path twisted round giant boulders and clumps of lantana. By now the house and Land Rover were like matchbox toys in a land of miniature cows and sheds. The sky was patched with hurrying clouds and the colours of the rainforest were deep and green. Finally, we reached the crest of the hill and the vista below was worth the climb: canefields and townships, a goods train inching along a distant railway, and through the morning haze the soft glint of sun bouncing off the O'Connell River.

"That's the bridge across there to your left," she said. "And that's where Dad's cane farm starts, near that power line, and that's the road up to our house. See way over there to your right, that blue line, that's the ocean."

I sucked in heaps of clean air. A lot of country lay below us. "Are we still on your granddad's land?" I asked.

"Yes, the State Forest runs along that ridge behind us and separates this farm from those on the other side." She touched my arm with her stick as she pointed. "See that escarpment to your left. That's the start of the track linking Nonno's farm to ours. Follow it past those hoop pine until it comes to a fork. Turn right and the track drops sharply into our valley, go left, and it takes you to the headwaters of the O'Connell River."

"Where Guido was killed," I added.

She glanced at me. "That's right."

"Have you been there, Maria?"

"I know the way, that's all."

"But you could find it?"

"Never given it much thought."

I went back to the farms. "Loretta said it's two hours walk from one house to the other?"

"Yes, because the track is so steep. It seems a long way now but in those days it was quicker than the road, unless, of course, you borrowed the farm truck which was an old pre-war beast that wasn't for *gadding about in*... Papa's words. I walked the track as a kid but I prefer to ride. Nowadays, if Loretta comes along we take the horses. She might be packing on the kilos, but she's a good horsewoman."

After I had finished admiring the view I was about to return to the house when Maria said, "Come, I've something to show you."

She led the way across the hill to a gully blanketed in rainforest. "Listen," she whispered. Moments later I heard the trickle of water falling over rock, then I noticed a spring gurgling merrily from behind a towering carabeen. Tiny finches and wrens darted in and out of the pool at the tree's foot. "The water is so sweet," she said. "Taste it."

I cupped my hands into the water and drank. It was delicious. I grinned at her. "We should bottle the stuff."

"Never," she said, and sluiced her face. "God's gift to the forest."

Pulling out a handkerchief, she dipped the cloth in the pool and wrung it out. "Come here. You'll drip blood on your new shirt." With her free hand holding my face to the light, she dabbed at a cut where I had walked into a branch. It was like I had imagined; the sensation that comes with a woman's touch, the impulse to touch the hand touching my cheek. She was business-like as she cleaned the wound and I stood before her like an old Labrador.

After rinsing out the handkerchief she gave it to me. "You'd better keep it until the bleeding stops."

"Thank you."

"You're welcome."

When she turned back to the track, I stopped her. "Can I ask you something?"

"Depends on what it is."

"That burn on your shoulder. How did you come by it?"

"Please, Jack."

"I've told you my story."

"Yours is different."

"How, *different*?"

After leading me to the crest of the hill, she sat on a flat stone. I sat on the grass a short distance away.

"Hot oil was spilt on me as a kid," she said without preamble.

I winced. "Bloody hell. How little a kid?"

"Nine."

"Go on."

"Don't push me, Jack."

"Sorry. I guess it's still painful."

"It is." Her face was about to crumple. She was quiet for several minutes. "Do you remember asking how my mother died?"

"Yes. In a car accident."

"That's only half the truth. After my aunt Maria... your mother... died in Moreton Bay, Dad was a changed man. From all accounts he had been a good-natured, hard-working man who gave his love to three people. I came first, of course; his baby girl. The other two were his wife... my mother... and his sister Maria who got killed by her husband a thousand kilometres away."

I made to protest, but she silenced me.

"Hear me out, please. After Aunty Maria's death he became moody and argumentative. Probably even wished Jack had lived so he could take out his revenge. But as happens in life, the person nearest is the one who suffers most. In this case it was Mum. Because her family hailed from Bowen, she had nobody in Calen to turn to. Little by little she took to the gin and tonic, mostly during the crushing season when I was at school and Dad away on the farm. When times were busy, he might be away all day and half the night. Well, that's how my shoulder got burnt. Mum had had a few drinks and one night stumbled over me with a pan of hot oil. I was driven into the Mackay hospital where after a few months of repair I returned to school, wearing long sleeves. Mum was terribly shaken by what she'd done. She swore never to touch booze again. Sadly, the promise didn't stick. She started wardrobe drinking. One day when I was twelve, she was taking lunch up to Dad and missed a bend in the river and rolled the car. That's how they found her. At the bottom of the river."

Maria ended her story and I said quietly, "I'm sorry." All this time I'd been bleating about my childhood, oblivious to the misfortune in others.

"That was seven years ago," she shrugged. "I lost my mum, and Dad lost both his sister and his wife. He laid the blame squarely on Jack Bellamy."

My father's conquest of the prettiest girl in Calen had triggered a domino reaction. One tragedy led to another. Although I felt awful about Maria's childhood, it seemed unfair that Dad was taking all the blame. Carl could've been more understanding of his wife, but wasn't; he could've supported his sister, but didn't; and Paulo could've counselled his brother, but hadn't. However, it was not the time to reassign fault. I asked Maria if she had considered skin grafts to hide the scar.

She gazed at me, then jumped to her feet. "You asked how I received the burn, so I've told you. Now you know everything and that's the end of it. Okay?"

"Sure. And I owe you an apology."

She flashed a smile. "That's alright, Jack. We'd better move along and mind where you put your feet."

The walk back to the farmhouse was much easier. All downhill, and the cattle that had blocked our path now lay in the shade chewing through their morning siestas. Maria and I sat together on the verandah steps with our tea and homemade scones, tossing crumbs to a party of mynas that fluttered near our boots.

After a time Maria said, "You must be confused about your parents. Loretta tells one story and Paulo another."

"Yes. And Carl a third."

"For what it's worth," she said, "I think Loretta is probably closer to the truth. She would've seen her older sister dragged round by the two boys, never allowed an opinion, and never asked who she wanted to marry. Everyone, grandparents included, would've matched her up with Guido. When Jack

Bellamy came along, he... well... opened a gate for her."

"Gate?"

"Yes. The gate Loretta called free choice."

I fell quiet at that. Maria would've been aware of the similarity between herself and her aunt. Another Jack Bellamy was unlatching the gate, or imagined he was.

"I agree with you," I said, trying to keep my voice even. "Loretta's story is the most plausible. If given the chance, I think Mum would've lived contentedly with her young Australian husband. As for Jack himself? Well, before the war he sounds happy-go-lucky, took life as it came. He was bowled over by Maria the moment he laid eyes on her, then won her heart fair and square. But where was the monster lurking? Even if he did bring it back from the war and Guido's death was an accident, why kill someone he loves?"

"How old were you at the time?"

"Four."

"Can you remember anything?"

"Not at all. Apparently Mum and Dad hired a boat for a day's outing. I would've gone along excited as a young puppy."

"Were there only three of you in the boat?"

"I believe so. According to the paper, a handful of people were on the jetty when we climbed aboard. That statement came from the boat-hire man."

"Did he hire a boat to others?"

"Nothing was mentioned in the paper. I doubt he took names as he just hires little boats. Why do you ask?"

"Well, there could've been witnesses to the shooting."

"The police would've checked all that."

"From what I understand, Jack, your father shot his wife, tied you to a floating oar, holed the boat, then shot himself. That's quite an effort for a man whose only motive appears to be war fatigue. Who picked you up?"

"According to the newspaper, a passing fisherman."

"Nobody with him?"

"Don't think so."

"Well, it sounds too neat to me."

"Maria, I've always said Dad is innocent and one day I'll prove it. But one step at a time. Right now we have the mystery of Guido's death to clear up. Once that's done we'll concentrate on the events in Moreton Bay."

Maria touched my arm. That was twice in one day. "Sorry, Jack. I don't mean to interfere, but I can't help thinking one mystery does hide another. I agree your mother was beautiful, but she was also a trophy men fought over. Somebody, perhaps the losers, wanted the trophy destroyed. The grudge against your father could have been an all-consuming rage."

"Carl had a grudge against him, and still does."

"That's not true. Dad was dreadfully upset when Jack broke up his family, but he doesn't bear grudges."

"He has a peculiar way of showing it."

CHAPTER 18

We left it at that. I wasn't in the mood for probing deeper into why three murders had taken place - and all involving Dad - but it was odd I remembered nothing about the events in Moreton Bay. Well, not entirely odd. One wet afternoon at the orphanage, a nun had explained why we were not only unruly, but retarded. Apparently when something bad happens to a kid, trauma sets in and every memory back to his birth is erased. So if the kid was three when the nasty thing happened, and he is now eight, the first three years of his life are obliterated, and he is left with the mind of a five-year-old. I had no trouble with her theory. When I was nine I still wet the bed and had the reading age of a second-grader. Although things had improved since then, my dunking in the bay remained a total blank, and while uncovering the truth was important, I was wary of Bernie Maroni's caution that the truth may hold a surprise I might just regret.

An hour later we had repacked the picnic basket and motored down the road to the Rise and Shine intersection where our morning began.

Maria braked beside the Norton and said, "So what's next?"

"Well, first up is a chat with Paulo. Dad stayed at the Avolio house in the early days and because Paulo and Guido were brothers, Paulo has to know more than he's admitted."

"Alright, tell me if you discover anything."

"Aren't you tagging along?"

"No, thanks. It's too awkward. As you know, Paulo is the father of my Sam."

I couldn't stop myself grinning. "You mean *lovely* Sam."

She let out a sigh. "Drop my guard and I get this."

"Maria, you misjudge me. I only want to help the boy."

"You're being horrid."

"Okay, I was out of order. He's... well... sweet."

Maria leant across, opened the door and booted me out. "Hey," I said, "that's no way to treat a cowboy."

She threw the car into gear and spurted gravel over my new shirt. I was no authority but even blind Freddy could see her boy needed therapy. Funny what love does to people.

CHAPTER 19

The next two harvesting days purred along, and as luck would have it we were scheduled to cut a block of Paulo's cane that Wednesday and Thursday. I turned up early knowing the farmers always tidied their fields to prevent the fire spreading to a second block. Sure enough Paulo was on a slasher cutting the grass along his headlands while Sam raked the cane tops from a previous cut.

After Paulo finished slashing he drove to the farm utility where I stood, and climbed stiffly to the ground. "Arthritis," he grumbled. "Runs in the family."

"Try cod liver oil," I said.

"Cod liver oil?"

"Yes, oil from a cod's liver. Nuns swore by it."

He looked at me strangely. "I like olive oil, and Italians for centuries have sworn by it. You're here early, Jack. Aren't we burning to plan?"

"We are, but I wanted a chat before the place got crowded."

He leant into the ute and took out a burner which he began to fill. "What's on your mind?"

"Paulo, you and Carl helped bring Guido's body down from the hills."

"Sure did. It's no joy carrying your dead brother."

"Yes, that would be awful. Sorry. Anyway, Loretta said the two men left home with one rifle, Guido's, but it was a different rifle that killed him. How do you think that came about?"

"What's in the police report?"

"She never told the police."

"Well, she needs to take care saying things like that. Some people might see it as an accusation."

"How's that?"

"By implying others were involved."

"That's hardly an accusation. Anyway, where were you and Carl that morning?"

"What's this, Jack, an inquest? We told the cops everything we know."

"No, Paulo, it's not an inquest, but there are holes in the official story. I've come to the conclusion that Dad was innocent in all this. The cops wrote Guido's death off as an accident, but an unknown person shot him deliberately and let the Italians think it was Dad."

"Don't look at me, kid. It was my brother who died, and I loved him."

"Nobody suggests you didn't love him, but any idea how a second rifle turned up?"

"The *second rifle*, if there was such a thing, would've been Carl's. Ask him."

"I have and he's not talking either. Only Loretta seems willing to cooperate. Maybe she's the one person with nothing to hide."

Paulo didn't like that and angrily threw his burner into the ute. In that brief moment his lawyer's features had turned ugly.

I held up my hands. "Sorry, Paulo. I'm not pointing the finger at anyone. I'm just teasing out the leads. Now here, I'll fetch the burner." I climbed into the tray and retrieved it for him, even using a rag to clean up the spilt fuel. While there I noticed a gun on the rack behind his seat, exactly as Loretta had described Guido's ute on the day of the shooting.

After he had settled down I said, "Paulo, do you remember a cop with a limp?"

"Yeah, now you mention it."

"He attended the fight between Dad and Guido. He also investigated Guido's death."

"He could've done. So what?"

I watched for Paulo's reaction. "He was Dad's brother-in-law."

And Paulo didn't let me down. He dropped the burner on his foot. "You're taking the piss."

"No. It's a fact. But it doesn't mean Dad was guilty of any crime. It only makes things look worse. People will think the pair conspired to hide the truth."

Paulo was stumbling for words. "This is all news to me, mate."

"I can understand you didn't know that Dad and D. S. Cleary were related. But you knew Cleary was the investigating officer. You couldn't have brought Guido's body down from the hills and not meet him."

I stared bluntly at Paulo waiting for a response.

"Yeah, it's true about Cleary. I swore I'd never utter his name again. He was a vicious bastard. Hated Italians, hated everyone, except maybe your father being a relative and all."

"They weren't blood relations. He was married to Dad's sister. What do you remember of him?"

"Not a lot. I think his investigation was what you'd expect from a white cop. Two men, a murder weapon - despite what Loretta thinks she saw - and the white hero declared innocent."

"Paulo, I'd like to see where the shooting took place. I need to do that for Dad's benefit and my own peace of mind. I also want to pay my respects to Guido."

"Pay your respects?" he said angrily. "As far as this place is concerned, you'd do better apologising. Your dad thought he was still fighting the Japs."

"The war changed him. That was hard on everyone, but he wasn't gun crazy."

By now Sam had finished raking the tops and set them on fire. A smudge of greasy blue smoke drifted over the paddocks, curdling the bright colours of the sunset. Slowly he drove the length of the fire checking that it couldn't escape, then motored across to Paulo's ute and jumped to the ground. He wore a pair of flared jeans and a body-hugging shirt. The curls in his hair shone in the orange light.

"G'day, Jack," he said. "You're here early."

"Yes, Sam. I wanted to catch up with your father. Ask some questions about Guido's death."

He rolled his eyes. "Twenty years of water under the bridge and Guido's ghost is still flipping and turning."

"Sorry, but I can't rest until Dad's name is cleared."

"It was an accident."

"That's the official line, Sam. But not what locals believe. I suppose you've heard about the second rifle? No? Well, it was a long time ago, before you were born. When Guido and Jack left the farm in the morning, they had one rifle, Guido's. When the police arrived at the scene, there was a different rifle. Odd wouldn't you say?"

He tapped the side of his head. "What's this fella on about?"

"Oh, some yarn that Loretta fed him," Paulo said. "Her heart might be in the right place but she's an old busy body with nothin' better to do."

Sam fronted me. "We can do without wanna-be cops stirring up the grief. You ought to bugger off, mate. Our family has suffered enough."

"Sorry, but I've got to hang about. Cane to burn. Say, why don't you set my mind at rest. Show me where Guido died, and that'll be the end of it."

Sam turned to his father. I had to admit that in profile Sam was handsome if you favoured the Caesar look. "Is there any harm in that, Dad?"

"Why should there be? There's nothing to see."

"Okay, Jack, I'll take you. It'll have to be Sunday week. But once you see the place, that's it. Finished."

"Suits me."

Just then the men from the harvesting gang arrived with their trickle burners and water sprays. We had cut so many blocks over the past months that we had the burning down to a fine art. And it was an art. Two men started firing carefully along the downwind side while the others watched for lighted leaf that could jump the break. Once the downwind rows had burnt in a few metres, the same two men dashed round to the top of the block and set it alight. The wind then pushed the fire to the heart of the field where it drew all sides into an inferno that lasted a bare ninety seconds. We stayed for another twenty minutes knocking out the embers, and once Paulo was confident all was under control, we upped stumps and drove home.

CHAPTER 20

All that week I was strangely on edge. Every afternoon the temptation was in me to ride into town and see Maria, but I couldn't think of a good reason. She had thrown me out of her Land Rover, and since I wasn't her boyfriend there was no point in turning up with flowers and a weak apology. As it happened, I needn't have fretted. Late in the week I heard there was an RSL dance at Calen on Saturday and Jimbo was taking his panel van.

Saturday night arrived cool and clear. It was one of those sublime winter evenings with a big moon rising over the canefields and frogs croaking merrily down by the creek. As I switched on the caravan light I decided I could pick the flaws in Sam only because I prided myself with good taste. I shaved every day, I visited the barber (not hairdresser) once a month, and I knew why the park had a laundry. Hoping to impress girls at the RSL, I washed and brushed my longish hair, then threw on a neat denim shirt that was neither wild west nor post-Vietnam hippie. I studied myself in the mirror. My dad was a handsome Australian with fair hair and a strong chin. I was all Latin, but when I smouldered my eyes I bore a likeness to Marlon Brando; so a girl at Maryborough had said one drunken outing. I gazed into that mirror for several minutes and, despite checking my profile from all angles, I found little resemblance to Dad or Uncle Carl. For one frightening moment I saw a likeness to Sam but, I decided, that was more about wanting whatever he had that appealed to Maria. Sadly I pondered Father Burke's observation that I could be a curly headed mongrel who should never have left Brisbane. Father's remark aside, this trip was supposed to be about Mum and Dad, not myself, so I turned off the light and closed the door. Out at the gate I climbed into the back of Jimbo's van with three sisters from the farm across the road and two boys from the cane cutters' barracks. As someone had thrown in a supply of rum and cola, we were singing cheerfully long before our destination.

Calen hasn't much to offer from the highway, but she shapes up nicely when you turn west and drive up the main street. St Helens' Creek borders the left side of town and Mount Consuelo dominates the south-west over a scattering of iron roofs. To give Calen her due she's the iconic Queenslander: footpaths aglow with tropical colour, and gardens heady with the distinctive spice of the north. Throughout the hot summer the place is drowsily quiet but during *the crush* (as the harvesting season is known) she jumps. The RSL Hall was like a bee hive when we arrived. Utilities and gleaming sedans were parked two deep, girls and their boyfriends crowded the entrance and the warm, happy sounds of a three-piece band flowed out the windows.

One of the sisters from the panel van grabbed my arm and led me inside. Ten seconds later I hit the brakes. While I was cocky enough in the darkness, the hall's interior bulged with self-assured strangers. At the orphanage there'd been precious little schooling on how to dance, and in Maryborough I mostly hung out with the football crowd.

The blonde sister who latched onto me was attractive in an earthy kind of way. She had good legs, motherhood tits and a smile that outshone the moon.

"Come on, son of a gun," she shouted. "Let's dance."

"I'll sit this one out. Get my bearings."

"Stuff your bearings," she said and dragged me onto the floor.

I couldn't dance to save my life, but this girl was a keen teacher and had me tearing round the floor with the rest of the larrikins.

A couple of brackets later, we collapsed onto a bench against the wall.

"Hey, that was alright, Jack," she gasped. "What's your full name?"

"Jack Bellamy. What's yours."

Her eyebrows flew up. "Jack Bellamy?"

"That's right."

"No connection with the bloke who shot Guido Avolio?"

"He was my dad, and he shot nobody."

"Good for you. There're more stories about Guido's death than the great war. It was almost set reading at school."

"What do you know about it?"

"I wasn't born at the time and I know the Italians keep it hushed, but the story goes that war hero Jack Bellamy shot Guido for cheating on his missus."

"That's a theory, but it's far-fetched. Dad was a highly decorated officer. There's no way he'd take Guido into the mountains and shoot him. He'd just box his melon on day one. All sorted."

"What if a man cheated on your wife. Would you box his melon?"

"Not if she was a nag. I'd say, 'Here, pal, your lucky day'."

She laughed. "Nagging can be underrated." Although her teeth were clean and white, the drinks in Jimbo's van had smudged her lipstick. "Let's dance, Jack Bellamy. My name's Tessa Woods and I ain't Italian."

She hauled me onto the floor just as the band eased into a slow number. Without warning, she cuddled up and there were precious few bits that didn't touch. God, I needed an ice pack. I had little idea how to handle a girl that was all over me. There'd been a few Maryborough girls who'd put out feelers, but they were chasing a roof over their heads and a signature on the register. Not that I was a complete mug in the sex field. A couple of older girls at the orphanage had made it their duty one dull Saturday to coach the First Eleven in the cricket shed. Although I was a member of that select team, I was still a kid at fifteen and the coaching technique of those girls would've blown Krakatoa.

When the dance ended we were sweating heavily and Tessa's crotch was imprinted on my jeans.

"Let's have a drink," I gasped.

"You'd better make it a double, Jack Bellamy."

We staggered out through the side door where a sizeable crowd was already into the grog. Most people were drinking lager, but a quantity of rum and cola was sliding down throats and several girls had dented the supply of cold duck. In the shadows a group of hippies passed round a flagon of rosé while a lone youth in a cheesecloth puffed furtively on a joint. After ordering two double rums I took them back to Tessa. By then her two sisters had found us, and I was shunted back to the bar for more drinks. I was halfway to my destination when Maria and boyfriend Sam strolled into the fresh air.

Looking back on it, the big mistake was that Maria and Sam were sober while I was half cut. To make it worse Maria's beauty was understated while Sam glistened like an oil can. Not to mention he was so far up himself he could hardly breathe. He had unbuttoned his shirt to the navel, he wore chunky jewellery like a pharaoh and his platform shoes lifted him into the ceiling. For all his faults, however, he was Maria's date and I should've been content with my three sisters. I was about to turn away when something twigged about his jewellery. The brightest medal, smack in the centre of his chest, was a St Francis of Assisi. The very same St Francis that Aunty Nell had given me.

I jabbed a finger at the medal. "Where did you get that?"

"None of your business."

Reaching inside my shirt. I pulled out my St Francis. They were identical. Maria and Sam gaped at it.

"Where did these come from, Sam?" Maria said.

"How would I know? Family heirlooms, I expect."

"Did it belong to Guido?" I asked. "Because this one belonged to my mother."

Sam was flustered. To him the medal was just a classy lump of silver. "I'll look into it," he muttered, and dived for the bar. Not to be outdone, I raced ahead and elbowed him aside.

"You'd better find out where it came from," I said, waving for the barman's attention.

"Maybe I will, maybe not. Hey, Tocko!" he bawled over my shoulder. "A baby champers and a Fourex."

"Get in the queue, fella," I said.

"Queue? No such word up here."

At that moment Tocko dumped two drinks in front of him and grabbed his cash.

"It's who you know, not what you know," Sam grinned and took the drinks back to Maria.

I can't recall if I tripped or got bumped, but three minutes later while heading towards the sisters I accidentally knocked Sam's elbow and spilt beer over his shirt.

"Whoops... sorry."

Sam bellowed a string of obscenities, shaking the windows and upsetting the hippies.

"Drop off the shirt," I offered, "and I'll handwash it for next Saturday."

Maria's eyes blazed at me. "For God's sake, Jack, leave us alone."

"Sorry, Maria. I was just passin' through with drinks for my friends... and, well, Sam must've got in the way. It won't happen again. Be more careful, honest."

She was furious. "You're so like your father. Picking brawls, making enemies."

"That's not true. And anyhow, you're very like my mother... so pretty, men fought each other."

It was a good thing Sam fussed with his shirt. "You've done enough damage, Jack. Good night."

I took the drinks over to Tessa and her sisters, and I confess I don't remember much about the dance after that, but around midnight I found myself alone in the back of Jimbo's van with the three sisters for the ride home. I don't know if I was in the mood to play up but they were, and more.

CHAPTER 21

The following morning my mouth tasted like the skin of a dead hare. I still wasn't chirpy at dark when we arrived at the Avolio farm to burn more cane. Sam was present but said nothing, just a curt nod in my direction. He made no attempt to hand over his soiled shirt and I didn't remind him of my offer.

All week while cutting on the Avolio farm, I was on best behaviour with Sam as I desperately wanted to see the place of Guido's shooting. It had become my pilgrimage, my need to visit a sacred site. But it was more than that. Guido's death in a remote forest seemed to be the tipping point for Dad, the final scene of Act One. After that everyone deserted him, almost like it was no surprise that he should kill his wife and himself. Meantime, I tried unsuccessfully to erase the sight of the identical St Francis medals. If Sam's had once belonged to Guido and mine to Mum, then perhaps Dad had muscled in on a genuine romance. It was an idea I refused to accept. Dad hadn't only rescued Mum from a stifling Italian community, he also loved her. Genuinely loved her and wanted to set up home with her, until the stupid war came along and let the Italians climb back in.

CHAPTER 22

Much as I needed to find out about the St Francis medals, I had to visit Kevin Cleary again. He was possibly the only one alive - apart from the killer - who knew the details of Guido's death. If a second rifle had appeared on the scene, Cleary would know who carried it. Besides, who raised the alarm? Did my father hurry back to the farm, or did someone, a third man, hear the shot and run to investigate? If so, the third man's tracks would've been seen, and it's possible he knew the killer - or was the killer himself. I was growing weary of tying myself in knots. Wherever I started it always returned to the single fact that nobody, apart from Dad, bore a grudge against Guido.

On the following Saturday I rose at daylight and headed for Townsville, reaching the city an hour before lunch. I grabbed a quick bite at the café in Flinders Street, bought a half-dozen buns and rode across to Cleary's house in Railway Estate.

The procedure to wake him hadn't changed. Knock and listen, skin crawling as curtains twitched in nearby houses. Knock again. More shadows in the windows. Knock louder. Finally, the scuffle behind the door, and an eye visible through a security chain.

"You again," he said.

"Yes, it's Jack."

"I told you not to bother me."

"We need to talk more."

"You're a pest." Scowling, he released the chain. "Well, don't just stand there."

I closed the door and followed him down the hall. My uncle looked more like a vulture than ever. Having shrunk in height, his bald head jutted from thin, hunched shoulders while his sticks balanced him like two broken wings. When he pointed me to a chair, I sat and opened the buns.

"I don't like sweet stuff. Eat them yourself," he said, filling an electric kettle. As he waited for the water to boil he spooned coffee into two cups. "I figured you might be back, and I don't have a lot of time."

"That's a shame. I was ready to give all day."

"Yeah, and I've got cancer."

"Sorry to hear it."

"Skip the pity. Prostate cancer killed my old man, and it's killing me. What's your question?"

"When Dad was stationed in Townsville, you had the sergeant's stripes taken off him. That was a mean way to treat a brother-in-law who did nobody any harm, just going home to see his wife."

Cleary splashed hot water into the cups, then with a grimace settled himself on a heavily cushioned chair.

"Your old man was my nemesis. I would've happily killed him a dozen times, but I didn't. And since you'll give me no peace, shut your mouth and listen. Nothing leaves this room, okay? Nothing."

"Of course."

I pushed the buns to one side and leant forward in my chair.

CHAPTER 23
KEVIN CLEARY

Cleary was born the only child of Irish migrants who landed in Brisbane shortly after the Great War. They congratulated themselves on escaping the Spanish Flu that swept Europe but had not counted on a wave of poliomyelitis to hit Brisbane when Kevin was barely four. The disease laid him in hospital for months, and eventually he was sent home with a pair of feeble legs. Over time his mother taught him to walk, first with a homemade frame, then with sticks, and finally unaided. At six years of age he began school where he embarked on a fresh round of misery. Unable to run or jump he was excluded from most sports, especially cricket and rugby which were the domain of the school's elite. Even more humiliating, classmates would toss the ball beyond his reach then laugh as he scrambled to make a catch. In time, they nicknamed him *emu* and banned him from their playing fields.

Despite these shortcomings, or perhaps because of them, he resolved that he would make something of his life. He trained in the gym where he built up chest and shoulder strength, and applied himself to his studies. Meanwhile, he found a counter-defence to the mockery he endured. Although he was a ready target for his classmates, they held a deeper contempt for wops and blacks. This suited him perfectly. He had someone in the pecking order beneath him, someone on whom he could dole out his own bitter medicine. He became the best taunter of Aborigines and Italians in the school. He used words that stung, he learned how to mock skin colour, and he tasted the exquisite delights of cruelty - the accidental snap of a ruler on the nipples or testicles, the cockroach in the lunch box, the glue on a victim's chair.

As the years passed and adolescence knocked on his door, he discovered the awful stirrings of manhood. His voice changed, scraggy hair appeared on his face, and erections sprang up at embarrassing moments. One such day in high school was to mark him for life. He and another boy in class had drawn the crude, naked image of an islander, which they had modelled on a pretty Samoan girl seated two rows in front. In their naiveté - and still to confront the enigmatic beauty of a living nude - they had drawn sex organs not unlike the cave paintings of antiquity. Kevin was strongly aroused by the sketch. Eagerly he shaded in the girl's breasts and thighs, failing to notice the class had fallen silent. Like a man emerging from a trance, he became aware of Miss Bernshaw at his elbow.

She leant over and picked up the sketch between two fingers. "Cleary, what is this?"

He tried to claw it back. "Nothing, miss."

"Stand up, boy."

He rose to his feet, hiding his mortification under a flimsy notepad. Unhurriedly, Miss Bernshaw studied the paper as he squirmed to the titters sweeping the class.

When the arousal had faded - in its own sweet time - she marched him past the rows of grinning students to the principal's office where he received six cuts on each hand and a warning that sick minds would never be tolerated at a Christian school.

The lesson wasn't lost on Kevin. Frequently he lay awake at night recalling the faces of the girls sneering at his discomfort. Although the bitches would never have seen an erection before, they would know such a thing existed, probably even discussed the phenomena during their lunchtime covens. However they weren't just laughing at his arousal, they were ridiculing the cripple with a donkey anatomy and two match-stick legs. His anger was not directed solely at the girls. He cringed as he pictured the guffawing of his male classmates, the bastards smug with good health and fine prospects, dipsticks who would never risk an indiscretion in public. They would content themselves with dreams about women, furtive emissions at night, waiting for the big moment when a pimple faced girl in Senior School might allow herself to be taken to the pictures. Kevin's imaginings always ended in misery. No Anglo-Irish girl, regardless of how plain or pimply, would ever be seen with him at a dance, the movies, or even one of the night booths common to Fortitude Valley. In time Kevin added women to his hate list of Aborigines and Italians.

The months spooled by in a routine of exams, school carnivals and boring holidays. One afternoon while strolling through Enoggera Park he stumbled upon an edition of *Man* magazine that was tattered from days of lying in the grass. To his gloomy mind the magazine's jokes lacked wit, the photos were uninspiring and the women's heavy-lidded stares were more laughable than seductive. As he flicked through the pages, he was about to despair of his luck when he came to the inside back cover. Pictured in full gloss was a beautiful Italian girl with soft brown eyes. Her thick hair curled to her shoulders and her even white teeth smiled at the reader. She was lightly dressed as she sat sideways on a carnival horse, summer clouds filling the background, her breasts barely covered and one hand holding down her skirt that showed a tantalising glimpse of white underwear. Her invitation to Kevin was so powerful that he grunted. An olive-skinned Italian woman - embracing all three classes that he despised - was beckoning to him. Carefully removing the page, he took it home and pinned it to his cupboard where he would often stare at it. One day he would find that woman and force her into submission. What he would demand was wonderful to dream about.

In Kevin's final year at school, his parents took him by tram into police headquarters to meet his cousin Jimmy - or 'James' as his mother insisted - who was the Acting Assistant Commissioner of Police. Although A.A.C. Jimmy Cleary had the surly good looks of his Irish descendants, he mixed readily with the state's English elite who welcomed anyone prepared to denounce Catholicism and working-class mores. Discovering at an early age that Jimmy had potential, his parents had scrimped to give him a private school education. Jimmy had not let them down. He studied hard, played in St Joseph's First XV rugby team and emerged ready for a university scholarship with the police service. More importantly, he had cultivated an old boy network that opened doors in the city. Now in his smart uniform glinting with decorations, he leant back in his swivel chair, hands behind his head, studying the lame youth on the other side of his desk.

"Kevin Cleary," he said, rounding out the vowels like a BBC announcer.

"Yes, sir," said Kevin, standing crookedly to attention.

"I've been watching you."

"Me... sir. Really?"

"Yes, you. Good at school, good attitude... but..."

Here we go, Kevin thought.

"Your parents say you want to be a police officer."

"Yes, sir."

"But you can't run. How could you stop a thief? Or any villain come to that?"

"He's very quick over a short distance," said Kevin's mother Jill who sat in an upright chair, gloved hands clasped in her lap.

"Fair go, Jimmy," muttered Kevin's father. "Some of them fat cops downstairs would have a heart attack if they ran a chain."

"Maybe so, but they weren't fat at seventeen."

"Please, James, give the boy a chance," Jill pleaded.

A.A.C. Jimmy Cleary stretched in his chair. "Alright, lad, we'll put you through the physical, and provided there's nothing else wrong I'll slot you into the academy. Mind, you'll have to march and box. Could you handle that?"

"Of course, sir. I'm already boxing in the gym."

"Okay, the next intake is on"... he glanced at a calendar... "third of December. Make sure you're ready."

"Oh, thank you, James," the mother said. "We'll always be grateful."

"Yeah, thanks Jimmy," said Kevin's father.

"That's alright," the cousin brushed aside their gratitude. "See the officer at the desk. He'll take your details."

Kevin became an exemplary police officer. His marks were always at the top of class lists, his work in the gym was second to none and his academic record impressed former teachers. Immediately after graduating with distinction he was assigned to Fortitude Valley with several of his classmates. There he discovered a police culture that hadn't been studied at the academy, a culture in which officers employed a blend of carrot and stick to maintain law and order. They used the carrot with any venture that made a profit, and they used the stick on the undesirables - the hoodlums, the blacks and the European migrants who were collectively known as wops. While Kevin had a natural bent for the stick, mostly in the watch house on Friday night, he willingly accepted rewards from the carrot. The procedure was simple. In early days on the beat he would follow a senior constable round the cafes and newsagents, collecting free coffees and newspapers. The bigger the shop, the greater the pay off. Likewise with the hierarchy of race. A Chinese businessman would pay more protection currency than an Italian, who in turn paid more than an Irishman. At a rotation of Irish barbers he might expect to receive his monthly haircut, but at a Chinese clothing shop he could demand a new suit including hat, tie, belt and shoes. Kevin approved of this system, and he subscribed to the belief that everyone was a winner. Power (the police) scratched the back of money (business) who scratched power's back in return. As the months passed from probation to permanent officer, he discovered that in the higher ranks the carrot took on a golden hue. Kickbacks to senior officers, and the old constables who did the footwork, were in the form of cash. Brothels left an envelope with the doorman, drug dealers handed over bank notes in alleyways, and gambling dens set aside a monthly commission. To maintain this co-existence Fortitude Valley police enforced the law zealously. If a drug dealer broke the rules and tried an under-counter sale, he was carted to the watch house where after a beating he was dumped back on the street. Prostitutes trying to work the alleys alone were sexually assaulted by plain clothes officers, and uncooperative betting shops burnt down in the night. The Valley was tough but Kevin adapted fast.

After a time at Fortitude Valley he realised, however, that his chances of promotion depended on two things. The first was to get transferred out of the convention-bound station where the network of old officers kept young colleagues poor, and the second was to find a bride as single officers, for no obvious reason, rarely moved up the ranks. Of the two options, marriage was the easier one; the challenge was in locating a suitable wife. He swallowed his pride, dressed in his Chinese-made suit, and headed for the police socials where nervous young women were drafted in to partner nervous young constables. As Kevin's sole motive was to find a bride, he diligently hunted for the girl who so lacked poise she might ignore his ghastly legs.

Following several false starts, he eventually found a candidate. First, she was Irish-Australian which placed her in the right social group. Second, her frizzy yellow hair, ill-fitting spectacles and birdlike features labelled her as defenceless. And third, even though she was barely into her twenties, she wore that fatalistic, left-on-the-shelf demeanour.

Kevin inhaled to steady his nerves and asked the girl for a dance. When she murmured a polite "That would be lovely", he steered her onto the floor where, as best he could, followed her surprisingly lithe body through a foxtrot. It was hard work. While his arms and legs were engaged in one direction, his mind was busy elsewhere.

Anxious to please, he said, "You have beautiful skin."

"Thank you."

"It must be the Irish in you. Irish always have beautiful skin."

She smiled. "Yes, my parents are Irish."

"And your hair. My favourite colour is gold."

"Gold? That's nice."

They manoeuvred across the floor. Two steps forward, two back, swing the lady.

"What colour are your eyes?" he asked. "They appear to be blue... deep, dark blue."

"Yes. Blue."

"I love deep blue eyes. They are the window to the soul."

"To my soul? Really?"

"Yes. I see the soul of a gentle, generous woman."

Even though bemused by his flattery, she avoided by so much as a glance any reference to his clumsy legs. When the number was over, she agreed to a second dance and, yes, she would like him to escort her to supper.

By the end of the night he knew her name was Ursula Bellamy. She had one brother, Jack, and two sisters, Nelly and May, the youngest of whom had died from consumption as a child. She admired his ambition to become a senior police officer, and she was impressed that he had graduated from the Police Academy with distinction. He was a young man going places.

Three months later she invited him for Sunday lunch where he met Mum and Dad, sister Nelly and brother Jack. Nelly was a married nurse whose eyes never left him, waiting for the mask to slip. The man was impossible to fathom. Sure, he had polio, not an issue in itself, but how genuine were his feelings for Ursula whose naiveté with boys was a standing family joke. And why choose a policeman? Seated at the table where one couldn't see his legs, he was well featured although going to early baldness with a hooked nose and cold eyes. But of greater intrigue was the man's discipline. Not so much as a conjunction out of place or a piece of cutlery incorrectly used. Kevin held Nelly's gaze and reckoned he was a match for this woman, but she needed to be watched, her prim mouth suggesting she would enjoy spoiling his hard-won prize. But Nelly aside, he trusted his instincts with Ursula. He had found the girl who would support his climb up the police ladder.

Ursula's brother Jack, a trainee teacher, came from a different mould. He was remarkably good-looking, confident, and had the easy grace of an athlete. When he spoke his face smiled, inviting everyone to be his friend; apart from sister Nelly who seemed impervious to his charm. To Kevin's mind a tension crackled just below the surface. While the strain may have come from a distant clash, it appeared more likely that Nelly was the priggish first-born while Jack's world unfolded blithely before him. Kevin found himself mirroring Nelly's sentiment. Brother Jack was too poised, too endowed with nature's gifts.

Bastard wouldn't know the meaning of struggle, he reflected.

Meanwhile, as the family of four checked him out, Kevin was never sure what views he was expected to hold. At one point Jack asked him about the plight of Aborigines, and he replied they shouldn't be on the street.

"Society wouldn't tolerate any other race that lay about drunk on footpaths," he said.

"Where should they be?" Jack asked pleasantly.

"I don't know. On a reserve where they'd be safe."

"Where they can't be seen or heard?"

"I don't mean to disparage them, but they'd be happier in the bush where they came from."

"Would you send them back to the reserves?"

"If I was the Prime Minister I would. The police are expected to clean up the streets, but nobody will give us the law to do it properly."

After extracting himself from Jack's snare on Aborigines, Kevin was asked about migrants. He was more guarded this time and said the country ought to be grateful for the hard work done by migrants, especially the Irish and Italians.

"Do you know any Italians?" Jack asked.

"No, do you?"

"Only at school. We called them Eyeties."

"Same here. That and wops."

Kevin felt the draft of another trap missing his fingers. This Jack was a crafty bastard, leading him onto dangerous ground. Well, he wouldn't be drawn on blacks or wops again.

The remainder of the lunch went agreeably, as did the next three occasions when the family concluded Kevin Cleary would be a suitable match for their daughter. Meanwhile, the social visits were rotated and Ursula arrived at Kevin's house where Mrs Cleary welcomed her with open arms. The girl was rather mousy, but thankfully Kevin had found himself a wife. In her dreams Mrs Cleary pictured herself as the happy grandmother minding the baby while Kevin and Ursula enjoyed a night at the movies.

Later that year the couple were married, and to Ursula's surprise Kevin applied for a transfer to Townsville. His move was perplexing because not once had he mentioned setting up home outside Brisbane, and in fact spoke glowingly of an officer's life in Fortitude Valley. He had also remarked how lucky they were to have supportive families in neighbouring suburbs. The transfer came through and within a year they had taken the thirty-hour train ride to Townsville where they bought a home in the middle class suburb of North Ward. Meanwhile, Kevin continued his studies and inside two years had earned the right to wear a detective's short-sleeved shirt and tie. It was also during this time he practised the skills he had learned at the Valley station, albeit on a lesser scale since the city of Townsville fitted several times into Brisbane.

Kevin's boat came in when Mussolini signed his Pact of Steel with Hitler in May 1939. The outcome was a racketeer's dream as any Italian threatening Australian state security could be interned for the duration of the war. Volunteering his services to the Federal Government, Kevin familiarised himself with the National Security Act, then devised a means of turning the Act into hard currency. The key to his scheme was extortion. If an Italian wanted to remain in the bosom of his family, he would have to pay a *freedom fee*, always in cash and never recorded on paper. At most, the grateful Italian might receive a handshake and a lift back to his house.

Kevin had plenty of fertile ground in which to work. A quick glance at a map showed he could choose north or south of Townsville. North of the city, from Ingham to Cairns, canefields stretched from the mountains to the sea. However, with war imminent in Europe the north had its dangers. What should happen, God forbid, if the country was invaded and northern farms confiscated? And he had every reason to be fearful. German warships sailed the oceans at will, the Italian army had flattened Albania, and the Japs were picking the eyes out of China. So with good reason he turned his sights on Townsville's south. His delighted gaze fell on Calen and its Italian community. Everything about the district was right, which he already suspected from the period he had spent at the two-man station during a training stint.

In June 1939 he sought a temporary transfer to Calen where, among his regular police duties back in uniform, he administered the National Security Act. Without consulting Ursula he travelled alone, leaving her in Townsville to pass the hours with her friends in the exclusive, though unremarkable, police wives' club. Besides, having tired of the role of caring husband, he welcomed the excuse to vacate the marital bed.

There was, however, one cloud raining on his picnic. His brother-in-law Jack Bellamy taught at a school near Calen, and much as the two avoided each other, they were forced to meet officially in their roles with policing and education. Moreover, Jack captained the local rugby league team which for the first time in years brought home the district trophy. On the night of the triumph Kevin was forced to acknowledge Jack's superior gifts. As expected, Jack held centre stage in the Calen Hotel when Kevin arrived to offer his congratulations. After shaking Jack's hand, Kevin ignored the keg and strolled through the bar checking for blacks who may have sneaked into the restricted area. He then evicted three half-castes from the winning team, mostly to annoy Jack, before returning to the bar where he removed his hat and joined in the celebrations. The only positive in this whole distasteful affair was that nobody knew the hero and cripple were related. If that detail ever emerged, the locals would probably seize the cripple and drown him like a two-headed cat. Later, back at the station, Kevin angrily punched his desk. Of all the luck to have Jack Bellamy sharing the town. It was like his marriage to Ursula had reignited the curse of his youth. From the door of his office he glared towards the pub where a triumphant roar filled the night sky. Even as he watched, his brother-in-law rescued the half-castes, apologising for Kevin's racial attitude which, he implied, had something to do with the man's unfortunate disability.

Throughout the winter of 1939 Kevin Cleary's efforts with the National Security Act bore little fruit in the face of solid Italian denials. Farmer after farmer pledged allegiance to the Southern Cross while loathing the fascist Mussolini and his *scandaloso* behaviour. Indeed, no man loved Australia more passionately than a Calen Italian. Meanwhile, Kevin and Jack stepped round each other like mistrustful card sharps, observing a truce that might've lasted for months had Jack Bellamy not dealt himself the Queen of Hearts.

Prior to the infamous flare-up at Cohen's Hall, Kevin was oblivious of three things: first, that dancing was a regular Saturday night event in Calen; second, that Maria Rossini even existed; and third, that Jack was a participant in the local romance stakes.

On the Monday following the first clash between Jack and Guido, Kevin's junior constable, coffee in hand and with time to kill, described the action. "I tell you, boss, it was worth the entrance ticket. It all started with this bloke Jack Bellamy who you met at the pub. Remember him? The footy captain. Well, he pinched a couple of dances with the Rossini girl. Can you believe it... right under the Eyetie boyfriend's nose. And did the Eyetie drop his lip. On the third dance he stormed onto the floor, grabbed her arm and ordered her back to her seat. Maybe earlier he had some influence over the girl -

you know, strong man, weak woman - but his Eyetie heritage was no match for Bellamy and his charms. She slipped out of the boyfriend's grip and clung to Bellamy, which I reckon had to be gutsy. Anyway, Bellamy took her in his arms - real flashy like - and did a few more turns. After that she danced with other Eyeties until midnight when her dragon brother marched up and dragged her out the door. Gee, it was like a movie, the Italians spluttering into their vino and the white folk cheering Bellamy like he was back on the footy field."

When he drew no response from Kevin, he said, "You ever laid eyes on this Rossini girl, boss?"

"Can't say I have, or want to."

"Then you should. She's some looker."

"Italian girls don't appeal, mate, but maybe I haven't lived here long enough."

"You don't have to live in Rome to fancy this one," the constable said, strolling to the back of the office where he rinsed his cup and fetched a clipboard of duties.

I'll have to watch that man, Kevin reflected. While nothing Jack did would surprise him, he had always thought white constables would prefer their women with a British heritage.

The fracas over the Rossini girl came to a head at the cut-out dance at the end of the season. When Jack Bellamy flirted publicly with the girl a second time, boyfriend Carl's response was so explosive that cane cutters bundled them outside and formed a ring. The contest was a no show. After a few feints and blocks Jack ended the scrap with a single punch. Dance organisers belatedly called the police, but by the time Kevin arrived the fighters had been secreted into the night. He didn't get to question Jack or the boyfriend, but he did see the girl, and that's really where it all started.

Maria Rossini was a sensation, her prettiness all the more startling in a backwoods town like Calen. But to Kevin's astonishment she was the girl whose picture he had torn from *Man* magazine in his days of raging puberty. However, unlike the photo model this girl dressed simply as if aware that her beauty was complete in itself, that any attempt to improve would be an affront to nature. She was the quintessence of all that tormented him. He imagined her sitting side-saddle on the carnival horse, wind blowing her skirt, the glimpse of naked thigh, the simple blouse exposing a lushness of breast. His restless nights came back to haunt him, the love-hate craving for a beautiful Italian woman. Worse still, his frustration spilled into daylight when he snapped at his constable who suggested that as she must have committed some offence in her life, she'd be worth a session in the watch house.

Despite the years since adolescence Kevin had not destroyed the *Man* photo, and on a weekend visit to Townsville he left the image on the sideboard for Ursula to find, which inside the hour she did. Alarmed because she had thought his sex drive was a distant, though not-unpleasant memory, she demanded an explanation.

He replied archly, "She makes a good comparison."

Ursula stared at him. "Who with? Me?"

"Who else?"

"You don't like Italians."

"This one is different."

"Different? How different? The size of her bust?"

"Among other things."

Ursula frowned. "Do you know her?"

"You could say that."

"It's only a photo. She's not even named."

"Quite right."

"Then how can you *know* her?"

"There are more ways than one to skin a cat."

"You're being silly."

"Am I?"

She tried to read his face. "Is there someone else? Another woman?"

"Yes and no," he said indifferently.

Hurt by this cryptic betrayal, Ursula took to concealing her body. And while she understood her own shape was too thin to be pretty, she had always believed his favourite erotic image was of a pale Irish girl with small breasts and a mound of yellow hair that hid a treasury of sexual delights. She consoled herself by arguing that much as he desired the Italian model, the photo could never give what she could; a real night in a real bed with a real woman.

Unknown to Ursula, Kevin had found the dream woman in Calen and, one way or another, he would get his real night in a real bed with a real woman. And it wouldn't be what Ursula imagined.

Since Kevin desperately needed to meet this woman, he seized on the cut-out brawl to invite the three parties into his Calen office. The occasion was also a God-given chance to humiliate Jack while exposing the Italians to the National Security Act.

He sat at his desk as Jack, Maria and Guido stood before him. He was tempted to lean back in his chair, hands clasped behind his head as A.A.C. Jimmy Cleary had done years earlier. It was a priceless statement of control, and he had rehearsed it to perfection, but not this time, not yet. Jack was livid. He had been drawn into the office on the pretext of Aboriginal truancy when Kevin closed the door and ordered him to stand with the other two. To Jack the brawl was none of Kevin's business, and since nobody was really hurt or filed a complaint, what was the upstart doing? By contrast, Guido was nervous. Kevin eyed him scornfully. The sweaty little wop was a double for the actor who seemed to feature in every Mafia film. With his smooth good looks, he was nature's gift to gullible women, but in truth everything about him was small, from his stature to his courage, and heaven only knew the size of his toy. Jack and Guido aside, it was Maria who fascinated him. While the two men were in his office to make the summons respectable, she was the one he wanted. She stood calmly before him in her country dress, hair piled loosely on her head, hands clenched at her side. She was pretty alright, damn pretty. For a full minute under her gaze he studied every line, every curve in her body until he had stripped her naked. Finally, he dared her to lower her eyes, but she refused. So the bitch was gutsy. He should've guessed as much.

"I've summoned you here to warn you that the law is the law, whether out in the sticks or on the streets of Townsville. Fighting in public is an offence."

He ignored Jack's glare.

"I could throw the book at you, but I'm letting you off with a caution. A repeat of Saturday's nonsense, and you'll spend a night in the watch house. Understood?"

"Is that it?" Jack demanded.

Kevin finished his coffee. "My advice seems to be falling on deaf ears."

"Okay, you've made your point. If there's nothing more, we have work to do."

"We?"

"Yes. We."

"Right. You may leave," Kevin said, and as the three moved to the door, he raised his hand to Guido and Maria. "Not you two. I have more questions."

Jack frowned. "What have they done?"

"It's none of your concern, Bellamy. Piss off."

Wavering briefly, Jack stormed from the office. Kevin turned back to the Italians and studied the names before him. "Maria Rossini and Guido Avolio. This is a serious matter. You heard of Mussolini?"

"Of course."

"Well, our government. Sorry, *my* government is worried about this Mussolini chap and how he's firing up patriotism. Once an Italian, always an Italian. Know what I mean?"

"We're not Italian," Guido protested. "We're born in Australia. We're Australians, like yourself."

Kevin jumped to his feet. "What a load of shit! You're Eyeties, wops, wogs - whatever you call yourselves. You're not Australians, never. When Mussolini whistles, you'll catch the first boat home. You'll desert Calen for a life with the enemy."

"That's not true," Maria said.

"Don't tell me what's true, girlie. We're at war. Scores of traitors everywhere. I ought to throw you in jail on suspicion. And it's probably the wise thing to do."

They were now shaken. This is how he wanted it. Break the girl's spirit. Droplets of sweat appeared on her cheek and temple. She wiped her hands on her dress. Kevin felt the power surge. This was his most exquisite moment in years; it was like the naked islander sketch, the spontaneous lift in his trousers.

"I'm actually a good guy," he said weakly. "Kind-hearted and fair. So tell me, bimbo, where do you live?"

"At Cathu. On Dad's farm."

"How old are you?"

"Nineteen."

"Finished with studies, I expect?"

"Yes, sir. I work at Mrs Wilson's store in Calen."

He could think of nothing else. "I know Mrs Wilson. I'll call in there one day. But take my advice. No more trouble at dances. Be off, girl."

Maria hurried out the door leaving the men alone.

Kevin paused to collect his thoughts. "Okay, lover boy, tell me who's who in the zoo?"

"Sorry?"

"See that room in there, it's soundproof," Kevin said, indicating a second office that contained two chairs and a table. "You can stay out here and tell me the names of wops who've visited Italy recently, or we can go in there and finish what Jack Bellamy started the other night. Well?"

"That's all you want? Who... who's been to Italy?"

"Correct." He then mimicked a news editor. "Selfless-young-patriot-helps-Australian-lawman."

Guido swallowed. "Noth... nothing else?"

"You'll leave with the Pope's blessing, or mine, which in your case may have more value."

"My brother Paulo," Guido blurted. "He... he's been to Italy."

"And where might I find this brother?"

"The farm at Pindi Pindi."

Kevin smiled and pointed Guido to the door, then he leant back in his chair. *Three fat birds with one stone, how good was that.*

Two days later Kevin paid a visit to the Avolio farm. In style and appearance it was similar to other Italian properties in the area. The three-bedroom house sat on low stumps to catch the prevailing breeze, small Italianate columns supported the railings, and pots of flowers clung to the rafters. Down one side ran the vegetable garden rich with zucchini, tomatoes and eschalot, while on the other side stood a large tree under which the farmer and his family enjoyed afternoon siestas. In the kitchen drying herbs hung from hooks on the wall, the warm scent of olives and cured ham filled the air, and a pasta sauce bubbled on the stove.

Kevin was all charm with the old folk who welcomed him uncertainly. They poured freshly brewed coffee, and cut slices of *prosciutto* to eat with homemade cheese and *grissini*.

Afterwards they sat across from him while the two sons, Paulo and Guido, leant against the bench at their rear. The old couple had never learned fluent English and still used their dialect in the house, but much as they dreamed of Italy, they had long rejected any thought of returning home. They were proudly Australian and, besides, this was the land of their children.

"I'm here as a friend," Kevin said, and glanced at his notes, "I know you were born in a village near Assisi, but that means bugger-all, sorry, very little to me. Your home is where your heart is, and I can see your hearts are in beautiful north Queensland."

The four Italians watched him.

"What I am saying, folks, is that we are going through tough times. Mussolini is seeking out his beloved sons and daughters. You may not list yourselves in that celebrated group, but it's my job to cull the sheep from the goats. Sheep being good old Aussies, and goats being naughty Italians."

He drained his coffee and pushed it across to the mother for a refill. Taking his cup, she rinsed it in the sink and filled it with steaming black liquid. As an extra consideration she added a splash of *grappa*.

"So what are you," Kevin asked, "sheep or goats?"

"We're all sheep, Mr Cleary," Paulo said from behind his parents. "Nobody loves Australia more than we do."

Kevin glanced at his notebook. "Ah, Paulo Avolio. You love Australia. Wonderful country. Nobody in his right mind would leave the place. Am I right?"

"You are, Mr Cleary."

"Then how come, three years ago, you sailed back to Italy? Away for five months if my information is correct."

Paulo's high forehead creased in puzzlement. "My grandmother was seriously ill. I had never met her. Her dying wish was to see one of her grandchildren from Australia. As I am the oldest, my family decided I should go."

"That was very noble of them. Tell me, Paulo, have you heard of the Black Shirts?"

"Of course. They're in the papers every week."

"Well, my information tells me that you had meetings with a Black Shirt commander in Assisi."

"What garbage."

The old couple stared at him.

"It's total nonsense. I have not spoken to a Black Shirt, and never would. This is my home, damn it."

"Sssh, *bambino*," his mother said, then in halting English. "I believe you. Black Shirts are snakes, pah! All *fascisti* are snakes."

Kevin toyed with his cup. He had heard of Black Shirt cells being formed in regional centres, but he doubted the local Italians had that kind of savvy. To his mind they were two-vinos-a-day, spaghetti eaters. "Our informants rarely get the pig by the wrong leg," he said. "Everything, as they say, comes out in the slop. Even sneaky little trips to Italy."

"You 'ave it-a wrong, sir," Mr Avolio declared. "Paulo is a good-a boy."

"We'll see," Kevin said, rising to his feet. "And in the meantime, Paulo, be a good chap and call at my office in Calen. Tomorrow at nine. Don't keep me." He collected his hat from the hallstand.

"Thanks for the coffee. You've got a classy home, folks."

A shaken Paulo Avolio arrived promptly at nine and inside thirty minutes was feeding Kevin the names of Italians who kept in touch with their homeland. A few of the names were dubious, like old Mr Rossini who couldn't read or write, but Paulo would rather overfill the basket than be accused of letting one traitor escape. The threat of imprisonment was real, and although Kevin had tossed the name Black Shirts speculatively onto the table, it had brought Paulo running. In a further sign of his eagerness, Paulo added a subcategory to the basket - those who had money and those who didn't.

Within days Kevin was knocking on Italian doors. As the local cop doing his duty, he handed over to federal authorities all those who, in his view, posed a threat to the country. Mostly they were the poor and the marginal, the ones who were living in their adopted land like an ungainly foot in an ill-fitting shoe. At first he suspected Paulo was withholding prize clients, but as the extortion money flowed in he dropped his suspicions. Once he was convinced of Paulo's loyalty, he outlined a business deal in which the *freedom fee*, as he dubbed it, would be shared on an eighty-twenty basis. Although Paulo was given the minor slice of the pie, he agreed readily to the terms. After the men shook hands, Kevin produced an agreement they both signed. The single-copy document recorded the terms of the *freedom fee* and was to remain in Kevin's possession. In the wrong hands the paper would be dynamite, but Kevin knew he held the security; Paulo's complicity.

During this time Kevin and Jack Bellamy took to walking opposite sides of the street. Although Kevin knew Bellamy frowned on his role as administrator of the National Security Act, the subject was never mentioned. Their common interests in Calen were viewed through a lens that contained only one person, Maria Rossini. Meanwhile, an observer would have noticed Kevin's shopping habits had changed. Once he had rarely shopped in town, now he bought his groceries at Wilson's store. Timing his arrival at the counter to be sure Maria served him, he projected cold authority like a Nazi officer confronting a pretty Jewess. But he was unfamiliar with the minds of strong women, and the more he glowered, the more she defied him. Grudgingly she would fetch his orders and accept payment, which she never took from his hand but had him place on the counter in a pile of notes and coin. Adding to his irritation, she welcomed Neanderthal boys from the local farms with a cheerful smile. These galling experiences reached a climax one afternoon when he called to fetch the daily papers. Maria and Jack stood together at the rear of the shop. She was gazing up at Jack, and he was certain Jack had been stroking her face. Maria pulled away, but Jack took her by the shoulders and kissed her on the mouth.

After releasing the girl, Jack turned to his brother-in-law. "I don't expect you've heard the news, mate?"

"What news?"

"Maria and I are tying the knot. You'll be invited of course."

It was all Kevin could do to hold his composure. He had heard that since the fight at Cohen's Hall, Jack and Maria had been dating openly. Although the old women in town might consider them a handsome match, the relationship was seriously out of order. Jack was an Australian whose country was at war with Italy. Even worse, beautiful Italian women were created for pleasure, not breeding. He should've nailed her when he had the chance. He had tried extorting her family, but they were as clean as the bishop himself, or maybe more careful. Kevin bit his lip. Surrendering control over Maria was bad enough, but losing her to Jack's bed was intolerable.

At the wedding in January Kevin wore his police uniform, rather than a civilian suit which would have sat more favourably with Maria's family. When Ursula asked him why, he brushed it off as protocol.

"Aren't they a gorgeous couple," she sighed as Jack and Maria stood before the priest at the altar.

Kevin gazed stonily ahead.

"He is my brother," she said. "You could show some enthusiasm."

"Shut up, woman."

It was at that instant Jack lifted the veil from Maria's face. In a moment of dreadful clarity Ursula saw the model in Kevin's photograph.

"Oh no," she wailed.

Nearby guests turned anxiously to Ursula but when they saw tears rolling down her cheeks, they smiled and said, "The bride is indeed beautiful."

That evening Kevin and Ursula joined others in the nuptial celebrations at the Rossini farmhouse on the O'Connell River. Despite the shadow of war hanging over the district, the Italians gave their daughter a traditional send-off. Several months later Jack said farewell to his new bride and boarded a troop ship to the Middle East where he fought with distinction against the German and Italian armies. Maria, meanwhile, returned to her parent's home leaving the Rise and Shine house vacant.

The wedding signalled a change in Kevin's life. With Maria's beauty now compromised and the network of payments operating smoothly, he applied for a return to Townsville. Before the transfer came through, however, Paulo sought him out and warned him of complaints reaching unwelcome ears.
"Whose friggin ears are you talking about?" Kevin demanded.
"The priest."
"That silly old drunk. What does he care?"
"He might not care, but he knows about us, and that's a risk."
"Then I'll go see him."
Kevin jumped into his car and drove the short distance across St Helens Creek to Kolijo where Father Michael Burke lived next door to the church. The Irish priest was in his garden, watering a bed of lettuce. At the end of each row, he reached into the watering can and drew out a bottle of beer. He drank appreciatively, returned the bottle to the can, then continued along the next row.
Kevin pulled his car into the driveway.
"Hey you, Father. I want a minute."
"Are you meaning confession, son?"
"Confession? Not from you, soak-head. But if that's the only quiet place, it'll do."

Nursing the watering can in both arms, Father Burke led the way into the church and sat in one of the back pews.

"It's too hot in there," he said, indicating the confessional box. "What's your problem, son?"

"Don't son me, pal. I know your game."

Father Burke was instantly sober. "What game?"

"You mean, apart from the illegal still? No, you can keep the grog, this is more serious. In Townsville there's a rumour circulating about an Irish priest who likes breaking the law. It so happens the priest lives out of sight, but he's not out of mind."

"So? Who is this priest? What law?"

"The rumour goes that the priest had a colourful past in Ireland. Now he's bringing Irish criminals into Australia, passing them off as labourers for the vineyard. He puts them up in his parish for a few months then filters them into Sydney or Melbourne. Now I wonder who this priest could be?"

"You're talking nonsense. Trainee priests can't just enter the country. They need the bishop's approval. Are you telling me the bishop is crooked?"

"I don't know how it's done," Kevin said, "but I can make it my business. So let's just say, we keep ourselves to ourselves. My lips are sealed, and so are yours, okay?"

Father Burke reached into the watering can and drew out the half empty bottle. His voice was calm as he handed it over. "A toast to sealed lips. You first."

Kevin stared in horror at the beer. "Not like that, soak-head. Get a man a clean glass, and a fresh bottle."

Father Burke tipped the bottle to his mouth then wiped the neck on his sleeve. "Drink up, copper boy," he said menacingly. "You're not the feckin clean cop you pretend to be. I know all about your extortion racket. You breathe one word about my good deeds in this parish, and I'll wrap your feckin legs around your neck. Now drink."

The men glared at each other. Ignoring the offered bottle, Kevin reached out with an open hand. "Okay Father, let's shake on it." When the priest took his hand, Kevin wrenched him forward and punched him hard in the stomach. Father Burke collapsed gagging on the pew. "You've got your deal, Latin-lover, but don't threaten me again." Kevin smashed the bottle on the floor and stormed from the church.

By the time Kevin returned to Townsville, war had blistered the façade of Europe and Japanese tentacles were reaching Australia's northern outposts. Keen to do his bit, he applied for the military police who desperately needed experienced officers to control the thousands of troops camped in the city. When the army accepted him despite his limp, he wore his new uniform with pride. At first, he was given the rank of corporal to reflect his experience, but within weeks was promoted to sergeant. If anyone at this time had bothered to ask, he would've said life was sweet. Paulo managed their joint interests in Calen, the whiskey priest had sunk back into his vat, and Maria's image had been returned to the drawer in the second bedroom where he now slept.

His military work also gave him space to indulge a second pursuit; harassing the Aborigines who gathered under the giant figs along the Strand. By day the blacks met in idle groups where they drank cheap alcohol and stared sullenly, but harmlessly, at passing whites. By night, however, against the background swish of the ocean their soft voices retold dreamtime stories of peace and contentment. But this was not how Kevin saw it. Because their presence created a 'bad impression' for visiting troops, he felt obliged to herd them across Ross River to the mangrove swamps where they 'belonged'.

All went fine until he and Jack Bellamy crossed paths.

Kevin had known his brother-in-law's battalion was stationed in Queensland after withdrawal from the European theatre. He knew Jack had won a medal in north Africa and - ironically for a man with an Italian wife - had been tortured by the Italians. He was also aware that the Australian soldiers, Jack included, had been mustered in Townsville from where a national defence would be launched. Jack was now wearing three stripes on his sleeve, and it was said he would have pips on his shoulders before the year's end. Kevin had no doubt Jack would go places. He fitted the classic officer's portrait - well educated, personal charm and a born leader. Blokes seemed to want to follow him through hell. However, he had an Achilles heel. He flaunted discipline, and although his name had come to police attention on several occasions, charges had never been laid. Kevin was about to change all that.

The confrontation had its origin on a quiet June afternoon when Jack stood at the mouth of Ross Creek trying to catch bait with a cast-net. A young

Aborigine, whose name he later discovered was Godwin, approached him through the mangroves.

"Hey, boss, I been watchin'. You tryin' to brain them fish?"

Jack grinned ruefully. "The damn net has a mind of its own."

"Boss, you throw like a piccaninny. I show you."

Godwin cast the net in a perfect circle. Moments later prawn and herring were skipping inside the mesh. Unhurriedly, Godwin dragged the net onto the bank where the two men scooped up the little fish.

"Now, boss, I teach you to catch barramundi."

"Hey, that'd be terrific," Jack said and dug into his army kit for a hand reel.

Godwin showed him how to thread a sinker, tracer wire and hook on the line. Next he attached a herring then threw the line on the ocean side of a fallen log. "Now hold this line, boss, while I set one near the bank. Barramundi thinks he is a smart fella."

Soon two lines were in the water and the men sat comfortably side by side.

Jack thrust out his hand. "My name's Jack Bellamy. What's yours."

"Godwin, boss. Just Godwin."

Jack reached into his bag and drew out a packet of dry biscuits and a tin of beef.

"I'm hungry, Godwin. You must be too."

"No, boss, I'm not hungry. You eat."

"We eat together or not at all," Jack said and broke the biscuits in half. As they munched on the food, a breeze picked up the empty packet and blew it across the mud. Turning to retrieve the packet,

Jack noticed dried blood on the back of Godwin's shirt.

"What happened there, Godwin? The mozzies get to you?"

"Yeah, boss," Godwin laughed. "Bad mozzies."

After fishing for a minute, Jack said quietly, "They're not mosquito bites, Godwin. What happened?"

"Nothin', boss."

"Lift up your shirt. There's ointment in my bag."

"No, boss. It's nothin'."

"Godwin, you could get a serious skin infection. Show me. That's an order."

Painfully Godwin raised his shirt above his waist. When Jack saw the material had congealed to the torn skin, he whistled and said, "You're coming with me, lad. Reel in these lines."

"No, boss, please. I fall on stones. It heal soon. I be alright."

"I don't know who you're frightened of, Godwin, but you're safe with me. Some bastard gave you a flogging, and one day we'll find him. In the meantime, you need medical treatment. I know exactly where to get that and nobody the wiser."

After Jack helped Godwin readjust his shirt, the two men walked through parkland to the base of Castle Hill where the Americans had set up a military camp. Leaving Godwin to one side, Jack approached the Negro sentry.

"How can I help, chief?" the Negro said.

"I found a man who needs medical attention. You chaps can help."

The sentry studied Jack's Australian uniform. "What's wrong with your medics or the local hospital?"

"The man is black," Jack said.

"Oh, right. I get you, chief. Wait here." He reached across to a field telephone and spun the handle. "Hello, sir. It's Raymond on the front gate. I need a medic, sort of urgent. Yes, sir. He's one of us."

He hung up the phone and turned to Jack. "Well, he is kind of one of us."

"Thanks, mate."

Moments later a Jeep roared across the open space and pulled to a dusty halt at the gate. "Where's the casualty, corporal?" demanded a lieutenant wearing a red cross on his helmet.

"Right there, Doc," the sentry said, pointing at Godwin who was seated on the ground.

"He… he's a civilian, corporal."

"Yes, sir, but he's a sick dude for all that."

Once the two men had removed Godwin's shirt, the medic cleaned his injuries.

"Who did this?" he said to Jack.

"No idea, Doc, but I'll find out."

"Somebody who'd be right at home in Alabama?"

"Yes, somebody like that."

After dressing Godwin in a fresh shirt from the sentry's kit, they took him on his first car ride to a camp on the far side of Ross River. Jack remained with him for some minutes.

"Tell me who it was, Godwin. We're in a fight bigger than Townsville. If there's a mongrel in the pack, we have to weed him out."

"It was the cop with bad legs," Godwin whispered.

"Indeed, I should've guessed. Make sure you cross into town at night only when you need to. We'll go fishing again soon, but this side of the river. Do you understand me, Godwin?"

"Yes, Boss Jack."

Jack strode back into the city. Outwardly he was calm, but inside he seethed as he hunted for Kevin Cleary through the cafes and bars lining Flinders Street. It wasn't only the cruelty to Godwin that burned in his gut. He recalled his humiliation in Cleary's office at Calen and his disgust at seeing the man's eyes strip a defenceless Maria. As he marched from one pub to the next, Jack wrestled with the dilemma of confronting Cleary with Godwin's injuries. Although he'd love to thrash his brother-in-law, he knew others would view the punishment as an act of cowardice. Effectively, Cleary had turned his disability into a weapon. Half an hour after leaving the river, he found Cleary drinking alone in the Exchange Hotel.

Jack paid for a beer then drew up a stool beside the MP who was in civilian dress.

"Mind if I join you?"

Kevin glanced up in surprise. In the years he'd known Jack, they had never shared a beer. "Sit where you like, mate. You lonely or something?"

"No, I want to make a deal."

"With me?" Kevin laughed. "You got counterfeit dollars?"

"Nothing like that. You ready to hear?"

"Sure. I'm all ears."

Jack leant forward in his seat. "Yesterday I found an Aborigine beaten half to death. The Yanks fixed him up, so he'll be okay. But more to the point, we found out who nearly killed him. Guess who it was? No idea? Then try this. A military cop with bad legs. That's right. You mightn't believe it but a Yank officer put us on to him. And there were reports from other sources. So how many Townsville MPs are there with polio? Just one. Sergeant Kevin Cleary."

Kevin stared levelly back at his accuser. Law and order in the city had nothing to do with Jack or the Yanks.

"Living with polio as a kid would've been bloody awful," Jack continued, "but it doesn't give you the right to be cruel to others."

"Is that so, Saint Jack?"

"I haven't finished yet, Cleary. If you touch one more black in this city, I'll let your bosses into your secret."

"What friggin secret?"

"Your extortion racket with the Italians."

Kevin laughed. "You're bonkers, Bellamy. Marrying the Italian whore has addled your brain."

Jack forced himself to remain calm. His information was mostly hearsay, but he had to call Kevin's bluff. "Some Italians down Calen way have kept records of every quid that went into the pockets of you and Paulo. And they have corroborative evidence. You'd know what that means. Your word against twenty others. Who do you think the courts will believe?"

"Twenty wops against one police officer. They wouldn't have a show."

"They're not all Italian. One day this war'll be over, and the hole you scurry down will need to be mighty deep."

Kevin had stopped breathing. A bloodless patch formed either side of his eyes. He then spat on the table next to Jack's hand. "It's you who'll get the friggin surprise, Bellamy. Right when you least expect it. Okay, I'll tell the bastard who's flogging the blacks to lay off, and you keep your trap shut about this Eyetie business. I'll never admit I've done anything, but mud can stick."

Jack stood up from the table without touching his beer. "I'll keep my end of the bargain, Cleary. You'd better keep yours." And walked through the door into Townsville's tropical glare.

That same day saw the end of Aboriginal beatings in the city. Although Kevin Cleary had become in recent months like a vampire addicted to native blood, he stayed home at night with good reason. One unhappy Eyetie back in Calen was a nuisance, a whole mob would be dangerous; and if Jack and the priest knew of the racket who else? Fuming at the rebuke, Kevin diverted his efforts into building a dossier on Jack's misdemeanours. And they were many. To Jack it was a caper sneaking out of camp after dark, drinking where he shouldn't, snubbing the army's petty orders. His commanding officer winced at each new report, but hid the papers in his bottom drawer. Although Jack was a pain, his troops loved him. He wasn't only their hero in these dark times, he was a brave, intelligent leader who would soon make officer. Kevin Cleary, however, was the ruthless hunter stalking the boar that had dug up the family plot. One silent footfall after another, one knot tighter on every trap. And bang, one day the boar would be gone.

The hunter's patience was rewarded on Friday, August 21, with the first report of battles at Milne Bay on New Guinea's southern coast, just a short hop from Australia's mainland. All weekend leave was cancelled and troops were ordered to start boarding ships from noon Monday. Jack heard the command but as he held a precious two-day pass, right or wrong he was on the train to Calen. At the same moment he slipped into the station precinct, Kevin Cleary received a despatch from headquarters ordering him to arrest any soldier trying to leave camp. A grin spread over Kevin's face. He was certain his nemesis would steal one last weekend with his Italian bride.

Taking twelve MPs with him in a truck, Kevin drove up to the railway station where he parked discreetly behind the goods shed. He then ordered his men to crawl to the rear of the platform and into the Station Master's office.

His instructions were clear. "I don't care what other bloke you grab, but Sergeant Jack Bellamy mustn't escape."

"What's he look like, sarge?"

"Athletic type. Fair skin, dark hair and fancies himself."

"Bit of a prick is he?"

"Worse than that. He sleeps with the enemy."

"How're we supposed to catch him? It'll be like ropin' a rogue bull."

"Don't worry. Our station master is a patriot. Now shut up and keep your heads down."

The minute hand on the station clock jumped to 9:37 as a goods train rumbled by the platform. Tightly wrapped wagons filed past followed by two wooden carriages and a goods van. When the train slowed, soldiers erupted from bolt holes and dashed for the carriages whose doors had mysteriously opened. In the blink of an eye they were inside and the doors clicked shut.

Almost precisely with the closing of the last door the train ground to a halt. Kevin and six of his men rose to their feet and marched from the Station Master's office. Six more MPs approached from the opposite side.

"Well, who have been naughty boys then?" Kevin demanded of the silent carriages.

He swung a baton in his hand. "So we're a spineless lot. Come out quietly, lads, and we'll stroll back to barracks and sort this out. No takers? Well, here's a pleasant thought, resist arrest and God knows how many skulls get cracked."

The doors opened and men filed sheepishly onto the platform. They stood in a row before him.

"I believe somebody is missing," he called to the gaping doors. "Now who could that be? Let's try the name Jack Bellamy. Got a nice ring to it, rhymes with felony. Sergeant Bellamy, you have the count of five to show your face."

Kevin counted to five then stepped up to a soldier and slammed his baton hard across the man's nose. Blood spurted onto the concrete as the man howled in agony.

"Bellamy, you're supposed to be a leader, not a frightened old woman. I'll try again. If you're not out by five, I'll smash this bastard's teeth."

A carriage door swung open and Jack emerged covered in dust.

"You've had your sport, Cleary. Take us in."

Kevin walked across to him. "I haven't finished my sport yet, Bellamy." And smacked Jack in the groin with the end of his baton.

Hissing in pain, Jack clung to the carriage door for support. Kevin thrust his face forward. Spittle clung to his lips. "Show that bruise to your Eyetie bitch... if you live that long."

The men were bundled into the MPs truck, and that same day faced a court martial. All men lost pay and privileges and a few, like Jack, lost rank.

CHAPTER 24

I had sat for over two hours on an uncomfortable chair as Kevin Cleary told his story. The man was exhausted and a terrible wheeze in the last minutes had drained him of all colour. When I moved to switch on the light, he held up his hand. "I don't want you staring at me."

"Is that the end?" I asked.

"What more do you want?"

"Well, you haven't told me what you know about Guido's death. Or about Mum and Dad in Moreton Bay. That was no murder-suicide."

"I killed nobody. You might think I'm a dog fit for poisoning, but I killed nobody. Not a soul."

"Then who did?"

He turned to the window. His nose was a thin lump of sinew that would've been aquiline years earlier. Now it curved over a sickly face covered in stubble.

"Tomorrow I start chemo again," he rasped. "It's as rotten a death as any other. I can't talk anymore. Come back in seven days, no sooner."

He didn't give the impression he would last a week. "Tell me, Uncle Kevin. Who pulled the trigger on Guido? Who did it to Mum and Dad?"

Slowly he faced me. "I told you to piss off. Now go." With that he leant back in his chair and closed his eyes. The faintest of pulses beat in his throat. Disappointed, I walked down the hallway and let myself out the door.

CHAPTER 25

The next morning I returned to Jolimont Creek, potholes on the highway jarring my wheels as though cast there by Cleary's evil spirit. He was one vile character. Everything he did had left contamination, like he was single-handedly trashing the universe. And I didn't know how believable his story was. Three of the main characters - Jack, Maria and Guido - were dead, and I doubted Italians would testify against a bully who was still alive. The only person that seemed willing to discuss this period was Loretta. She might be able to fill in some gaps, and besides, I needed her to explain the mystery of the two St Francis of Assisi medals.

By the following Thursday I had thrust Kevin Cleary from my head. Hard work in the field is an excellent tonic for glum faces, and in any case we owed it to each other to stay focused on cutting and hauling cane. When the afternoon arrived, and we were excused from burning for the next day, I jumped on the Norton and rode across to Loretta's house. She was out front with a garden fork digging under the hibiscus. As the bike pulled up she straightened slowly.
"Hello cowboy. What can I do for you?"
"Cowboy? What's with this *cowboy*?"
"Maria told me about the Roy Rogers gear. She said you cut quite a sight."
"She did?"

"But she didn't elaborate. You're a sight anyway."

"I'm not the only one," I countered. "Loretta, I want to test your memory."

"Not about St Francis medals?" When she saw my eyes pop, she laughed. "I'm not psychic. Maria asked me the same on Sunday, so I've had time to think. The story goes back to the thirties when Paulo sailed to Italy to visit his grandmother."

She plumped herself on the front steps and beckoned me to sit beside her. As there wasn't room for two I leant on the railing.

"Paulo was always the deep one," she continued. "He was a few years older than his brother and rarely mixed with the three musketeers. He had these weird eyes - kind of emotionless - and a spiteful laugh. I mean spiteful in that he saw the funny side of disaster. Like the day he stood on the verandah and laughed when Carl took a nasty spill off his bike. With Maria though he was different. I think he secretly had a crush on her."

"You've got that part wrong," I interrupted. "He called her a trollop."

"Maybe after she ditched Guido, but not earlier. It wasn't so much anything he said but how his eyes never left her. Once when she fell out of a tree he jumped forward to help, but she found him too creepy and brushed him aside. Another thing about him, he liked shooting. I recall the time somebody dumped stray kittens near our farm. Paulo climbed on his bike, rode back to the house for a rifle, and calmly shot every one of those kittens. A bit scary really. Almost like the Avolio brothers were beaten with the same cruelty stick. All that aside, I think he preferred his own company, even travelling alone to his parent's birthplace called Assisi. It was there that he visited the local church where he bought three St Francis of Assisi medals. I know he had three because he showed them to me when he returned to Calen."

"Do you know if he met the Black Shirts while in Italy?" I interrupted.

"Black Shirts? Who are they?"

"Mussolini's thugs."

"I can't recall that. Why?"

"Just curious. Go on."

"Well, I expect he kept the first medal for himself and handed the other two to Guido who, I do know, gave one to Maria. I had always thought Maria's went to the grave with her. Since Guido didn't marry, his medal would've gone to Sam, and the one that Paulo kept I haven't seen since. Maybe his wife Elsa received it but if she did, she keeps it hidden."

"I've not met his wife," I said.

"You're not likely to either. She doesn't leave the house, and if a visitor comes round she barks at him. Even rude to Paulo when it suits."

"Maybe she needs St Francis."

"Who doesn't, Jack?"

Who doesn't indeed? I thought to myself, but said aloud, "Was Elsa always like that?"

"I didn't get to meet her until she was seventeen or eighteen. When she came down from Mirani she had a lot of zest; you know, drink the boys under the table… and their dads if they were bold enough. She even cultivated a legend around football nights. The saying went that any boy from the winning team left standing could have her for the night. I suspect that was all bravado, but it shocked the old folks. To my mind I don't believe she was loose because her heart, even then, was set on Guido. That's right, Guido, not Paulo. Unfortunately, Guido had his eyes on Maria who was the real catch of the district. Elsa was attractive in a waspish kind of way, and if Maria hadn't been in the picture, men might've thought she was pretty. Her luck changed when Jack Bellamy stole Maria from under Guido's nose, and for a time she was able to call Guido her own. According to local gossip, the pair went too far one night, and she fell pregnant. Since Guido was still yearning for Maria - even though she was now married to Jack - Elsa had to carry the baby alone, which was scandalous in a Catholic community. Anyway, her baby was born in the Mackay Hospital, by coincidence on the same night Maria gave birth to little Jack."

"Little Jack? Me?"

"That's right. You and Sam were born on the same night."

I slapped myself on the forehead. "Bad luck follows me."

"Don't be silly. Your mother Maria was a beautiful, caring woman… don't ever forget that." She frowned at me, then went on. "Not long after Sam was born Elsa disappeared with him to Brisbane, re-emerging as Paulo's wife eighteen months after the tragedy in Moreton Bay. Despite what everyone was thinking, she insisted the boy was fathered by Paulo, who certainly treated Sam as his own. In any case, Elsa wasn't the same girl. All the fire had gone from her. Never went to a party or drank anything stronger than tea. When the old couple died she and Paulo moved onto the farm he had inherited. They only had the one child Sam who was spoilt rotten. But knowing what she did about him, she had no choice."

"No choice in what? Concealing the real dad's name?"

"Yes, that... and... um... well, everything really."

"You're not making sense."

"I guess you're right. Sorry. Just a foolish old woman rambling to herself." She sighed. "We've strayed off the subject. You asked me about Paulo."

"We'd moved onto Elsa. She sounds an odd bird. Could she be mixed up in the shooting?"

"Anything's possible, but I doubt it. The men were fighting over your mother, not Elsa."

When Loretta made to lift her bum off the step, I changed subject. "Fancy me and Sam being born on the same night in the same hospital. You can't tell me that's not weird."

"You weren't the only two. It's a big hospital."

"At least I've discovered where I was born."

"Not just where, but when."

"I'll have to recalculate my birthdays."

I could feel her gaze like she was doing her own sums: age, places, events. Time to take a step deeper into the cave. "Tell me, Loretta, has Sammy always had his eyes on Maria?"

"That's none of your business."

"It's too late for that."

"Well, of course they were friends. Nearby farms, the same school, close Italian families."

"Does she... ah... sleep at his place?"

"That *is* none of your business."

"Please, Loretta."

"Okay, no, she doesn't. Although she loves Sam, she finds his mother a bit difficult. And as for Paulo, well, he suffocates her."

To my ears Loretta had used the word *suffocate* deliberately. Did Paulo's future daughter-in-law so resemble the woman he once admired that he couldn't leave her alone? Or was I getting the story wrong? Did she mean Paulo smothered her with affection as the fiancée of his only son, Sam?

While I pondered this word association, I absently flicked a green ant off the rail into Loretta's big hair. "I dunno what's worse," I observed. "Growing up in an orphanage where you can't pee without everyone knowing, or an Italian family that tells you when and how to pee."

"Don't be vulgar."

"Sorry. Just reflecting."

The ant had rappelled down to her scalp where it was gnawing on the roots of her hair. She thumped it dead with her palm then flicked it onto the lawn. Vaguely I felt bad for the ant, but it would've known life with these Italians was a risky business. Dad had discovered that truth years earlier. Once satisfied the intruder worked alone, Loretta said, "Life's full of coincidence; you and Sam born on the same night, you and Sam arriving at the dance with identical St Francis medals."

"Even so," I said, "if there is a third medal, I'll give it to Maria. The three musketeers again."

Loretta climbed to her feet and fixed me with a double barrel glare. "Now you listen to me, Jack Bellamy. Maria is not only a pretty girl and all, she is… well, very special. Right now she's at a vulnerable age and young blokes like you could hurt her. She's content here. She loves Calen, and she loves cane, cattle and kids, exactly what Sam Avolio has to offer. You're a handsome lad, and you've got a cheery manner, all things considered, but you're footloose, and you come from a dark past that involves Maria's family. So please, for everyone's sake, stay out of her life."

Loretta pulled a rag from her pocket and fussily blew her nose. Her eyes didn't leave me. I hadn't noticed them before. "You've got nice eyes," I said. "Just like Maria's."

I didn't see the hand coming. I guess it was all that training she'd done on grasshoppers, but she clapped my ear like a bell ringer.

"Far canal," I yelped. When the clanging had eased I said, "Sorry Loretta. Didn't mean to be disrespectful, but Maria is… well, special to me too."

"We all know she's special, so mind it's left that way. Now, I've made enough pasta for an army. Come upstairs and eat."

Loretta was right, she'd made a huge pasta dish. I was half way through a second plate, wondering if I might score the left overs, when Maria's voice sounded on the verandah. As the door had been left open she just barged in, catching me with a mouthful of noodles. "Hello Jack. I saw your bike outside. Aunty knows how to cook *Italiano*, eh?" She spoke all in one breath and kissed her aunt on the cheek. Then she laughed at my astonishment. "I guess

Aunty didn't tell you I'm secretary of Farleigh Rural Youth. I eat here after the meeting."

Once Maria was seated at the table, Loretta handed across a bowl of pasta. She then settled herself opposite and the two chatted away like old chums. At times, I studied Maria, imagining what it would be like to have her sit across from my table at night, eating dinner together, big moths flying in from the darkness and somewhere in a back room the kids asleep. I believe Maria sensed what I was thinking because she turned and gazed at me, and when I held the gaze, even old Loretta knew an interest was piqued that no cuffing of the ear would kill. She spooned more pasta into Maria's bowl then waddled round behind my chair and massaged the damaged ear. "God help you, boy," she murmured. "God help us all."

After returning to her seat, she wiped her nose on her apron. "I told Jack about the three medals," she said to Maria, "and that I haven't laid eyes on them since before you kids were born. The legend behind St Francis of Assisi is that people should exchange these medals as a sign of their love."

"I'm not doing a swap with Sam," I said.

Loretta wasn't amused. "Be serious, Jack. If Sam is wearing Guido's medal, and you wear your mother's, maybe there *was* love in the mix."

"One day we'll find the third, and you can wear it, Maria," I declared, avoiding Loretta's stare.

"No," Maria said quietly, "I'll only wear a St Francis that I exchange with the man I love. That's how it should be."

I could feel my medal burning my chest. I was tempted to take it out and lay it on the table between us, hand it to her like a primitive love token. I could've wept, an idea so idiotic that another smack on the ear would've done me a kindness. Clumsily I rose to my feet and wiped my mouth. "Sorry, I've gotta leave. Have an early start tomorrow, and a big walk Sunday."

Both women swung on me. "Big walk Sunday?"

"Yes, Sam's taking me to the place where Guido was shot."

Loretta blessed herself. "Nothing can come from that, young Bellamy. You'd do well to stay away from there."

"Steady on, Loretta. The place is not voodoo or stuff."

Maria pushed back her chair and stood by the table. Her eyes were troubled. "Aunty Loretta is right, Jack. That's a bad area you're talking about. I'm not superstitious, but even the cattle won't graze there."

The two women were so earnest that I opened my palms. "Okay, I surrender... for now. Since we're working at the Avolio farm tomorrow I'll tell Sam I've got a prior engagement. We'll have to drop the walk."

"Thanks, Jack," Loretta said.

An awkward silence followed. Maria was the first to break it. "I've got an idea. Well, it's just a thought really. I'm mustering steers at the Rise and Shine in two weeks. Why don't you help out, Jack? And Loretta, you come too. If we finish late, we can all... um... stay over."

Loretta inhaled loudly. "Okay, love, but I hope we don't pay for it."

"Of course not." Then Maria turned to me. "What about it, Jack?"

"Promise no horses."

"No horses, cowboy. We've got a padded rail you can sit on and watch."

We laughed, and as I left the room, I heard them planning the supplies needed for a night at the Rise and Shine.

CHAPTER 26

Friday afternoon arrived with a warm north-easterly pushing the smoke haze back into the Clarke Ranges. Soft cumulous clouds rose through the haze and a trio of black cockatoos sculled lazily towards their lofty mountain home. It was one of those placid afternoons that typically heralded a fine weekend. After servicing our tractors, we parked them in a line near the harvester then I walked across to Avolio's shed where Sam was on the floor fixing a set of rakes. I wasted no time explaining that our hike upriver was off because I'd had to amend my plans.

"Last week you were in a tearing hurry to see the place," he said from under the rakes. "This week you've gone cold. Make up your mind."

"Sorry, Sam, but work comes first."

"What work?"

I lied cheerfully. "Jimmy has to fit an elevator on his harvester. I've been asked to give a hand. Why don't you come along and pass the spanners?"

"No, mate, I can find better things to do."

"Like what?"

"Like having fun."

"Fun? Sure you got the right word?"

"Look it up. Three letters starting with f. Anyway, Carl is branding steers over the next fortnight. We help him, he helps us."

"Carl's steers?" I squeaked.

"What's wrong with that?"

"Carl runs cattle at the Rise and Shine. That's a long way from here."

"Maybe if the steers were there, but they're not. They're on the O'Connell River farm." He laughed. "Why don't you join us? Make Carl's day."

"Dunno about Carl's day, but I could brighten Maria's."

Sam's hackles rose and I kicked myself. The last thing I wanted was him thinking Maria needed a bodyguard. I was sorry and showed it. "Didn't mean that, Sam. Maria's a good kid. You'll have to take me up the O'Connell River after the cut-out."

He couldn't answer right then as he'd caught his lime and purple shirt on one of the tines.

I changed tack. "Sam, don't you think it's odd we own identical St Francis medals."

"They probably cut millions," he replied absently. His shirt was caught fast and the steel wasn't giving in.

"Sure, but I've never seen one before. Where did you get yours?"

"I found it."

"Where?"

"In a box."

"What sort of box?"

He wasn't listening, so I did the right thing and lifted the end of the rakes. The shirt popped free.

"Of Uncle Guido's things," he said after checking the damage. "Dad kept it in a cupboard in the spare room. One day I opened the box and found this medal, so I took it out and started wearing it. Dad wasn't happy. Said it had special meaning. Supposed to tie lovers together or something." He was suddenly embarrassed. "I wear it because I like it. Same as you."

I ignored the last remark. "Did you notice another medal in the box?"

"Can't be sure. It was full of papers. Why do you ask?"

"Loretta said there were three medals."

"Maybe your dad sold the third before he started killing people."

"Yeah, that'd be right."

As I walked out the door, I said, "Is your mum at home?"

"Guess so, why?"

"I want to call on her. Say hi."

"You?"

"Why not? I'm a friend of the family. Almost kin."

"What a scary thought."

CHAPTER 27

Leaving Sam to his rakes, I strolled across to the farmhouse that was unchanged from the account Kevin Cleary had given: a sprawling timber home up on stumps, little marble columns guarding the front steps and baskets of flowers hanging from the verandah. It was somehow more inviting than I had expected, and besides, who in the family was likely to have grown the flowers? Paulo Avolio was a quiet, humourless man who didn't come across as a flower lover, Elsa lacked heart and soul (according to Loretta), and Sam, well, surely not the boy who inherited his taste from a Beatles cover.

I knocked on the door and waited. Shortly an Italian woman answered. No smile or greeting, just the open door and a blank stare, not much different from my first encounter with Loretta. She was perhaps fifty with a surprisingly attractive face despite the greying hair and pointed, waspish nose. She had a swanlike neck on a body that broadened out from the shoulders to wide hips then narrow again to tiny feet, like God had run her through a sausage machine. She wore a black head-scarf and the black dress of a grieving peasant.

"Mrs Elsa Avolio? My name is Jack Bellamy."

"I know who you are."

"I've just finished work. Do you mind if we have a chat?"

"It's not convenient, but... alright... come inside."

She sat me at the table. "You hungry?"

"A bit. We don't stop for lunch Fridays."

"I'm aware of that."

With that she poured a bowl of milk coffee, then laid out a board of *polenta* and cheese. When I started eating, she sat opposite and studied me as if I were a painting for sale. "So, Jack Bellamy, why this visit?"

"Elsa, you knew two people who were important to me. They died violently and one of them, my father, was also accused of shooting your brother-in-law, Guido Avolio."

"He wasn't my brother-in-law then."

"True, but you know who I mean. Did you know racketeering was going on here during the war?"

She thought hard about her answer, twisting the ring on her finger. "Yes."

I hadn't expected the frankness, so I pushed straight on. "Were you aware of Paulo's connection?"

"Who told you that?"

"Kevin Cleary."

"That abomination," she hissed.

"Elsa, your husband was in it up to his ears. Not the organiser perhaps, but just as guilty."

"You have been poking around," she said flatly.

"Not poking, Elsa. Inviting. I've been inviting people to flush the toxin from their system. After they tell their story they feel better."

"So that's how you go about it? You've got Paulo and Cleary talking. Now it's my turn."

I cut a square of cheese and fed it carefully into my mouth. *What's it to be, Elsa?*

"You are the first person to raise the topic," she said. "All these years I've waited, and finally it's come from Jack Bellamy."

"It had to start somewhere."

"But fancy with the orphan. Nobody expected that. Is Father Burke on your list?"

"We had a chat though I didn't learn much."

"He's no angel either."

"I discovered that from Cleary. You mightn't have heard but Cleary's in Townsville dying of cancer. I'll ride up again this weekend. It seems he wants to get the dirty water off his chest."

She glanced at the open door then said quietly. "The extortion racket is what cost Guido his life."

"Go on, Elsa."

Removing the ring from her finger she laid it on the table. A full minute passed. "I always loved Guido. He was different from the others. I realise that some people, Loretta for one, disliked him and he did have his faults. But he had good qualities too. He was loyal to Carl, and he was generous. Anything he had, he shared. Unfortunately he didn't recognise I loved him until Jack Bellamy stole his girl Maria. Up 'til then I was no match for her, same as no girl today can match Carl's daughter... and I'll say it now, my Sam would do better finding another girl."

After reflecting on this, she shook herself back to the present. "In any case it was nice having Guido to myself. At times, he snapped at me, but I accepted that because of the humiliation he'd been through. He wanted revenge on the man who had trumped him, and he wanted it badly. He even dreamed up this horrid scheme of getting Maria to divorce Jack, which is how he happened to be at the church one afternoon in the hope of catching Father Burke. When he arrived, he was surprised to find Kevin Cleary's car in the driveway. Wondering what the pair might be up to, he sneaked up to the door. Apparently they were arguing over the extortion money. In return for his cooperation Father Burke wanted a greater cut from the racket while Cleary wanted to use the Irish migrants - well, Irish thugs - to force Italians into speedier payments. As Cleary also had a score to settle with Bellamy, he hoped the priest might be able to help."

Elsa paused and mopped her eyes. A quarter of a century on she was still dressed in mourner's weeds, but grieving for whom, or what, I couldn't honestly say. Surely it wasn't Guido.

"Guido's next move was his death warrant," she continued. "He should've walked away, but was driven by the same greed as the others. He barged through the door and demanded they give him a hearing. The two men in the church were furious, but they had no choice."

Abruptly, she pushed the bowl of coffee under my nose. "You haven't tasted it."

"Never mind the coffee."

After a long, uncomfortable stare in my direction, she covered her face with her hands. "I remember as clearly as if he was here now. Every last, frightening word."

She began to speak with the sharp, narrative detail of a radio play.

ELSA'S RECOLLECTION

Guido was now in his mid-twenties and had striking good looks. Although small in stature, he was confident with women but out of his depth with men who regarded him as a spiv rather than a farmer or fisherman, their traditional occupations. After demanding he be heard, he took his seat between the two conspirators.

"I'll rid you of Jack Bellamy," he declared.

"Keep talking," Cleary said.

"It's connected with Maria. She wasn't a virgin when they married."

"Who was the rooster?"

"Me," Guido said proudly. "First time when we were sixteen. It happened down at the river. The day was hot and Maria had no togs, so we…"

"Spare us the detail. What're you getting at?"

"Jack and Maria's marriage can be annulled. I've been talking to her. She's not happy. Well, who would be? Stuck out in the middle of nowhere with an Australian hotshot."

Cleary turned to Father Burke. "Any merit in this annulment thing?"

"Guido has a point. Annulments can take forever, but even for Jack to know she has applied would break him. Too mortifying. His wife has slept with another man. Like he's been neutered. He won't hang around."

Cleary tapped the seat with his knuckles. "Okay, it makes sense and I can't see any risk to ourselves. We'll do it your way, Guido. And we'll open your account the day Bellamy leaves the district."

Guido protested. "That could be years."

"No, mate. The war in Europe is finished, and the Japs are almost buggered. He'll be home soon. That's when you play your ace."

"What good will that do? Once the war is over, Italians will be free. No more payments."

"Don't kid yourself. Attempting to bribe a police officer is a criminal offence. They'll keep paying until I'm good and ready."

Cleary unfolded a sheet of paper from his jacket and laid it on the seat. At the top was a date from 1939, another from 1941, and the locality Pindi Pindi. Beneath, a simple statement read; 'We hereby promise that all monies paid towards the Italian *freedom fee* will be shared justly among the undersigned.' Across the next three lines were scrawled the names and signatures of Cleary, Paulo and Father Burke. Kevin Cleary drew out a pen from his jacket and told Guido to write his name and sign underneath. When the ink had dried Cleary folded the document and returned it to his pocket. "That's my insurance," he said. "Not that I don't trust priests and Eyeties, but one can't be too careful."

The three shook hands with a further warning from Cleary. "If word of this gets out, wop boy, you're dead."

CHAPTER 28

Elsa opened her eyes, and when she saw I hadn't moved she crossed to the stove and lifted a pot onto the bench. After adding spinach and beans, she returned the pot to the stove. Next she took a couple of breaths to collect herself, and walked back to her chair.

"Guido and Father Burke set about 'releasing Maria' as they described their little scheme. I wasn't too happy, knowing that once Maria was divorced I would lose Guido. Besides that, the scheme was flawed. It might sound uncharitable, but Guido was no Latin lover. Although he demanded sex as his due, he never... um, well... consummated... the union. I was keen to carry his baby, but on the times we slept together his... um... taxi left the rank without me. Maybe it was my fault. Maybe he only ever wanted a child with Maria, I don't know. It was on one such night that he revealed the church meeting. Naturally I was anxious for him, but since I was now exposed to the secret, I was more concerned for myself. You had to remember that Cleary, Father Burke, Paulo and Guido all faced jail if the story broke. So guess who they'd identify as the source of the leak? Guido's girlfriend, me. Cleary's reputation for nastiness wasn't something you'd want to put to the test.

"Anyway, the war ended and Jack returned home. He wasn't the same cocky Jack though who could blame him after the awful things he'd been through. I believe he and Maria still carried a torch for each other, but - and this is the saddest part -

every Italian in the district had had five years of nibbling away at her. While she readily accepted that Jack had good prospects and would make a decent father, taking him back into the Italian community was like mixing oil and water; or so she'd been told. Meanwhile, his old friends had gone, his teaching job no longer existed in Calen, and his rugby days were over. The boys at the RSL were proud of their local hero, but even hero worship has its life. I think he became depressed and lonely, and it's just possible Maria did raise the subject of annulment. I'm not saying she mentioned infidelity, but it couldn't be ignored as most blokes round here were under her spell. However, there are other reasons for seeking divorce, and incompatibility is one of them, which simply means they should never have married in the first place. Despite all that, sometime after Jack arrived home, she did conceive a child. I recall the announcement was made prior to Guido's death, which was interesting as Guido had boasted her firstborn would be his. As it turned out he never lived to see the child, much less press his claim."

I interrupted her. "You were also pregnant at this time."

"That's right."

"Who was the father? Guido?"

She avoided eye contact. " I... I wanted to have a baby with him but couldn't, as I told you. Paulo is the father of my Sammy. We had a one-night affair... celebrated too much after the Jap surrender... around the time the boys came home. Why? What are people saying?"

"What do you expect? You didn't marry until months later."

"That was out of decency to Guido who'd just been killed." Elsa tore off a sheet of brown paper and wrapped the *polenta* that was starting to crust. "Anyway, we're not here to talk about me. You were Maria's little boy, and she always insisted Jack was your father." After sliding the plate into the fridge, Elsa leant against the bench and faced me. "But it's curious how you don't resemble either man, Jack or Guido. Not so much as a freckle."

"I've argued that point a dozen times."

"But has anybody followed it through? First there was Guido, then Jack. Maybe a third Romeo was hiding in the bush."

I shook my head. "Despite how much you people like slandering Mum, she was loyal to the man she loved, my dad."

"One believes what one must."

"What's that supposed to mean?"

"Well, if the gossips won't accept Paulo is the father of Sam, why should your situation be different?"

"That's easy. Guido was hopeless in bed, and 'Romeo in the bushes' is a fantasy of yours."

"Only Maria can answer that, and she's not around."

"You mean she's not here to defend herself."

"That's not what I meant."

She waited until I cooled down before resuming her story. "So Jack, from whichever angle you look at it, a hunting trip into the mountains for your father and Guido was madness. I suspect one of the other three - Cleary, Father Burke or Paulo - arrived at the idea, but they're hardly likely to admit anything. We all know what came next; Guido was shot dead, and nobody was charged."

"Do you believe Dad was innocent?" I said.

"Yes."

"You serious?"

"I never thought otherwise."

"Then who killed him?"

"Cleary," she replied bitterly.

"When I put it to him in Townsville, he denied it. Wasn't even there at the time."

"That snake would eat his offspring."

"So what happened after Guido's death?"

"I took my baby and fled to Brisbane. If Cleary had pulled the trigger on Guido, I was next."

"Did Mum and Dad go with you?"

"No. Maria wasn't fit to travel. She was still recovering. I suppose you know that you and Sam were born on the same night."

"Yes, Loretta told me."

"What else did she say?"

"Nothing really. Why?"

Elsa picked up the ring and slipped it back on her finger. "Well, it was a long night at the hospital for both of us. My little Sammy struggled through the night, but it was worse for Maria. She lost one of her twins."

I sat upright. "Pardon?"

"Oh, you hadn't heard. Maria gave birth to twin boys, but the second was stillborn."

"I had a twin brother?"

"Sorry, I thought you knew all this."

"No, of course not. What else should I know?"

"Well, it was a dreadful time for your mother. You were such a big healthy lad, almost too big, and you came out hard. Nurses thought they had lost Maria when at the very end a second boy emerged. But the poor little fellow was already dead. Nobody guessed she was carrying twins, not even the doctor. I heard about it next morning."

I sat dazed at the latest revelation.

"Once they had discharged me, I left town while Maria stayed in hospital. She was there a month or more, and it was during this time Jack convinced her they would have a better life in Brisbane. When she was strong enough to travel - early the following year, I think it was - they took the train south where they bought themselves a nice house in Coorparoo, and Jack went back to teaching. Every month or so I caught the tram out to their place for a Sunday visit, and I honestly believe they were happy. You were a pretty little boy doted on by loving parents."

"Did Sam and I... um... play together?"

"No. I never took Sam with me. It would've hurt Maria after losing one of her twins. All that aside, she appeared settled in Brisbane and the anger had gone from Jack. Life would've moved on wonderfully except for..."

Abruptly she burst into tears, burying her face in her hands. Her distress was so awful I feared that Sam might come running from the shed. I crossed to the sink and fetched a glass of water. After taking a mouthful she calmed down enough to realise I was waiting for her to continue.

"Except for what, Elsa?"

"Cleary is the most evil person I've known."

"I agree. Go on."

"He found out where I lived in a flat in Spring Hill. He rang me late one night, and told me that if I didn't follow his instructions he had a friend who was partial to Italian mothers - he called it *sesso mamma* - and the friend didn't care if she'd had one child or ten. I was to steal Jack's revolver - the one he'd kept from New Guinea - and leave it in a bag in my flat when I took Sam for a walk. Somebody would collect it. I demanded to know how this somebody would access my flat, and he said, 'We've got keys, love, and I wouldn't dry my knickers over the bath. My friend gets turned on by that lacy stuff. After you steal the gun, tie a blue wrapper to the fence near the letterbox.' Next day, when Sam and I came home from town, my underwear in the bathroom had been torn in half. I was terrified. Well, I had no choice. The following Sunday I went over to the Coorparoo house where I pretended to use the toilet while Jack and Maria were playing with you on the lawn. It wasn't hard to steal the gun as Jack was careless, leaving it in an unlocked drawer with a packet of spare bullets. He probably guessed I was the culprit, but he never said anything."

She started weeping again. "They were both killed, and it was my fault."

"No, you were frightened and alone. So who pulled the trigger?"

She sobbed and shook her head.

"Please, Elsa, tell me."

"No, Jack. Leave me alone."

In desperation I crouched down in front of her. "Please, Elsa, why can't you tell me?"

"You'll be next. That's why."

When she refused to continue, I let myself out the house. Over in the shed I could see Sam's legs where he sprawled on the floor mending the rakes. The glint of spanners lit the motes of dust slanting in through the door while a light breeze stirred the cane trash at his feet. Briefly I wondered if it was possible that by knowing a killer's identity, one's life could be in danger twenty years later. I also wondered if I was exposing young Maria to the same risks. The farm scene lying before me was chocolate-box tranquil, and besides, times had changed; young Maria was educated and independent, and I was no devil-may-care teacher.

CHAPTER 29

After riding back to my caravan that night, I was at a loose end. Most Friday nights saw me at the Calen pub with the rest of the haul-out drivers, but after the time I had spent with Elsa, I was in no mood for rowdy drinking. It seemed incredible that Elsa had stolen the revolver for Cleary. She had lived two decades with this secret, hiding it from everyone except maybe Paulo who, apart from being her husband, was Cleary's co-conspirator. Paulo, I decided, was a character who needed watching. He lived in a shadowy world where the light of day never quite penetrated. Aside from my comment about the two rifles, which had puffed him up, he played my questions with a straight bat, and although he was undeniably corrupt and a lover of guns, he hardly had the profile of a murderer. The only case against him was Loretta's unflattering remarks, which were anything but evidence. After all, he was unlikely to shoot his brother in Calen then go to Brisbane and kill another two people for the hell of it. All the signs continued to point to Cleary who, as Elsa had said, would eat his own offspring. In every imaginable way he was evil. His behaviour had even forced his long-suffering wife Ursula to commit suicide under a tram.

Meanwhile, my gloom deepened when I recalled I had shared the womb with a baby whose eyes never opened, a twin brother who had never said my name, a best mate who had never breathed. Sighing, I collected a pack of beer from my fridge and went in search of Jimbo who I found trapping fireflies in a tin. Flipping open a beer, I handed it to him. We clinked bottles. "Cheers."

"No pub tonight, bro?" he said.

"Don't feel like it. The same old drunks beating the same old drums. They need fresh things to gripe about."

"Dat's okay. We all talk dat way."

"Yeah, I guess so. Anyhow, what's with the fireflies?"

"Night fishin'."

"It'd be simpler to buy a torch."

"No, bro. Dey be like lanterns. Fish tink it's da moon. When dey come to da surface, I catch em."

"You crafty bugger. So why do fish come to the moon?"

"Dey like da light. Better to see by."

"Why is that? To check your boat licence?"

Jimbo laughed. "What boat licence? Hey, bro, you're no fool."

"I am with things that matter, Jimbo, but I get by as a haul-out driver. We passed the ten-thousand ton milestone this week."

"Den what next?"

"I wish I could say," I confessed wearily. "You know how I've been trying to find information on my parents. Well, it just gets worse. At every turn I find somebody hiding something new. And none of it is pleasant."

"Make da fish come to da moon."

"How am I expected to do that?"

"Like I said, bro, you're no fool. You'll find a way."

We sat in silence, drinking out the six pack while Jimbo continued to fill his tin with fireflies. Then I realised I was already stirring the fish from their dark holes. Sooner or later one of them would strike at the moon.

Next morning about an hour before daylight rain cascaded from the sky, and was still pounding on my roof at seven when I dragged myself from bed. Peering through the window, I saw water surge beneath the caravans towards Jolimont Creek where boats lay upturned in the rising flood. I snatched a raincoat over my head and ran to help Jimbo drag the boats to safety.

"Where did this rain come from?" I shouted.

"Radio man says big low formed off da Whitsundays. Dey tink it will rain like dis two, t'ree days."

"Damn. I was planning to ride to Townsville."

"Best you hurry into Calen and buy tucker, bro. Roads will soon be cut."

I took his advice and pushed the Norton Commando out into the rain where it started reluctantly. Then, dragging on the only jacket I owned, I rode up the highway. At times the rain whipped at my goggles while torrents of water poured down headlands and under the bridges. Occasionally I passed cars that had spluttered to a halt in the wet. Most of the drivers sat glumly in their vehicles waiting for help while others tinkered with wires under the bonnet. At culverts I rode over swirling floods and once, just south of Kolijo, I dismounted and heaved the Norton through water that almost covered the axle.

When I reached the store in Calen, I guided the bike under the awning and wrung myself out before stepping inside. To my surprise Maria stood at the counter with two boxes of groceries.

When she saw me, she raised an eyebrow.

"Been for a swim, Jack?"

I grinned ruefully. By comparison, she was straight from a photo shoot. Pretty blouse, pretty skirt, pretty shoes. Lots of make-up.

"What are you doing here?" I asked.

"Went out last night with friends, then we were planning to see a matinee this morning. Had to hurry home instead. They said the road will be cut at Blackrock Creek."

I pointed at the boxes. "You taking those out to the car?"

When she nodded, I said, "Here, I'll do it. I'm already soaked."

Before she could reply, I grabbed a box in either arm and charged out the front.

"This way," she called, pulling on a raincoat and running ahead.

Careful to avoid an avalanche of junk, I dumped the boxes inside the rear doors, shouted, "See you next week," and hurried back to the store.

When I turned at the counter, she was behind me.

"How are you getting your stuff home?" she asked.

I held up the leather bag I wore across my shoulder.

She laughed. "That keeps groceries dry?"

"It doesn't need to. Wet stuff dries out."

"Not always. I'll wait and drive you."

After I had finished my shopping, I checked with the store owner before pushing my bike into a shed round the back. Next I made space on the Land Rover's front seat and climbed in beside Maria.

By now St Helens Creek was frothing angrily as water poured out of the mountains and through the canefields. "What happens if the bridge floods and you can't get home?" I shouted at Maria.

"I'll phone Dad and he'll come in the tractor to fetch me."

"Don't bother him. I'll make up a bed in the caravan."

"Very thoughtful, Jack, but it won't be necessary."

The inadequate wipers on the Land Rover beat at the rain driving towards us in sheets. Maria sat forward over the wheel searching for the white line in the centre of the road. Occasionally the line appeared as a pale blur but mostly it lay under swirls of running water.

"Slow down to first gear," I said. "These old tyres could aquaplane."

"They're not old tyres," she retorted, and eased back to a crawl. The rain thundered on the roof and danced across the bonnet. Maria's raincoat was unbuttoned and rivulets of water poured from the gaps onto her clothes. I couldn't see any point in the car having a roof. While Maria concentrated on the road, I stemmed the worst floods teeming from vents that were rusted open.

"Thanks, Jack. I've never seen rain like this."

"Jimbo says it's a low in the Whitsundays."

"Who is Jimbo?"

After I had told her about Jimbo and the park residents, she said, "You've come to know lots of interesting people."

"I wouldn't say I know them, apart from Jimbo. They're wandering souls who've made a home in a caravan park. You know interesting people too: staff at Venardos, the Rural Youth Club, friends who go to the movies."

She was quiet as we navigated a culvert that had water streaming up to the guide-posts. Two bedraggled egrets clung to a branch, and fences bowed under the weight of debris caught in the wire.

"I hardly meet anyone," she said. "Sheltered life, I guess."

"Tell me about yourself."

"You already know about the farm and where I work."

"I know very little. We talk about things that happened years ago."

"Which is how we should leave it."

"Give me a break, Maria. You sound like your old man. Let's start with your school days. I can see you as a skinny kid in plaits driving the boys wild."

She turned and glared.

"Hey, watch the road," I shouted.

"You talk garbage, Jack."

"So tell me."

"Well, I was a bit of a rough child," she began hesitantly. "But that's because I didn't have other girls to play with. It was just Dad, Mum, Nonna and myself on the farm. My best friend was a horse named Toby and I had a dog called Whiff. Don't laugh. We had great adventures and we explored everywhere from the Rise and Shine to the

O'Connell River. But don't think I was a lonely kid. Other people were often at our place to see Dad, and if school was out they brought their kids along. I suppose that's how I got to know Sam. While Dad and Paulo talked sugarcane, Sam and I would hang out together. He understood a lot about machinery and cattle, and he liked horses. After a time I looked forward to seeing Paulo's ute in the yard. But apart from the days we had visitors, Saturday was the best day at home, especially while Mum was alive. Sundays weren't so relaxed because the day began with Mass which could sometimes go through to lunch. Before you knew it Monday had arrived and the bus was out front taking kids to school. In a way I enjoyed school. I was a better-than-average student with nice teachers and I had friends who were mostly Italian, except for a time I was close to the headmaster's daughter, Helen. We still write to each other."

"Did Sam attend your school?"

"Yes, he was a grade above me."

"Should've been more, but…" I shrugged "… can't be helped."

"What do you mean?" she prickled.

"He's my age. Born on the same date."

"Really?"

"True. Our mums gave birth the same night in Mackay Base Hospital."

"Who did you get that from? Loretta?"

"And Lisa. I had coffee with her yesterday. She told me lots about the events of that night. And how she and Mum took their babies to Brisbane." I didn't mention my dead twin because I didn't know how to.

It was like a dark layer beneath all the other dark layers.

"Is Sam aware of this?"

"Probably not. Anyway, you said you were in different grades at school."

"Yes. We caught the Calen bus together, then he started carrying my books and watching out for me. I was grateful as some of the boys were becoming pests."

Ah, the new generation of suitors. I had slipped the blade into the oyster shell and was prising it open. But my fingers were clumsy. "Maria, the pests hung around because you were pretty. But what if you weren't? Would Sam have been so noble?"

"Yes, because that's the kind of man he is. Anyway, this stuff about being pretty is nonsense. I grew up as an ordinary girl who likes ordinary things."

"You were never ordinary, you're, well… special. That's what Loretta said."

"Maybe special before God. Everyone is. In any case, Jack, what girls do you know? Can't be many, that's for sure."

As we motored south the rain began to ease. Trees appeared along fence lines and the screen cleared except for when the occasional truck whooshed by. While Maria concentrated on the road, I mopped up the water that squirted into the cabin.

"Did you play sport at school?" I asked.

"Everyone did. In high school it was compulsory. One year I won the blue ribbon in long-jump."

"No surprise there. Or aren't I allowed to say that?"

She ignored me. "High school was more than sport, it was a new world. Chemistry, physics, maths. I couldn't get enough of it. That all changed in Year Ten when the accountancy firm Venardos advertised for a junior clerk. My teacher said that as maths was my best subject I ought to post off an application, which I did. A week later they held an interview, then rang and said I could start Monday. Four years on I'm still there and enjoying it."

She banged the windscreen to free a wiper that had stuck on the glass. The blade jumped up then flapped to and fro like a crow's wing.

"Maria, do you know any farmers at Yalboroo?"

"Some. Why?"

"Well, the first bloke to admit knowing my mum was from Yalboroo."

"What's his name?"

"Not sure, but he said studs queued for miles to have a crack at her. Does that sound true?"

"I'd say he drinks too much."

Ten minutes later we pulled into the caravan park. While Maria remained in the car, engine running, I climbed out with my box of groceries.

"Wait a minute," I said. "I have a present of sorts."

I dashed into the van and grabbed a woman's magazine I had taken from the Townsville hotel. On an inside page was an article on plastic surgery for people with burns.

Back at the car window I handed the magazine to Maria with the page open. When she saw the article, she said, "Please Jack, not that. I only showed you the scar to…"

"To what, Maria? Tell me that you had a rough childhood? Well, I'm tackling mine. You can too."

"Jack, I've long forgotten the burn. It doesn't affect me anymore."

"Doesn't it? Why do you wear long sleeves?"

"Because…" she began.

"Because, like me, you're living with something awful."

We stared at each other.

"Goodbye, Maria. And thanks for the lift."

"Bye, Jack," she said and turned the heavy Land Rover onto the road.

Despite Jimbo's forecast of a wet weekend, the rain had stopped by four in the afternoon. Within minutes the sun was splashing light on the millions of streams that plunged across the land. By five o'clock fences were visible and sodden rows of cane began staggering to their feet. Like everybody else in the park, I stepped warily outside. It was a powerful yet dismal scene - powerful to see Nature's hand at play, dismal for the erosion and uprooted crops. As this wasn't my first deluge in the north, I knew that although the surface water would soon clear, harvesters would be banned from the fields for at least two days; enough time to revisit Kevin Cleary.

CHAPTER 30

Sunday dawned hot and steamy. I hitched a ride into Calen where I collected my Norton and directed its nose towards Townsville. This was now my third trip, and I was growing used to the road, especially the potholes and rough shoulders either side of Bowen. At Ayr my journey halted when I picked up a nail on the Burdekin River bridge and was forced to push my bike into town for repairs. The elderly mechanic was in no hurry, recounting stories about the Norton and how it was the machine to beat in the 1920s and 30s. As the morning wore on he tapped a spanner on the Norton badge and swore one day the English would reclaim mastery over the Europeans and Japanese. This was all fine, but I was anxious to be in Townsville before Kevin Cleary found another reason to lock me out.

When I arrived and banged on his door, he answered inside a minute. There were no greetings, just a grimace and a thumb pointing to the kitchen where again I sat on one of his hard chairs. Cleary had aged years in the week since I last saw him. He could barely walk, even on sticks, and his head flopped about like a man trying to keep awake. He still wore a cardigan despite the heat while the end of an intravenous bung projected from under the woollen sleeve.

"If you want coffee, make it yourself," he rasped.

Walking round to the sink, I made two coffees, topped them up with sugar and milk, and left one near his hand.

"Tell me what happened after the war," I said.

He tasted the coffee and winced. "I can't be bothered."

"You promised."

"I said I'd think about it. Why should I say anything more?"

"Ease your conscience for a start."

"My conscience is clear."

"Then talk to me. What took place after the war?"

He scowled. "You mean when Jack Bellamy returned to Calen?"

"That's right. And especially Guido's death."

"Okay, I'll give it to you straight. Guido Avolio had a bullet coming and Jack Bellamy was the prime suspect. Simple as that. Guido was a slime ball who'd been into Jack's missus for years, and made no secret of it. So what happens when the war hero comes home? He decides to set things right, and Guido ends up in the morgue."

"There's also the business of Guido being an unwelcome part of your racket."

"Don't know where you heard that. Guido was no partner of mine. The shooting was all about Maria, two men chasing the same woman. That Guido was an idiot, should've moved on. Can you believe he wanted Maria to get an annulment? Claimed he'd first screwed her as a kid. I reckon he was all show, but it didn't help Jack's blood pressure."

"Dad was no hot head. He was innocent, and others agree with me."

"Not surprised. The world is full of suckers."

This conversation was going nowhere. Cleary had seen the inside of more courtrooms than I'd had hot dinners. "Were you on the scene when Guido died?" I asked, like a barrister.

"As chance would have it, I was in Calen doing follow-ups for the government. My Italian revenue was drying up, so me and the priest were cooking up fresh schemes. Around ten in the morning I received a call that a shooting had taken place in the mountains and some poor bastard was dead. Well, I drove into the foothills then climbed the rest of the way, which was bloody hard work. Sure enough, one fella was on his back in the clearing, covered in blood, and another four were perched on rocks like crows waiting for daylight. I can tell you, it was a cosy little group. The stiff was Guido, shot through the chest, and the four crows were Jack Bellamy, Father Burke, Paulo Avolio and Carl Rossini.

"So what actually happened?"

"Jack said he was wading through the river when he heard a shot and turned to find Guido lying on the ground. Not a chance. Jack fired the shot himself."

"Twice you've said Dad was the culprit. But did he admit anything?"

"He didn't have to, though he spun a yarn about the rifles being swapped. Like somebody had waved a wand and... *boof*... a different rifle."

"Maybe it wasn't black magic."

"We're talking factual evidence here. The bullet had come from Jack's rifle, which was lying near the river where he had dropped it."

"And whose rifle did Dad say it had been swapped with? I bet it was Guido's."

"You're right. But Guido's rifle was still at the farm. Where you'd expect it to be."

He lifted his watery eyes at me. *Okay, orphan boy, where to now?* the eyes were saying.

"Maybe Dad was set up. Had you thought of that?"

"Every crook's first defence, 'I was set up, your honour'. Jack claimed he hadn't seen his rifle in a week, yet the bloody thing was there staring up at him."

"He could've been telling the truth. Somebody else took it up the mountain with the intention of shooting Guido."

"Come off it. Next we'll be blaming dear old granny."

"Okay then. Who told you Guido's rifle never left the farm?"

"Nobody. I checked for myself."

"When? That day? The next?"

He let out a breath. He was holding onto his temper. "Read my notes, mate."

"I'm sorry, Uncle Kevin, but don't you think it odd?"

"You're what is odd."

"No, that everything was so neat. Why would Guido go hunting without his own rifle? These are country boys we're talking about. Whose fingerprints were on Dad's rifle?"

"Everyone's. Even the idiot priest."

Cleary began to cough and I let him drink half his coffee which had gone cold in the Police Service commemorative mug. Wiping his mouth on his sleeve, he reluctantly faced me. All these years he'd been nursing a premise that I was untangling, and he didn't like it. "Anyway," he said, "this is the guts of what happened next. Take it or leave it. After checking Guido for a pulse, Jack ran across to the Rise and Shine house where he told Carl Rossini. Carl made three phone calls. The first was to Father Burke - last rites sort of thing - the second to Paulo, the dead man's brother, and the third to me. After the calls, according to Carl, he and Jack collected stretchers and blankets and returned to the clearing where they were joined by Father Burke and Paulo. Since Guido was already dead, they sat and waited until I arrived."

"Did you question them separately?"

"Of course. Each of their stories was plausible, except for Jack's. After I'd finished with the crime scene, the priest did his holy stuff and the four men carried Guido's body down to Paulo's truck. From there he was driven into Mackay where forensics told us the obvious, that the man had died from a bullet fired from Jack's rifle. They also said the death couldn't have been suicide. Anyway, as Jack was the only suspect I dragged him into the Calen lock-up to question him further."

"You would've loved that."

A glint of life appeared in Cleary's eye, but it died as he turned back to the window. "Yeah, for the first time I had the bastard on a grill, and I was gonna see him roast. I told him that he was likely to make history as the last man hanged in Australia. Think of the honour, the prestige. The case against him was water tight. No matter how much he pleaded innocent, the jury would condemn him. The gun was his and the motive couldn't be more obvious. We didn't need Sherlock on this one. Well, I had him skewered. The bastard was tough, which I guess the Eyeties in Africa had already discovered, but not so tough the gallows didn't frighten him. He was going to pay, like it or not. It was then I came up with this brilliant idea. Why not drop the charges as there was no strong evidence either way? In return for a finding of accidental death he could make a contribution to my happiness fund. 'You can walk from here a free man, but here's the deal,' I said to him. 'I want to screw that woman of yours. Any night I ask, she's mine. And you can sit outside the door and listen to her moan. If she stuffs me about, or you hold her back, I dig up fresh evidence, and you swing on a beam.' Well, Jack was smart enough to know he didn't have a choice. I released him, the coroner agreed it was a tragic accident, and life returned to normal. Except there was no more Guido sticking his nose in, no more talk of annulment, and every fortnight the lovely Jack and Maria invited me up to their cosy farmhouse for dinner and sweets. And, man, were the sweets fantastic."

"You're disgusting."

"Hey, kid, show more respect. I could be your father."

"The thought of it sickens me." I glared at him in the poorly lit kitchen. "Why did you force Elsa to steal Dad's revolver? Hadn't you caused enough misery?"

"That revolver wasn't for me, pal. I never shot Mr and Mrs Jack Bellamy."

"Maybe not, but you orchestrated it."

"Rubbish. Your old man taunted me all his life and his missus loved flashing it about, but that doesn't mean I wanted them dead."

He began coughing phlegm. "Now piss off, kid, and don't come back."

"I'll be back," I said, rising to my feet, "and I'll have the police with me. I don't care how riddled you are with cancer, the only place for you is behind bars."

He was gasping for breath. "Your word against mine? Get real, Bellamy."

I took a room that night at the Great Northern troubled by the possibility that Cleary's story contained more truth than lies. Especially revolting was the notion that he just might be my father. To help stay calm, I forced myself to bear in mind that he could be delusional from all the drugs they were pumping into him. Even so, the vulture knew exactly what befell Mum and Dad and I was determined to wring the truth from his scrawny neck.

The next morning I arose following an awful night's sleep, which didn't improve my frame of mind. A drunk with a smoker's cough had wheezed and spluttered from closing time until two in the morning. After being driven close to insanity, I banged on his door expecting to find Satan, but instead I was met by a gutted old man whose eyes were red holes in a sad face. My anger dissolved, and we sat on the verandah drinking tea under a naked bulb. The cold light exposed walls of flaking paint, and above our heads the fanlights held spider ghettoes where each filthy web was a boneyard of insect shells. Although my companion was keen to fill the pre-dawn hours with stories of Townsville's early days, and how he'd once been a good family man, I paid scant attention because it wasn't history

I needed but solid sleep. Finally, when I turned in after sunrise my mind drifted back to Kevin Cleary. I drew the conclusion that the retired detective had invented his sick fantasy solely for my benefit. Besides, Elsa had said that when she visited the couple in Brisbane they were happy. Something didn't add up, and although I was inclined to believe Elsa, I needed Cleary's explanation of what had taken place next.

Around eleven, I ate a late breakfast, threw on my leather jacket and rode across to Railway Estate. Halfway down the street I was met with a cordon of police cars that blocked off Cleary's house. I pushed my way to the front where a young constable guarded the door.

"What's going on?" I asked.

"Who are you?"

"Kevin Cleary's nephew. What's happened?"

"He's deceased."

"What?"

"Sorry, mate, your uncle's dead." The constable called out to an officer in plain clothes. "Sir, I've got a fella here who knew him. His nephew."

When the constable handed me across to the detective, who introduced himself as D.I. Morgan, I said again, "What's happened?"

Before D.I. Morgan would reply he asked about myself, why I was in Townsville, and where I lived and worked. Not wanting to be tied up in formalities, I avoided mentioning any of Cleary's previous life, or the story he had told. I explained that I was visiting an uncle I hardly knew. Yes, I had seen him the afternoon before, and I was returning to say goodbye before riding back to Calen.

D.I. Morgan then led me into the house where Cleary lay sprawled on the kitchen floor. His shirt was soaked in blood and all the bitterness was gone leaving a serene, grey husk. Although my face revealed a grieving nephew, inside I fumed because someone had torn the last chapter from a book I was close to finishing.

"Is that Kevin Cleary?" he asked.

"Yes, sir. That's the man. How did he die?"

"A bullet. What were you expecting?"

"The man had cancer. He was dying anyway."

"But not this soon. He was killed around two-thirty this morning according to neighbours who heard the shot. We think it was a hand gun, maybe an old service revolver, but we can't be sure. Do you know if he was related to Kevin Cleary, the ex-policeman?"

"Yes, sir, it's the same man. You'll have a file here in Townsville."

"I've already seen it, but it makes no mention of his current address. Apparently some officers liked him, others didn't. From what I hear he had a reputation. No time for blacks or Italians."

"I heard the same."

D.I. Morgan ran his eyes over my features. "So how come he had an Italian nephew?"

"That was through marriage. He married my Dad's sister who was of Irish descent. Dad's choice of wife was Italian."

"So a mixed marriage. Tension in the family?"

I lifted my palms in the classic Italian disbelief. "Steady on, Inspector. This has nothing to do with family. As you say, he hated dark people. Perhaps someone with a long memory got his hands on a revolver."

"Maybe," he said indifferently. "Anyway, where were you at two-thirty this morning?"

I told him about the wheezing drunk at the Great Northern. "My alibi will be easy to check, just follow your ears."

After writing 'follow your ears' in long hand, the detective asked, "So Mr Bellamy, you are half Italian. What's the other half?"

"Australian."

"Where are your folks now?"

"What's this to do with Kevin Cleary? My mum and dad died in a boating tragedy in 1951. I don't have siblings, and apart from a cousin in Brisbane, Cleary was the only relative left on my father's side. I have no idea who'd shoot him."

D.I. Morgan led me into a small bedroom that served as an office. Cabinet doors stood ajar, papers were scattered across the floor and a broken lamp lay on its side in the corner.

"Ever been in this room, Mr Bellamy?"

"No, sir, never. I came to see him three times, and always in the kitchen."

"Three times? You told me you saw him for the first time yesterday."

"I never said that."

"I'll check my notes. People often change their story." He tapped his nose; it wasn't a handsome nose, but it looked well-tapped. "I can smell deceit a mile away."

"Well, sniff me all you like."

"One day I just might." The detective crouched on his haunches and picked through the documents with a pen. "Did Cleary hint at valuables somebody may have wanted?"

"No, sir. Maybe he startled a burglar."

Rising to his feet, the detective sighed. "So a startled burglar draws a revolver and shoots Cleary in the heart. About as likely as finding a fat beggar in Delhi. Personally I believe an offender, as yet unknown, called here to locate an item that Cleary had in his possession. One way or another Cleary got himself shot for it. Whatever it was, I doubt it's still in the room. And I have a feeling in here"… tapping his nose again… "that more of the story is to come, sooner rather than later. What's your view, Mr Bellamy?"

"I'd say you're on the money. But keep me out of it. The man was my uncle."

"I've heard what Italians do to their kin."

"That's Mafia. And besides, I'm not Italian, I'm native Australian."

"Whatever you say, Jack Bellamy. You can go for now, but don't change your address without telling us."

With that D.I. Morgan showed me to the door. I was half way down the steps when a green Ford pulled up. Out of it stepped two men, Father Michael Burke and Paulo Avolio.

My mouth dropped open. Slowly I shut it. What were they doing here?

"You blokes know each other?" D.I. Morgan asked, then he grinned, "I didn't expect things to happen this fast."

"Of course I know them," I replied. "I work as a haul-out driver in Calen where Paulo is a farmer and Father Burke is the parish priest."

"Paulo who?"

"Avolio," Paulo said. "Second generation cane grower."

"It's a long drive from Calen to Townsville," the detective said. "What brings you this far north on a Monday?"

Father Burke stepped forward and introduced himself. He was the smooth, relaxed professional. "I was at the cathedral, detective, at ten today saying Mass when I ran into an Irish lad who, please God, I'd helped settle…"

"Get on with it."

"Well, he told me that poor Mr Cleary had passed away. He knew Kevin Cleary had worked in Calen, and he thought… me being the parish priest and all… that I ought to be told. So we skipped coffee and came straight here. Is it true your man was shot?"

Ignoring the question, D.I. Morgan rounded on Paulo. "And you, Mr Cane-grower? What's your story?"

"I drove up to Townsville yesterday with Father Burke. We left straight after Sunday Mass. Father is not only our local priest, he's a family friend."

"When did you arrive?"

"Late afternoon. We stayed in West Townsville at an empty house that's kept for visiting priests. Then at nine this morning, when the office opened, we visited Customs and Immigration to collect paperwork for an Irishman we are sponsoring to Australia. It's part of our parish commitment. Next up, as Father said, we attended the cathedral where we heard about Kevin's death."

Shoving his hands in his pockets, D.I. Morgan leant against the fence. His jacket was crumpled from hours in a car seat and his shoes hadn't seen polish in months. On his head he wore a battered Akubra that sprouted a cockatoo feather from the band. Pushing the hat back, he scratched tiredly at a mop of brown hair. "It's a funny thing," he said, "how you three arrive out of thin air. All with good alibis and loving the man. So what do I make of it? Maybe the killer was an Italian with a long memory and short temper. Or maybe Mr Cleary had a little treasure that somebody wanted badly. And that somebody happens to live in Calen. Odd as it may seem, you blokes are the only lead we have apart from a gunshot wound. So before you wander off give your details to the constable." He readjusted his hat and disappeared into the house.

At the bottom of the steps we studied each other. We were all familiar with Cleary's history and we all had reason to want him dead. But I couldn't help thinking the pair knew I was in Townsville and had organised his murder to protect a grubby secret. It seemed very possible that Cleary's *freedom fee* document was in the mix. However, you wouldn't know that from their faces. Like good Catholic boys they offered their condolences while grieving the loss of a dear friend. Easing past them, I buckled on my helmet and rode back to Jolimont Creek.

CHAPTER 31

The following Saturday after a trouble-free week in the cane and no word from D.I. Morgan, I kicked the bike into life and rode along the track that led to the Rise and Shine farm house. Maria's Land Rover was already parked under the Burdekin Plum and three horses were saddled and tied to the rail. I didn't relish the significance of that; three horses and two riders, plus myself. As the Norton Commando putted up the track, Maria came onto the verandah and waved. Blocking the doorway behind her was Loretta with a broom in her hand.

"Hi, Jack, you're late," Maria said.

I lifted the bike on its stand and swapped my helmet for the cowboy hat. "What's with the third horse? You know I'm no rider."

"I hadn't forgotten. You can sit on Topsy while he walks up the track."

Loretta bustled onto the verandah. "My, doesn't he look the part. All he needs are the spurs and a bandana."

"Give us a break, ladies." I pulled a duffel bag from the rear of the bike, tossed it over my shoulder and stepped onto the verandah. "Where does the boss sleep?"

"Her room is out of bounds," Maria said, then pointed to an enclosed space at one end of the verandah. "The hands sleep down there... where they can't get into mischief."

After throwing my kit onto a monastic bunk, I wandered into the kitchen. The two women hadn't wasted their time. The floors and table were spotless, the wood stove crackled and a kettle sang on the hotplate. In the centre of the table they had stacked a load of sandwiches which I tackled dutifully, then I asked long questions about beef and dairy cattle, herbicides and insecticides, stray dogs and wild geese; anything to delay mounting a live horse.

After a time they dragged me outside and Maria showed me how to put one foot in the stirrup and throw my weight into the saddle. Thankfully Topsy dozed in the shade brushing flies with his tail.

"Okay, cowboy," Maria said to me. "Try not to get excited when the cattle run."

"If Topsy sparks into life, I'll jump off," I replied.

Maria and Loretta swung onto their mounts and jogged towards a bunch of cattle that watched them suspiciously from the corner of a distant paddock.

"Come on, Topsy," I said. "Wakey, wakey."

The old nag ambled into the sunshine and headed towards the gate the women had left open. When he reached the first shady tree past the gate, he killed the ignition. Cautiously I heeled him, then I slapped him with the reins and sank in a boot, but the bag of bones just hung his head and snoozed. Meanwhile, I felt silly as Maria and Loretta cantered into the distance. The minutes passed. Noise and dust billowed from the far paddock then suddenly cattle thundered into the open. An angry mass of sinew and horn bore down on me like a curse from the Old Testament. Crikey, this was no place for a white faced cowboy, but Topsy barely opened an eye as the mob swirled past. At the end of the track Maria swung her whip and turned the herd into a steel corral which she then bolted shut. Once the action was done the women rode across to my grandstand position, their faces streaming with sweat and dust.

"That wasn't difficult," Maria said, sucking in draughts of air.

"Yeah, too easy. Now what?"

"It's time to start work in the yards."

We all looked at Topsy.

"Let's crank it up, fella," I said.

Maria reached across to the tree and broke off a green twitch. Topsy straightened and eyed Maria as she handed it across.

"Smack him on the haunches with that," Maria said, "and he'll do as he's told."

Maria was right. I hardly touched his skin with the twitch when he exploded into a ball-breaking jog. A minute later he eased from the jog to a gentle canter that was at least bearable. Another two minutes he changed down gears and walked me back to the yards where I gladly disembarked. Over in the distance Loretta was nudging a cow and calf towards the corral while Maria perched on the rail counting heads. Three hours later the work was over and we returned to the house where the ladies had me carry buckets of water into the laundry. There I mixed hot water into a kerosene tin, screwed a rose to the bottom of the tin and hauled the primitive shower to the ceiling. After Loretta and Maria had finished their showers and I'd had mine, we retired to the verandah where they arranged a bottle of cold, sweet wine for themselves and a beer for Roy Rogers.

It was achingly peaceful out there. Below us the cattle settled in the yards and the dying light brushed the distant hills in shades of pink and blue. From where the women sat in their padded chairs their voices carried softly to the top step where I drank beer and let the evening descend around me. Every so often I glanced across at Maria whose outline was just discernible in the fading light. She wore a loose fitting skirt, one leg tucked beneath her as she lay back in the chair twirling the glass in her hand. A smooth white foot and an ankle were visible, and the paint on her toe nails glowed like polished bronze. She had her face partly towards me, and she smiled as she talked, revealing a faint gleam of even, white teeth. After a time Loretta levered herself upright and lit a pressure lamp for the kitchen. She ordered us inside to eat reheated stew, then while I cleared the dishes, the girls refreshed their glasses and returned to the verandah where it was now growing cool and the carpet of stars spread from hilltop to valley.

"Penny for your thoughts, lad." Loretta said as I flipped the cap from a beer.

"Oh, trying to imagine this place with Mum as a little girl, then afterwards when she and Dad were married."

"Yes, I think your dad liked the bush. He was a city kid brought up with noise and concrete. Out here everything was quiet, and your mum would've been comfortable because this was the world she knew. She probably hoped he would find a permanent job in Calen."

"And only one fly in the ointment," I said.

"What was that?" Maria asked. "The war?"

"Well that too, but it came and went. The spoiling fly was her Italian background." I nodded to

Loretta. "You once said Dad gave Maria new life. Do you think she felt let down?"

Loretta sipped her drink. "Not your mother. She was a cheerful girl who never looked back, and she would've known that marriage included sacrifice. Maybe friends were not as common out here, but she was a farmer's daughter, not a socialite. So it would've been natural for her to put on old clothes and climb into the yards. As kids, we often came over in the holidays to help Nonno and Nonna. Most mornings we'd do chores and after lunch we'd play games or visit secret haunts."

Maria laughed. "You had secret haunts, Aunty? You never told me that."

"It never occurred to me."

"What sort of haunts?" I said.

"Nothing special. Little fairy caves, that sort of thing. Though there was a hidey hole I do remember. It belonged to everyone but it was mostly for the boys. They found it, and they cut the stone to seal it off."

I was now intrigued. "Where is this secret hole, Loretta?"

"Up along the ridge. Maybe a kilometre. It's a tough climb."

"When were you last there?"

"Not since I was a kid. No, that's not true. On the day before Maria's wedding we exchanged little cards with pressed flowers. We put them in the hole."

"Let's check it out tomorrow."

Neither of the women were convinced. "I'm not sure, Jack," Maria said. "There might be family skeletons up there. Best we leave them to sleep."

"Maria's right, Jack. Some of my childhood is in that hole, and I'd rather it wasn't disturbed."

I wasn't to be put off easily. "Come on, girls. There's a lot of mystery about Mum and Dad, and it's not all sweet. If it's personal family stuff, we'll leave it in the hole and say nothing, but if it's about Mum and Dad, I think we ought to know."

In the pale wash of the lamp I could see Loretta exchange glances with her niece. "Okay, lad. We'll climb up there tomorrow if I can make it."

Shortly after that we called it a night. Maria lit a small kero lamp and handed me fresh sheets. "Goodnight, Jack. And thanks for your help today." As I took the sheets our fingers touched.

"That's okay, Maria. Cow herding ain't what it's cracked up to be." I then took her by the arm and kissed her full on the mouth. She didn't resist, and it was the softest, warmest, most awesome thing I've ever done.

Her eyes were full into mine. She said quietly, "Night Jack," and was gone.

Hard as that cot was I slept like a baby. You know, awake every couple of hours with dreams that had Maria about to touch me, or perhaps she was warning me. Regardless of the message, her beautiful face drifted through my sleep until daylight when it wasn't Maria waking me but Loretta thumping the door frame.

"Up and at 'em, cowboy," she called. "It's Sunday morning and brekky's on the table."

"Take it easy, Loretta. The birds aren't awake."

"This is a farm, lad, not a holiday resort."

I dragged myself from the bed, climbed into my cowboy gear, and after sluicing my face at the outside tank, staggered into the kitchen. By now the sun had flushed the horizon and late starters in the trees were clearing their throats. On the sideboard a pressure lamp flared while the aroma of bacon and coffee filled the kitchen. Loretta flipped eggs on the stove and Maria sat at the table dicing pieces of fruit. Both women were freshly dressed in contrast to my soiled outfit from yesterday.

"Morning," I grumbled.

"Beg your pardon?" Loretta cupped a hand to her ear.

"Good morning, folks."

"That's better. Now park your frame on a chair and eat while it's hot."

I looked across at Maria. "Hi, cowgirl."

She smiled. "Hi, cowboy. How did you sleep?"

"Okay, but I dreamt a lot."

"What about?"

"You."

There was a distinct pause in the kitchen. Even the pan stopped sizzling but I didn't look up. Just piled bacon and eggs onto my plate and forked them into my mouth. "This is terrific, Loretta. You ought to cook for me every morning."

Loretta folded her arms over her abundant breast. "You're a cheeky devil, and you need to train your mouth." She turned back to the stove. "Anyway, I came in at the tail. Maria lit the fire and did the bacon."

"It's great tucker, Maria. Thank you," I said, glancing up at her.

She busied herself with the fruit platter, and maybe it was the heat of the stove but a flush lit her cheeks. "You're welcome, Jack."

During breakfast the women talked business about the cattle and cane and what needed fixing on the house. I then ushered them onto the verandah with their coffee, so I could wash up. Afterwards I said, "When are we tackling the mountain?"

"As soon as we've done with Mass and the calves," Loretta said.

"Mass?"

"Yes, seven-thirty at Calen. You're coming, I expect."

"Can't wait."

"Good. Shave and put on fresh clothes. We leave in ten minutes."

I did as told and soon I was perched on fencing gear in the back of the Land Rover as we bounced down the valley to Sunday Mass. Nobody said much on the way, and if Father Burke was surprised at my presence, he hid it well. Back at the farm we changed into our cowboy gear and tramped over to the yards where we fussed with water and gates. An hour later we halted in the shade and Loretta pointed to a granite outcrop about half way along a spur to the south of the house.

"That's where we're headed. So we'd better get moving."

I have to give it to Loretta. Climbing that mountain was no fun for anyone, but she hauled her great weight through the long grass and lantana bushes without a murmur. Because there were no tracks to follow, we sort of dragged ourselves from one level to the next. Not that it was true mountain climbing - more a steep, rugged pull - and at times we had to edge sideways to clear stands of granite. We drank lots of water and the higher we climbed the more we stopped for a breather. At one point when lantana blocked the path, Loretta suggested it was a waste of time and maybe we should return to the house. Maria and I swapped glances and shook our heads. We had come too far not to poke our noses into this cubby hole. With that we tied my pocket knife to a stick and hacked through the lantana. From there we emerged onto a narrow terrace.

"That's it, up to the left," Loretta said. "We need to approach it from the other side."

The face of the mountain was now steep and dangerous. Our boots dislodged pieces of granite that rattled down to the grass in the paddocks below. Carefully we edged towards the rock that was as big as a city office and almost as grey. Narrow wallaby tracks led under the overhang from one side and reappeared on the other. We crawled along one of the tracks, and when our faces were against the wall, Loretta seized my knife and dug into crevices searching for a chisel line. Five minutes went by and she had prodded every hole she could find. Nothing.

"You sure we're on the right mountain?" I said.

"Don't be silly, boy."

Maria had moved further along the rock and was dusting the surface with her fingers. "Look. There's an indent here, and it's been squared off."

I took the knife from Loretta and scratched along the indent. Loose pieces of stone trickled from behind the blade. "Somebody went to a lot of trouble to cover the hole," I said. After a few minutes I had exposed the wedge of rock that was the size of a house brick. "It's ready to come out," I called to Loretta.

"Just do it, boy."

I prised out the wedge to reveal a large cavity. In the dim light I could make out a few packages. I drew out the smallest one, a brown envelope, which Loretta untied awkwardly to expose the cards that she and my mother had exchanged years earlier. Loretta glanced at the cards then folded them into her shirt pocket. Seeing her sister's handwriting after all this time had clearly upset her. Her bottom lip trembled. "Go on, boy, what else is there?"

I pulled out the second packet which was a lumpy paper bag fastened with string. I shook it open to reveal two war medals on a ribbon. My mouth opened in amazement.

"Keep going, boy."

Reaching in, I dragged out a third, heavier package wrapped in oiled canvas. Slowly I unrolled the covering. The women gasped. A service revolver, black and menacing, lay in my hand. Tied to the barrel was another packet that I unfastened to reveal several rounds of ammunition. We stared at each other. I don't know what we expected, but it wasn't that.

I folded up the packages and stuffed them inside my shirt. "Come on. We'll study these things at the farm."

"Put the stone back first," Loretta said.

But Maria stopped me. "Was that all?"

Again I slid my arm into the hole and felt about. When my fingers touched something hard, I drew out the object and held it in my palm. It was the third

St Francis of Assisi medal, still shiny after years inside a rock.

We were gawking at it when I shoved it at Maria. "Here, this one's yours."

The girl flinched. "No, it wouldn't be right. It doesn't belong to us."

"Wrap it up with the gun, boy. We have to find out who owns these things."

After doing as ordered, I pushed the granite wedge into the hole and led the way down the mountain.

Back at the house we were in a state of disbelief. Once I had placed the gun, the war medals and St Francis on the table we sat around moodily drinking coffee, staring at the booty.

Finally Maria whispered, "What happens next?"

"Yes, who do we tell?" I said. "My guess is the revolver was Dad's from the war, and those are his medals. So why are they hidden in the rock? And what medals did Aunty Nell throw in the river years ago?"

"Maybe he won two lots of medals," Maria said unconvincingly.

"Well, that's possible, but on the climb down I've been thinking. I firmly believe Aunty Nell's mind had flipped. Because she wanted to close the book on him, she thought that by discarding his medals - even if they were fake - she would erase his memory. She was also making sure I got the message."

We were silent as we let this idea penetrate. For Maria and I the morning had uncovered pieces of a jigsaw that were baffling, but for Loretta we had dug up her past, and it was hurting.

"What do you make of it?" I asked her gently.

She fingered one of the war medals. "These look genuine to me, and maybe Jack hid them in the rock for safe keeping, though I can't imagine why. But the revolver, that's awful"... she shuddered... "Jack was supposed to have shot Maria and himself with it, and the whole lot went to the bottom of the ocean. What's it doing here?"

"It's here because Dad was innocent. This gun is the first hard evidence in his favour. He never shot anyone. Whoever killed Dad has killed Kevin Cleary."

When they stared at me, I told them what I had learned from Cleary, leaving out the ugliest parts of his story. I also recounted how Elsa had stolen the revolver in Brisbane then arranged for it to be collected by one of Cleary's mates. I finished by telling them that Cleary had been shot dead in Townsville and police suspected a service revolver.

"Do you notice one chamber is empty?" I said. "My guess is somebody fired it last week."

Loretta hurriedly blessed herself.

"Had you heard of the *freedom fee*?" I asked her.

"Not until recently."

"A lot of Italians were caught in the web. Even your family. At worst, they could be charged for bribery, though that's unlikely as no records were kept, and it's doubtful any of them hated Cleary enough to kill him. Which leaves us with one main suspect. And he was a taker, not a giver."

"Paulo?"

I nodded and said, "Would he have known about the cubby hole?"

"I'm not sure. I only went there with Carl or Maria."

"Well, he's the last of the gang, apart from Carl."

Maria riled. "My dad is *not* involved in this."

"Okay, where was he last Saturday night?"

"Jack, you're cruel. He was home watching TV. I can't believe you'd think he's a killer."

"Your dad is hiding something, Maria, and that's a bad sign."

When I held her glare, Loretta slammed the table causing the revolver and medals to jump. "That's enough, you pair. Carl does have his problems but he's not a criminal, Jack, and it was heartless to suggest it."

"Sorry."

"You don't look sorry."

"Then maybe I'm not. Everyone snaps at me when I ask about family. Carl is no saint, nor am I, but at least I'm open with these things."

"Jack please, I love my dad," Maria said unhappily. "I couldn't bear anything to happen."

Loretta touched the girl's face. "We all love him, child, and we'll make it our business to prove he's innocent. Isn't that right, Jack?"

I felt cornered. "Of course, provided he *is* innocent. Anyway, if it's any consolation Paulo is still the main suspect."

"Or the priest," Loretta said.

I sighed. "Yes, the priest though I can't see it."

There was a long pause as we stared at the revolver.

Maria recovered first. "So I guess next stop is the police."

"Yes, the gun needs to be handed over. If it was Dad's, they will have to reopen the case."

"That was twenty years ago," Maria said. "The leads will be cold. And we're only guessing it was the gun that killed Cleary."

"I don't know how they check these things. I'm not a cop. But I'm sure D.I. Morgan will talk to Elsa who was the last known person to touch it. I want to keep Dad's war medals. As for the St Francis, I guess that's for you to decide."

Loretta bit her lip. "It would belong to Paulo. He brought it back from Italy."

"Very well, Maria," I said, "you give it to him next time you're at the farm."

"No thanks," she winced. "That's a lover's medal. He might get the wrong idea. And after what you've told me, I'm not sure I can face him."

"That's fine, I'll do it. We still have a block of his cane to cut. But you can offload the gun when you drive into work tomorrow. Leave it at the police station, tell them where we found it and let them contact D.I. Morgan."

"There'll be lots of questions," she protested.

"I expect so."

She wasn't excited by the task, but nodded her head. We wrapped the revolver inside the cloth then dropped it into a shopping bag. After that we packed up and headed home.

CHAPTER 32

By now the harvest cut-out was less than two weeks away. The mills were crushing around the clock, and lost time had been recovered on the breakdowns. We still had cane to harvest at the Avolio farm, but I never got there. While hauling an empty bin along a gravel road near Pindi Pindi one morning, my Ford 4000 blew a tyre and rolled. As my ribs took a bruising, the boss ordered me onto light duties while the rest of the team kept steaming ahead. Although time off work might sound a lark, five enforced days in a shed bored me witless, so I rode across to Calen to see Father Burke who had some explaining to do.

When I arrived he was at the back of his presbytery, oiling a yabby pump. He glanced up in surprise.

"No work today, Jack?"

I lifted my shirt to reveal the bandages. "I rolled a tractor last week. They've given me a few days off."

"Want a refreshment?" he said.

"No, it's a bit early."

"So how can I help?"

"Well, Father, let's start with that drivel about you and the IRA."

"I was in the IRA," he objected. "Nasty business."

"I'm not saying you weren't a card-carrying member. What I meant was the crap about British soldiers forcing you to take a boat to Australia. You came here because the IRA needed a pipeline for crooks, so-called trainee priests and labourers for the vineyard. Then after six months they disappear with a new name and a new life. It was a clever racket, and you made good money."

"Lad, take care with allegations like that. In Ireland men die for less."

"It happens here too. Men like Guido."

He lowered the yabby pump onto a bench. "I need sustenance even if you don't."

"Help yourself, Father. I've got all day."

He led me into the rear of his presbytery where he opened the laundry fridge and selected a beer. After snapping, it open with the blade hanging by a cord, he perched on the back step as he'd done on the first day. I hefted a pineapple crate into the centre of the laundry and sat facing him.

When he had swigged half the can, I said, "You knew my parents. Why deny it when I asked?"

"Like I said, Jack…"

"You knew them alright, Father. You were the parish priest here. But you didn't marry them or your name would be on the wedding certificate. Why?"

"Okay, Jack, I did know them, and I should've married them, but I was in Townsville."

"Doing what? Collecting a shipment?"

"That or taking much-needed holidays."

"Father, you're hiding quite a story. You'd better open up."

He snorted. "And get myself killed like Cleary? You'll take a bullet too if you're not careful."

"Who are you afraid of?"

"I've lived thirty years on the edge of the law. There are people around who'd like to see me dead."

"Are you a real priest?" I asked bluntly.

"Yes, that part is true. In name anyway." The bounciness had gone out of him. He stared over my shoulder and spoke in a low voice. "Like I said, I was an orphan, and priesthood was the gateway to a better life. The downside was that my sponsors were not about to waste my education on petty crime. So they groomed me in immigration law. After eighteen months the IRA shipped me to Queensland where I sought a job as parish priest in a small town. I failed to get that posting but worked as a curate in Fortitude Valley where I did meet Kevin Cleary. We meant nothing to each other. I was an insignificant junior priest and he a junior cop. Over time he shifted to Townsville and I was transferred to this diocese. After the death of the parish priest in Kolijo the bishop offered me this vacancy which I accepted. For almost two years, right up until your parents were engaged, I worked on my invisibility, the mild-mannered priest in an obscure little town. Then one day I received the letter I dreaded."

"Dreaded? You loved your part in the racket."

He frowned. "May I go on?"

"Try and stick to the facts."

"My chiefs in Belfast wanted me to start the work I was trained for. Using a code we had prepared beforehand, they told me the migrant's name, his occupation, the ship he would be on, and its date of arrival. Nothing else was given, and I never asked questions. At this end I completed the paperwork that allowed me to accept responsibility for whoever they sent. And it wasn't a tough ask as none of these boys dared offending in their new country. The IRA has bloody long arms."

I stopped him again. His revised narrative was flowing too easily, a fresh angle but the same drill. "Father, when I knocked on your door almost six months ago, I was a total stranger. You knew where Carl Rossini and his daughter Maria lived. But you fed me a pitch about how you handed Joe O'Reilly over to British soldiers in return for a secret passage to Australia. That was a drunken fantasy. Is this more of the same?"

He drained the first beer, flattened the empty can with his shoe, then angrily opened another. "I hate this feckin life. Afraid of my own shadow, and which feckin shadow is mine anyway? That of a parish priest, or smuggler of Irish filth? I concocted the story about the British soldiers because I wanted you to believe I was someone. People look into my eyes and see a hopeless drunk. Well, I was a good priest once. Yes, that's right. In the early days I was God-fearing and decent. I admit Joe O'Reilly never came to my church. My parents were never in the IRA. Like millions of other wretches they died of the flu. Because the homes of my aunts were bursting at the seams, I was sent to an orphanage where the nuns schooled me in the three R's. And yes, I was aware of little orphan Jack Bellamy and how your parents were killed in Moreton Bay. I knew all about your father and Guido Avolio. I knew who your mother was and how her beauty drove men to fight each other. God forgive me, but I also lusted after her on terrible nights. Tell me who didn't? I never voiced my feelings, even to the Lord, but I am a man for heaven's sake. I joined the priesthood to escape poverty, not live like a hermit."

His voice now hoarse, I thought he was on the point of breaking down. Instead, he ran his tongue over wet lips. "Each month I received a treat other men dream about. Aye, it was a treat because good Catholics attend the confessional regular as clockwork. My highlight was Maria's confession. I drew out of her sins she would never tell her mother."

I broke into his reverie. "Father, did she ever mention she'd had sex with Guido."

"I can't reveal those things."

"She was my mother and they're both dead."

"She told me of her battle," he said after a pause. "When Guido demanded we try for an annulment, I asked her if she had been unfaithful. I said that if she didn't answer truthfully, she would be committing a mortal sin. She swore upon the name of the Virgin that she and Guido were never intimate. She told how they had touched and explored, and occasionally - when they were a bit older - Guido had tried to force himself on her, but she refused. She said the gift of a blessed marriage would never be theirs if they slept together."

"What about with my father, Jack Bellamy? Carl said he'd *had his way* with Mum before they were married."

"Carl got it wrong, as he often did. Maria told me about her relationship with Jack. He pushed her further - *unbearably* I remember she had said - and his personality was stronger, but she remained a virgin to the day of her wedding."

Although uneasy about probing my mother's sex life, I was determined to press on. "Kevin Cleary said that after Guido's death, he took Dad into the watch house and forced him to make a deal."

Father Burke squinted at me. "What sort of deal?"

"Sexual. Cleary could have Maria whenever he chose in return for a finding that Guido's death was accidental. Cleary talked of his love-hate lust for her."

"I never heard of such a deal, and she never mentioned it."

"Do you think it's possible?"

"Although your mother was beautiful, I never saw her flaunt herself. Cleary was a crass man and usually got his way, but I can't imagine Jack ever trading Maria. No matter the price."

Behind Father Burke I could see down the hallway to where the church's stained-glass window was framed by the front door. Soft yellows, reds and blues filtered through the window and spilt onto a young lilly pilly that was growing from an earthen pot. Piety flowed from the image of the Holy Family and the small leafy tree, but Father Burke sat with his back to it, drinking from the third can he had fetched himself.

"Father, why do you think Guido was killed?"

"Ah, I knew that question was coming."

"Did it have anything to do with Dad?"

"He was the excuse we needed."

"Who needed?"

Abruptly he grabbed my arm like I was the ancient mariner. His eyes were bright. "Jack, can't you feckin see? Cleary is dead and I am next. I've been a damn awful priest and a hopeless liar, and now it's finished." He released his grip, but not the watery glare. "I've always had my snout in the trough. And why? Feckin greed. I wanted to have good things. I wanted to be respected, be someone in this town. But I'm none of that. Good old flat-footed, bumbling Father Burke. To be sure, I earned cash from the racket, and I took some grand holidays, but I was a nobody. Living out my days... accepting my lot... until Cleary poked his dirty nose in. I already knew about his extortion racket from Italian confessions, but I said nothing, it was none of my business. Cleary guessed I had twigged to it, and warned me to keep my mouth shut. He also said he knew about the Irish illegals. He was only fishing for evidence, but he was a cruel, vicious fecker. Things changed when he returned to Townsville in '43 and joined the military police. He hadn't been in the army a month when he collared an Irishman serving with the Australians. Somehow the Irishman let slip he had a secret. That was too much for Cleary who beat the secret out of him. Next thing Cleary was at my door demanding a cut in the migration racket. I said fair is fair, and asked for a cut in his. He agreed, though not before roughing me up, and just to keep me honest, he forced me to sign a paper. Typical of Cleary, he kept the only copy of that document, which had three signatures - himself, Paulo and me."

Father Burke opened a fourth can of beer, poured some down his throat then reached behind the tubs for a bottle of clear liquid. When he drew the cork I recognised the smell of an illicit still that one of the gardeners kept at the orphanage. From experience the stuff was white lightning. After topping up the can he took a pull and shook like a wet dog.

His voice had changed. "One afternoon Guido came roun' to tell me about his 'nulment idea, and stumbled upon Cleary and me in the church. Cleary reckon'd I was takin' too much of the *freedom fee*, and I complained he was takin' all my Irish payments. Guido heard 'nough to recognise a racket and wanted a share of the money. Cleary cut him in, but only on condition he force Bellamy out of the distric'."

Father Burke's eyes were like malfunctioning search lamps. One minute up at me, the next on the floor. A bead of saliva had formed on his lips. "I know what you're thinkin', lad. Why pick on Jack Bellamy? Why be so tough on your father? Well, he brought the roof down on himself. He was too feckin good for the likes of us. Poor, foolish Guido bragged his plan was a winner. He reckon'd that once Jack heard 'bout Maria's treachery, he would self destruc'. Sure, Jack had changed from the early days, but it wasn't war memories makin' his life so wretch'd. It was the shit that Cleary, Guido, Paulo, me - and even Carl Rossini - were dumpin' on him. But Guido got it wrong. Perhaps Jack would've been happier fightin' the Japs, but he wasn't handin' Maria over to a gang of brutes."

I recalled young Maria's words at one of our first meetings. She said Jack had become moody after the war and was often heard sobbing at night. While her family blamed the nightmares on his time in a prison camp, they never took into account the five-man vendetta against him.

Father Burke was hooking into the grog. He drank white rum straight from the bottle - one swig of rum, one beer - and his hands shook. At this pace he would be dead inside a month. No need for a bullet.

He turned and squinted.

"Jack, what I tell you stays inside these walls, eh?"

"How many times have I heard that?"

"Heard what?"

"Never mind. Go on."

"One day the three of us sat together - right here it was, right in this feckin laundry - and worked out how we'd get Jack and Guido to go huntin' together."

"Which three of you?"

"Me, Paulo and Cleary. Anyhow, good huntin' in the hills. Lots of wild pig. Good eatin' if you catch 'em young. So off they go, but - and here's the crafty bit - Paulo had nicked your dad's rifle. That was easy 'cos it was kept at Carl's place in a big cupboard with other guns, and one night while Paulo was over visitin', he just feckin nicked it. So your dad and Guido had only one rifle, but nobody else knew we had the other one."

"Loretta did."

"Did she now? I always said she's a smart one, but she needs to wass herself."

"Anyway, what next?"

Father Burke tried to sit and lurched sideways, dropping the bottle of rum. It hit the floor and shattered. At once, he was down on his knees picking up the shards of glass in his fingers. Blood from his knees and hands ran across the floor with the rum. It was suddenly beyond him. Covering his face with his hands he began to weep.

I put my arm round his shoulders. "Hey, Father. It's okay. Sit back and finish the story. I'll clean up the mess."

"I've done a bad thing. Sweet Mary, I'll rot in hell."

"Why is that?"

He garbled something about the mountain and a gun.

"Please, Father, was it Cleary or Paulo? Just say the name."

He sobbed. "No, it was two of us. We're the guilty feckers."

With that he began rocking back and forth, crying like a child. I found a pan and brush to sweep up the broken glass, then I hosed out the laundry. Although the place reeked like a distillery, it was now clean of blood. When I returned to Father Burke, I wondered what I could do for him. Apart from the blood and rum trickling down his trousers, his face was a mess from where he had sobbed into his hands. He had been so close to revealing his secret. My fear was that whoever had got to Cleary would silence the priest, but I had no choice as he was now a shivering, crying wreck. I quietly let myself out the back, closing the door behind me.

CHAPTER 33

Concerned about Father Burke's mental state, I had planned to return to the presbytery next morning, but the boss left a message in the shed demanding a full crew for the remaining paddocks along St Helens Creek. As a concession to my bruised ribs, he said his wife would help push the empty bins onto my trailer. Having seen the woman lift a derailed bin one-handed, I accepted his offer and joined the team at daylight. Over each of the following days I called at the presbytery, but Father Burke was never in. No messages, no car, nothing. I had no alternative but to shut him from my mind. When cut-out day arrived on Thursday, the gang was in high spirits like the last day of school. At two-thirty the harvester slashed through the final row of cane, and we followed years of tradition by hanging our ragged boots and hats on the last bin. Meanwhile, cane locos from upriver rumbled past with more boots and hats, and the loco drivers sounded their horn at every gang they passed.

Late in the afternoon we serviced the machinery for the last time then helped the boss's missus unload a carton of beer from the rear of the ute. After draining the beer we were driven home to change for the cut-out binge at the farmhouse that night. Laid on by grateful farmers, the party was for everyone who had played a role in bringing in the harvest. The only two absent faces were Paulo and his son Sam who, according to know-all Wacko, didn't appear because they were at the mill directors' binge at Farleigh. And of course Maria wasn't present as her father's cane was harvested by a different contractor in a different group.

Cut-out parties were the curtain raiser to the big event, the harvest dance. All the sugar towns had some kind of festival to observe the end of the season. Some of the Italian and Spanish mobs further north held religious processions to thank the Almighty, but at Calen our celebrations were more earthy - food, drink and dance.

Saturday night arrived clear and warm with the hint of an approaching summer. Flying foxes swarmed soundlessly through the darkness and stars glittered ahead of the humidity rolling in with the northerlies. I waited at the gate for Jimbo and his panel van, tossing stones at the toads that hopped out on their foreign invasion. The harvest's ending had left an emptiness. It was like something you had wanted to be finished, but once it was over you were unhappy: the mornings with a purpose, the mates in your gang, the tall rows of mature cane. I would miss all that. And what lay ahead? I had tried not to think beyond the harvest dance because I always believed I would solve my parents' mystery then send down roots with a special woman who'd bear me a clutch of kids. Having come so close to both endeavours but failing, I decided reluctantly to head north where recruiting was underway for the construction of the Townsville to Greenvale nickel line, a job that was tough, dirty and relentless like the one I was leaving. The lifestyle was something I could handle and there was no point hanging around Calen when family like Carl Rossini couldn't see the back of me quickly enough. Maria was the most awesome girl I had laid eyes on, but - kinship aside - she was bound to Sam, and the background to Dad and Mum's life had become impossibly complex, hidden under layers of malice and deceit. Not to mention the discovery of a stillborn twin. To be honest, the view from the clock tower was fading into the gloom each passing day.

    I felt like the toad I'd clouted with a rock when Jimbo arrived and bundled me in with the three sisters who were passing round a silver flask. After taking a mouthful of rum and Tessa's left breast had nudged my arm, the fit of miseries evaporated. Minutes later we pulled into the bright lights of Calen where a crowd swept along the footpaths in a colourful boozy river. Big Jimbo motored slowly past the hotel then pulled into a no-parking zone at Cohen's Hall. He unlatched the rear door and the sisters and I tumbled out like puppies.

    "Hey Jimbo, you coming with us?" one of the girls called as we linked arms for an assault on the hall.

    Jimbo shook his curly head. "Dat dancin's a game for crazies. I come for da two-up."

    I think Jimbo had a point. I'm no dancer, as I've noted before, and my technique with women is ordinary but the sisters that night weren't after technique, they wanted fun. And fun they had – off the floor and on. However, despite my flaws I was kept hopping and bouncing, especially by Tessa, the girl with a wide smile and breeder's body.

    But dazzling as the sisters were, the planet I sought in my heavens was Maria. When she finally arrived my pulse quickened. The girl was a genuine Italian starlet: the dark hair framing a beautiful face, the simple but elegant dress, the classical figure. The only downside was boyfriend Sam hanging off her arm. And he wasn't just hanging there, he was the Siamese twin. I had a real dilemma. The sisters were twirling around me like a carousel and the one girl I wanted had a limpet attached. God knows how I would prise the bastard free.

It would appear God was alert to the moment because shortly afterwards fate intervened. Sister Three and I were tearing across the floor in the Barn Dance when the strap on her shoe broke. It was like a blow-out on the freeway. Suddenly she was out of control, down on her fairing under a collapsed ankle. Meanwhile, up ahead Sam was so absorbed in his own galaxy that he didn't see the wreck coming. One instant he was vertical, the next on his back dragging Maria into the squealing heap. Unable to spot Sister Three, I dived for Maria and pulled her free, but she was scarcely grateful as she thought I was the rogue dancer who had caused it all. She also glowed from a splendid exhibition of flashy lace knickers; side view, front view and a clever inversion to finish. In the meantime, Sam was using the winded sister's chest to lever himself upright, but she was in no mood for his discourtesy and smacked him where it hurt. Sam grunted like a sick lion and flopped back to the deck. At this point Tessa strode into the melee to rescue her sister and the shoe, and I was left standing with Maria in the centre of an appreciative audience.

"Wow, Maria. That was some pile-up."

Her eyes blazed. "It was dreadful. And let me go, I'm not a cripple."

"Sorry," I said, releasing her arm. "Do you need to tidy up or something?"

"I'm fine." With that she stormed off to the washrooms trailed by a hobbling Sam.

The crowd settled back to the dancing and I saw Sister Three, shoeless, going at it on the dance floor with another bloke. I had to admire the girls. They pumped out more energy than the Callide Powerhouse and were country happy with it. Meanwhile, feeling a bit deflated, I loitered near the washrooms waiting for Maria to emerge, which she did fifteen minutes later. She had her dignity back in place but was still attached to Sam, although he had a distinct limp and a gentler hold of her arm.

Fixing on my best smile, I stepped into their path. "Sorry about that, Maria. The crash was my fault. I was dancing too fast with the girl when her shoe broke."

"It's already behind me, Jack. Accidents happen."

"Lunatics should dance out on the grass," Sam butted in.

I turned to him. "Why are you walking funny, Sam?"

"That bitch."

"You can't blame the girl. Your elbow was crushing her tit."

He rubbed his groin. "If she was a man, I would've retaliated. Crack her nuts and see how she reacts."

"Fair comment. Shame if the damage is permanent."

"Jack, stop it!" Maria said.

"Sorry, Maria. I was being sympathetic. Poor Sam can hardly walk."

"I'm not poor bloody Sam," he growled. Apart from the limp he had smudged his terylene shirt and his curls had lost their bounce.

"Sam, why don't you rest your thing while I dance with Maria?"

"Be buggered."

"No, that's okay, Sam," Maria said resignedly. "I want to talk to Jack about the farm."

Sam blinked at her. "What farm?"

"The Rise and Shine. Where his parents stayed after they married."

"I'd appreciate that," I said.

Although Sam snarled under his breath, he didn't have a choice. He hobbled off to a bench against the wall while I smiled at Maria and held her for the Gypsy Tap. She ungripped my hand and said, "Relax, it's not a horse race." When the music started, she took the classic dancer's pose and led me into the first of the waltzes. We coasted round the hall and although my memory of the dance is mostly blurred - snatched words about the farm and the booty we found - I do recall saying, "If only things were different."

"Why is that?" she asked cautiously.

"If things were different, I could say that I've... well... loved you since laying eyes on you."

Her fingernails dug into my arm. "But nothing is different. It is as it is."

"Humour me a minute."

"No, not even one second."

"Maria, remember the kiss the other night at the farm?"

"I won't answer that, Jack."

"Well, it was a lover's kiss."

She dropped her face. "Oh, stop it, please. I felt sorry for you, and now I wish I hadn't."

When the music ended I led her across to the bench where Sam held centre court. On his left the sister responsible for the injury talked him through his pain while Tessa sat close on his right. Meantime a couple of mates hung about giving free medical advice. When we arrived Maria chased the sisters with a blistering look, followed by the two mates.

Sam rose gingerly to his feet. "So how's the farm?" he demanded.

"Good," Maria and I said in unison.

Sam was no fool. "Those sisters are your style, Jacko. Go and do your farm stuff with them."

At this moment all three sisters had returned to the floor, all barefoot, and having a ball.

"Will do, Sam. Those girls yearn for real men... you know, mountain men."

"Or dead beat haul-out drivers," he said.

"Nothing wrong with a haul-out driver. We're the blokes who deliver the harvest, come hell or high water."

"That's right. The job that needs no brain. But what do you expect from the son of Jack Bellamy?"

The bastard had punched me onto the ropes. "How do you mean?"

"Shit, man, don't act dumb. Your dad flogs his rocks around like an alley cat, then when he tires of that he makes off with Guido's woman; yeah, you know who I mean, your mum. And when he's had enough of playing hubby, he goes on a shooting spree. Not a great career start for his only son."

"You're a gutless wonder, Sam. My dad's long dead, and you know damn all about what happened.

You've lived as an overfed ponce since birth, and you think it gives you the right to be a prick."

A crowd gathered as Maria hopped from foot to foot. "Shhh, shhh. This is childish. Cool down."

Sam pushed his face into mine. "The facts are clear, Jacko. Call me what you like, but you're the gutless wonder. Can't face up to the truth about your old man."

I lined up to smack him, but someone shouted, "Outside, boys! Get 'em outside!"

I was about to head through the door when the thought struck me. This was Dad and Guido all over again; Bellamy fighting Avolio for the Rossini girl. I took a steadying breath. "Okay, Sam, let's cut the crap. Take me up to the site of Guido's death."

"I would but I can't. I'm fertilizing cane all week."

I opened my hands and turned to the crowd. "Is that a dumb excuse, or what?"

At this point Maria broke in. Her voice trembled. "Take him, Sam, please. He... he has to go sometime. The family owes him that."

Sam was now the one on the ropes.

"We owe him? Him... Bellamy? Alright, tomorrow at eight, at Carl's farm."

"You'll have to make it Monday," I said. "I've got Mass tomorrow."

After that I let them be. I mucked about with the sisters and shortly after eleven Jimbo stuck his head through the door and said he was leaving in ten minutes. Although the girls were disappointed at the early call, we trudged out the door and headed for Jimbo's panel van. Maria appeared beside me.

"Jack," she said urgently, "Can I have a moment?"

"Sure."

I released the girls and followed Maria into the shadows.

She stood in front of me, her eyes wide. "Be careful on Monday."

I laughed. "Sammy couldn't hurt a bandicoot."

She was in no mood for laughing. "Jack, listen to me. The farm boys get nervous whenever they ride near the place. There's something bad about it."

"I'll look after myself, Maria. Nothing remains there but an old memory. Once I've seen the spot, I'll be fine."

The pulse at her neck beat in the faint light. "Jack, when you're finished there, will you do me a favour?"

"What's that?"

"Leave here. Leave Calen forever."

"No, Maria. I said I love you."

She was angry. "That's being cruel… hurtful to everyone. We can never fall in love."

"Yes, we can."

"No, Jack, please." She fought the tears. "We mustn't ever… not ever, please."

I said to her, "Kiss me, Maria."

She stared at me helplessly then flung her arms round my neck and kissed me hard. With that she was gone, running back into the hall.

In the rear of the panel van on the way home the girls were in a playful mood, but I had sobered up. I know there's a saying, three birds in hand is better than one in the bush, but Maria's face - the frightened eyes, the soft lips - were etched on my brain. I'd like to pretend differently, but to the three sisters I was a disappointing mountain man.

CHAPTER 34

I did go to Mass next morning in Calen, which opened the eyes of good folk at the caravan park. Loretta of course wasn't there as her church was St Patrick's in Mackay, but Maria and her old man did attend. The pair were already snug in the family pew when I arrived, seating myself up in the back with the rest of the lukewarm Catholics. Father Burke wasn't his usual unctuous self, instead he was a right mess. His face was chalky grey, covered in fine scratches from where he had rubbed his glassed hands. Twice he stumbled on the altar to the alarm of the congregation, and at one anxious moment in the Offertory forgot his lines. Like everyone else that morning I shuffled up to communion where, as I took the host, I stared into Father's eyes but the pupils were blank, unseeing holes. In truth the man presented less like a priest than a sheep awaiting the butcher's knife.

Despite the priest's confusion, Mass went quickly enough. Following the last blessing everyone crowded for the door and fresh air. Maria and her father Carl waited for me under a stand of cedar that shaded the western porch. To their left several grevillea and a bed of late-flowering marigolds separated the carpark from the presbytery. Father Burke was nowhere to be seen.

Carl beckoned to me, his face grim. I ignored him and smiled at Maria who touched my sleeve with one finger. "Hello Jack."

Carl grunted. "Maria has told me about the gun in the cubby hole."

"Yes. Who put it there?"

His broad nose wrinkled like I had tossed him a rat. "I wouldn't know, Jack, and even if I did, I'd think twice about telling you."

"Carl, that's the problem here. Everybody has a secret that's causing a pile of grief. You've known all along Dad never shot Guido. If you'd been straight with me, we'd be sitting over a coffee right now smiling at each other. Not facing off like two block-headed wops."

"Your father was not innocent. He did shoot Guido."

"Were you there when the gun was fired?"

"No. Only the two of them were."

"Well, that's where you're telling fibs. A third man pulled the trigger, and you know it. But…" I said before he could jump in, "…you may not have understood the reason. Guido was killed because he knew too much, and he was greedy. He was a small thug in a local racket, something called the *freedom fee*." When Carl flinched, I continued. "So you do know about the extortion money. You might've kept your nose clean, Carl, but your silence makes you guilty. You're as corrupt as your pals."

"You smug little bastard. You don't know what it's like to be threatened with five years in an internment camp. If we hadn't paid up, our families would've been thrown behind wire. And why? Because of our olive skin and curly hair. Is that a crime? Answer me that, smart arse."

"That's not the crime, but if men like you had spoken out, Guido would still be alive, and so too my parents."

Maria eased her old man round to face her. "Come on, Dad, we agreed to work with Jack on this. We haven't made a good start."

Carl gazed into his daughter's eyes then steeled himself for his next words. "Sorry, Jack. I... we... I owe you an apology. Come back to the farm. We'll have coffee and talk it through."

I don't recall staggering at Carl's unexpected apology but it caught me off guard. I had barely recovered my senses when a bright orange glow lit the trees around us. I turned to see the presbytery lifting off its stumps as though by a giant hand, then settle back into a cloud of smoke, dust and fire. The old timber building was an inferno in seconds.

"Holy Mother of God!" Carl exclaimed. For the next minute Carl, myself and a handful of parishioners ran about like crazy ants. Despite the urgency, we were clueless what to do next. There was a tap beside the church but no hose, there was a hose under the bell tower but no fittings, and the water dish at the back of the church was for thirsty dogs. Maria's brain recovered first and she sent for the fire brigade while Carl broke open a storeroom searching for hoses and buckets.

It was then I remembered Father Burke.

Grabbing a hessian sack from one of the men, I covered my head and ran to the laundry at the rear of the presbytery. Through the open door I could see blue flames snaking in rivers from the remains of a large glass container. More flames poured from every door and window. Taking a deep breath, I rushed into the laundry where I found Father Burke sprawled on the floor. A mass of blood covered the back of his head and coils of flame licked at his flesh. Seizing him by the belt, I carried him out through the doorway and into his lettuce garden.

He was barely conscious.

"Father Burke, can you hear me. It's Jack Bellamy."

"Aye, Jack," he whispered. "I said I'd be next."

"Who did it?"

When he fumbled for his waistband I thought he wanted one last, heroic pee. "Here, Jack. The paper's down here."

I dug my hand into his trousers and pulled out a yellowed square of paper. When I unfolded the sheet I saw it was Cleary's *freedom fee* document, containing the brief statement and four signatories. Of the original party, Paulo and Father Burke were the only two still alive, and the latter's grip on life was slipping fast.

"Did Paulo do this, Father? Talk to me. Did Paulo light the fire?"

Father Burke started mumbling. I bent closer. "Forgive me, Lord, for I have sinned for which I am truly sorry…"

"Sorry for what, Father?"

"Lord, forgive me… Jack, are you there? Please, Jack, I'm sorry… it was me. I… I wanted Guido's death. It was never your father. He was a good man." Father Burke's voice was fading. "I had to shoot him. He swore to tell the bishop. I… I couldn't have that. They would've killed me."

"Who would've killed you?'

"IRA. They kill everybody. And… and Cleary and Paulo stole the rifle. I carried it up the mountain."

"Who pulled the trigger, Father? Was it Cleary?"

"Cleary and Paulo… always covered each other."

"Yes, I know that. It had to be Cleary. He was the cruel one."

"So was Paulo."

"And what about you, Father?"

"He told me the gun wasn't loaded. But I didn't care. I shot Guido." He fumbled for my hand. "Destroy that paper. It's all over now."

"Not before I catch Paulo."

"No. No more killing."

"I'm not a killer, Father, but Paulo is. I have to stop him."

"God be with you, son." Then he relaxed among the lettuce. "God help me," he whispered and was gone.

I was aware of men running towards me. Among them was Carl. I shoved the document into my pocket.

"Did he light the fire?" Carl said.

"No. The poor bugger had it coming, but not like that."

We stood in a circle around his body. Somebody checked his pulse and another covered his face with the hessian sack.

"We can't stay here," Carl said as bottles continued to explode inside the building. "It's too dangerous. Come across to the roadway."

Feeling the need to do something religious, I knelt and awkwardly made the sign of the cross over the priest's body. Despite his illicit money, there was nothing to show for his time on earth: the shoes that needed mending, the frayed trouser cuffs, the shirt patterned in beer stains. For all his faults, however, he was still entitled to his one-on-one with God.

Climbing to my feet, I was about to follow Carl when a man in a suit stepped up beside me. It was Detective Inspector Morgan from Townsville.

"Crikey, you fellas are on the ball," I muttered.

"But not quick enough, Bellamy. You must be a trainee undertaker, such an instinct for death. Cleary was barely cold and you were there. Now the priest. I'll get a fright if you knock at my door."

"His death had nothing to do with me, sir. I was at Mass this morning with these other people. We were standing over there talking when bang, the priest's still went up."

"How did you know he had a still?"

"Can't you smell it? Anyway, sir… you beat the fire brigade."

He took his time studying me. "If you want to know, Bellamy, I have good reason to be here. The priest's story had holes you could drive a truck through. He and his mate Paulo were nowhere near the so-called house for visiting priests in Townsville. Why did he lie? Odd thing for a holy man, among other odd things…" his voice trailed off. I wasn't buying in, though he gave me every chance. "So it was these little puzzles that led me to Calen. I was a half-hour late for the priest, and there's no sign of Paulo. I guess that's my next job - after tidying up here - to find Paulo. Following that, Mr Bellamy, you and I will have a serious chat." He glanced in his notebook. "Two o'clock tomorrow at the Calen police station. Understood?"

"Yes sir, I'll be there."

Relieved to escape, I climbed on my bike and followed Carl and Maria back to their farmhouse.

CHAPTER 35

After digging out fresh clothes for me from a bag of Sam's cast-offs (something about donations for St Vincent de Paul), Maria fussed in the kitchen while I showered and dressed. The clothes fitted perfectly, although I felt like a goosed-up Puck on a quiet Sunday. Strolling onto the verandah, I found Carl already seated at a wicker table. When he saw me he started, then pointed to a chair. A major change had overcome Carl since leaving the church. He was like a Michelin Man whose skin has been punctured. The bent woolly head and the gnarled hands toying with the sugar bowl spoke of a man who has been cast adrift from his mooring of twenty years. But remorse was the flip side of a confession, and he was letting nobody near the coin. At the church Maria had forced him to admit he'd always known of Dad's innocence on the mountain, and he'd mumbled an apology. However, his second grievance - that Dad was responsible for his sister's death - was buried deep, and he wasn't shifting ground on that.

Maria spread out the breakfast dishes on the table then disappeared to her room where she spent an eternity.

"We'd better start eating," Carl grumbled, spearing a slice of bacon.

Just then Maria emerged in a change of clothes. In my preoccupation with recent events I almost missed something remarkable. Maria had chosen a sleeveless dress to wear at the table. Like a fool my eyes locked onto her bare shoulder where the scar, naked against such perfection, was an ugly blemish. She winced.

"You look great," I said contritely.

Her eyes were wet. "Thanks, Jack. How are the eggs? They're from our farm."

But I hadn't finished. "Maria, you look wonderful in that dress."

Grizzly old Carl raised his head from the plate. "Give it a break, lad."

"No sir, I mean it. Don't you think that dress suits her?"

For the first time in years Carl peered at his daughter and saw she had exposed her flaw to a stranger. His compliment was heartfelt. "She is a beautiful girl. Always been my princess... always brave, and thoughtful."

Maria rose from her chair and kissed him. "Stop it, Dad. This is embarrassing," and brushed aside a tear.

After that we ate in silence. It wasn't until we were into our second pot of coffee I raised the dreaded subject. "We have to trap Paulo. He's behind all this." I pulled out the sheet of paper and handed it to Carl. "Three of those four men are dead. It only leaves Paulo. He and Father Burke rifled Cleary's house a few weeks ago looking for this document. I'd say Paulo guessed that Father Burke had found it, so with one match to the distillery up goes the paper and the priest. And I have no doubt he lit the fire because Father said he was expecting it. Did anyone see Paulo in the church?"

"I saw him talking with the priest before Mass but that's not unusual," Carl said. "He's an occasional church-goer."

"I'm one of those too, Carl, but I wouldn't set fire to a man's house."

"No? Look at the trouble your father caused…" he began then corrected himself. "Sorry, Jack. You were saying?"

"Hold on, Carl. My father caused what?"

"I've said I'm sorry. Let's move on."

I forced him to look at me. "Carl, you've got this canker eating away in your belly, and the canker's name is Jack Bellamy. I'm supposed to believe you hated Jack because he stole your sister off Guido then married her, which somehow resulted in her death. Sure, you and Guido were mates but to hate my father so much? Every card is now on the table, except yours and Paulo's. You say, let's move on. Show your hand so that we can."

After the briefest hesitation Carl pushed away the sugar bowl, locked his fingers on the table and spoke in a fierce monotone. Maria and I lowered our cutlery.

CHAPTER 36
CARL ROSSINI

By early 1938 the three musketeers were no longer youngsters exploring the district on pushbikes. Carl and Guido earned their living on their parents' farms, and Maria had found a job at Wilson's store in Calen. Jack arrived a quarter of the way through the year to run a school that was nine kilometres from town on the bank of a narrow, mountain-fed stream. Canefields chequered the level, fertile land behind the tennis court, while more farms on the opposite bank merged into the distant rainforest. Since the freshly painted, single-room school was a short distance from the Rossini farm, the Rossinis often boarded the new teacher. While this arrangement suited everyone in the dry months, it was impractical in summer when monsoonal rains flooded the causeway linking the farm and school. On the night of his arrival at the Calen Railway Station - the only place with a lamp burning - the station master, in pyjamas and slippers, directed Jack to the Avolio farmhouse which stood safely above flood level although five kilometres from the school via an all-weather road.

It didn't take long for Jack to be noticed. Although his charm and good looks helped unlock the tight community, he had other assets. He was an amateur boxer, he was skilled at rugby league, and he owned the smartest motorbike in the district; a 500cc Norton International. Carl Rossini was among the first Italians to make Jack welcome. Since childhood, when an uncle from Ayr had ridden into the farm on a Moto Guzzi, Carl had secretly nurtured a passion for bikes. He could name all the winners of the Isle of Man TT, and when he first sighted Jack's Norton he was able to recount its pedigree, including the historic 1932 win when Stanley Woods, the Irish Dasher, riding a black International M30 reached 78 mph to beat Wal Handley on a Rudge. Carl had hugged a crystal set to his ears until the early hours of the morning listening to the race details, and although it was the closest he ever got to a track, he still shivered with excitement at the memory. It was no surprise that within three months he and Jack had cemented a friendship. On warm afternoons with the sun low and the children gone, the two men sat on the school verandah and talked motorbikes. In time Jack propped the Norton on a centre-stand, and they began to tinker. Carl quickly showed his mechanic's touch when in the space of two hours he stripped and reset the faulty carburettor. Next he toyed with the rear suspension, and a few weeks later rebuilt the exhaust to harness more thrust. Those afternoons became the highlight of Carl's life.

"I remember one evening standing outside the school gates after Jack had set off for the Avolio house. It was late, and I ought to be getting home, but I listened to the bike until I heard it climbing the far side of Murray Creek. My ear was tuned to the exhaust note, waiting for a missed beat, and I imagined myself in pit lane servicing one of the great racing bikes of the era. I recall thinking I was not a poor farm boy, I had greatness in me. Given the chance, I would make my fortune." He snorted at the recollection. "So much for flying too close to the sun."

Jack and Carl's companionship grew steadily. Unless Jack was at football or Carl busy on the farm, they met in the school grounds where they exchanged ideas on bike performance. Carl challenged Jack with his knowledge of mechanics while Jack spoke of seconds gained through better riding techniques. As the weeks passed, Jack took the bike across to the farm workshop where Mamma Rossini invited him to stay for dinner.

"If Jack noticed Maria in this time," Carl said, "he never mentioned it. We only ever talked bikes. Papa would throw his hands in the air at our endless prattle and threaten to lock us in the shed. I suppose by now I had grown out of the three musketeers and was looking for new pursuits. Outwardly though, little had changed in the house since we were kids; a crowd of noisy Italians - Guido and Nonna included - gathered round the table, stabbing the air with our forks as we talked. I think Jack thrived on it as he had come from a small family, and remember we weren't play-acting for his benefit, we were genuinely welcoming an outsider to our home. All the same, I don't recall if Jack and Guido ever chatted together. They might've done, but it wasn't anything to be noted."

Carl explained that during this period the expectation was that childhood friends, Guido and Maria, would go on to marry. In any case Jack appeared to have little time for socialising as he was busy with teaching, football and his precious motorbike. Five months into the new year he formed a club of bike owners who were keen to show off their machines. While some of the men were social riders taking their girlfriends on pillion, Jack set the pace for the others on his Norton. The club met Sunday afternoons twice a month at Tocko's farm where a track had been cut through the trees and planks bolted together for rough benches. As bikes roared along the road towards the track, Jack would first turn in the opposite direction to collect Carl at the farm gate then race the slower bikes to Tocko's. With each bike he passed he saluted cheerfully and the riders returned the wave. In the pits - a flat area cleared of bush - Carl and Jack formed a close team, tuning the bike between races that were one-on-one skirmishes in a series of elimination rounds. If Jack lost a race, which he rarely did, Carl at once lifted the bike on its stand and attacked the engine with spanners.

As it happened, Carl was the only Rossini to show an interest in the Norton. Loretta in her final years of school preferred horses and was surprised that her brother knew anything of bikes, much less had a passion for them. Her older sister Maria, conditioned by Italian tradition, was directed into home making, and husband-to-be Guido spent his weekends tilling the farm with brother Paulo or chasing sweetlip and trout on the reef.

The term holidays were fast approaching when one afternoon at the track, Carl lowered his tools and pulled Jack to one side.

"Have you heard of the Townsville Speedway Club?" he asked.

"No. Who are they?"

"Just as the name says, but they're a good club. Quite big, well respected. Anyway, they're holding a 10th anniversary race to mark their first meeting."

"Where's this happening?"

"At the showground in Townsville."

"Old showground, old bikes. Doesn't sound much fun."

"It'll be fun, Jack. They're racing all kinds of bikes. Three different classes and sidecars."

Jack picked at a stone caught in his tyre. "Does my bike fit into any of these classes?"

"Too right. I checked."

"You've checked? That sounds keen. And how do you think we'd go?"

"There's only one way to find out."

Jack laughed. "They'll call me the Bellamy Bullet."

"You have to win first."

Although Carl had been cautious in putting up the idea, he was thrilled with Jack's response. This was the opportunity he had dreamed about. The two men donned serious faces and worked through the hurdles in their way, especially the task of getting the bike and tools up to Townsville. When Carl outlined his plan of borrowing the farm truck, they agreed the race was on. Next day while Jack phoned Townsville and posted off a nomination cheque, Carl raised the subject of the truck during a rare silence at the dinner table.

His mother shook her head as she ladled sauce over bowls of homemade *lasagna*. "It's too dangerous, *bambino*," she said in Italian. "You will kill yourself."

"Mamma, I'm taking the bike to Townsville on the truck," he replied in English. "That's not dangerous. Jack Bellamy is the rider, and I'm his mechanic."

"Have you ever ridden the bike?" his father growled, also in Italian.

"No, Papa, I swear it."

"So who else is going on this mad adventure?"

Maria saw her chance to escape the farm. "I want to go too, Papa. It's boring here. Motorcycle races are such fun."

"How would you know?"

"I've heard Carl talk about the races at Tocko's."

"What races at Tocko's?"

"Oh, some chaps ride around on their bikes," Carl said, affecting nonchalance. "But I'm not one of them, I'm Jack's mechanic. Anyway, his bike is perfect for Townsville."

"Says who?"

"Me, Papa. I have looked into it. Jack has a very good bike, and I'm a good mechanic."

From the head of the table Mr Rossini glared at the pair then banged his knife on the table. "*Allora*. Take the truck, but no riding Jack's bike, and look after your sister."

"It'll be hot and dirty. She mightn't…"

"She can go if she wants. And you," he said pointing his knife at Maria, "stay close to your brother."

"Yes, Papa. Of course."

Later Carl and Maria stood at the sink washing the dishes. Carl bubbled with excitement.

"Ask Guido to come too," he said, "but he'll have to sit on the back."

"I wish he could, Carl, the three of us together like old times. But it won't happen. He's organised a fishing trip." Maria then smiled disarmingly. "I'm sorry to spoil your outing, but it can be so dull at home."

"That's okay, Maria. It doesn't bother me but I'll have to ask Jack."

"He'd better agree, or nobody goes."

When Carl relayed the condition to Jack next day, he could've saved his breath. Jack's only concern was that Carl had secured the truck and they were off to Townsville.

After loading the bike on Thursday afternoon, the three left Calen early next day. Carl drove, Maria sat in the centre and Jack against the window. For the first hour Maria was invisible as the boys talked bikes across her face. She listened, trying to absorb the language, wanting to be a part of the outfit. It had been like this in the early days when breaking into Carl and Guido's little escapades. Listen carefully, then speak. But it wasn't a childhood friend at her side. She was conscious of Jack's leather coat brushing her arm, and her senses quivered as she'd never been so confronted by the presence of a man who wasn't family. At first, she regretted her mother's advice to dress formally, but stockings and gloves seemed ridiculous on a motorbike adventure that asked for sun dresses and windswept hair. Meanwhile, the truck chewed up the miles and Jack's easy confidence seeped into the cabin. His only thought was the race. Leaning forward, he argued the advantages of Stanley Woods' style of body-low cornering.

When he paused to demonstrate, she said; "Where did you learn to ride?"

"Brisbane."

"Who taught you?"

"I taught myself."

"Ah."

He looked at her. It was the first time he'd actually taken notice of the woman. She was certainly very attractive, but she was Guido's girlfriend and, well, this racing was no place for a woman.

"What do you mean 'ah'?"

"Ah, you must be good."

"At teaching myself or riding?"

"Both, I suppose," she said, then met his gaze. "Are you good at both?"

"The truth will come out tomorrow, Miss Rossini."

"Maria, please. My name is Maria."

Several minutes passed before the men returned to talking bikes, but this time Maria was free to ask questions. Although the answers barely enlightened, she was no longer invisible.

Shortly after lunch they arrived in Townsville where their first task was to visit the track. Jack completed the marshal's wordy forms and paid the five shillings balance on his registration fee. Next they drove along Flinders Street until they reached the Exchange Hotel where they booked two rooms for two nights. Maria took the room at the top of the stairs while Jack and Carl shared the next room down the corridor. From there they walked into the city so Maria could buy herself a 'decent' hat, and Jack a set of gloves and leather helmet. Because the sun was still high, he suggested returning to the showground where he could join other novices in practice.

Maria raised an eyebrow. "Novice? This morning you were a trained rider."

"I am, but Townsville is not Brisbane."

"Ah," Maria said for the second time that day.

Jack soon discovered corners one and three were fast, demanding the correct racing lines which he struggled to hold against the camber. On the long straight, however, he felt his Norton International had the power to elbow aside the slower English and European bikes that were built for leisure not speed. After several laps he and Carl agreed the bike's setup was close to perfect, and as they had stripped away the track's mystery, they decided final preparations could be left until morning. Climbing into the truck, they returned to the city where they ambled along the Strand until a weary sun slipped behind Castle Hill. Minutes later, darkness replaced the short tropical twilight and the breeze shifted ninety degrees from Palm Island to the open waters of Cleveland Bay. Maria shivered in the cool change and urged the men to return to the hotel for a quiet dinner and an early night.

Saturday dawned clear and mild. The scent of frangipani drifted up from the hotel garden, through the glass louvres along the eastern wall, and into the rooms where the race goers were beginning to stir. Jack was the first to rise, and after a brisk walk along Flinders Street returned to the hotel where he called Carl and Maria down for breakfast. On his program he noted that the feature race was scheduled for three-thirty in the afternoon with qualifying sessions in the morning. A practice round had also been assigned for each class, and the minor races, including sidecars, were to start from one-fifteen. The sun was barely an hour into the sky when the three drove out to the track that was throbbing with the exhausts of fifty or more engines. Once into his leathers Jack was a fearless rider, but as he had not raced formally before his first qualifying round was plagued by mistakes. Back in the pits Carl's tireless fingers danced over the engine while Maria attended to the officials who were forever changing the blackboard. Maria also played host, providing coffee and the finger of Bell's Irish whiskey that Jack requested at the start of his second qualifier.

"This stuff would do better in the engine," she warned.

"Whose engine?"

"Not yours."

As Jack's confidence grew, he pushed the bike lower and faster through each corner. Slower riders were content to let him past, and apart from one outstanding machine from Brisbane, nobody came close to matching his time.

An hour before the start Maria returned to Carl who was tightening spokes on a spare wheel, and whispered that a man appeared to be operating a book on the race. He was in a tent behind the stand pretending to sell hot chips.

"What's that to me?" asked Carl whose dreams of money had never extended to betting.

"Nothing, except they have Jack as second favourite."

Carl straightened from the wheel. "Behind who?"

"That team," Maria said, pointing to the group in blue and white overalls crowded around a gleaming bike.

Even as she pointed one of the men glanced up and laughed. He was a tall, bull necked man whose hair had been cropped in a military prickle that was still unfashionable in the north. At the centre of his chest the blade of a dagger tattoo disappeared into the vee of a loose, cotton shirt. He wore short sleeves unlike the rest of his team, and on his left arm he displayed a scar that ran from the elbow to the wrist like a disused rail line. He was a strong, self-assured man whose barking laugh could be heard above the roar of engines.

"Who are they?" Maria said.

"BMW Motors from Brisbane. I've heard they are professional. Won races at most tracks along the coast. Their team rider - that fellow in the dark glasses - has even raced in Sydney."

"Does Jack know about them?"

"Of course he does, but look at him. Do you think he cares?"

Jack leant against his bike, puffing on a cigarette as machines hurtled down the main straight. Helmet and jacket unfastened, he was the essence of quiet confidence. He turned as Bull Neck from the BMW team sauntered up to him. For several minutes the conversation appeared friendly, then Jack stiffened. The two men argued fiercely before Bull Neck thrust his nose into Jack's face, wagged his finger, then turned and stormed back to his team who had watched the encounter with interest.

Alarmed, Carl and Maria hurried across to Jack.

"What was that all about?" Carl asked.

"The bastard wants me to throw the race. Worth fifty quid to stay in his mirror. *Limp home if you have to*, he said. I told him to piss off, or he'd have a limp, and it wouldn't be home."

Something about Jack's hubris stung Carl. Racing was a serious business and fifty quid was a lot of money, more actually than Carl had ever seen. He sensed Jack laughed at the world because it owed him nothing while Carl was a beggar at the rich man's feast. He had always dwelt on the poor side of the track; hand-me-down clothes from Italian neighbours, pushbikes rescued from the dump and a skin colour that labelled him as a grateful migrant. He prided himself as a loyal family man who lived in a tight knit, supportive community, but next to Jack he was travelling through life in a second class compartment. Only one thing had more value than family, and that was wealth. Every shilling Carl earned went to his mother who doled out pocket money sparingly. On the Thursday before driving to Townsville, she had handed him thirty pounds to cover against breakdowns and living expenses. When he returned home, he would need to account for every penny. But... what if he used the balance to earn some proper cash, give the Rossini family a kick-along, even buy his mother a treat, maybe a new hat and gloves for her daughter's wedding. He would no longer be the honest worker, he would be the clever one. Rapidly the idea formed. Put the money on the BMW bike and ensure Jack lost the race. He couldn't feel sorry for Jack. It was only a game to him. Townsville would soon be forgotten as he chased another prize.

During a break in the practice session Carl sidled up to Bull Neck who was to one side arranging tyres for the BMW.

"Can I have a word?" Carl said.

Bull Neck glanced up at his visitor. "Go ahead."

"What would it mean to you if the Norton lost?"

Bull Neck released the tyre. "I might sleep easier at night. Why?"

"Fifty quid and I'll see he loses."

"Fifty quid is a lot of dough."

"How badly can't you sleep?"

"Okay, mate. I'm listening."

"I'm Jack Bellamy's mechanic. Before the last race I'll add water to the fuel."

"That won't stop him."

"Maybe not, but it'll foul the bike. Fouled bike means a slow bike."

"Very well. Twenty-five quid now, and twenty-five after the race."

"Sorry, friend. I want the fifty quid up front."

"How do I know you're for real?"

"You don't."

Bull Neck glowered. "So what's your security?"

"I don't have any. Only my word."

"Not good enough. Who is the girl?"

"What girl?"

"The pretty one. She your missus?"

"No, my sister."

"Well, there's your security."

Carl gulped. "No way. I've given my word. The Norton will not win."

"No security, mate, no deal."

Carl glanced across at Maria. She would never know her part in the arrangement, only that she had a brother who was going places and taking the family with him.

"Okay, we have a deal."

After shaking hands, Carl stashed the fifty pounds in his waistband, then took another twenty from his mother's roll and sought out the bookmaker. Unknown to him, Maria at that moment had arranged to buy lunch and found him whispering in the bookmaker's ear.

"What are you doing?" she demanded.

Carl jumped. "Oh, just talking odds."

"What odds?" Her eyes widened. "You've put money on the race, Carl."

"It's alright, sis. The money's safe."

She blocked his path. "What money is safe? Who have you backed?"

"Nobody in particular."

"Was it Jack?"

"Yes... of course. Jack to win."

"I know when you're lying, Carl. Who was it?"

When he refused to meet her eyes, she said, "Not the BMW?"

He nodded.

"Carl! The BMW over Jack. That's awful. How could you?"

"Jack can't win, Maria. They're much too professional. They've raced for years. This isn't Jack's race. He simply can't win."

"You know something else, Carl. What have you done?"

"Please, Maria," he squirmed. "Give me a break. I'm doing it for us, so we can get ahead. Not live like wops all our lives. It means nothing to Jack. Look at him. He's happy just being here."

"That's not true, Carl, he does want to win. You can't deny him that. And it's better for him, for us, than those bullfrogs."

"Maria, please. Leave it alone. I have laid the bet."

"How much?"

"A lot of money... at three to one."

"Good Lord." She stared at him. "You started with the cash from Mamma. Who gave you the rest?" As she asked, she looked to the BMW camp where Bull Neck shared a joke with his rider.

"No, Carl. Don't tell me he paid you."

"Maria, stay out of it. Leave it be."

The beautiful almond eyes searched for the brother she had grown up with. "I will for now, Carl, because I don't have a choice. But there'll be a price to pay, I know it."

The main race was set down for mid-afternoon. Fourteen bikes had entered the race, but all eyes were on the Brisbane BMW whose odds had shrunk after Carl bet his seventy pounds. Ten minutes out when Jack dashed to the men's toilet, Carl grabbed a wet rag and squeezed water into the fuel tank. From her table near the truck Maria unhappily watched the sabotage. Only that morning she hadn't cared if Jack won or lost this game of motorbikes. She didn't even know the value of the prize, if indeed there was one. She had imagined both men wanted victory for the love of it; why else the long drive to Townsville in a farm truck? She puzzled over Carl's abrupt change of heart, his unexpected treachery. She had never seen this side of her brother, never would've believed he was disloyal or ruthless. Adding to her misery was her complicity in the crime. Carl had forced her to take sides. Suddenly, she wanted Jack Bellamy to win. Carl had pitched 'family wealth' onto the table as his trump card, but Maria's instinct was to match his bid with 'loyalty'. Money versus principle, avarice versus an honest swashbuckler. She could've wept. As Bellamy hurried from the toilet, strapping on his helmet, she handed him a small whiskey. "God be with you, Jack."

"Hey, it ain't that bad."

"Promise you won't get angry if you lose."

"Cheer up, Maria. Who said anything about losing."

"It's possible, that's all. They're very fast."

Tossing back the whiskey, he grinned. "We'll show the smug bastards."

Jack hit the lead early and went at the first corner like a terrier. With each lap he pulled a half-second's lead on his BMW rival who appeared to be comfortable sitting in the Norton's shadow. Two laps to the finish Jack's bike spluttered, but the misfire was barely audible, the faintest of coughs. Jack squeezed on more throttle and the bike responded with a surge, but as it entered the corner, it coughed a second and third time. In pit lane Carl glanced nervously at Bull Neck who saluted with a smile. Jack eased off the throttle and the engine regained its rhythm, but he had lost precious seconds. The BMW now sat a half-length behind and Jack was unwilling to risk more power. Two corners to go and the BMW closed the gap. Within moments he was level with Jack's wheel. Jack went into the apex tight and drifted wide pushing the BMW onto the grass, but the bike returned unharmed to the track. When Jack eased open the throttle for the last turn, the Norton broke into convulsions and the BMW seized its chance, spearing down the inside for a pass. Clenching his jaw, Jack threw the bike across the BMW's nose forcing the rider to brake hard. As the BMW dived on its front forks, the rider lost control, hitting Jack's back wheel which threw the BMW into a wild slide. For an instant the rider hung suspended by the handlebars before crashing heavily to the track. Now riderless, the BMW galloped into the barriers where it crumpled and died. With his adversary gone, Jack eased off the throttle and limped across the line ahead of a group of bikes that swept through in his wake.

Carl was dumbfounded. He had lost the unlosable. The Norton had survived. This wasn't fate, this was a curse on the underdog, the beatitudes flipped on their head. While Jack circled the track waving to his admirers, Carl dropped his face into his hands. Seventy pounds. With the horror dulling his eyes he turned to Maria.

Despite her thrill at Jack's win, she felt for her brother. "It's okay, Carl. Money is not everything."

"I lost the man's fifty pounds," he whispered.

"He gave you fifty? Good heavens. What was the actual bet?"

"That Jack wouldn't cross the line first."

"Well, don't surrender yet," she said without conviction. "They might challenge the result, declare it null and void. Start the race again."

"Sure."

"Anyway, fifty pounds is not impossible. Spread the debt over six months."

Carl shuddered. "It's worse than that. We had a deal."

"What deal?"

Before Carl could answer, Bull Neck stepped forward and grabbed the front of his shirt. "So we couldn't lose, eh wop?"

"I'm sorry," Carl mumbled. "But how was I to know your man would crash?"

"This had nothing to do with the crash, fella. You gave me your word."

"I said I'm sorry."

"Not half as sorry as you will be. Where are you staying?"

"The Exchange Hotel."

"Seven-thirty at the Exchange tonight. Fifty quid, or I take the security."

"No, you can't," Carl moaned.

"Can't I? Try me." Then he looked at Maria. "You'd better be worth it," and stormed off to load the crashed BMW into the back of a van.

When he had gone, Maria said, "What did he mean by that?"

"He wants the money tonight."

"I gathered that. What else?"

"He... wants to have a drink with you."

"We can drink together."

"Alone."

"With me? Alone? For God's sake, Carl, what's happening? I'll ask Jack for the cash. He won't mind giving a loan."

Carl was losing control. First he had lost money in a dreadful miscalculation, then he had lost the respect of Bull Neck who took him as a man of his word. Now it was no longer a question of Maria's pride at risk, it was his too. He swung on her. "We're not taking any damn money from Jack. He already laughs at us. We have self-respect too, you know. The Rossinis are a decent family. We won't borrow from anyone. Leave it to me, I'll think of something."

By now Jack had climbed off his bike and stood in a group of teenagers, mostly girls, signing autographs. At one point he lifted his head, caught Maria's eye and winked. When the admirers had gone, he unzipped his jacket and strolled across to the pair who waited sombrely near the truck. He punched Carl on the shoulder. "Congratulations, Carlo. Best mechanic in the north. Spot of dirt in the carby but we made it, eh pal?"

"Yes, Jack, we made it."

"Hey, what's up? Faces down to your boots. We won fair and square, so don't feel sorry for the BMW. See how he tried to pass me? Right across my racing line. Cheeky blighter. Come on, help load the bike, and we'll find a bar."

After wheeling the bike onto the truck, they were securing it with ropes when an official called Jack for the victory presentation. Carl excused himself from attending. "You go ahead, Jack. We'll finish up here."

Maria sat on the running board. "Carl, this is impossible. I can't do what you ask. You seem to forget I'm marrying Guido."

"I haven't forgotten anything. Look, Maria, I made a promise. Nobody need know."

"I will."

"Well, it won't come to that."

Taking a spanner and screwdriver, he began stripping parts off the truck: the mirrors, tool box, seat cover, tonneau and spare wheel. Loaded with these goods, he strode across to the temporary bar that was now crowded. The first item to sell was the watch his parents had given him for completing scholarship, next went the hardware. At the end he was still twenty pounds short.

Shadows lengthened on the showground, and the few remaining officials joined the diehards at the bar. When Carl and Maria were unable to locate Jack, they drove slowly back to the hotel where they ordered a meal against their account. As they ate, Carl raised the idea of fleeing town before Bull Neck arrived.

"We can't leave Jack behind," she said miserably. "Carl, how could you do this? It's all gone horribly wrong, and getting worse."

"He might be content with the thirty quid," Carl suggested.

"Ask him to wait until Jack gets here."

"Never. This is none of Jack's business."

Right on seven-thirty Bull Neck appeared in the lounge bar, demanding his cash. He wore the same clothes from the track, but his face was now red from a mix of sunburn and drink. He was in an ugly mood.

Carl rose hesitantly and offered the thirty pounds, which Bull Neck grabbed, counted with a quick riffle then shoved into his pocket. "Another twenty, wop. Fifty quid was the deal."

"He's not a wop," Maria said.

"Shut up, pretty face, your turn's next."

Carl stammered. "Take it out on me. Leave my sister alone."

"Saving her for the Norton rider? Mustn't spoil his trophy."

Maria threw her drink over him. "You're crude."

"Hey, watch that temper, girl. I'm the one who's cranky. Drove all the way to Townsville to be frustrated by a greedy wop. Not a good look for me, but worse for BMW." He punched Carl viciously above the heart. With a muffled yelp Carl dropped onto the bench and lay writhing in pain. "That's for treating us like fools."

He grabbed Maria by the wrist. "Come on, girl. We've got twenty quid's worth of business to get through. Show us to your room."

She flung off his hand. "I'm going nowhere. Touch me again and I'll scream."

"Try it and I'll smash your brother's face."

"You're a sadist."

"No, honey, it was a deal. So you'd better get in the mood, or else…" Leaving the sentence hang, he punched the whimpering Carl a second and third time.

Maria shivered helplessly. "Stop it. Please, stop it. We'll find the money. Look, take my necklace, my watch. Anything."

"Don't worry, I will. Upstairs, sweetheart, now."

Seizing her by the hair, Bull Neck dragged her across the lounge and up the stairs.

"Which is your room?"

When Maria nodded dumbly at the first door, he thrust it open, pushed her inside and kicked the door shut. The couple had scarcely disappeared when Jack staggered into the lounge like in a scene from a French farce. Smoke hung from the ceiling and empty glasses littered the tables, but apart from the injured Carl the lounge was empty of patrons who had vanished at the first punch. Jack walked up to the bar and thinking Carl was already drunk, ordered a bottle of champagne and asked after Maria.

Carl's reply was inaudible.

Jack bent over him. "Hey, I say, mate. It's too early for bed. Where's Maria?"

At that moment Carl was unsure whom he reviled most - sadistic Bull Neck, happy-go-lucky Jack Bellamy, or himself for his wretched misfortune. He also felt for Maria, but she was strong; she could take this punishment and move on, be herself in a week. But not him. His pride was shattered. He lay miserably on the couch unable to speak.

"You don't look too flash, mate," Jack said. "Champagne's on the way. Where's Maria?"

"Piss off," Carl groaned.

Jack was startled. "Sorry, mate?"

Carl lifted himself to a sitting position. "She's upstairs. Where did you think she'd be?"

The drink was playing tricks on Jack's brain. "What, in bed already?"

"Yeah, in bed. With that BMW prick. It was the pay-off for your stupid win."

"I won that race fair and square. What pay-off?"

"You blind or something?"

"No," Jack muttered. "What has my win to do with Maria?"

"It's the price he demanded. That's what."

Jack shook his head. "She was never mentioned."

"Well, go rescue her," Carl snarled. "You caused the mess."

"Like hell," Jack said and bounded up the stairs three at a time. As Bull Neck was not resident at the hotel, Jack guessed they were using Maria's room. He tapped on the door.

"What d'you want?" Bull Neck growled from inside.

"Manager here. We've got an emergency."

When the door opened a crack, he saw Maria seated on the edge of the bed in her white slip. Bull Neck's eye appeared. "What emergency?"

"This one," Jack said, throwing his weight at the door. Bull Neck's nose snapped like fresh celery and a stream of blood followed the crashing man to the far wall where he lay stunned under an open towel. Blood dribbled onto the dagger tattoo and down his belly to the makings of an erection that wobbled in disbelief. Maria lifted her tear-stained face in alarm as Jack stood granite-like near the door, unsure of his next move into a woman's room.

"You alright, Maria?"

"Yes, thank you," she nodded, and swallowed.

"Carl said I… um… caused it. Sorry."

She shook her head. "No, it wasn't you. You were brave. It was… Carl and me. We got out of our depth."

"What do we owe him?"

"Not you, us. Another twenty pounds."

"Twenty? Exactly your share of the win. I meant to hand it over at the track. Sorry."

Jack stepped across to Bull Neck, but as the man had no pockets, Jack shoved the notes in his mouth. He and Maria then looked awkwardly at each other.

"You'd better cover him up," she said, glancing away.

"Even better, I'll drag him onto the street."

"That would be nice, thank you. I'll come down in a minute."

After pulling on the man's trousers, Jack bundled up the remainder of his clothes and dragged him through the doorway. As he paused to negotiate the hall, Maria said, "Thanks again, Jack, for... um... saving..."

"Glad to oblige," Jack replied and threw the unconscious Bull Neck over his shoulder.

Some ten minutes later Maria appeared in the lounge freshly showered and dressed. Jack was at ease sipping an Irish whiskey while Carl sullenly toyed with a beer. They rose to their feet as she arrived.

"Like a drink, Maria?" Jack asked.

"I need one. Gin and tonic. And make it a double, please."

When Jack returned with the drink, he said, "Okay, tell me the full story."

"It's done and dusted," Carl mumbled.

"No, it isn't," Maria said to her brother. "Tell him everything."

With that they forced the details from Carl, and at the finish an uncomfortable silence filled the bar.

Jack threw back his head and laughed. "Boy, that was close. I nearly lost the race, and Maria nearly lost her"...he reddened... "honour."

Relieved at having avoided a personal disaster - and Jack's censure - Maria laughed with him, but Carl sat at the table, head lowered. He had never felt so wretched.

CHAPTER 37

Silence followed Carl's story. Unlocking his fingers, he latched onto the sugar bowl and began rotating it, three times one way, three times the other. I butted in. "Carl, you've lost me here. Jack saved your skin and Maria's self-respect, yet you hated him. I can't be hearing right."

"Oh, it's for real. Every time I looked at him from that day I squirmed. God forbid, I had sold my sister to cover a dopey bet. Jack never said as much, but he must've despised me. And I despised him in return. He and his bike."

"So how did Maria feel?"

"On the outside she didn't change. Still my little sister though she had every reason to disown me. Mind you, she didn't go out with Jack or anything. Stayed loyal to Guido. But I made a second stupid mistake. Instead of letting the episode die I blathered to Guido, and claimed it was all Jack's fault. Naturally Guido turned on Jack, started baiting him. I did the same hoping my conscience would clear, or at least fade from memory once he was gone. As I should've guessed, the plan backfired. While we snapped at Jack's heels, Maria felt sorry for him and - I belatedly discovered - began falling in love. Everything came to a head the night of the dance at Cohen's Hall. While I drove the truck taking us in, Guido and Paulo were on the back goading Jack about not mixing with girls, only having a bike for a woman. At first, he took it in good spirits but midway through the night he walked up to Maria and asked for a dance. I've heard Paulo say she was no angel, but he's off the mark. Although she'd always been a good kid, the incident in Townsville had shaken her, and we were making it worse. She readily accepted the dance and, well, they became inseparable. The truth is, I had lost my little sister years before the events in Moreton Bay."

Wordlessly we digested Carl's story. The sun was climbing to its zenith and a pee-wee faced up to a troupe of mynas that had settled uninvited in his leopard tree. To the west cumulous clouds formed above the Clarke Ranges and their soft grey underbellies snagged against the trees, spilling showers into the foothills. Carl's voice was barely a whisper as he struggled with his emotions, and Maria sat with a hand on his arm gazing into his face.

"I caused it all," Carl said bitterly. "I hated Jack, but I should've hated myself."

"No, Dad, never that. The hatred's over. It's done with." She took her father's hand and reached out for mine. "Dad, you and Jack take hands too."

We sat awkwardly in a circle, Carl holding one of my fingers like a cornered homophobe.

"Take his hand properly," she ordered.

He did so.

"Jack has found his family now. Isn't that right, Dad?"

Carl nodded.

"So from today we'll behave like family. He'll always be welcome in this home. Okay, Dad?"

"Yes," he mumbled, then lifted his head and said clearly. "You'll always have a place in my house, Jack."

"Thanks, guys, I appreciate that," I said, releasing my hand from Carl's rough paw. Alas, Maria did the same with mine.

I rose from the table to let Maria and Carl be alone for a few minutes. When I returned Maria was drying her eyes and Carl had found a bottle of grappa which he slopped into three glasses. Desperately needing the stuff, Carl and I tipped it back without calling a toast, but Maria left her glass untouched.

I took a clearing breath and tackled the subject in hand. "Now we've got serious work to do. Our friend Paulo was last seen talking to the priest. I'll swear that while Mass was in progress, he lit the fire then jumped into his car. By the time we found Father Burke, Paulo's feet would've been tucked under the breakfast table at home. D.I. Morgan will be out there now doing an interview, but clever Paulo won't be caught with a speck of evidence. All witnesses are dead, and even if I handed D.I. Morgan the *freedom fee* document, it doesn't prove murder. No, Paulo has to be trapped into an admission."

"He's too wily for that," Maria said.

I drummed my fingers on the table. "Tomorrow, that's when we trap him. D.I. Morgan wants to see me at two. Plenty of time to climb the mountain. My bet is that when Sam takes me to the murder site, Paulo will appear. He has to silence me because I've interrogated everyone including his wife. Besides that, there's a remote chance I found the signed paper."

"I'm not happy with this trap idea, Jack," Maria said. "Take the paper to D.I. Morgan, and while you're there, give him the revolver. It's still in my bag."

I was about to chastise her for not handing in the gun when I was forced to make my own admission. "And I haven't parted with the St Francis medal. I like to imagine it belonged to my father, a companion to the one my mother wore."

She refilled our glasses with water. "That would be nice if it was true."

"One person would know, our man Paulo."

I couldn't get Paulo out of my head. I guess he was filling the space once occupied by the now-dead Cleary.

"Anyway, I agree with Maria," Carl said. "Paulo is too dangerous for us. Leave it to the police."

"No. It would be my word against his, a blow-in orphan versus a respectable farmer. We'll catch him tomorrow."

"How?"

"Sam is collecting me at eight in the morning. I want you to ring D.I. Morgan tonight when it's too late for him to object. Take him up early from the Rise and Shine to be sure you're there before us. Once Paulo makes his presence known, I'll bait him. He will expect to nail me cold. Sorry Maria, but you'll have to stay and watch the base station."

Carl shook his head. "It's too risky, Jack. Too many what ifs. And how do you know you can trust Sam? I don't mind the fellow, but you've hardly been his best friend."

I pushed back my chair. "I don't trust either of them, but like I've said for weeks, I'm visiting the site where Guido was killed, and tomorrow at eight Sam is taking me. If nothing comes of it, we'll tell the police all we know. After that, I'll do the right thing and leave you in peace." When neither argued with me, I said, "Well, I'll be gone. Maria, thanks for the breakfast, and Carl, I'll see you tomorrow as arranged."

Maria escorted me to the bike. "Jack, remember what I said last night. Be careful."

As Carl had his back to us, I took her by the hands. "Maria, can I tell you something?"

"I might not want to hear it," she said.

"It's about us… you know… going the next step."

"Jack, please." She steeled herself. "I'm sorry it's gone this far. I think I have, well… done the wrong thing by you. No, I'll be truthful. It's been entirely my fault. I opened a space in my heart and invited you in… maybe felt sorry for you… I don't know… smiled or let you kiss when I shouldn't have. Now the opening is wide, and I ought to have been stronger. We're cousins." I made to interrupt but she held up her hand. "And anyway, to be honest, I'm practically engaged to Sam."

"Can I speak now?"

"It won't change things."

"Maria, I understand what you're saying, but let me explain myself. When I was in Townsville, I read this story about two cousins who were rock stars in Europe. They were in the same band, and one thing led to another. They eventually got married and had a bunch of great kids."

"I read that story too, Jack. It was in the magazine you gave me."

"So you will have heard of the phrase"…and I said it slowly… "a consanguineous marriage."

"Yes, but…"

"Hear me out, Maria. After our night at the Rise and Shine, I made an appointment with a doctor in Mackay. He said a marriage between first cousins is not unusual, and is perfectly safe. In fact, these consanguineous marriages were frequent in the early days of white settlement. Problems arise when the offspring marry each other. So you see, it's alright for us to be in love."

She was close to tears. "It doesn't solve anything."

"Well, at least I can say I love you without feeling guilty."

She forced a smile. "You can say what you want."

I took her bare shoulders, one hand touching the scar, and drew her close. "Maria, I love you."

"Thank you, Jack. I know you do."

And she let me kiss her.

Old Carl had turned to watch and I could see the sadness in his face. Without another word I buckled on my helmet and rode back to the caravan park.

CHAPTER 38

Next morning early, I gobbled down breakfast, threw on my cowboy shirt and rode up to Carl Rossini's farm to meet Sam. Although Carl's ute was gone, I was disappointed to find the Land Rover also missing as I had prepared final advice for Maria. By and by Sam arrived in his four-by-four Land Cruiser. He had tossed away his fancy gear for hard-wearing shorts and a khaki shirt.

"Get aboard," he said, and made a point of shoving a .303 rifle onto the rack behind us.

"What's that for?" I said.

"Feral pigs. They root up the cane and spook the dogs."

"That bad, eh? Well, keep in mind pigs have four legs."

"I'll try."

With pleasantries out of the way we drove up the O'Connell River valley. As each kilometre passed the road grew rougher and the Clarke Ranges pressed in from both sides. Occasionally we skirted an abandoned farm house where the early selectors had battled against the rainforest and monsoonal floods. Ugly wash-outs scarred the river bank and rusting fences marked the extent of human endeavour.

"Where does the path come across from the Rise and Shine?" I shouted at Sam.

"Up ahead," he grunted, then after a pause, "You planning a walk?"

"Not at the moment."

We came to a length of track that had been scoured away by the river. Sam changed into four-wheel drive and edged round the embankment. When the wheels on my side began scrabbling towards the river, I grabbed for support. Sam eased the Land Cruiser back onto the track and turned to me. "Scared, eh?"

After a time the track could go no further, and we pulled into a small clearing. To our surprise Maria's Land Rover was there.

"What's she doing up here?" Sam demanded.

"Dunno, but when we meet next, I'll ask."

"You haven't long to wait," Maria said, appearing beside my window. "I'm going with you."

"No, you're not," Sam and I said together.

"Try and stop me," she replied, and for an instant I heard my tomboy mother answering Carl and Guido years earlier. Maria was joining the party, fellas, like it or not. Mirroring Sam's outfit, she wore a khaki shirt and bush-walking shorts, and on her feet a pair of sturdy boots. Her hair was tied in a ponytail, and she carried a small canvas pack on her back. The pretty Vespa girl had switched her guise for a tough Alpine hiker.

Sam lifted the rifle from its rack behind the seat and grabbed a pack containing water and food.

"Did you bring anything?" he asked me.

"Not really. We'll be back by lunch."

"If you're lucky," he said and threw across a water bottle. "Don't lose it."

After checking the gun was on safe, he led the way along a path that followed the bank of the river. I fell in behind him and Maria drew up the rear. By now we were into heavy rainforest: giant trees held erect with buttress roots, orchids hanging in damp clusters from mossy bark, and whipbirds cracking sharply through the green canopy. Up here the O'Connell River was a small creek that bubbled over rocks and fallen trees while flowing towards distant Repulse Bay. Either Sam was fit or he was a convincing show off. He never once broke stride as he pounded his way up the track that Carl's cattle kept in passable condition.

After forty minutes of hard climbing we emerged onto an exposed ridge. Sam stopped and pointed. "You asked about the Rise and Shine. That's it over there to the south, and we left the ute through that gap on the left."

"Thank you, Sam."

"You can just see Dad's roof from here," Maria said, using her stick as a pointer.

"No, it's his shed," Sam countered without looking up.

I took a slug of water. "How much further?"

"Twenty minutes. More if you dawdle."

Sam marched on and we followed. I was getting used to the sight of his back, and I wondered if a hairdresser curled his hair and waxed his ears. Even in tough safari wear he looked unsuited to a girl like Maria.

Suddenly the track opened onto a wide grassy clearing. The river gurgled in a semicircle to the east while a tumble of rock and leafy trees bounded the west. Maybe it was my imagination but the air had turned clammy and all but a single wren had fled into the scrub.

Sam walked to a log in the centre of the clearing and sat down. "This is it," he said. "This is what you came for."

"Maria, have you been here before?" I asked.

"Once. We were looking for cattle, but I didn't like the place. Too creepy."

"You were told not to come," Sam said.

The clearing wasn't quite what I expected. I studied the grass and the water. "Where was Guido when they found him?"

"About here where I'm sitting."

"And where was the rifle?"

"Near those rocks. No, over this way more. Your dad was near the rocks."

I walked several paces towards the river. A small ledge jutting into the water had created a weir with a shallow ford below it. "These rocks?"

"Yep, thereabouts."

Maria had wandered across to the stream where she removed her boots and socks. She now stood ankle deep in the clear water sluicing her face.

I began combing the ground. "The two men trudged up here to hunt feral pigs. The place should be full of tracks, but I don't see any."

"The pig is here alright," a voice boomed from the treeline. Paulo appeared at the edge of the clearing with a rifle cradled in his arms. Despite ourselves, Maria and I jumped. So my guess about him had been right. I tuned my ears for Carl and D.I. Morgan who were meant to be in the trees waiting to spring the trap.

When Maria stepped out of the water towards me, Paulo lifted his hand. "Sweetie, take your boots and disappear. Next time you'll stay at home where you belong."

"I don't *belong* in any *home*," she retorted and began drying her feet.

"Mind your tongue, girl."

After that he seemed to lose interest in her. He took his rifle by the barrel and using it as a crutch, hobbled from the shadows with blood streaming down his right leg.

"Flamin' hell, Dad, what happened?" Sam said.

"Fell on some rocks earlier. Cut myself bad. You got a first-aid kit in that pack?"

"No, just food."

"Then you'll have to go to the ute and fetch it. Get a move on. I have business to attend to."

"Sure, and I'd better take Maria, eh?"

"Yeah, it was dumb bringing her in the first place."

"I'm going nowhere," Maria said, lacing up her boots.

Sam glanced at his father and shrugged.

Paulo pointed a finger at her. "I don't abide disobedience, girlie. Go with Sam. That's an order."

"I'm going nowhere," she repeated, hands on her hips.

"For once do as you're told."

"No."

"I'll sort you out later," Paulo said, controlling his anger. Then he turned to Sam. "Okay, get on your way."

Without losing any time, Sam grabbed his pack and rifle and headed down the path.

When his footsteps had faded into the scrub, I said, "Right, Paulo, drop that gun, and I'll take a squiz at your leg. I can tear up my shirt as a tourniquet."

"It's fine. I'll live."

Maria stood beside me. "It looks dreadful, Paulo. Let Jack apply a bandage, at least stop the bleeding."

"Alright, I give up," he grinned. "It's a fake. The blood is from a boar I shot this morning."

"I guessed as much," I said. "It was prearranged, so Sam could make himself scarce. When he returns in two hours, the dirty work is done, and he rehearses some yarn you've invented. But I'm glad he's gone because he's innocent, too big a twit to be otherwise. He doesn't have to know everything about his old man."

"Don't get too smart, Jack, I'll crack your skull open."

"I'm not smart, but I'm no mug either, Paulo. You don't think I came up here without insurance. You tell me what happened to my parents, and I'll hand over a sheet of paper. Then we can all go home."

"What sheet of paper?"

"You need to see a quack about your memory. The paper you hoped went up in flames with the priest, the same paper you murdered Kevin Cleary for. Well, I have that document and your signature is on it."

"You're lying. Show me."

"Not so fast, bro. I said it's insurance. We could do a deal. Remove the bolt from that rifle and chuck it in the river. Then I'll hand over the paper."

"How do I know you've got it."

"You have to trust me."

"Okay." He lowered the rifle and drew back the bolt which ejected a bullet onto the ground. Next he released the bolt and tossed it underarm towards the river.

"Right. Now for that sheet of paper."

Taking the document from my pocket, I stepped forward and laid it on the ground. "There, Paulo. I've kept my word. You've got the incriminating evidence. Now you tell me what happened to Mum and Dad."

Paulo grabbed the paper and read it quickly. As the tension flowed out of him, he became cocky again. He glanced at Maria. "Send the girl down the track. One day she'll be my daughter-in-law, and doesn't need to hear any of this."

"Do as he asks, Maria," I said, indicating the way Sam had gone. "I don't need a witness."

"Jack, don't be silly. Of course you do."

"Please. The less you know the better."

"I'm staying," she replied vehemently. "If it's about family, I must know what's going on."

We both turned to Paulo.

"Okay, Paulo," I said, "it's over to you."

He then followed the same moves I had observed weeks ago at the farm when I approached him about my past. He pulled out a tobacco tin and papers and rolled a cigarette. This time the strong hands were assured. He then felt for matches in his shirt. Unable to locate them he began patting his trouser pockets. "Hold on, what's this I've found?" and drew a small automatic from his back pocket.

"Well, I'll be buggered," he chuckled. "It must've been there all the time."

Cocking the pistol, he pointed it at my head. "So you're not as clever as you think, orphan boy. Not nearly as bright as Sam. He wouldn't fall for that old trick." He pulled a length of cord from another pocket and threw it at Maria. "I don't want orphan boy running loose. Tie him up."

Maria did as told, but her fingers were light on the knots. Paulo watched her. "Come on, baby, do it properly. He's not a friggin kitten."

"Don't swear at me," she said.

"I'll say what I like, and you need a shake-up. My lad devotes his life to you, but you'd rather horse about with a loser cousin."

"That's not true. I've always been faithful to Sam. It's a pity he had no choice for a father."

"Is that right, baby? I regarded you as my daughter-in-law, but I'm changing my mind. You're a cock teaser."

"Ignore him, Maria," I said. "He forgot to take his pills this morning."

Paulo stepped across and kicked me hard in the ribs. As the pain flared through my gut, I retched and almost passed out. "Next smart remark, and you'll get a kick in the teeth," he said and strolled back to his perch while Maria knelt on the grass holding my face out of the vomit. After five minutes the nausea had passed, and I was able to sit upright.

Rolling a cigarette in one hand, Paulo said. "Okay orphan boy, you want the story on Guido. First up, the culprit was not your old man. Didn't have the balls. It was the dipso priest. First time he fired a gun."

"You and Cleary set him up," I said.

"Maybe, but that doesn't make us guilty."

"A judge might think otherwise. In any case, the priest confessed before he died. So let's move on."

"Good old Father Burke. As they say, no fool like an old fool. Anyway, Jack Bellamy was a pain in the arse to everyone. We had two choices with him. Get him to accept a payment - then he's guilty like us - or find a way to piss him off. Guido's idea of an annulment was weird, but it sowed doubt in his mind. And he had every reason to worry about Maria. Half the district wanted to shag her."

"You're vulgar," Maria said.

Paulo swung on her. His face was white. "Me vulgar? I heard about your little trick at the dance last week. Flat on your back, showing everyone your fanny."

"Hey, damn you, Paulo," I exploded. "It was an accident. A girl's shoe broke in the middle of a dance. Half a dozen people were knocked down, including Maria."

"Broken shoe, like hell. I've heard other stories about our little princess. Not to mention dancing and kissing with this freak of a cousin. So don't talk to me about morals. You're no different from the original Maria Rossini. She was always on heat."

Maria was quick. She took two steps and slapped Paulo across the mouth. His eyes popped in shock then his voice went icy cold, "You'll pay for that, bitch."

"Get on with your story," I said.

Deciding the girl could wait, Paulo swallowed his fury. But there was a new edge to his manner. "That dog Bellamy was untouchable. He wouldn't take a bribe, and he wouldn't hear bad things about

Maria. So it was a brainwave getting him to hunt pigs with Guido."

"Whose brainwave?"

"Don't remember. Maybe Cleary. He was full of bright ideas."

"Did he ever mention his pact with Dad?"

"What sort of pact?"

I kept my voice level. "That in return for Dad's freedom, he could have sex with Mum whenever he wanted."

"The stinking, rotten bastard."

"So you never heard of it?"

"Oh, it's possible. Why else would he have Bellamy released? We had him cold over Guido's death. Hanged or in prison for the rest of his life." Paulo spat on the ground in disgust. "You don't know who to trust anymore. Even that scum Cleary was into her pants. I'm glad he took a bullet."

Maria's fingers trembled as she gripped my shoulder.

A branch snapped in the trees behind us. Paulo was instantly down on one knee, pistol at the ready. When a wallaby bounded across the clearing, he relaxed. I had to keep him talking. "In early 1948 Dad took his family south to Brisbane. Three years later he was killed. Why?"

Paulo grinned. "He stumbled on my pals."

"Your pals? You mean the extortion ring?"

"To hell with those sponges. No, my business contacts."

"Of course. The Black Shirts."

"You're close. In Italy I met a *comandante* who showed me how to form a patriots cell in Mackay. As luck would have it, Cleary's racket with the *freedom fee* slotted in perfectly. It gave me the contacts I needed. We called our little mob the *Patrioti*. Great fellas every one of them. Loyal to a fault, to Italy that is," he chuckled. "But otherwise they weren't that special. Just a few businessmen and professionals funding clever tricks during the war. Like getting a sugar mill to break down, or a tram derailed. It cost the industry a mint. When things started falling apart for us in 1951 we had a meeting and decided Jack was the blabber mouth. We drew straws and bang, Jack was dead."

"Why Jack? Cleary could've been the betrayer. He hated Italians."

"We're not fools. The *Patrioti* kept Cleary in their pocket."

Flicking his cigarette into the river, he said, "Right, boy, you've got what you wanted. This is where we say goodbye."…he studied my bleak face… "Cod-liver oil, eh? You'll wish you stayed on the shit."

CHAPTER 39

As Paulo walked to the edge of the river to collect the rifle bolt, I looked up to Maria and shrugged apologetically. She had been wise to toss me out of her father's house on that first visit. Pity she hadn't thrown cold water over me.

Paulo became like a chef about to prepare a meal. He tapped his fingers against his cheek. "Too bad the original plan is stuffed. We need an accident, but how can we get orphan boy to die accidentally? His march into the hills with Sam should've led to his demise, but the foolish girl wouldn't stay in her kitchen. We can't have that accident now, too messy. Hey, I know." He punched the air. "Twenty years ago the nasty Jack Bellamy shot Maria in Moreton Bay, then turned the gun on himself. Clean finish, deceived everyone. Years later Jack Bellamy the son tries to rape young Maria in distant mountains and in defence she shoots him. Yes, I like it. Neat and believable. Just need to roughen your shirt up a bit, girlie. So let's clean the bolt and slot it back into the rifle. No worries. A tidy ending and a spot of fun for old Paulo."

An awful coldness settled in my belly as he talked through his fantasy. He was no different to Cleary. No wonder they were each other's best mate.

"I'll tell the police everything," Maria said. "You won't get away with it."

Paulo slapped his thigh. "Hell, I'm dense. The girl's not loyal to Sam anymore. She'll squeal to the cops. I'll have to change the ending. Jack tries to rape

Maria. Maria grabs the rifle and shoots her attacker. Is the man dead? She cocks the rifle again. He doesn't move. Her first bullet has finished him, no need for a second. She is so upset at what she's done, she runs blindly into the forest where she trips and falls on the gun. Boom. Maria dies. Newspapers report double tragedy and my poor Sam mourns the loss of his beautiful bride-to-be."

He smirked then lifted the pistol and aimed it at Maria's head. "So let's get started, love. A few scratches on Jack's face to make it look real."

Colour had drained from her lips. "Never."

"I'm the boss here," Paulo said and walked across to her. With the barrel of his pistol he drew a line down her forehead, stopping between her eyes. "Now move, or I'll take a knife and do it for you."

Sobbing, Maria dropped to her knees and held my face in her hands. "I love you, Jack."

"Touching last words," Paulo said. "I hope I don't choke."

A fuse blew inside me. "Paulo, you chicken dick. You're brave with a gun, but underneath you're chicken. Little man, little dick. A dick the size of a worm. No, worm's too big. Maggot. Smaller than a..."

"Another word from you, orphan, and you'll get a bullet in the mouth."

"Yeah, Paulo, shoot a bloke when he's helpless. Like you did with Dad."

Paulo dragged his eyes off Maria. His tone was vicious. "He got what he deserved. And all that war hero crap. Just rubbish."

"He was a hero. I've got his medals."

"No, you don't. They're hidden where nobody will ever find them."

I twisted my hands round and drew the medals from my pocket. "These don't look hidden to me."

He stared. "Where did you get them?"

"I found them. And I found other things. So drop the gun, and let's talk back at the house."

"What other things?"

"A St Francis medal. Like the one Sam's got, and I have too."

"Who else knows this?"

"Lots of people," I lied.

"It'd have to be bloody Loretta," he snorted.

He turned back to Maria who had climbed to her feet. When he lifted the pistol, I started gibbering again. "We've got other stuff on you, Paulo. That sheet of paper's not the only thing."

"Not half what I've got on you, kid."

"Like what?"

"The boy Maria carried wasn't Jack Bellamy's. It was mine. How do you think that looked to a war hero?"

I gaped. "You?… my father?"

"Sure am."

I know I should've laughed, but his voice was matter-of-fact. Because of the shock, reality fell out of sync with itself. Like in a movie house that starts the second reel before the first has ended. Even worse, as I sat in that clearing like a tethered goat, I sensed real time had crashed on the rocks years earlier and was only reaching me now.

My jaw must've dropped because I heard Sam chuckle. I hadn't even noticed him sneak into the clearing. No first aid kit, no pack, just a rifle. "That brightened your day, Jacko. You should've kept your nose out of things."

I ignored him. "I don't believe you, Paulo. Mum didn't fall pregnant until after the war. Dad was home then."

"Not always."

"You're all deranged," I groaned. "Guido claimed to be my father. Then it was Cleary. Now you."

Paulo didn't answer. He fidgeted with the trigger of his gun. "I told them pricks to stay away from her. She was mine. I was the one who loved her. And she loved me. She was going to marry me when it was all over."

"When what was all over?"

His voice dropped to a hiss. "When we'd cast off the leeches. Bellamy and Guido. When she was alone again."

The nightmare kept cranking out new scenes. His own brother a leech? "That's why you had the priest shoot Guido," I said incredulously. "It was never about money."

"He was warned."

"And then you shot Dad in the boat. Was Mum next? Destroy the gilded bird?"

He waved the gun about and stabbed the air with his left hand. Sam had dived for cover and Maria was kneeling on the ground with her pack in her hands. She was trying to undo the straps.

"She was a bitch. She said she loved me. She took the St Francis medal I gave her. But in the end she was a whore. She slept with Guido. She slept with Jack, but she made me beg for it."

"Beg…? This is crazy. So why did you save me, the little kid?"

"That was Elsa's idea. Some crap about twins."

"Mum was in this too?" Sam gasped.

"She followed orders, so button your lip."

Sam's eyes were like saucers. I turned to him. "If you let him shoot me, you're as bad as he is."

"No, Jack," he bleated from behind his rock. "You've reopened old wounds and you've pestered my girl, just like your father did. How do you think that hurt me? And my family? You brought this on yourself."

"Come on, Sam," I cried. "Get that conscience working."

And where the hell were Carl and D.I. Morgan? Some bloody cavalry.

"This has nothing to do with me," Sam said.

"Get real. You're as deep in the mess as your old man."

"Rubbish, Jack. You should've gone south when told. And all that talk about poncy Sam."

"Well, just look at yourself."

Paulo grabbed the rifle off his son and thrust him out of the way. "Did anyone tell you we like cleanliness in these parts? I've shot pigs and roos all my life, and you gotta do it to keep the place clean."

It was about then I started taking my prayers seriously. No more lukewarm Catholic for this little black duck. Sam turned his back decently while Paulo cocked the rifle and aimed at my head.

"Ta ta," he said.

I gulped and looked straight into the madman's eyes. God, this was it. Suddenly there was a loud click from my right. Maria was holding Dad's service revolver, and it was pointed squarely at Paulo.

"Put the gun down," she ordered.

Paulo's mouth opened and shut but nothing came out. Sam gaped at Maria like he was seeing the Holy Mother.

"Do as you're told," Maria said, then at Sam, "And I thought you had more sense."

Sam was at once meek as a lamb, but not Paulo. He was off his brain.

"Shoot me if you like," he snarled. "But this prick's had it."

His finger tightened on the trigger and I remember a double explosion and a roaring pain as I flew backwards into the grass.

CHAPTER 40

A day later I awoke in Mackay Base Hospital. The ceiling and walls drifted in and out of focus and every part of my body hurt. To make it worse I was unsure if I'd crossed the divide and had only returned to collect my papers. Then I heard a voice. A woman's voice. I don't know what she said. I nodded then floated back into that grey world where you're neither awake nor asleep, alive nor dead.

Sometime later I woke again. Although the eyes were clearer the pain was much the same, and since a fierce, double-chinned nurse was taking my pulse, I knew I couldn't be in heaven.

"How're you feeling?" she said.

"Awful."

"Well, brighten up. You've got visitors."

Loretta and Maria stepped quietly into the room and took turns to kiss me; Loretta on the forehead, Maria on the cheek. They drew up chairs next to the bed. "How's it feeling, lad?" Loretta asked.

"Can't feel anything. Might've fallen off."

Loretta turned to her niece. "Morphine makes them silly."

"Sillier than usual," added a passing nurse.

I reached for Maria's hand. "What happened?"

"Well, Paulo took a potshot at you, same instant as I pulled the trigger…"

"Spoilt his aim," Loretta interrupted.

"…but luckily his shot wasn't fatal, and well… I missed everything too. I had never held a revolver before, but it kind of woke everybody up. Dad and Sam grabbed the rifle off him…"

"Did you say Dad? Where did Carl appear from?"

"It wasn't his fault he was late. His ute wouldn't start, and once he had it going he couldn't raise D.I. Morgan who got tired of waiting and decided it was a hoax. Apparently he'd tried phoning the house, but nobody was there. So he returned to the police station taking what he thought was a shortcut, which got him lost. By now Dad was at the Rise and Shine anxious about events on the mountain. Knowing he would need the horses to reach the clearing in time, he rang Loretta who came straight over. They saddled up and rode across, and... well... it was touch and go."

"I won't hold my breath again."

"Be grateful you're alive," Loretta said.

"Anyway, while they were holding down Paulo, Loretta bandaged your shoulder. She used to be a nurse remember. After that we built a litter and carried you down to Sam's ute. From there it was across to the hospital."

"Where is D.I. Morgan now?"

"He found his way out eventually and took Paulo to the watch house. Charges are expected to be laid for all four murders; Jack, Maria, Cleary and Father Burke."

"I hope they stick," I said glumly.

"They should. Remember he had the document on him, and now he's been exposed a lot of Italians are ready to testify. A witness also saw him at Cleary's house on the night of the murder, and his fingerprints are on the revolver."

Loretta stood up and began fidgeting. She poured a glass of water and took a few sips, then she straightened the flowers in a vase.

"Hives playing up, Aunty?"

"You're obviously on the mend," she growled, then asked, "Where is that third St Francis medal?"

"In my pocket."

As the hospital had done my washing Loretta opened the little bedside cabinet and lifted out two St Francis medals; one I had been wearing and one from the cavity in the mountain. While holding the medals in her palm, she coughed and said, "Do you understand their significance?"

There was silence from both of us.

"Yes we do," I blurted, then added, "but Maria is marrying Sam."

"Honestly, I don't know what to think," Maria began slowly. "I've always loved him… and he, well, feels the same way… loves me. We were like that from school days. Always looking out for each other." She bit her lip. "Really, my head's a jumble, I don't know what to make of it. He's shown a side I don't care for, even aside from the business on the mountain." She looked up at Loretta and shivered. "His father was horrible but he didn't have to go along with it."

"Don't be too harsh, love, but there is another issue."

"We've already discussed that," I said. "Cousins can fall in love and get married. It's called a consanguineous marriage."

"I'm aware of that, Jack, and you're right it's permissible. Families need to adjust, that's all."

"And if they can't?"

"I guess they'd still want Maria and Sam to marry, even when he hasn't been his usual self. However..." She stood and walked round the bed. My eyeballs ached following her. "I'll tell you a story which has niggled me since you arrived. I kind of pretended it was best left in the closet. But things have changed in the past few months."

"It's okay, Loretta. Nothing more can hurt me."

"I'd still brace myself."

She paused, holding my eyes. "Sam is your twin brother."

I almost choked. "Sam? My twin?"

"Yes."

"Can't be. My brother died at birth. Elsa told me."

Maria's eyes were darting from one to the other. "Sam Avolio died at birth?"

Loretta held up her hands. "Shhh. Shhh. Settle down and hear me out. Elsa was not entirely honest. It's true you and Sam were born on the same night, but you were twins born to Maria. Yes, that's right. Maria's twins. You see, it was Elsa's child who had died stillborn, not Maria's. However, Maria was so weak from your birth, hardly alive in fact, we gave her second boy to Elsa. Perhaps it was the wrong thing to do, and perhaps we thought Elsa would return him if Maria survived, but that never happened. And, to be truthful, I don't think Elsa ever allowed Maria to lay eyes on him. Elsa was afraid she would lose her Sammy, and she reared him as her own, not even telling Paulo."

We gaped at each other in silence.

Maria spoke first. "Does that mean Sam, Jack and I... all three of us... are cousins?"

"Yes."

"Did my dad know any of this?" I asked.

"No."

"And is he my real father?"

"Yes. I have no doubt he was your mother's only lover. Guido's claim about sixteen year olds was always fanciful. And as for Cleary and Paulo, that was utter nonsense. I mightn't know many people, but I knew my sister."

In the stillness a phone rang at the nurse's station. It rang out, then I heard squeaking shoes hurry down the corridor. When the phone started ringing again, the nurse picked it up and looked our way. "No, sir. He's still unconscious." Then she hung up. "Bloody coppers."

"Did Mum ever suspect the truth?" I asked Loretta.

"No. In those days a dead baby was whisked away, no formal records, nothing. I was Maria's sister and I told her that her second baby had died. My conscience is clear because if we hadn't given him away, he would have died, and Maria mightn't have survived either. She loved you, Jack, as her only child."

My head was spinning. Sam Avolio my twin brother?

"Are you sure about this, Loretta? Everybody's had the pleasure of telling me I'm a misfit. Not a Bellamy, not a Rossini. Nobody."

"That's because they wanted you to disappear. It was a dreadful time with your father. And other people - myself as well - were frightened you'd uncover terrible secrets… even change things. But we underestimated you. I'm truly sorry, Jack. We've all been cowards in this."

When she sniffled and turned away, I reached out for her hand. "You're not a coward, Aunty. Never were."

After a time she withdrew her hand and blew her nose. "You'll have to talk to him, Jack. Sam's your family."

"Yes, I'll talk to him. But warn him first. We'll need time to adapt... both of us."

"All of us will. Even Carl."

"Dad is a new man already," Maria said.

"Yes, but go easy."

Loretta was at once businesslike. "I want a cuppa. We all do." Dropping the medals on the sheet, she waddled out the door leaving Maria and I alone.

We gazed at each other, avoiding words.

"Jack..." Maria began. A tear rolled down her face.

"Don't say it, Maria."

"Say what?"

"That, well, everything's a shock, but..."

She put her finger on my lips. "I said on the mountain I love you, Jack. I meant it."

"You also wanted me to leave when it's over."

"Yes, I know." Then she began sobbing. "Last night outside your room I thought you were going to die. It was awful. Everything in darkness, just the machines. Loretta said she had information she couldn't divulge unless we were together. And I thought it would be something horrible."

"It wasn't that bad. Anyway, does that mean we can... you know...?"

"It means we can find a way where yesterday there was none. Sam also needs me right now."

"I'll take that answer," I said, then I held her eyes. "Maria, what do you think about Sam and me being twins?"

"I think it's the blessing you didn't expect."

"And you?"

"I'm sure there'll be a blessing in it for me too. I just have to find it."

I took one of the St Francis medals in my good hand. "Maria Rossini, I love you." When I couldn't lift the medal over her hair, I hung it on her ear, right above the scar.

Despite her tears she giggled as she draped the second medal round my neck. "I love you too, Cousin Jack, and I've realised what my blessing is. Our St Francis medals. Love times three equals the new… well… musketeers. You, Sam and me. Thank you, dearest Jack." And kissed me on the mouth.

I felt a million bucks and the view from the clock tower was very clear, and, yes, the frame was wide and deep and I was in it.

Best of all, though, Mum and Dad were finally at peace.

EPILOGUE

Long years have passed, and I wavered over penning an epilogue. Wisest, I thought, to let readers imagine the three of us lived happily ever after; all sharing the one house, three separate beds, three roles on the farm, three dinners on the table. The truth is, my twin brother did marry Maria, which was right for both of them, and they had two fine-looking boys, the older of whom they named Jack. Not surprisingly, I drifted into the wide arms of Tessa and returned to Maryborough where we raised a family. I'm now a grandfather lying in bed listening to the clock chime six, a light shower scudding across the iron roof. At eight-fifteen this morning I'll pick up the grandkids - twins, Sam and Maria - and take them to kindergarten. They don't half know how much I love them.

INDEX

CHAPTER 1 .... *11*
CHAPTER 2 .... *15*
CHAPTER 3 .... *33*
CHAPTER 4 .... *39*
CHAPTER 5 .... *57*
CHAPTER 6 .... *65*
CHAPTER 7 .... *75*
CHAPTER 8 .... *81*
CHAPTER 9 .... *87*
CHAPTER 10.. *89*
CHAPTER 11.. *97*
CHAPTER 12..*111*
CHAPTER 13..*117*
CHAPTER 14..*131*
CHAPTER 15..*135*
CHAPTER 16..*149*
CHAPTER 17..*157*
CHAPTER 18..*169*
CHAPTER 19..*171*
CHAPTER 20..*177*
CHAPTER 21..*185*

CHAPTER 22	*187*
CHAPTER 23	*189*
CHAPTER 24	*229*
CHAPTER 25	*231*
CHAPTER 26	*241*
CHAPTER 27	*245*
CHAPTER 28	*251*
CHAPTER 29	*259*
CHAPTER 30	*269*
CHAPTER 31	*283*
CHAPTER 32	*297*
CHAPTER 33	*307*
CHAPTER 34	*317*
CHAPTER 35	*325*
CHAPTER 36	*329*
CHAPTER 37	*353*
CHAPTER 38	*359*
CHAPTER 39	*371*
CHAPTER 40	*377*
EPILOGUE	*385*

Printed by Printforce, United Kingdom